PENGUI
He's

Jessica Yale grew up in Shropshire, UK, before moving to the
United States to work in veterinary science. She began writing to
remind her of home. *He's A 10* is her debut novel and won I AM In
Print's 2022 Romance Writing Competition. Jessica was an avid Man
City fan and, when not watching football with her husband, loved
yoga and walking her lurcher.

He's a 10

JESSICA YALE

PENGUIN BOOKS

PENGUIN BOOKS

UK | USA | Canada | Ireland | Australia
India | New Zealand | South Africa

Penguin Books is part of the Penguin Random House group of companies
whose addresses can be found at global.penguinrandomhouse.com

First published by Penguin Books 2024

001

Copyright © Jessica Yale, 2024

The moral right of the author has been asserted

Set in 12.5/14.75pt Garamond MT
Typeset by Falcon Oast Graphic Art Ltd
Printed and bound in Great Britain by Clays Ltd, Elcograf S.p.A.

The authorized representative in the EEA is Penguin Random House Ireland,
Morrison Chambers, 32 Nassau Street, Dublin D02 YH68

A CIP catalogue record for this book is available from the British Library

ISBN: 978-1-405-96253-7

www.greenpenguin.co.uk

The book in your hands represents what can happen when a thoughtful, fashion- and dog-loving young woman becomes exposed to a lot of football on TV. Jessica was slowly drawn into the world of football through her husband's interest, and came to appreciate the intensity of professional footballing life and develop an empathy with the stresses on players. The sight of fit young men running around a pitch didn't hurt either. Jessica loved working on this novel and included details that reflect her own enthusiasms, aiming for a book that was easily readable, entertaining and emotionally satisfying. If football be the food of love, play on.

*Covenly Town Football Club, Covenly,
Midshire, England.*

'Where is Tony Garratt?' Monica asks, scanning the office as if she genuinely believes I've hidden a 6'1" attacking midfielder under a desk, or stashed him in a drawer for safe-keeping.

I sneak a look at my phone, desperately hoping I've missed a reply to my string of texts. But it's still one blue speech bubble after another:

Today, 09.10
Hi Tony, Welcome to Covenly. Do let me know if there's anything you need to help your first day go smoothly. Also absolutely no pressure, but any idea on an ETA?
Delivered

09.11
BTW this is Genie Edwards from Player Care, if you haven't had a chance to add me to your contacts
Delivered

09.17
If you're having trouble finding the stadium, give me a call
Delivered

09.29

Sorry to keep bothering you, but any updates on arrival time?

Delivered

09.51

If there's a problem, please let me know

Delivered

10.02

We've pushed the press conference back to 10.30

Delivered

10.18

Could you call me? Please

Delivered

It's now 10.21. That's not good. Monica clears her throat. I've kept her majesty waiting. That's worse.

'I'm sorry, I'm having a bit of trouble getting hold of him.' I hate that I sound cravenly apologetic. This is definitely not my fault. But our club's owner is intimidating at the best of times, and when angry, she's terrifying.

'So, you have called him?' Monica demands.

'Um, no, not exactly.' I make a conscious effort not to shrink away. 'He, um, well, it seems he doesn't do phone calls.'

Monica goes to run her fingers through her immaculately straightened hair, then clearly thinks better of it.

I try to resist the urge to pull at the collar of my blouse. 'I have texted him.'

Monica takes a deep breath. 'And have you found he *does*

text messages?' Her brows flicker as she stresses the 'does', just in case I've missed that expectations are not being met.

'Generally.'

I mentally cross my fingers. In the two weeks since Tony's transfer was finalized, I've made countless attempts to contact him. In return, I've had a series of increasingly abject excuses from his agent and precisely two text messages from Tony. The first was to give me the car registration numbers to set up his parking. The second was a curt 'OK' to the hotel I booked after no response to my offer of help finding housing. So, 'generally' is maybe putting a positive spin on things.

But Monica's got to be needing some positivity. I mean, when the club's record signing fails to show for the welcome press conference, you have to wonder, was he worth his multi-million price tag? And it can't be much fun for Monica, mulling that one over. Not after she twisted the board's collective arm to get the deal done. So, if I can sprinkle some sugar on the situation for her, I will. Not because I like her. I don't. But I love my job. Put it this way, I don't get nail extensions in case they make it easier for Monica to prise me out of my office.

She's been dying to get rid of me ever since she stole my husband, who happens to work here too as our senior doctor. I get why, no one likes seeing someone they've wronged. Except honestly, she didn't. I'd have happily donated Gavin, if she'd asked. But Monica's not exactly a touchy-feely, let's-talk-things-out sort of boss either. So, instead of having a sensible conversation, I've mastered walking on eggshells while wearing stilettoes.

Today, that means sweetening some unpalatable truths about Tony Garratt's level of enthusiasm for a move that pundits have universally judged a step down. Only it looks like this is turning into a repeat of one of my marital baking misadventures. Monica's puckering her lips, exactly like Gavin after he sampled the anniversary cake I baked using salt instead of sugar. Any second now, she's going to explain how even a half-competent player care professional could've transformed joining Covenly FC into a tempting treat.

I prepare to bite my tongue. Tony's walking away from a London club that's Premier League royalty. Cut me and I bleed Covenly grey, but even I can't pretend we're not a financially shaky upstart by comparison. Since Monica's genetically programmed to force her family's tractor manufacturing company into any conversation, there's a strong possibility she'll lead with the agricultural delights of the West Midlands when he finally shows up. And I haven't actually met Tony, but my slight weakness for creative midfielders translates into knowing a disturbing amount about him. Enough that, if Monica mentions the joys of rural peace and quiet, there's a definite risk I'll laugh in her face.

Thankfully, I'm rescued by Skylar, one of the two junior members of my team, sauntering in.

'Any sign?' I ask, my voice determinedly cheerful, but trying to communicate by laser-focused eye contact that now is not the time to be light-hearted.

Skylar does her best to look serious. ''Fraid not. Katia's going round to the punters' car park, in case he's come in at the wrong entrance.'

Monica drums crimson fingernails against the elbow of her beautifully tailored blazer. 'So, the only contact you've managed to attempt with Garratt is via text messages, which he may or may not read. Is that correct?'

I can't stop myself looking at the floor like a guilty schoolgirl. 'Um, yes, I'm sorry, it is.'

'Well, that's really not good enough.' Monica's finger-tapping turns into an exasperated wave of her hand. 'What is the purpose of a player care department if you can't even keep track of said players' whereabouts?'

That's enough to conjure up an image of me, Skylar and our admin genius, Katia, wandering the terraced streets around the stadium calling for Tony like a lost dog. Which is unfortunate, because it makes me want to laugh. Well, more cackle hysterically. Once I reach this stage of anxiety, the next thing I say will inevitably be inappropriate. So, when Monica orders us to come up with a solution, I find myself suggesting, 'A DM from Skylar's Instagram might do the trick.'

As soon as it slips out, I regret it. If you've opened a paper in the last year, you'll get what I mean. Tony Garratt's way more likely to respond to a random pretty blonde on Instagram than messages from his new club. But Tony's now unforgivably late, so I doubt Monica wants to be reminded of his reputation. But Monica looks at Skylar properly for the first time. 'Will that work?'

Skylar makes her face exaggeratedly serious. 'I can only try.'

She starts getting out her phone, but I'm saved from having to prevent a workplace #MeToo incident in the making by a voice behind me. 'I'm after Genie. Am I in the right place?'

Luckily, over the years, I've watched more than enough post-match TV interviews to recognize Tony's east London drawl. That gives me ample time, before I turn, to hide that I could cheerfully strangle him. In fact, as I hold out my hand, I'm almost sure my expression is every bit as warm as any new signing could expect from the head of Player Care.

'You are. I'm Genie. In fact my name is Charlotte but for some reason I've always been known as Genie. It's nice to meet you.'

He smiles, the lazy smile that must've won him just as many fans as his ability to make passes so perfect, strikers salivate at the sound of his name. 'Hello, love. You've been texting me, yeah?'

I hope my smile hasn't become any less bright. 'That's right.'

He makes the face all players practise, the one that says, 'It's a fair cop, ref, but I didn't mean nothing by it.' If you're not a football fan, it's roughly the same as the one that children use to get an extra biscuit out of doting aunties.

'Sorry. I've not been the best at getting back to you, have I? I've been making the most of a couple of weeks off, you know how it is.'

His tan is almost a match for the gold of his watch, so I guess that means lying on the beach was more import-ant than replying to me. Usually, I'd be sympathetic. The English football calendar has got so stretched, players barely get a summer break before it's time to get back for pre-season. But Tony was out most of last year with a recurrent hamstring injury, I can't believe he went into the off-season exhausted. Only it's not my job to get into that, so I turn up the smile. 'It's not a problem. We're just pleased to have you here now.'

That was a mistake. It gives Monica a chance to add, in a distinctly unwelcoming tone, 'Even if you are extremely late.'

Tony squints, distorting his perfectly symmetrical mask of dark stubble. 'I don't get you.'

'You were expected at 9 a.m., to be briefed for a 10 a.m. press conference.' Monica's voice remains every bit as icy as her expression.

Tony turns his head to one side. 'Nah, I got a text last night. Saying it'd got pushed back to eleven thirty.'

Monica pounces on that like a tabby on a particularly succulent mouse. 'A text message. From whom?'

Tony looks at me, and the smile's gone. 'You, I guess.'

I shake my head. 'No, I'm sorry, but it wasn't.' I hold my phone out to him, open on my texts. 'But I did contact you this morning for an arrival time. Repeatedly.'

He glances at the screen. 'Yeah, you was persistent, weren't you?' It doesn't sound like he considers it a positive quality. 'Only I was out for a run. I'd not got my phone on me.'

Pre-season doesn't start until tomorrow. I'd put the chances he's done any sort of exercise today at pretty much zero. But whatever, or probably more accurately, whoever was keeping Tony occupied this morning, I doubt he'd care to share the details with Monica. Possibly that shows in my face, because his mouth changes from flatline to a sneer. 'And I can't prove what I got sent last night, cos unlike some, I don't hoard my texts. But it said it was from Player Care all right.'

Monica snaps round to stare at me. 'Is this true?'

I'm almost a hundred per cent sure it's not. I definitely didn't change the time, and I can't believe either Skylar or Katia would have contacted Tony without my say-so. Plus, in the last few months, there've been enough stories about Tony's discipline having gone walkabout, I suspect he's covering up having overslept. Obviously, that's intensely annoying, but down the corridor, there's a room full of journalists. And they'll all be itching to put out the story that Covenly FC has bought the world's most expensive white elephant, so now is not the time to argue about it.

I make my voice bland. 'I think there's been some confusion. But perhaps we could look into it after the press conference?'

Monica goes through a visible battle between her desire to kill a villager every hour until the truth is established and the need to minimize public embarrassment. Thankfully, the latter seems to win out and she sighs loudly. 'Very well.'

I turn back to Tony, not bothering to smile any more. 'Do you need us to delay for a few minutes, so you can look over the talking points?'

He shakes his head, screwing up his face. 'Nah, I know the drill. You wants the usual? How it's time for a fresh start, couldn't want for a better set of lads, manager's the business. All that, right?'

I would love to tell him the press office has come up with something truly original, but they haven't, so I raise my brows at him. 'That should cover it.'

'You got the shirt here?' he asks, his voice matching mine in chilliness.

Skylar passes across the gunmetal grey and blue home kit shirt, freshly printed with Garratt 10. It looks wrong, he's been Garratt 27 since, well, forever. Apparently, though, he was quite insistent about making the switch, which is the exact opposite of what I'd expect. I mean, obviously there's status attached to the number 10 shirt, but it's not like Tony needs to announce he's a playmaker. And even if he's not the type to get superstitious over numbers, you'd think he'd want to preserve his brand. But clearly I don't have the best read on Tony, because I'd also expect him to walk out into the corridor to change.

Instead, he peels off his bright white t-shirt and drops it on the nearest desk. And I guess I'll have to reassess the odds he was out running this morning. Because Tony might have finished last season out of condition, but there's no denying he's perfect now. We're talking dictionary-worthy muscle definition. Which, if anything, makes the whole thing even more maddening. Just to put the cherry on top, as Monica marches him out, Tony looks over his shoulder and winks at Skylar. Infuriatingly, she grins back.

2

Skylar, who had come straight from women's team training, pulls a towel from her gym bag. She holds it out to me. I turn my head, confused.

She smiles. 'I thought you might need it.' I look at her, still bemused, until she laughs. 'To mop up the drool.'

Usually, I'd laugh back, team discipline not being one of my managerial strengths. But today, I'm definitely not in the mood and my, 'I can assure you that won't be necessary,' comes out snappy.

Skylar withdraws the outstretched towel, but she's still grinning. 'Honestly? I'd have thought Tony Garratt stripping in the office was your idea of heaven.'

I could do without the reminder that I might have mentioned, once or twice, that Tony's an extremely watchable player.

'It turns out, in person, he doesn't live up to my expectations.'

Skylar laughs. 'Really? He definitely exceeded mine. With his shirt off, anyway.'

I do a shrug/sneer combo. 'A few hours in the gym hardly make up for being such a liar.'

Skylar's face clouds. 'Yeah, I assumed you hadn't texted him.'

'No, and I take it you didn't either?'

'Nope.'

'And I think we can be absolutely confident Katia wouldn't have done.'

'No chance.' Skylar sounds distinctly smug. Katia is in almost every way a better employee than Skylar, but her Achilles heel is shyness. It's vanishingly unlikely Katia would've contacted a player she didn't know. Not without running multiple drafts of the text by me first, anyway.

Thinking about Katia, it strikes me that she may still be vainly searching the outer reaches of the stadium's car park for a missing midfielder. I try her phone a couple of times. It goes straight to voicemail, and I end up sending Skylar off to hunt for her. I was hoping that by the time they got back, my temper would have recovered, but it turns out pacing around the office for fifteen minutes isn't terribly calming.

Katia is telepathic when it comes to tension. The second she and Skylar walk in, she's apologizing for not answering my calls. I decide against interrogating her over the text and make myself smile. 'It's OK, Kat, don't worry about it. We just wanted to make sure you weren't still waiting around for Garratt.'

Katia shakes her head, vigorously enough that her braids vibrate. 'No. I got caught by Monica. She wanted one of us in the press conference, in case they needed anything.'

'Did it go OK?' I ask. I should've gone myself. That'll be another point against me to add to Monica's tally.

Katia nods this time, still a little exaggerated, so my pretending to be relaxed can't be too convincing. 'Yes, fine.'

Then she smiles, her most genuine smile, warm and sweet as freshly baked pie. 'He was good. Great, actually.'

'Well, that's something, I suppose,' I say, grudgingly. 'At least it'll sell a few shirts, which is what Monica bought him for, after all.'

Skylar tries not to openly laugh. 'What's happened to "He's the best of his generation, top assist maker in the Premier League, the missing link that's all we need to make it in Europe"?'

'He was the best of his generation, but not any more,' I snap. 'And anyway, he's thirty. His generation's on their way out.'

'I don't know that's true,' Katia says, so quietly I'd have missed it if Skylar hadn't followed on with a long list of players who've continued at the top level well into their thirties.

They're both obviously right, but I'm not going to admit it. 'Yes, but they all work like dogs to keep up their fitness, don't they?' Pushing back a strand of hair that's escaped from my attempt at a French twist, I rush on before either of them can answer. 'Garratt's never had the discipline, and now he's got to the age where his talent can't cover up the laziness any longer. I should think his last club practically bit Monica's hand off when she got her credit card out. Getting Garratt off their books must be the best bit of business they've done in years.' I crinkle up my nose in disgust. 'And now we're the lucky ones paying him a fortune to sit on the bench.'

Objectively, that's only partly true. His whole career, Tony's been a tabloid journalist's dream. But there's a big difference between staggering out of nightclubs with a stranger on your arm in the off-season, and doing the same before a big game, or when you're supposed to be focused on coming back from injury. Those stories only started last season. About the same time rumours began to circulate that Tony wasn't turning up for training, and that when he did show, he was instigating trouble in the dressing room. And I've been doing this long enough, I know perfectly well that's a sign something's gone seriously wrong.

But I'm really hitting my stride. So, instead of remembering that it's my job to make sure he settles here, I'm revving up to dissect every error Tony's made on and off the field. Luckily, Skylar pulls a warning face, stopping me just in time. A second later, Tony's in the doorway.

'I'm here for my shirt,' he says, voice flat.

I turn and gesture towards the t-shirt, still screwed up on the desk. 'You're more than welcome to fetch it.'

That came out a shade or two ruder than I'd intended, but he just gives me a nasty smile and lounges across to collect it. I gather together the shreds of my professionalism and try to inject some warmth into my voice. 'Actually, if you have a minute, there are a couple of things we need to cover.'

He glances at his Rolex. 'Yeah, I guess we might as well get it over with.'

I suppose that's better than a refusal, but only marginally. And it's unfortunate we're in the shared stadium admin area, instead of the Player Care office in the training ground. Here, the cubicles are all uncomfortably intimate. I manage to find one that's fractionally larger than the others, and sit at the desk. Hopefully, I don't look as unenthusiastic as Tony, who's doing an excellent impression of a teenager en route to detention. Skylar would clearly love to listen in, but Katia pulls her off to help with an unspecified task.

Tony drags across a chair and slumps down opposite me. He's heavy enough across the shoulders that standing, it's easy to underestimate his height. But sprawled out under the desk, his legs are so long that I almost pull back my feet. I'd put money on that being what he's expecting, me tucking my heels under my chair like a good girl. After all, he has just watched me cower in front of Monica. But Monica pays my wages, and Tony doesn't. So, if he thinks I'm going to give up my space, he's very much mistaken.

That would work better as a rebellious gesture if it didn't mean that, halfway through the opening sentence of my new-player spiel, the outside of my ankle grazes the inside of his. Tony pulls half his mouth into a closed-lipped smile. I don't smile and I don't break eye contact. But I do wait for him to move his foot. He doesn't. And I'm not going to move mine, because as we've already established, why should I? So, while I'm describing all the helpful things my team offer, my heel is up against his trainer. That's extremely distracting. Although not quite as distracting as noticing Tony's eyes are the exact same grey that's on our home kit.

Under the circumstances, I think I'm really doing quite a good job of being coherent. But I'm clearly not achieving persuasive. Every suggestion I make, Tony shakes his head and alternates between 'Not necessary' and a monosyllabic 'Nah'.

Eventually, he tilts back on his chair, which at least moves his shoe away from mine. 'Look, love, I get you're not paid to know 'bout the football, but you've got a rough idea of who I am, right?'

There's no way I'm admitting to having watched virtually every match he's played since hitting the first team at the ridiculously young age of seventeen. 'I do, yes.'

He nods slowly, making it clear he's being patient because I'm obviously intellectually limited. 'So, you get I've played for a couple of other clubs, yeah?'

'I am aware of that.'

He tips his chair forward and leans across the desk towards me. 'OK. Then maybe you could just take it as read, I know what Player Care's here for.'

Everything about him is out to provoke. I make sure to sound ultra-calm. 'Perhaps you could give me a quick summary? Just to be sure we're on the same page.'

He still doesn't show his teeth when he smiles, but both sides of his mouth are involved this time. 'Anything I need done that I don't fancy sorting myself, you girls take care of. Right?'

I allow myself a small and similarly cold smile in return. 'No, not exactly.'

He sits back again, hands stretched behind his head. 'Go on then, enlighten me.'

I'm careful to mirror him, leaning deep into my chair. 'If there's something a player needs, to help them settle in or to allow them to perform to their full potential, we aim to make that happen. But we're not personal assistants. Most of what we do, the players aren't even aware of. And while we do handle requests, within reason, we answer to management.'

He laughs, though he doesn't look particularly amused. 'Is that you making it clear there's services you don't offer?'

I don't smile this time. And I don't want him thinking he can make me back away, so I put my elbows on the desk and rest my chin on my hands. 'No, but you can take it that's the case.'

'You might want to rethink your work outfits then.'

Despite myself, I glance down. I must have been seriously yanking at my collar when I was shrinking away from Monica, because my shirt has come open at least two buttons too low. There's a lot of pale skin on show against the bottle-green silk, and Tony must have a clear view of the claret red of my bra. And there's no way he's bringing it up to flirt or as a joke. It's to make me feel ridiculous. Like I've done it deliberately, like I'm so deluded, I actually believe he'd look at me twice. And it really stings, so for the first time in the whole conversation, I'm not annoyed, just humiliated. Well, not just humiliated, defeated too. It must be what it's like for defenders when they realize, as the ball slips past, that Tony's been ahead of them from the opposite end of the pitch.

I do the buttons up without looking at him. I'd love to crawl away as quickly as possible, but whatever I said before, signing Tony Garratt is a huge deal for the club. I can't drop him, even if he is loathsome. I try to make my voice sound like nothing's happened. 'The last thing is housing. If you let us know your needs, we can come up with some possibilities. Or we can just set up a rental, if you prefer not to be bothered with it?'

He looks at me for a long time, his face blank, then runs his fingers through the hair that hasn't been shaved into his low fade. 'Nah, it's all right. I can take care of myself.'

I give a small shrug, then stand to indicate that we're done. 'Well, you know where to come, if that changes.'

3

My feet pound on the treadmill. Usually, I like this bit, when it doesn't feel like dying any more. But I know my playlist so well, I could rap along if that wasn't deeply culturally inappropriate. And I'm staring at the white wall of an empty gym, so I've got zero distractions from worrying about Tony Garratt.

We're only a week into pre-season. Already two of the coaching staff have pulled me aside with concerns Tony isn't settling. Next time, it'll be the manager. And just like everyone else on the staff, I adore our manager, who's a genius and a gentleman. But to say he's intense is the understatement of the century, and I can't face a prolonged discussion about Tony. It's not like I can pretend I don't see the problem, it's definitely there.

Since it's opening week, I've made sure to drift into the first team's canteen a few times. That way, if there's something a player needs, they can drop it in among baby photos and holiday stories. Tony never says hello, which is fine by me. What isn't fine is that he's always sitting separated off from the team, phone in hand. I can just imagine the look on the manager's face, like a disappointed deity, if I have to admit I haven't done anything to fix that.

It's not that there's nothing I could do. Just getting Tony out of the hotel would be a step closer to making

Covenly home. And it isn't that I'm not trying because I don't like him. My job's to help, regardless. But he's made it abundantly clear he doesn't want my help, and I don't understand why. Because, once I calmed down, it struck me that our first meeting had actually been quite odd.

If he was making up that text, why stay angry after Monica left? It would've made more sense to make out it was a misunderstanding. Maybe Tony takes a method approach to lying, to the point that he ends up believing his own story. But it seems more likely he really did get a message. And if he did, maybe he'd work with me if I apologized?

I'm not above saying sorry for a text I didn't send. If that would smooth things over with Tony, I'd do it in a heartbeat. And yes, I'm aware that sounds pathetic. But it's incredibly important to the club that Tony's a success here. Unhappy Tony equals underperforming Tony equals our entire transfer budget wasted. It's irrelevant that I might, maybe, in the past, have found him the tiniest bit attractive. Even if there was the slightest chance he'd be interested in me, staff contracts have zero-tolerance fraternization clauses. I'd never put my job at risk, not even for a man who reads games like they're comic books.

So, if fake apologizing is what's best for Covenly, I'll do it. Only, if there was no text, Tony's going to think I'm crazy. And who wants help from a crazy person?

I run that round and round, until my brain's more tired than my legs. As I step off the treadmill, pulling out my earbuds, I turn and jump out of my skin. Because there's Tony, finishing up on an exercise bike.

I grab at my throat. 'Oh God.'

He dismounts and lolls back against a neighbouring elliptical. 'Bad as that, is it? Finding yourself in the same room as me?'

'No, of course not.' I gulp in air. 'Sorry, you startled me. I thought I'd the place to myself.'

'So I saw. It's the norm at this place, is it? The office girls using the first-team gym?' His tone is sneery, and irritatingly, his breathing is already close to normal.

'Um, well, no, not exactly.' I try to discreetly mop sweat from my face, then make myself look at Tony. 'Actually, no, it's absolutely not. I shouldn't be here. But it was pouring this morning, and I couldn't face running outside. And the women's team were already using their space, and . . .'

Tony cuts in before I have to forcibly stop myself babbling. 'Whatever. It don't bother me one way or the other.'

I'm practically squirming. 'But I really shouldn't be in here. So, if you could keep it to yourself, I'd appreciate it.'

'Funnily enough, I'm not too keen on letting on I'm in here a couple of hours before everyone else.' There's a closed-mouthed smile that doesn't reach his eyes. 'Don't want no one thinking I'm putting in extra effort. Not when everybody round here knows I'm a washed-out has-been, here to sit out the rest of my career on the bench cos I've squandered my talent. Isn't that right?'

My eyes widen, like he's just slapped me. 'Oh. Tony, I'm so sorry. You heard what I said?'

'I could hardly miss it. You wasn't exactly keeping the volume down.' In contrast, his voice is quiet, conversational almost, except there's a hiss to it.

Professionally, offending the star signing on his first day is by far the worst thing I've ever done. For a split second, reaching out and touching his arm feels like the right thing to do, a physical connection to show how sorry I am. Luckily, I manage to stop myself just in time. The first rule of this job is don't touch the talent. Or, maybe that should be the second rule, after don't insult them.

I stare down at my running shoes until I've got myself together enough for eye contact. 'I'm sorry I said it, and even more sorry you heard. It would've been unforgivable, even if I meant it. But I obviously don't.'

He shakes his head and his voice is dismissive. 'Forget it. I can't get too worked up over what the secretary thinks 'bout my stats.'

I'm definitely still the one in the wrong so I resist the urge to point out I'm not the secretary. 'Except it's honestly not what I think. The start of last season, you were on track to hit the year before's numbers, probably better them.'

When he smiles this time, his eyes are starting to narrow down. 'I know everyone goes on 'bout how you keep this place running, but I weren't aware you ran the numbers and all.'

'I don't. I'm just an enthusiast.' I open my hands to him. 'And Tony, that's why I said what I did. We sold players, good young players, some for less than they're worth, to buy you.'

'And you thought I weren't taking things serious, yeah?'

I nod.

'And you reckon those kids, they'll go and do a job for

22

someone else, and the money I bring in won't be enough to replace 'em?' He's gentler now, like he's genuinely curious.

I fiddle with the strap of my sports bra. I'm not sure he needs to hear all of what got me so pissed off. I mean, I grew up in my parents' house. If anyone understands the crushing weight of other people's expectations, it's me.

'Come on, love. You might as well tell me. It can't be no worse than what you've said already.' His voice is teasing, but I guess that's true. Honest has to be better than mean.

'It's not just the money. It's that some of them have probably made the wrong move. Our academy players who were settled here, building up to something big. One or two of them, they'll just disappear at new clubs, because they weren't ready. And if you don't show up for us, that'll be for nothing. You know?'

He nods and his smile has got pillowy soft. 'Yeah, I do know. And Genie, it's nice, you caring 'bout that. But that's sort of why I'm here.' He screws up his mouth. 'This, it's kind of embarrassing.'

'Then don't tell me. It's not like you owe me an explanation.'

'Only maybe I does, cos I was a bit of a dick when I first showed up.'

I start a polite denial but he laughs and shakes his head.

'Nah, I was, no need to pretend otherwise. But what I was going to say was, it's true, last season went off the rails for me, can't make out it didn't. Being injured, it don't agree with me. Devil makes work for idle hands, and all that.' He ducks his head for a second. 'And I had some personal stuff feeding in that I won't go into. But you're basically right, I didn't put in the graft to get back.' He looks away again, and this time it seems to take effort to look back at me. 'And I did a bang-up job of blaming everyone else. But when my contract came up for renewal, I had to admit to myself, I'd been going through the motions with the physio and stuff.'

He stretches back, and it's like opening his shoulders frees him up, because the words start coming more easily. 'So, I decided I could go one of two ways. Either exactly what you said, signing for my last big pay-day and go to a club that is known in the market for paying over the odds for a star, even when they're not who they once was, or come back to a club like where I started. The sort of place where even the girls paid to fetch and carry care if you're making your fitness targets.' He shrugs. 'And here I am.'

I think I'm forgiven, because everything about him is relaxed now. In fact, lazing back against the handles of the elliptical, he looks like he'd happily spend the rest of the morning chatting in the gym.

I smile apologetically. 'Well, we're very glad you chose us. And my actual job isn't to fetch and carry, it's to make you feel welcome. So, even though I've obviously made a terrible start, if there's anything I can do to make settling in easier, please let me know. Or, if you'd rather work with one of the other members of the Player Care team, we can arrange that.'

He grins, his eyes almost closed this time. 'As it happens, I can think of a thing or two you could do for me. But maybe we'll start out small. Like finding a place to live, that's not gone too well. And I want out of the hotel asap. Do you reckon you could find a few options?'

I nod, making sure my face doesn't give away that I caught the innuendo in his opening sentence. Not that he would have meant it. 'Absolutely. Do you have any specific requirements?'

'Nah, not really. Not city centre, though. I want something quiet, reasonably private. If there's a pool, I'd like that, saves coming in here every time I fancy a swim. Oh, and I'm not like the young kids, I want a kitchen I can actually use from time to time. Other than that, garage, obviously, and that's about it. I'm not too fussed 'bout nothing else.'

I give him an air-hostess style smile. 'That sounds easy enough.' It actually isn't. Not the pool anyway, most people round here don't want the bother. But it's doable. 'Shall I send you some possibilities, or would you prefer I do the initial viewings?'

'You busy this afternoon?'

'Nothing I can't change,' I say, managing somehow to hide my surprise.

'Then see what you can set up for after training, and we'll go look at 'em together, OK? I'll only get lost driving round them little lanes.'

'Of course. Come to my office when you're ready.'

I start to walk out, anxious to shower and change before anyone else arrives. A little stressed about the time I have to find suitable properties. And if I'm a tiny bit weak at the knees, it's definitely just glycogen depletion. When I'm halfway through the door, Tony calls, 'Genie?'

I look back at him, hoping this isn't going to be an excessively outlandish house-related requirement. 'Yes?'

25

'Bit of time on the treadmill suits you. Puts some colour in your cheeks.' Which doesn't do justice to the colour that's actually in them as I head into the changing room, but I have to say, I'm super happy I grabbed my nice workout clothes today.

4

Tony's pulling up just as I get to the door. These days, most players go for a discreetly luxurious SUV but Tony's definitely more of a Lambo sort of guy. In red, obviously. Clambering in wearing a pencil skirt might be more challenging than sumo squats, but it's worth it for the interior, all nude leather and gold. And that's before you get to the engine, which purrs like a tiger happy to find his steak tastes reassuringly expensive.

Our training complex is on a busy A-road, and the first few minutes are spent with me giving directions and Tony concentrating on traffic. But once we turn off onto one of the sleepy B-roads that snake across the county, neither of us can pretend driving still requires Tony's full attention. Since the only things I can think to say are, one, I'm so sorry again, for being appallingly rude, or two, you have by far the most attractive thighs of any man I've ever met, it's quite a relief when Tony takes the conversational initiative.

'You wanna drive?'

'Thank you, but no.'

He gives me a quick glance. 'Honest? I got the idea you was looking at the car with a bit of a hankering.'

I shake my head. 'No, I love sports cars in an entirely uneducated way, but only as a passenger.'

He looks at me again, head on one side. 'That's unexpected.'

'Why?'

He shrugs and makes a sideways movement with his mouth. 'Just I'd got you down as someone who likes being in the driving seat.'

'Not at all. I'd much rather be driven.'

There's an inadequately concealed smirk. 'Interesting.'

I can't allow myself to get drawn down whatever road he's heading. Our chat in the gym explained why Tony's here, but not why, behind his back, the first team are calling him the banana. Given their current enthusiasm for emoji-based rhyming slang, I'm fairly confident that works back to moaner or loner. Either way, it needs fixing, and opening up a bit myself might get him in a confiding mood. I try, 'I grew up around here. Learning to drive when there might be a tractor lurking around every bend left me pretty traumatized. As far as I'm concerned, it's the best thing about hiring Skylar, she's always dying to drive.' Well, that and how she reliably makes me laugh, which fully compensates for her appalling timekeeping.

'She's the blonde, right? With the tats?'

It doesn't surprise me in the least that he's noticed Skylar. 'That's right.'

'And the other one, the one that was in the office with you just now, what's her name?'

Interest in Kat is equally understandable, but I'm not sure his curiosity bodes well. 'Katia. She's LeMar's girl-friend.' Hopefully, even Tony can see it's not a good idea to offend our striker, even if Katia's personal appearance is every bit as polished as her organizational skills.

He laughs. 'Don't worry. No need to warn me off. She's a bit young for me.'

At twenty-one, Katia is only two years younger than Angharad Jones, the beautiful model-cum-influencer Tony was seeing on and off all last year. It would be rude to point that out, so I let the conversation lapse and focus on enjoying the drive. Midshire countryside isn't ideal for ultra-powerful cars, but with Tony, there's none of the usual fighting up and down our steep hills. Plus, every time he changes gear, I can't help noticing he has really nice hands. On the small side, like most players' hands and feet, but clearly strong.

Tony leaves it a minute then asks, 'They're both local girls and all?'

'Katia is. She and LeMar were at school together. She got the job to keep our star striker happy, but turns out she's fantastic at it. We scouted Skylar from London for the women's team. But their wages aren't exactly in line with yours, and Kat and I needed some extra help, so Sky fits in a few hours of player care after training.'

He nods. 'So, it's like your local club then? All of you?'

'That's right, I used to go with my grandfather when I was a child.'

'Not your dad?'

'No, the sporting gene missed a generation.' I hope that sounds casual, and doesn't hint at how deeply my parents disapprove of my job and life choices in general.

Luckily, if any resentment creeps through, Tony doesn't seem to notice. 'And the owner, it's like a family firm, right?'

'Sort of.' I make a profound effort to give Monica the

praise she's due. 'Except the whole time her father was in charge, we were a mid-level Championship team. It's Monica who got us into the Premiership at all, let alone the top four.'

Tony grimaces. 'Sort of terrifying, though, isn't she? Eyes like calculators, that one.'

I laugh despite myself. 'Well, you did cost a literal fortune. You can hardly blame her for continuously working out your investment-to-return ratio.'

'I'll be worth it all right.' Tony winks. 'It's a shame though. I've not played for a club owned by a woman before and I was quite into the idea. So far, she's not exactly lived up to expectations.'

High hedges and twisty turns straighten into stubble fields. Tony grabs his chance to accelerate past a horse-box. While he's focused on the road, I sneak a glance at his profile, all sloping cheekbones and a long nose that's been fixed so well, you hardly notice the break. 'It's more a board of investors, headed by a chief shareholder, who happens to be a woman. And Tony, I know my professionalism hasn't been stellar so far, but if you only take one bit of advice from me, don't do anything other than take Monica very seriously.'

He makes a sideways sort of smile. 'Understood.'

'Also, don't make any sort of joke about Monica, or to her. She doesn't understand them.'

He laughs good-naturedly. 'Good to know. But from our first little chat, I'd got the impression you was more likely to be passing stuff up the chain than keeping me out of trouble.'

'To Monica, no. My loyalty's to the manager, no one else.'

'I can understand that, cos I'm pretty enthused 'bout working for him and all.' Tony makes an ironic face. 'But he don't pay your wages, does he?'

'Except he's the one keeping us winning, so indirectly, he kind of does.' My voice starts out stern, but I can't help adding, 'And he only listens to what he really needs to hear,' in a much softer tone.

Tony nods. 'Fair enough.' Then he looks at me full-on, which is slightly terrifying as we're approaching a ninety-degree bend, and nods again. I'm ridiculously pleased that I seem to have given the right answer.

5

The first house I've managed to find is part of a small gated community. We're just about commuter belt enough to have a few new developments trying to look old, but given away by the shininess of the brick and excessive number of bedrooms. They're not to my taste, but players often go for the security and comfortingly high-end fittings, so it makes sense to start here. As we pull up on the mustard yellow gravel drive, still damp from this morning's rain, I start apologizing when there's no sign of the estate agent.

Tony waves it away but adds, 'Do you mind if we get out the car though? I'm a bit stiff.'

'Of course. Nothing serious, I hope?' I try to sound casual, but I'm sure Tony's more than conscious everyone's paranoid he'll pick up another injury.

He shakes his head. 'Nah, I just went pretty hard this morning. It's normal soft tissue stuff, nothing more.'

Only I can't help noticing the minute he's out of the car, Tony's leaning his weight against the driver's door. I'd really rather not keep him standing around outside when he's in discomfort. But peering through the bars of the black metal gate, the estate agent's car definitely isn't already inside.

I have another go at apologizing but Tony yawns and makes the same dismissive gesture with his hand. 'Don't worry 'bout it. Having to wait a few minutes'll give us a chance to clear something up anyhow.'

I make my face into a polite question.

He looks me right in the eye. 'The press conference. I did get a message from the office changing the time.' His voice isn't aggressive, but there's an intensity that's new.

'I thought you might have.' I'm careful not to break his gaze. 'But it wasn't from me.'

He purses his lips. 'Yeah, I've been thinking maybe it weren't.'

'I promise you, it wasn't. There are a few of us who may have messaged you about this, just signing off as "Player Care" as we usually do in case texts are coming from different members of the team, but I can't think who would have done that, or why.'

Tony nods, still serious. 'If you say so, that's good enough for me.' He looks down and draws a line in the gravel with the toe of his trainer. 'Since I got here, any time I've asked anyone anything, they've said go talk to Genie, she'll sort it. It don't make sense them being like that if you was the type to get something wrong.' He shifts his weight, but I think it's more about being uncomfortable in the conversation than any lingering muscle strain. 'And I know I got you in trouble with the boss over me being late, and I'm sorry 'bout that. I shouldn't have jumped to conclusions.' When he looks at me, his eyes are scrunched up, he's so keen to show contrition. 'It's just the trust thing, it's a sore spot, you know?'

I smile gently. 'I've never met a player where it wasn't.'

He half laughs. 'Yeah, that's probably true.' He pulls an

uncomfortable face. 'And I think maybe that's not all I've got to be sorry over. Cos before I left, that first day, I did try to, like, lighten things up. But I don't reckon it came out as funny as I was hoping.'

I work to hide how pleased I am. Now, when I daydream about Tony, it needn't hurt my pride. Which is a relief, the last few days have been agony. 'Don't worry about it. I must've missed the joke. And Tony, I'm sorry too. I was just as bad, assuming you were making something up to explain your being late.'

He grins. 'Yeah, you should've realized that weren't likely.'

I nod, feeling bad.

But he crinkles his eyes at me. 'Funnily enough, first day at a new club, it's not top of my list, pissing off the best-looking woman in the place.'

I laugh to hide how taken aback I am. And I admit it, how pleased. Though working with Skylar and Katia makes it obviously untrue, I can tell it's nicely meant. 'And you wonder why I might think you're capable of lying?'

He laughs too, harder than me. 'The sad thing is, Genie, you're only proving you can't see the truth when it's in front of you.' His face changes suddenly back to serious. 'But joking aside, you were just as bad. You was trying to gloss over it, even when you reckoned I was passing my mistake off onto you.'

'Honestly, it's fine, completely forgotten.' I frown. 'Except, it's odd, don't you think? Why someone sent that text? You sure it was signed off from Player Care?'

He shrugs. 'Maybe. Thinking it over, do you think some

journalist, looking to make a story out of me not showing up for the signing photo-op might have been able to hack one of the Player Care phones or something?'

I shrug. 'Well, it doesn't matter now, though I would like to find out who did that.'

We start making small talk about training and fixtures, but I'm more focused on the journalist idea. It makes sense. Or is that me leaping on an easy way out? I can't bear to think it was one of my colleagues. Unless maybe I confused one of them? It's crossed my mind I might have said something confusing to Katia, who genuinely thought the time had changed? Maybe when she found out it hadn't she was too scared to tell me what she'd done. It's only the last couple of years that I've had anyone to supervise, before that, Player Care was just me. I try to think if there is anyone else who could have sent that text that I could have also confused. The management side I'm not sure is exactly my strong point, so it could be that the whole thing's my fault. Which is a worry because . . .

Tony cuts into the spiral of self-doubt. 'You all right, Genie? You seem a bit distracted.'

'Sorry, yes. Just wondering where the estate agent's got to.'

I call their office, and the woman on the end of the phone tries to pretend there's confusion over the appointment. But whatever other errors I might have made, I can't believe this is down to me when I only set up the viewing this morning. If it was just my time they were wasting, I could be pleasant about it. But keeping Tony hanging about when he's tired from training is unforgivable. I make that point quite forcefully. In the end, the receptionist is so desperate to get me off the phone, she provides the codes for the gate and the lockbox.

Tony holds the front door open and I glance up at him as I walk in. He's obviously amused.

'What?'

He widens his smile, flashing white teeth. 'Just you're a bit of a fierce one, is all.'

'That's why it's called Player Care, not Estate Agent Care.' Damn, that definitely sounded sulky.

Tony raises his hand. 'I'm only laughing cos of how hard you tries to cover it up under the nice manners. Personally, I like a bit of an attitude. Keeps things interesting.'

His smile is exaggeratedly flirty, and I fight back the urge to banter back. Apart from it being highly unprofessional, I don't think I could hide that, while Tony's obviously playing at flirting, I'm having to constantly remind myself not to touch him. And not in a non-specific be-careful-of-his-personal-space sort of way.

I keep getting these intrusive hyper-colour flashes in my mind's eye. Like he's wearing this tight black t-shirt that leaves most of his upper arms bare, and as he pulls the door closed, I get this crystal-clear picture of reaching out and stroking from the hard muscle of his bicep down to his fingers. The effort involved in stopping myself doing it for real makes me dizzy. I try to clear my head, forcing myself to remember every tedious detail of the house's specs.

Tony takes a polite interest in the shiny white walls and glass staircase in the entrance hall. But as he races through the living room, I can't help that the involuntary image of him bending me over the sleek leather sofa is still sharp as we head into the kitchen. There's barely a glance at the top-of-the-line appliances before he turns for the door.

'Is this one not for you?'

He pulls a don't-care face. 'No, it's fine. I mean, I could live here.'

'But?'

He looks down at the stainless-steel countertop then back to me, as though I've caught him in a weakness. 'It's not very homey, is it?'

I smile to show I'm not offended that my first pick doesn't appeal. 'No, it's a bit sterile for my tastes too.'

He nods, obviously relieved. 'Yeah, that's exactly right. And like I say, if the others are the same, it's not the end of the world. I guess I just thought getting out of London, it'd mean I could find something that's not a white box. You know what I mean?'

'I do. And sorry, the next one's similar, but we can skip it. The third house is maybe more what you're hoping for, but it's got its downsides.'

He grins. 'Like what? A ghost in the attic or something?'

My smile is nervier than I'd like, but this is delicate, to say the least. 'No, nothing like that. It's a bit smaller. Not tiny, but not ideal if you're planning on having loads of visiting friends and family, or big parties.'

He shakes his head briskly. 'I'm not. Like I said this morning, I'm making a break from everything I was doing, the people I was hanging round with, all that. And I'm not that tight with family right now. One bedroom'd do me just fine.'

That's good to hear even if I can't see a monastic exist-ence lasting long, but it doesn't make the next bit any easier. I twist the collar of my blouse, then panic and glance down to check the buttons. Tony's mouth twitches.

'Um, Tony, the other thing, it's, well, awkward.'

He does a 'tell me' gesture with his hands.

'I know you wanted privacy, and I did try to steer clear of anywhere too close to other players or club staff. But there really aren't many houses around here with a pool, and this one has by far the nicest . . .'

Tony interrupts, and thankfully, he's smiling. 'OK, tell me the worst. Who's next door? The gaffer or the owner?'

'Neither. I'm afraid it's me. But there are lots of trees, so at most, I can see the roof.' I sound distinctly sheepish.

Luckily, he doesn't react like I'm a potential stalker. In fact, quite the opposite. There's lion's-roar-style laughing, then, 'That's all right. I promise, having you as a neighbour, it'd not be quite the ordeal you seem to think it'd be.'

'So, you want to see that next?'

Tony nods like a parcel-shelf dog. 'Yeah, for sure.'

6

Halsbury Lodge is a lovely house. It's partly seventeenth century, so all tiny red bricks and tall chimneys. As we swing around the last curve of the drive, the sun comes out properly for the first time, glinting on the white of the window frames. And the estate agent's still running late, so I can let Tony soak it in without the hard sell. That's perfect. He can stroll around, gazing up at the high ceilings, and craning his neck to get the most out of the view from the French windows.

I'm fairly sure it's a good sign, Tony behaving like an overgrown puppy who's wandered into Wonderland. Though it's not until he's staring out over the front lawn, fingers on the faded velvet of the curtain, that he says anything. It's just, 'Yeah, I likes this place.' But it's quiet, so I think he really means it.

'You haven't seen the best bit yet.'

He looks over his shoulder at me. 'What's that then?'

'Come and see.'

My heels click on the checkerboard tiles of the hall. He follows a step behind, trainers silent. I open a door that must once have led out into the yard. Now, there's an all-glass corridor leading into the old barn. Only, instead of hay bales, there's a brilliant blue pool, long enough to swim proper laps, and from my perspective, much more importantly, a hot tub. I know I'm supposed to say they're tacky, but I utterly adore them. It's nothing to do with the suburban wife-swapping associations, they just combine two of my absolute favourite things, being in the water and being warm. Though I might have more trouble than usual denying the appeal has anything to do with sex, with Tony so close. I can almost feel his breath on my neck.

But that's not something I should be focusing on, so I use the fact the stone flags are not stiletto friendly as an excuse to stay in the doorway.

Tony smiles at me from across the room. 'Yeah, I see what you mean. Not bad.'

I try to regain my professional focus. 'Umm. It's by far the best pool set-up in the area.'

His laugh echoes against the bare brick walls. 'You, my friend, have missed your calling. You should be selling houses.'

I look puzzled.

He grins. 'Anyone'd go for this, if they saw your face. Like you're staring at a real tasty bit of cake.'

I bite my lip and smile. 'It is quite dreamy.'

'Well, if I rent this place, you're welcome to come swim any time.'

I don't want to give the impression I'm going to get under his feet, so I tone down my smile. 'That's kind.' Then, over my shoulder, as I'm walking away, 'Shall we go and look upstairs?'

The current owners haven't made themselves known in the village, but most of the first floor's a little shabby, so I guess they ran out of money before the restoration was finished. Luckily, Tony's only interested in the master bedroom and bathroom. The bathroom is nice in a generic *Architectural Digest* sort of way, but the bedroom is mouth-watering. The woods behind the house block the sun, but instead of trying to make it look lighter, the walls are the colour of Valpolicella. The damask curtains and the bedspread match perfectly; lying in bed must be like floating in wine.

'I get why you were so enthused 'bout this one now. This room looks great on you,' Tony grins, pointing me to the silver mirror and indicating that I should take a look at myself.

Surprisingly, I can see his point. I'm the sort of pale that looks smudged against white walls. Here, my skin's almost dramatic and my hair looks more Belgian chocolate than its usual Dairy Milk. Only I know, even when I look at my nicest, I don't come close to a woman like Angharad Jones at her worst, so I shrug. 'The mirror helps, the antique ones soften out the edges.'

He shakes his head, his face play serious. 'I dunno 'bout that. You look like the lady of the house to me.'

I smile back, flattered despite myself. 'Only this is an old hunting lodge, so very much a bachelor pad. The only women who'd ever have set foot in here when it was first built definitely wouldn't have been ladies.'

Tony tilts his head. 'Here's hoping.' He looks at the brass bed, then at me, eyes narrow, and this time I can't stop the blush. 'Speaking of which, this place comes furnished, yeah?'

'It does.' I try to keep my face bland.

'Then how 'bout kicking off them heels and trying this out for size for me?'

Obviously, if he said that to Katia or Skylar, I'd be seriously annoyed. But always being everyone's big sister, or for the academy kids, their second mum, can get depressing. And that's my only defence for giving Tony my best confused Bambi look and saying, 'But I so much prefer keeping my heels on.'

It's pleasing that for a moment he's completely quiet, but a twitch of the brows widens his eyes into diamonds. His tongue flickers between his parted lips and he runs his forearm across his mouth. Then he laughs. 'Got to admit, that's a visual I wasn't expecting.' He stops for a second, looking at me sideways, then smiles slowly and slides his hand along the bedpost. 'But thinking 'bout it, maybe I should've.'

I'm actually confused now, rather than pretend confused. 'I can't think why.'

He grins. 'Well, you told me you like being driven. And if you're into someone else taking charge, this has gotta suggest a possibility or two.' He holds his wrist flat against the bedpost, so the gold of his watchstrap looks like the world's most expensive restraint.

He's so obviously played me at my own game, I can't help laughing. But it's probably for the best that the estate agent appears in the doorway before either of us can say anything more, apologizing but claiming I had made the appointment for tomorrow.

When I see it's Bunty Conroy, all the confusion over the appointments makes sense. I've dealt with her often enough to be convinced she was hired solely to sell this sort of house to her relatives. It's the only rational explanation for anyone paying her a wage.

'Oh good, you found your way up here. So sorry I'm late.' As usual, Bunty's voice is pitched to be heard from the opposite end of a hockey field.

I do brief introductions, after which Bunty asks, 'Well, what do you think, Mr Garratt? Is it for you?'

Tony's smile is of the happy crocodile variety. 'Oh yeah, I think it's for me all right. How 'bout you, Genie? You reckon it'll suit?'

Luckily, since Bunty's not the sharpest knife in the box, I don't think she notices anything out of the ordinary in my expression when I say, 'I can see it has certain attractions.'

Tony laughs. 'Too right it does.'

I decide it's time to return to being professional, or actually, that it's long overdue. 'OK, Bunty, we're looking to move Tony in asap. Can we get the paperwork done today?'

She looks horrified, and really it wasn't a sensible suggestion. Her office will be closing soon and Bunty almost certainly can't set up a DocuSign without assistance.

'Or tomorrow morning?'

Bunty shakes her head. 'I'm sorry, Genie, I really am. But the credit check always takes a few days. We could maybe do a move-in date early next week . . .'

'Bunty, this is Tony Garratt.' My voice is prickly.

She looks perplexed. 'Yes, you did introductions when I arrived.'

'He holds the record for most Premier League assists in

45

a season.' The irritation's still there, but I manage to coat it with a thin layer of patience.

'I don't quite see how that relates to the credit check?'

Tony gives her his laziest smile. 'Bunty, love, I think what Genie's getting at is I make a serious amount of money.'

Bunty looks to me for confirmation. I nod and mouth his salary.

'A year?' she yelps, and I hope that means she's re-evaluating the need for a credit check or anything else that will delay getting Tony out of an anonymous hotel room.

I shake my head. 'A week.' I can see she's poised to say something unforgivable, so I reach out to briefly brush Tony's elbow with the tips of my fingers. 'And if anything, he's undervalued. So, if we could get the paperwork rolling?'

We leave Bunty battling the security system and stroll to the car. Tony smiles down at me. 'Thanks, Genie, for getting that sorted.'

I smile back. 'I hope you'll be happy here.'

He looks over his shoulder at the ivy draped tastefully over the lead of the porch. 'Yeah, I kind of think I might be. I weren't sure the country'd be for me, but this place, I'm quite taken with it.'

'It should be the perfect home for a player.'

'How's that?'

'It was built to be somewhere to come home to after a hard day's hunting. You might be after goals instead of foxes, but it's the same principle, minus the cruelty.'

He grins. 'Not sure that's always absent, but you know,

that's a nice idea. Makes me feel like I've got a bit more in common with the previous residents than I'd have guessed.'

Interestingly, that suggests a thoughtful – at a stretch even romantic – streak I hadn't guessed was there. But it's best not to dwell on that. I try a joke to change the pace. 'Only there might be more similarity with the hounds than the humans.'

'You could be right.' He laughs. 'And as it happens, you're not the first woman to point that one out.'

'I don't imagine I am.'

He opens the car door and leans on the roof, watching me walking to the passenger side. As I'm about to lever myself in, he says, 'You know what? We might've got off to a rocky start, but I reckon you and me, we're going to get on.'

7

We're halfway down the oak-lined drive before Tony says anything else, and when he does, he's unusually hesitant. 'Look, I hope we do get on. But did I take it too far in there?'

'You mean the bed thing?'

'Yeah.'

'No, if I'd been offended, I wouldn't have joined in joking around. But I'd avoid that sort of thing with the younger female staff. Just in case, you know?'

He could brush it off and pretend easing the car round the gentle sweep of stone-grey gravel requires too much concentration to reply. Instead, he keeps staring out of the windscreen but nods quickly, face solemn. 'Don't worry, I get it. I don't wanna make no one feel uncomfortable. And I know, times have changed and all the old-school banter and stuff, it's dying out.' He sounds distinctly wistful, but he rushes to add, 'Not that I'm saying that isn't a good thing.'

I lean back in my seat, and maybe it's how luxurious the leather feels, but suddenly, I'm saying something I really should keep to myself. 'Don't you think, sometimes though, it's all getting a bit serious?'

There's a shout of laughter. 'Didn't have you down as a rowdy one. But yeah, I do, I'm afraid.'

Realizing I've just made myself sound like the sort of

woman who could be seen to be letting other women down, I try to walk it back. 'I mean, obviously, it's good that we've stopped thinking it's OK for female staff to get casually sexually harassed from time to time, or that the academy kids have to learn to take a bit of bullying, or . . .'

Tony interrupts. 'Yeah, course. And looking back, some of the stuff, it went way over the line. But I dunno, sometimes, it feels like it's gone a bit far the other way, you know? Like I came up through a couple of real old-school dressing rooms, so I get I'm more of a dinosaur than most. But it didn't do me no harm, cleaning boots, getting the piss taken out of me by the first team, all that.' He glances at me again, and you can see in his face the teenager that he must've been, equal parts bravado and determination. 'And you and me, we're about the same age, I'm guessing?'

I'm three years older, but I don't feel the need to point it out. 'Close enough, anyway.'

'So, you'll remember, how it used to be easier to have a real laugh about some of this stuff?'

'We certainly did.' It might just be that we're physically close, but I feel like there's a connection that wasn't there before. Even if it's only that, in a game where thirty is dangerously close to retirement, we're both feeling old. It makes me more confiding than I'd usually be with a player. 'I loved that side of working at the club when I first started. At home everything was always educational, always serious. But here the culture was completely different.'

Tony pulls a face. 'Is that code for fucking terrifying? The stories 'bout this place back in the day are pretty legendary.'

'Well, by the time I started, Monica had been in charge long enough, and most of the worst excesses were over, but there were a few of the old guard left. And I was a bit of a frightened little rabbit to begin with, but you know Gary King?'

'Yeah, I do. Your captain at the time?'

'Umm, that's right. Gary took it on himself to teach me my job, including how to give as good as I got. And one day I just felt like I fitted in.'

Tony's eyes flicker away from the windscreen for a second. 'That was a bit of a novelty, was it?'

I'm taken aback that he can tell. 'Maybe, yes.' He doesn't say anything, and since I don't want to sound like I'm wallowing, I smile brightly. 'So, I'm proud we're more care-ful these days, and much more diverse and inclusive too, and I think it's a big part of why we got successful. But sometimes, I know I shouldn't admit it, I do miss Gary ranging round my office after training, telling dirty jokes.'

Tony glances round at me and smiles, not the usual grin but something quite soft. 'I get that, cos I like having a playmate and all.' The smile becomes conspiratorial. 'And I reckon I could make a reasonable job of subbing for Gary, if you're interested?'

I'm not sure that's a good idea, but apparently my mouth disagrees, because I'm saying, 'That sounds fun.'

'That's me, the fun guy.' He's stopped smiling and when he looks at me next, it's like he's doing mental arithmetic. 'It makes sense actually, Gary having an influence. Cos your approach to player care, it's a bit non-standard?'

That hits a nerve. 'Is it? I mean, I don't exactly know

what other clubs do, it's always a bit secretive. And there are training courses now, but I tried one and every session made me want to vomit, it was so management speaky. But no one's ever complained, so I've kept doing what I've always done.'

Tony shakes his head. 'Oh, I've no complaints. It's just Gary's always been big on man-management, and you're kind of the same. Like player care guys I've worked with before, they'd be busy giving me a rundown of house stuff, what day bin day is, all that.'

I jump in quickly. 'Oh, you don't need to worry about that. I'm going to get you an excellent cleaner.'

He laughs. 'I'm sure you are. But what I mean is, your version of helping me settle is less fixing to get my car valeted on set days, more kidding round, then telling me personal stuff, cos you reckon I'm lonely, right?'

I'm mortified again, unsure how to react. I guess maybe I do. 'Are you? Lonely?' I keep my voice easy, but this might be it, the thing that's stopping him settling at Covenly. And this is the ideal way to talk about it, with him having brought it up. Tony stares straight ahead and I pretend to do the same while keeping half an eye on his profile.

There's a longish gap, then he twists his mouth and sighs. 'Honestly? Yeah, a bit, I guess. Does that make me sound pathetic?'

I shake my head. 'No, not at all. It's pretty standard when players come on their own.'

'Only they're like nineteen-year-olds, aren't they? Guys my age, they normally have a wife and kids in tow.'

'That doesn't always help. What I meant more was

players often bring someone along, at least in the early days, to soften the transition. Even if it's just somebody that's worked for them for a while, or a friend that's at a loose end. You could try that, see if it helps?'

'Yeah, only like I said, I'm cutting ties.' He drums his first finger against the steering wheel.

I deliberately relax my body, so what I say next won't sound like criticism. 'But Tony, do you mind me saying, trying to do everything on your own, it might not be the best approach? In the long term anyway.'

'How do you mean?' he asks, and there's a warning in his voice.

'Well, you come across as naturally social, someone who gets their energy from being . . .'

He half smiles. 'Centre of attention is the phrase you're looking for?'

'Perhaps. But that's not a bad thing, if you can turn it to your advantage. And obviously, I'm not saying spend every night in a club or anything like that, but . . .'

'Find something to feed my massive ego?' He smiles properly this time, so I think I've avoided crossing a line.

'No, something that lets you be you, instead of fighting it.' I want to stroke his hand, resting on the gear stick. I focus on keeping my voice gentle. 'Because if nothing else, what you're doing now seems to make you hard work for the others.'

'You had complaints?' he asks quickly.

'No, but I get the impression some of them find you the tiniest bit intimidating.'

He shrugs with one shoulder. It's less smooth than most

of his movements, so I think he's already aware of what I'm telling him, and a touch ashamed he hasn't done anything to change it. 'Well, they're kids, aren't they? Like the average age in the dressing room, it might as well be a creche.'

I smile, but keep my voice cajoling. 'I'm not saying you'll end up lifelong friends, but a bit of mentoring, a few war stories, they'd love that. And it might make it more fun for you too?'

He sighs. 'I could probably manage a bit more arm-round-the-shoulder stuff, I suppose.'

'That'd be nice.'

'Yeah, maybe.' That would be more encouraging if his tone wasn't quite so suggestive of a condemned man.

I really, really want to put my hand over his now, but I channel that into making my smile as warm as I can. 'Oh Tony, there's no need to sound so miserable. Give it a week or two and it'll start to feel like home, and if it doesn't, we'll find another solution.'

'I reckon you're overestimating your powers.'

There's a roughness to his voice, and his hand is tense on the steering wheel. I wait, not sure if he's upset with me or himself. At the gates, I expect him to rush back onto the road. Instead, Tony kills the engine. His eyes are fixed on cows grazing in the field opposite and he's back to looking like a kid again, the bravado gone. I get another of those images that have been pushing into my mind all afternoon. Only instead of the shirt-ripping, hands-all-over-him kisses that kept popping up at the lodge, it's me pulling him in and kissing his hair. But obviously, any sort of kiss would be deeply inappropriate, so I make myself statue still, trying not to intrude into something he's not ready to share.

After a minute or so, he puts a hand to his forehead and drags his fingers down his face. When he twists to me, there's a smile, though not a particularly happy one. 'Sorry, Genie. I didn't mean to get snappy or weird or whatever.'

I shake my head and say softly, 'It's all right. It's normal, you know? For this to be an adjustment.'

He shrugs. 'I guess, only this, it's not all new, you know? Some of it, I brought with me. So, like, don't worry 'bout it, OK? There's no point you putting a ton of effort into something I don't reckon's fixable.'

I decide now is the moment to become brisk. 'Oh no, we won't give up. I like a challenge. Do you have hobbies?'

'What, like golf?'

I nod.

'No.'

'Thank God for that.'

He looks at me questioningly. 'This would be so much harder to solve if you were boring,' I explain.

That seems to do the trick, because he sits back and laughs. 'Yeah, I reckon I was right, I'm definitely gonna like you.'

'Well, that's a start in the building of social ties, isn't it?'

'Did you learn that one on your training course?' He's teasing now, so we're definitely back on track.

'I did, yes. And although the phrase is obviously awful, it's not a bad idea in terms of settling in. So, are you in a hurry to get back?'

He runs his fingers over the gradient of his fade, tracing down to where his dark hair merges into stubble. 'To the hotel? No, the reverse.'

'Come and meet the man in my life then.'

He wrinkles his eyebrows together. 'If I'm honest, love, I'm not sure we're likely to hit it off.'

'You might be surprised. He's quite adorable.'

8

My lurcher jumps up at me the minute the door's open, paws flailing and tail wagging like crazy. I say over my shoulder, 'This is Rouden, Roudie to his friends. You'll have to excuse him. He's untrainable.' That draws Roudie's attention to Tony. Roudie pauses for a moment, eyes like saucers, then turns tail and runs into the kitchen. 'Sorry, he's not super keen on men. He usually gets over it, it just takes a few meetings.'

'Sounds reasonable,' Tony says, as I usher him into the kitchen.

Tony looks around for somewhere to sit, and settles for lounging against the cupboards.

'This place is, um . . .'

He's obviously searching for something nice to say, and I laugh. 'It's all right. Skylar's always teasing about how it looks like the bailiffs have been.'

'You not been here long?'

I grimace. 'Three years. But after I bought the bare minimum of furniture, I sort of ran out of steam.'

Even leaving aside my minimalist approach to decorating, no one could claim my cottage, which was built for farm labourers, is grand. But normally, it feels perfect for me and Roudie. The terracotta tiles can take any amount of muddy paws and dirty running shoes, and the log burner means it's always warm, even in the dead of winter. Today though, it seems cramped. I guess that's to be expected. I can't imagine Victorian ploughmen took up anywhere near as much space as Tony, or had quite such big personalities. And if it was just small that wouldn't be a huge issue, but I have to admit, it's looking neglected. Like I've always meant to re-do the kitchen but it's never made it to the top of the to-do list. The laminate worktops peeling at the edges are definitely a contrast to the lodge's smooth granite.

Bringing Tony here was a mistake. I'm being paid to help him feel at home. It's got to be off-putting that I haven't even hung a picture in mine, unless you count the photos stuck on the fridge, three from Katia's birthday, random photos of friends out of work, two of Roudie and one from Skylar's first start for the women's team. Not a single one of my ex-husband, obviously. I attempt to at least discreetly push the unopened letters scattered on the work surface into a tidy pile, which sends half of them toppling to the floor. Tony stoops to collect them and as he hands them back to me, he's trying not to laugh.

'You take the same approach with players' mail? Just let it pile up?'

'No. I promise, none of my players has ever had so much as an overdue parking ticket.' I should leave it there, but I hear myself adding, 'It's just, left to my own devices, I'm not terribly domesticated.' I meant it to sound jokey, but it comes out more prickly. I stare down at, inevitably, a chipped tile, and prod my fingers into a tense spot on my neck. 'Sorry, it's not a great advertisement for my professional skills, is it?'

'I dunno 'bout that. Seems like you're pretty good at looking after what you care about.' His voice is soft and when I look up, he points over at Roudie, lying on his ultra-deluxe memory foam bed.

It's unexpectedly kind. But it wouldn't do for Tony to see I'm getting all melty, so I limit myself to offering a drink and praying he doesn't want something involving milk, since I doubt there is any. Luckily, he asks for water.

I've had an idea, and as I fill a glass, I ask casually, 'Do you fancy coming for a walk with me and Roudie? He'll feel cheated if I don't take him out, now I've come home early.' When I turn to hand him the water, Tony looks decidedly wary so I backtrack. 'But if you're not into walking, that's fine, I'll let him out in the garden quickly and then we'll get going.'

'Nah, it's not that.' His voice turns gruff. 'Just I could do without pictures in the paper tomorrow of me adjusting to country living.'

'That's unlikely,' I say, hoping that's true, and berating myself for not thinking of that myself. 'It's one of the best things about coming to play here, we're too out of the way for the paparazzi to bother much.'

'Yeah, but half the time now, the tabloids, they're just buying stuff off people's phones, so someone else might see me.'

My smile is extra reassuring. 'Everyone in the village is ancient. Most of them probably can't use the cameras on their phones, and the rest wouldn't be able to send the photo as an attachment. And even if they could, they'd have to recognize you without their glasses. I honestly think it would be fine, but there's no pressure.'

He grins. 'Then yeah, a walk'd be great. You and the pup can show me the sights.'

I run upstairs to swap silk blouse and vegan leather skirt for leggings and a t-shirt, maybe knotted a touch tighter at the back than is strictly necessary. But given all the work I put into re-acquiring my waist post-divorce, I feel I've earned the right to show it off now and again. I also grab a baseball cap, on the basis that, even if I were to get a ridiculous urge to kiss Tony, the long brim would act as a makeshift chastity belt.

When I get back into the kitchen, Roudie's resting his head on Tony's knee, allowing his ears to be pulled.

'How on earth did you manage that?'

He shrugs. 'I dunno. He just came over.'

Roudie delicately licks Tony's hand.

'That's astonishing.'

Tony bends to ruffle Roudie's fur. 'I reckon you've just got good taste, haven't you, mate?'

He looks up at me through his lashes, and I let the eye contact linger a second too long, before pointing to the lock on the bin. 'That seems to argue otherwise.'

Tony laughs. 'Well, that's me told! Now, are we taking this fella for a walk or what?'

We head out and Tony looks at me closely. 'You told me I didn't need to worry 'bout press, yeah?'

'I really don't think so here.'

'So, what's with the hat?'

'Just keeping the sun out of my eyes.'

He smiles slowly, and I've got a horrible feeling he's guessed the actual reason, though it's such mad logic I know really that's impossible, but all he says is, 'Fair enough.'

I won't lie. Over the years, I've spent numerous imaginary afternoons in Tony's company. But they always involved hotel rooms, or if you held my feet to the fire, I might admit to the odd dressing room encounter. Definitely no pleasant country walks. And today's walk is genuinely pleasant. It starts out on a narrow path between tall holly hedges, Roudie in front, Tony padding behind. Then it opens out into springy green pasture and we're side by side, quiet, the late afternoon sun strong on my back. It's weirdly peaceful, except for Roudie dancing at the end of the lead. Once I'm sure it's sheep free, I let him off to gallop around. He does some cursory sniffing but there's nothing worth hunting, so he's mainly running circles for the hell of it.

Tony stops to watch Roudie whizzing past us, a sleek tan and white blur. 'He's dead elegant, isn't he? Like we should have him playing on the wing, he's that fast.'

I beam at Tony, an appreciation of Roudie being a major source of bonus points with me. 'That's exactly what I think. Imagine being able to make one killer pass for him to run onto? He's perfect for breaking down a high press.' Roudie races towards me and I dart at him. He feints right then turns left. 'And see, defenders would hate him almost as much as they hate you.'

Tony waits until I'm back beside him, then tilts his head to acknowledge the fully deserved flattery. 'You do like your football, don't you? And I get the dog now. He's not

61

what I'd have guessed for you, but he's just right for a sporting sort of girl.'

For half a second, his palm is on my back. It's the first time he's intentionally touched me. Nothing's peaceful any more. I swallow hard, digging my nails into my palm until I'm sure there'll be no sign of the rush of desire so strong, it's close to nausea.

'What would you have guessed?' My voice is thankfully at most slightly teasing, not breathlessly eager, which was a genuine concern thirty seconds ago.

'Something small and sort of cuddly. Not . . . Actually, what is your dog?'

'A lurcher. Well, really a long dog, because he's probably half greyhound, half saluki.' Maybe sticking to informative facts is the secret to keeping up a professional front? Let's hope so. If memorizing chunks of Wikipedia is the answer to prolonged exposure to Tony, that's going to make my life a whole lot easier.

He shrugs. 'So, you might as well have said that in dog language for all I understood it.'

'He's a hunting dog. They breed them round here for rabbits and deer and things. But they tend to get so carried away chasing something, they get lost, and end up in a shelter.'

'Don't the owners come look for 'em?'

'It's illegal, hunting with dogs, so no.'

Tony takes half a step away so he can grin at me directly. 'Well, I bet he's pretty happy with how it turned out. You seem like you'd make a top-class mistress.'

OK, so sadly, dry facts aren't the antidote. I make my face haughty. 'There's no point smiling like that. Now

62

you've said I seem like someone who'd have a small fluffy dog, you're dead to me.'

He laughs. 'Sorry, only I've never heard of a greyhound Suzuki, or whatever you said, so I couldn't have guessed that. And I don't have much experience of dogs anyhow. I like 'em though.'

Most players do. You never have to worry if it's you they love, or your money. Which is where my idea comes in, and it sounds like now's the time to lay the groundwork.

'Why not get one?'

He shrugs. 'I dunno. I've thought 'bout it a few times over the years. Only it's sort of like why I don't have the wife and kids neither. I like the idea.' He twists his mouth. 'But responsibility, let's just say it's lucky that doesn't count toward my FIFA rating.'

It's the perfect in, and I have to make a serious effort to sound off-hand. 'You can always borrow Roudie, if you like. He's deeply resentful of the hours I work and he'd love the odd post-training walk.'

Tony jumps at it like an aerial ball in the box. 'Yeah, actually, I would like that, if you're serious?'

'Of course, you'd be doing me a favour. There's a spare key under the mat, pick him up any time you want. Just keep him on the lead until he's used to you.'

Tony gives me a really happy smile, all teeth and crinkly eyes. 'Yeah, I will. Thanks.' He watches Roudie, then asks, 'So, is it bad, my first anchoring social tie being a dog?'

'Well, when I described him as the man in my life, I wasn't joking: he is my longest-lasting relationship, so I can't exactly judge.'

Tony's smile dims. 'Yeah, well, you've only had to open a paper the last few years to know I can't throw stones on that front myself.'

I change the subject, pointing out the view, how you can see the training ground and even the roof of the stadium in amongst the mini tower blocks and factory chimneys of Covenly. But that means Tony's so close behind me, it would only take half a step back for me to be leaning against his chest. And there's the inevitable visual flash, his arms around my waist, his lips against my neck.

9

'You got my keys, Genie?'

I dangle the ring from my fingers and jangle the keys at Tony, propping up the door to the office, hair still wet from a post-training shower and coffee in hand.

He saunters over and puts the paper cup on my desk. 'For you. From the players' lounge.'

I hold the coffee up, inhale it like wine, then smile up at Tony. 'Mmm, contraband. Thank you.'

He grins. 'I wasn't seen, so if you hide the cup after, I've probably got away with it.'

For that to make sense, you have to understand that coffee is the most recent weapon in the endless cold war between Monica and the manager. He takes espresso seriously and insists on a continuous supply of his preferred brand. Shortly after Tony arrived, Monica went on a buyer's remorse-fuelled rampage over financial extravagance. Coffee topped the list. To be fair, it's eye-wateringly expensive, and the manager's claim it offers a performance benefit is almost certainly spurious. But it's also a drop in the ocean in terms of our outgoings and a fraction of what other clubs must spend on caffeine supplements. Plus, it's delicious, and thankfully, it's survived Monica's cost-cutting, proving even she can't bulldoze a solid wall of charming obstinacy reinforced by strategic lapses in English comprehension.

Only that means, roughly once a week, there's a club-wide email reminding us the good coffee is for players and senior management only. So, it's sweet that Tony's standing with the serfs. Sweet but unsettling. I'd expect Tony to be absentmindedly amiable with staff who are useful to him, but the coffee feels like something more. Because he's noticed how I take it, almost as if he's watching me as much as I'm watching him. And if he is, he might see the real me. That can't happen. She needs to stay hidden behind work me, who definitely wouldn't have woken up this morning already imagining his lips on hers.

Tony holds out his hand. I give myself a mental shake. Obviously, he went with black, no sugar as the easiest option. I drop the keys into his palm. He tightens his fingers around them, eyes half closed. 'Thanks. It's going to be quite a relief, getting into somewhere a bit more permanent.' He pulls at the zip of his club tracksuit jacket, then looks back to me. 'And, um, I was wondering, is there anything I can do for you, like in return?'

'There's no need, it's my job,' I say, surprised.

He twists one side of his mouth down. ''Cept you went a bit above and beyond. Finding me somewhere that's a touch out the ordinary, getting the lease rushed through, all that.'

'Not really.' I smile, trying to smooth over a relatively common awkward moment. Players get so used to everything being transactional, they forget club staff aren't expecting a tip or a designer handbag. 'And from what LeMar's said about training, it sounds like you're providing excellent service yourself. I don't see why you shouldn't expect the same from us.'

Tony isn't a man embarrassed by praise and his face is extra happy, but verbally, he shrugs it off, 'Well, it helps that lad can nick a goal out of half a chance.' He tones the grin down and his voice drops a notch lower. 'But Genie, it's not only the house. I wanna make sure I've said sorry properly, for how I was at the start.' He pushes a hand into the pocket of his joggers, scrunching up the fabric. 'I was thinking, maybe dinner? I know it's not exactly fancy round here, but a couple of the lads were saying there's a nice place on the river.'

I do my best to control my reaction. There's an extremely nice place on the river. Or so I'm told, it's somewhat outside my budget. Though honestly, I'd happily eat service station sandwiches if I could do it staring at Tony. But it's against club rules, not to say potentially massively awkward. I mean, who wants to star in a tabloid exclusive revealing that bad boy Tony Garratt is such a softie, he'll stoop to taking a plain Jane out for a thank-you treat?

I pull an apologetic face. 'I'd love to, but I'm sorry, the staff contracts are pretty strict about player interactions. Unless it's an official thing, dinner is definitely not permitted.'

'Sorry, didn't realize.' He looks excessively embarrassed, but then everything about Tony is quite full on. 'But, um, is there something else I could do? Just like as a thank you.'

I shake my head and make my voice firm. 'No, as I said, it's all part of the service.' Usually, Tony's face is malleable, a jester's play of what he's thinking. But he's become very still. I worry he's offended, so I think about it for a second then smile. 'Well, actually . . .'

Tony jumps on the wheedling pause. 'Go on. Tell me.'

'I don't suppose I could sign you up for an evening chatting with the academy players? It'd only be the older ones. And just to talk nutrition, motivation, that sort of thing, nothing too personal.'

Tony holds his hand up. 'Yeah, course, I'd be happy to. No need to make it sound such a big ask. You sure that's what you want, though? Cos I don't wanna take advantage of genies being more used to taking requests than making 'em.'

I laugh. 'No. If you honestly don't mind, that'd be lovely. The diary system hates me, but I'll have Katia put it on your calendar when she gets back from lunch.' As I say it, I look up and see her hovering in the doorway.

Katia fidgets with a strand of her twist out. 'Sorry, I didn't want to interrupt.' She sidles over to her desk. 'Am I late back? I thought Skylar would be done by now.'

'Training must've run over, and anyway, you're not late.'

Tony frowns at Skylar's empty desk. 'You in a hurry to get off for lunch, Genie?'

'Not at all.' As confirmation, I scoop the empty salad bowl off my desk into the recycling. 'Is there something else we can do for you?'

'Two things, actually.' He fiddles with the keyring, pulls off one key and hands it to me. 'That's the spare, right?'

I nod.

'Since you're practically next door, do you reckon you could hang on to it?'

I widen my eyes. I'd expect him to be ultra-guarded about his privacy, not happy to hand out keys to staff. 'Um, of course, if that's what you'd like.'

'It makes sense. And I was thinking, your thing with the key under the mat, it's not the most security-conscious. I'll be in and out for the dog anyhow, how about I hang on to one of yours?'

I can almost hear Gavin, my ex, going on at me about keys, and planning ahead to make sure I don't end up walking home alone, and how activating Find Your Friends is a sensible precaution. But it's unreasonable to expect Tony to guess I hate helpful suggestions. Especially from men. Actually, especially from attractive men. I make an effort to bite my tongue.

By the time I reply, I think I successfully avoid sounding snappy. 'Please don't worry. You'll get sick of me locking myself out when I've been running. And Halsbury's not exactly a hotbed of crime.'

I'm dreading him arguing back, but instead of nagging me about being irresponsible, Tony glances over at Katia. She's the picture of concentration, bent over her keyboard and biting down on a pencil that perfectly matches her hot pink lipstick but I can tell she's listening to every word. He crouches down on his heels, hands on my desk, and looks up at me.

'Have I overstepped, love?' His voice is whisper quiet.

I narrow my eyes and half smile as I say just as softly, 'Maybe a tiny bit.'

He nods briskly, eyes serious. 'OK, understood. Won't happen again.'

I make my next smile extra friendly. 'It's fine, no worries. What's the second thing?'

He straightens up and perches on the edge of my desk.

'So, if this is too far off the books, say. Cos I get you two aren't like concierges or whatever, but can I get your input on something?'

'Of course, we're here to help. Whatever you need.'

Before he can reply, Skylar slouches in looking disconsolate. I'm guessing Jenny, her rival for a starting spot, had an excellent training session. I smile at her consolingly and Tony gives her a brief nod, before leaning into me.

'You know I mentioned the family thing?'

His voice is quiet again. I murmur yes, trying to make my face just the right shade of sympathetic, so he can see it, but Katia and Skylar won't. Family's a tricky one. Players almost always say it's their biggest support system, but it's rarely that simple, and somehow from what he's been saying, I doubt Tony Garratt got to be who he is on a diet of parental praise. So, this could be quite delicate. And he seems to be having a bit of trouble getting started, fiddling with a pen from my desk.

'Would you prefer to shoot me an email for this one?' I ask, my voice bright.

He shakes his head and puts the pen down. 'Nah, this, it's not a big thing. It's that my niece, my sister's kid, she's just passed her A-levels. She'll be the first one in the family to go to uni.'

I nod and try to make my face congratulatory but not prying.

'I've not seen much of her the last couple of years, but I wanna get her something to say well done, you know?'

'That's nice.' Still as bland as I can make it.

He gets his phone out and pulls up a photo before

passing it over to me. 'So, I was thinking these. What do you reckon?'

It's of a pair of ginormous diamond earrings. They would be absolutely perfect for a dowager duchess, or a young woman who's recently learnt to recognize truly expensive jewellery. I mean, let's say, just as an example, you were buying a present for your twenty-three-year-old girlfriend. And she happens to be an influencer, so it's got to be something that, when she posts it, proves she's worth following. Then these would be absolutely on the money. But for an eighteen-year-old off to university, they're not ideal, unless she's planning a study trip abroad in the Hapsburg empire.

I try to convey that, only in a nicer way and without anything spurious about Tony's ex-girlfriend. Or, more accurately, his probably ex-girlfriend, because he hasn't actually confirmed anything on that score.

Tony still ends up looking crestfallen. Skylar glances up from her computer. 'Don't worry. Buying jewellery for other women is one of Genie's specialist skills. You can trust her, she always picks something perfect.'

I shake my head. 'No. We need Katia for this. Because like I said, these are gorgeous, but your niece would probably prefer something more young and fun.'

Tony appears deeply unconvinced. 'Don't you think that'd look kind of cheap?'

He so obviously wants to get this right, I have to make an effort not to smile. 'There's a jeweller, Claudia, in town. She makes beautiful pieces, all proper stones, just less formal.' I can see he still isn't sure. 'LeMar's bought some lovely things there for Katia, and she's incredibly fussy about jewellery.'

Katia looks up for the first time since she sat down. 'That makes me sound like a gold-digger.'

I laugh. The only time she and LeMar argue is when Katia tries to insist on paying for things. 'No, just highly valued. Come and show Tony your bracelet.'

She walks across and holds her hand out from a distance, obviously uncomfortable. I can't say Kat's warmed to Tony, he's too rough around the edges for her tastes. But she's far too polite to let that show, so I think it's more that she doesn't like showing off her jewellery in front of Skylar, who couldn't possibly afford it. Tony doesn't make a big thing of admiring the tiny diamonds and rose quartz linked by a web of fine gold strands. Instead, he approaches as if a child's showing something precious, keeping his face grave. 'Thanks, love. Yeah, it's nice. Very pretty.' He looks at me. 'So, something like that, you reckon?'

'I think so, don't you, Kat?'

'Definitely. Something she could wear every day.' Katia's smile is so persuasive, Tony would have to have a heart of stone to resist.

I smile too. 'Umm, much better than something that lives in a safe or a drawer most of the time.'

'That way she'll have lots of photos, from freshers' week and parties and things, where she's wearing it. And when she looks back at them, she'll remember who gave it to her.' Katia sounds wistful, though I'd pick LeMar over my university experience every time, and I bet Katia feels the same.

72

Tony nods and his eyes are soft. 'Yeah, that's a nice idea.'

I beam at Katia. 'Do you think you could pick out a few options? And maybe Tony could drop by Claudia's studio after training, and decide which he likes best?'

Katia's more than happy to oblige. There's an intense discussion about stone preferences and price range, then Tony thanks Katia before turning to me. 'Knew I was coming to the right place. Thanks, Genie. And I'll get the dog back in one piece, promise.'

'Just don't let him con you into believing I let him eat human food or get on the furniture.'

He laughs. 'Don't worry. I've already got the message loud and clear.'

I grin. 'Enjoy yourselves.'

Katia calls Skylar over to look at Claudia's website, which is kind, since she can't need assistance.

Skylar waits until Tony's out of earshot before, 'Is there something you'd like to tell us, Genie?'

'Can't think of anything, no.'

'So, you and Garratt aren't suddenly very friendly?'

I can't help smiling back at Skylar. Partly because Tony seems to put me in a good mood for no particular reason. But mainly because she's being very nice about jewellery selection. And if anyone knows how it feels to look at gorgeous things you can't have, it's me.

Every time I see LeMar, he's full of how well pre-season's going. A happy striker ought to equal a happy attacking midfielder, so I shouldn't be worrying about Tony. But our first match is Saturday, and Roudie's still getting walked and Tony's still popping into the office for plenty of after-training chats. It's nagging away at the back of my mind that if Tony really had settled here, he wouldn't need us any more. So, I shouldn't be pleased when, at two o'clock on a Friday, Tony's head appears around the office door. That I'm not just pleased, I'm delighted, should probably raise a whole other set of concerns. But we'll worry about that when he's gone.

He takes a quick look around the office. 'Just you again?'

'Not for long. Katia's saying goodbye to LeMar before he goes into pre-game mode.'

'What 'bout Sky?'

Ah, so that's the explanation for the ongoing office visits. Skylar's gorgeous, as you'd expect for a twenty-year-old who spends half her life working out. I suppose I should be happy that it's not because Tony's still feeling lonely. And there definitely shouldn't be a snippy ring to, 'Kicking a ball around somewhere, I suspect.'

Tony raises his eyebrows. 'Can't help noticing that's a bit of a theme. Does that mean you're run off your feet?'

I'm actually busy indulging my paranoia that I'm going

to screw up booking hotel dates for our Champion's League opening-round games. I can't afford to get this wrong: qualifying to play in Europe was unimaginable even a couple of seasons ago. But I have to admit, the players aren't the only ones feeling the pressure. Having double- and triple-checked the dates against the UEFA website, I've almost got up the courage to click confirm. Only it can't hurt to let myself soak in a few minutes of Tony first. 'Not if you need something.'

He lounges in, not bothering to close the door, and slouches against Katia's desk. 'This is a quick one. What's this thing on my calendar for Sunday night?'

He holds out his phone. It's the sponsors' drinks evening, the least popular fixture on the players' timetable. Given how much complaining it triggers, I'm not surprised Monica's PA has slipped it onto the calendar without any explanation. I pull a sympathetic face. 'Sorry, it's the price of coming to a club that's not owned by a sheikh or an oligarch. Monica requires you all to make nice to the sponsors after the first game of the season. It's not too bad, only a couple of hours. And it does help them feel they're getting their money's worth.'

Tony screws up his mouth. 'Kind of like we're circus animals?'

I smile. 'More dancing bears, I think.'

He grins back. 'Of the sore-headed variety, I take it?'

'There's usually a general lack of enthusiasm. But it's better than it used to be. For years, Monica insisted on having it actually on the same day as the first home game of the season. At least now you play Saturday and do this Sunday.'

He leans against the desk, his weight on his palms, presumably stretching out tightness left over from training. 'Well, I guess it's an incentive to win first time out, anyhow. Better to spend the evening wallowing in a bit of praise than making excuses.'

I try to pretend I'm not fixated on his shoulders, the muscle obvious under the t-shirt. 'I suspect that's part of Monica's thinking. But, anyway, it's at her house. We can set up a car, but most of the lads prefer to drive themselves for this one.'

'For a quick exit?'

'Exactly.'

'Yeah, that's fine with me. I'm on mineral water in public, anyhow. Don't want no one thinking this season is going to be a repeat of the last one.'

I manage to prevent myself from pointing out, given how good he looks at the end of pre-season, it obviously won't be. Instead, I keep my voice cool, gesturing to the pile of paperwork on my desk as I ask, 'Is there anything else you need, or should I tackle these?'

'Just what am I supposed to wear?'

'If you can bear it, a suit.'

He pulls a face, roughly equivalent to the kind a child asked to dress up for a wedding would pull. 'Yeah, I would. Only suits, they makes me look like I'm going to court.'

Looking at him, that's so obviously true, I can't help laughing. 'Then aim for the get-past-a-small-town-night-club-bouncer look. Black trousers, white shirt, proper shoes. And we're selling the lifestyle aspect, so some conspicuous wealth display wouldn't hurt.'

'Rolex it is then,' he says, his eyes sardonic.

'Sounds perfect,' and I imagine he will look perfect, and that he'll play the part required beautifully.

He takes a bow. 'I aim to please. And I'm guessing it'd please you right now if I left you alone.'

I'm tempted to say nothing would please me less, but successfully hold my tongue. Tony makes for the door until the trinket on my desk catches his eye. It's the present our ex-captain, Gary King, gave me when he retired, a Moroccan lamp, studded with red stones, which look like rubies but sadly aren't. Tony takes it, twisting it in his hands. The gold's perfect against his tan, which has faded a touch since he first joined us, but is still obvious against his neatly manicured nails.

He smiles, and it's the gentle one that shows in his eyes. 'So Genie, this is the lamp you take refuge in, is it? When you're tired of taking care of everything?'

It's not the first time I've heard this kind of quip. 'It does cross my mind it'd be nice to hide in it, from time to time,' I grin.

'I bet it does. Only whoever gave it you got it wrong, didn't they?'

I look at him questioningly.

'The story, it's that you pick the shiny lamp and there's no genie. You've gotta go for the simple one to get what's worth having inside. Isn't that right?'

'In real life, I don't think that's how it works.' I break his gaze, which has got very serious. I'm not sure what game we're playing. 'Not in this business, anyway.'

'I dunno, maybe we're the ones that should be paying

more attention to that kind of stuff than most.' He shrugs and then he's back to smiling, even the start of a grin now. 'You'll be at this thing Sunday anyhow, won't you?'

'Uh-huh. We'll be helping out the hospitality team.'

His grin widens. 'And you'll be at the match Saturday?'

'Yep, doing the friends and family stuff.'

He's at full grin now. 'That's all right then. No need for me to be worrying about the lamp working for wishes.'

'That's a truly terrible line,' I splutter, laughing. Underneath my pretend frown, I'm not sure if I'm relieved or disappointed that he was evidently building up to that all along.

He tilts his head and the smile becomes lopsided. 'Yeah, it weren't my smoothest.' He laughs, his eyes squinting like a happy Staffie. 'Never mind, sounds like there'll be plenty of chances to get some improvement in, the next few days.'

'Get out and let me do some actual work.' I throw my pen at him, which annoyingly he catches one-handed as he leans over and replaces the lamp on my desk.

He strolls to the door. 'Well, it's nice to know you don't count helping me out as work. See you Sunday.' I've got a nasty feeling I'm grinning like a love-sick teenager when he reappears. 'Unless you fancy coming over tonight?' A mischievous look enters his eyes at this point. 'Cos I could do with working off a bit of pre-game tension, if you knows what I mean?'

'I believe true professionals channel it into match performance,' I say tartly, enjoying the joke, but still trying not to go pink.

He shrugs with a cheeky grin. 'Never found that works for me, but I'll give it a go.'

He wanders away and I decide doing anything that requires serious focus would be a mistake. So, instead of finalizing hotel bookings, I get up to check with Natalie in Hospitality exactly what we need to do for Sunday. And it seems Tony chose the busiest time possible to have that recent conversation with the office door wide open. As I walk out, Natalie's at the photocopier, the medical and physio team – including to my horror my ex, Gavin, on his way to the medics' meeting – are turning the corner to the conference room, and Skylar and Katia are emerging from the supply closet, giggling.

Skylar, who's got the world's second most carrying voice after Tony, says, 'We thought we wouldn't interrupt. But like you're always saying, he's obviously not the slightest bit keen.'

Hmm, I guess everyone heard Tony's parting joke. Including Gavin. It shouldn't matter. It must've been obvious we were only playing around. No one could possibly think I'm under the impression Tony's serious. All the same, I feel hot and shivery at the same time, just like I used to when I'd go to take Gavin's hand and he'd yank it away.

11

It's not hard to work out which door leads into Monica's bedroom. From the top of the stairs, I can already hear her interrogating Natalie over why guests are arriving early. I've no clue why I've been summoned, but I'm guessing it's not good from how Monica barks, 'Come,' in response to my knock.

As I shuffle in, Natalie makes a break for the door, muttering, 'I'll just, um . . .'

Monica keeps me waiting while she applies an extra coat of lipstick. I can't help noticing the state of her dressing table is the exact opposite of mine. I bet Gavin loves the perfectly aligned row of tastefully packaged products, instead of my mess of half-empty bottles and circus-worthy collection of eyeshadows. All the same, getting ready for tonight was definitely more fun at mine. Though somehow, I can't see Monica fighting with Katia for the mirror, or joining in with Skylar, teasing about Tony.

Monica blots her lips then brandishes her tablet. 'What possessed you to approve this?'

Tonight's invitation is blown up until the start time fills the screen. And it's an hour earlier than it should be, which explains why the reception room is thronging with guests when Monica's still in a dressing gown. I can see why she's angry, but not why it's directed at me.

81

'I'm sorry, but I didn't.' I feel bad, throwing Natalie under the bus, but I have to add, 'Player Care's just helping out tonight. Hospitality did all the arrangements.'

Monica achieves a scowl that her Botox shouldn't allow. 'I instructed Hospitality. They should have been responsible for all arrangements. But it appears not.'

She pulls up a Slack conversation. And she's right, there's me, saying:

> The invitation is good to go. Let's get it sent to the sponsor's list before EOD.

But I've got zero recollection of seeing the invitation, let alone sending that message. And when do I ever use EOD?

I'm still staring at the screen, mouth open, when Gavin walks in, fiddling with a cuff link. 'Monica, there are people . . .'

He spots me. There's a hunted dart of the eyes. I suppose that's understandable, finding your ex-wife in your bedroom has to be uncomfortable.

'Oh. Charlotte.' God, I hate it when he calls me that, even if it is my christened name. 'Are you . . .'

Monica wheels around to him. 'She's explaining how she signed off on an incorrect start time.'

Gavin puts a comforting hand on her shoulder. I guess she can't see that he gives me a small consoling smile. 'Perhaps it's best not to dwell on that, my dear. The start of the season's a busy time. It's understandable if sometimes staff are overwhelmed.'

Foot-stamping, toddler-temper-tantrum rage bubbles up. I'm not overwhelmed, this isn't fair, it wasn't me. Only Monica's just proved that it was, so it's fortunate that she gazes up at Gavin and nods rather than anything worse. And looking at their faces in the mirror, perhaps this is why they work? Monica seems genuinely grateful for Gavin's guidance, when I'd be bridling over him interfering. Though I have to say, I've seen her give the director of football much the same look after a shrewd transfer suggestion. Perhaps that's Gavin's role? Director of behaving like a normal human. If it is, I guess hiring decisions are Monica's only business blind spot.

But whatever, at least it means I can start to back out, murmuring about helping Natalie.

'One moment, Genie.' Monica waves to the two outfits laid on the wrinkle-free bed. 'Which one?'

I definitely wasn't expecting that. Gavin clearly wasn't either. He looks at my own dress and frowns slightly. To be fair, it is more figure-hugging than is strictly work appropriate. But after Katia found burgundy jersey silk at the back of my wardrobe, I'd got no chance of leaving the house in a sensible black midi. Gavin's disapproval is enough to make up my mind.

'That one, definitely.' I point to the white sheath dress, slit high enough to show Monica's legs are wasted, hidden under the board table.

As I walk out, Gavin's already busy persuading Monica that the decidedly matronly skirt suit is a better option. And maybe it's relief that I'm not the one being talked into dressing like a fifties housewife, but when Monica and

Gavin's twins rush out of the playroom with their nanny in hot pursuit, I don't feel the usual twinge of envy.

Only I don't think it is that. Because walking downstairs, I'm trying to work out what happened with the invitation. Could someone have fired off a quick Slack message from my work station, without signing me out? It doesn't seem likely, but even so, me not rushing to take the blame, well, that's major progress.

I'm pretty sure that's down to Tony. The second he saw me today, Tony did his 'you've just made my day' smile. I'm fully aware that's a well-rehearsed part of his repertoire, not spontaneous delight at my presence. All the same, it's kept me floating for quite a while. Plus, I'm privately amused that he's every bit as good at charming the sponsors as I'd expected.

He looks like a sartorially aware mafioso, with his gleaming white shirt setting off the carefully sculpted six o'clock shadow beautifully. And obviously, he's fantastic with the wives and daughters. What's more surprising is that he's equally good with the men. Unfortunately, that means he's been stuck with Ian and Christopher Craig for at least fifteen minutes.

The brothers' software business isn't our biggest sponsor but they're old university friends of Gavin's, so they have a direct line to Monica. Sadly for Tony, they're also two of the most boring men I've ever met. I doubt there's much conversational common ground and Tony's back-slapping full-on masculinity might have charmed everyone else, but he's getting drowned in the Craigs' general wetness. Tony's started scanning the room for an escape with an intensity he usually reserves for hunting out a player who's slipped free from their defender. But the brothers have him trapped in an awkward corner between a mirrored sideboard and an oversized orchid. So, when he catches my eye and calls across the room, 'Genie, get over here and say hello,' he's obviously looking for help.

I hesitate, remembering the throat-closing mortification when it became clear we'd been overheard on Friday. But Tony's eyes are pleading and I do want to spend time with him and . . . and maybe it's best to just brazen it out?

The only problem is, I'd forgotten why I've only worn this dress once since buying it to celebrate losing the last few pounds of marriage-related weight gain. But I remember now, the slightest movement is enough to send it creeping up my thigh. With Sky's choice of heels forcing me into supermodel-length strides, it's practically indecent.

Not that Tony seems to mind. The second I'm beside him, his arm is around my waist, like it's a life preserver. I say hello and manage to resist resting a hand on his rolled-up sleeve. He smiles back with the hint of a wink.

'Hello, Genie.' His voice is soft, like he's talking only to me, though this whole thing is for the benefit of the Craigs. 'You all right, love?'

'I am, thank you,' I reply. If you're going to be a prop, you might as well get a little subtle flirting in too. 'Am I allowed to tell you how good you were yesterday, or are you sick of hearing it?'

He manages not to laugh, but his eyes have got extra diamondy, so it must be taking a reasonable amount of effort. 'Funnily enough, I can take a fair bit of that.' He tightens his hand on my waist and I snuggle in. "Specially when it's coming from someone who knows the game so well. You look amazing by the way,' he adds, a look in his eyes that I hope no one else can spot. He turns to the Craigs. 'Don't Genie look nice, fellas?'

I'm the one who wants to laugh now. They're forced into making polite agreeing noises, while looking deeply uncomfortable. It's delightful. I'd bet a year's salary they've had numerous little chats about how Gavin's done better second time around.

'You know each other, I'm guessing?' Tony asks, which I suspect means he can't remember their names.

I stretch out my hand. 'Ian, Christopher, how nice to see you.' They shake back limply and I make my face conspiratorial. 'Do you mind if, while I have Tony's attention, I ask him something?'

They shake their pale blond heads, while exchanging the sort of smiles that go with infants offering to perform their party pieces. It's the same tolerant amusement Gavin perfected during the mid-stage of our relationship, when he was dutifully standing by me despite my being a massive disappointment. If anything, I preferred the final phase, characterized by continuous barely masked irritation. So, I'm not going to feel remotely guilty about teasing the Craigs, I'm going to thoroughly enjoy it.

Tony smiles down at me and his hand begins to migrate from my waist to my hip. 'What's it you wanna know, beauty?'

That throws me off. He hasn't called me that before. Though I doubt I'm the first woman he's used it for. But

86

actually, it works quite well, me gazing up at him for a second too long, then fluttering my lashes to break the eye contact. It creates a pleasing contrast when my voice becomes business-like. 'Yesterday's rotation in midfield. Do you think it'll hold up against teams that are more fluid defensively?'

Tony gives me an approving nod and launches into an intense discussion of the difficulties inherent in exploiting half space. It's reward enough that he's getting a break from computer programming or the motorway system of the UK, which would be my top guesses for the Craigs' cocktail party conversation so far. But it's a nice bonus that the brothers are staring at me as if I'm a Labrador who's just expressed a considered opinion on cryptocurrencies.

I could happily spend the rest of the evening at Tony's side, but it's not long before Gavin looms over. As usual he starts to irritate me almost immediately. Maybe it's the way he leans in to show he's actively listening; or could be the all-boys-together, rugby and rowing club way he loops an arm around the Craigs, ready for a tour of his collectibles? In the dim and distant past, I might've found Gavin's love of sci-fi an endearing chink in his otherwise intensely serious personality. But I can't say it was ever remotely interesting, so I peel myself away from Tony and make a break for the kitchen.

As I push through the revolving door, I glance back. Tony's been scooped up with the Craigs. He catches my eye and mouths, 'Help me.' I grin and mouth back, 'Have fun.' From the expression of Mrs Forrester, the ultra-churchy wife of a manufacturer of industrial coolants who happened to be watching, you don't have to be an expert lip reader to pick up on the 'Bitch' he sends my way in return. Which means I'm laughing as I walk over to tackle the washing-up.

Monica's kitchen intimidates me, which was probably her brief to the designer. It's a smooth sea of gleaming white perfection, untainted by handles. Opening cupboards is like hunting for a secret passage, pressing and tapping until something springs open. And you can guarantee, whatever it is, it won't be what you were hoping for. After spending forever trying to put away glassware and finding refrigerated drawers, which I didn't even know were a thing, and failing to find the recycling and the dishwasher, I give up. So, as I wash, wet champagne flutes are stacking up around me into a fragile prison.

I hear the door swing closed and then it's Tony's voice I hear. 'How's this your job?'

I twist round, hands still in the sink. 'I don't mind. Better than small talk anyway.'

Tony leans against the marble breakfast bar and looks up at the ceiling, eyelids droopy in a play of exhaustion. 'Yeah, I know what you mean. I slunk in here for a bit of a break from putting on the Tony Garratt show.'

I like that he can see the split between who he is and the public persona. But it's not my business so I make my voice jokey. 'I got the impression collectibles weren't quite your thing.'

He grimaces. 'I'm an adult man, so yeah, that's a

reasonable assumption. I notice you made a pretty quick exit and all.'

I smile. 'I can't say I've ever seen their appeal, but then, I'm an adult woman.'

He nods and begins to lounge over. 'Exactly. Why would I wanna stand around looking at old junk? 'Specially when there's a woman like you next door.'

I don't know what to say to that. He sounds like he does when it's banter to fritter away a few minutes after training, but his face is different. He's looking at me the way he studies the set-up before he takes a free kick, weighing up his options. I can still hear the chatter from the party, but it seems a long way off. For a split second, I think he's planning to kiss me. My heart starts bounding like Roudie after a rabbit. But realistically, a kiss is unlikely, and the last thing I want is to look like I'm expecting one. So, I just stand there, waiting, and when he's a step or two away, Tony stops. There's the same frustrated smile as when he realizes there's nothing on and he'll have to make a back pass, just to retain possession. Instead of coming any closer, he turns and begins prodding at the kitchen cupboards.

'Is there no way to open these?' There's an edge to his voice. It's understandable, the kitchen does seem deliberately infuriating.

'You have to tap the top right corner then push up.' I sound artificial, I'm so keen to hide my disappointment about the lack of a kiss, even though I know I'm being ridiculous.

'Surprised they don't need a password or nothing.' When Tony turns round, holding a pile of tea towels, he's at least back to smiling. 'It's all right. Found 'em.'

He rolls his sleeves a little higher. I doubt that's good for what is obviously an extremely expensive shirt, any more than it's going to help me hold back from ogling him. Because now I'm dying to run my fingers along the vein cutting across the crook of his elbow, prominent against the muscle of his forearm.

He walks across to me, reaches for a glass and begins to dry. And I have got to get rid of him. There's no way I can keep pretending, with Tony half a step away, that I'm not dangerously close to hyperventilating, I'm so desperate for him. I try, 'I think this is a bit beneath your paygrade.'

He shrugs. 'And yours. Or it should be, anyhow.'

'Sadly, it's not. And Tony, seriously, please leave it. You're here for the sponsors, not to help out in Hospitality.'

'Like I said, I'm bored with that.' He looks at me, his eyes as hard as his voice has become. Then he smiles, closed-lipped and not particularly friendly. 'Look, Genie, I can take no for an answer, all right. So, if you want to, just tell me to fuck off and I'll leave you alone, OK?'

Before I can stop myself, I hear my voice saying, 'That's not what I want.'

'Yeah, I'd been thinking maybe it weren't.' I'm expecting him to look amused or self-satisfied, but his face is puzzled. Then there's one of his click-of-your-fingers quick changes in expression and he's grinning at me. 'Which is good, cos I get you was only playing along in there, but when I was saying how fine you looked, I meant it.'

Obviously, that's nice to hear. Except, I know if I looked at his contacts, at least half the numbers would belong to gorgeous women ready to drop everything any time Tony calls. But honestly, that's not what's holding me back from grabbing Tony's hand and running off to find the nearest room with a lockable door. It's that I don't look remotely like those women, and I couldn't bear to see his face when he realizes just how big the difference is. Because there's no use pretending that wouldn't happen the minute he got my clothes off.

But it's not like I can say that to him, or not without sounding tediously insecure, so I opt for shrugging off the compliment. 'You should tell Skylar and Katia, they're responsible for the outfit.'

His smile is very cat who got the cream. 'Felt the boss had someone to dress up for, did they?'

He's right about Sky, but I'm not going to admit it. And he wouldn't understand how badly it would hurt Katia's heart to leave this dress trapped in the wardrobe. So, I settle for, 'No, Skylar's always nagging me about dressing too old. She caught me at a weak moment tonight. This is the result.'

'And very nice it is too.' Tony pauses, seemingly pondering something of vital importance to world peace, then shakes his head. 'But she's wrong. It's not that your clothes are too old normally, it's that they're too dressed up. Like you're all look don't touch?'

I bite my lip. It's a recurring theme in this conversation, me not knowing what to say.

Tony's still earnestly intense when he adds, 'Like you go for a lot of stuff that's fitted, so it does show off your body. But the fabric, it's like holding you in – not letting you relax.' I'm just about to say something huffily offended when he laughs. 'You know what, though? I'm an idiot for telling you that, cos I'm dead into the whole sexy-teacher thing.'

I make my mouth prim. 'I can't imagine why. You must've been a terrible student.'

He grins. 'Yeah, I weren't the most attentive, but I'd have been well up for a bit of extra tuition from Miss Edwards, I can tell you.'

His face is so exaggeratedly lascivious, I can't help laughing.

'So, don't you go chucking out them tight skirts, or the heels, cos I reckon I can find a use for 'em. Only your role-playing had better be more convincing than your good-girl act.'

I raise my eyebrows. 'Who says it's an act?'

There's a snort of laughter. 'Just like everything 'bout you. How you move, your smile, the way you laugh.' He steps back and takes a long look at my stilettoes. 'Plus, first afternoon we spent together, you let me in on where you like to wear them heels, and that's been playing on my mind ever since.' His face becomes mock-serious. 'Not to worry, though. I'm up for a bit of role reversal, if you're needing a few acting lessons.'

I almost break the glass in my hand, I'm gripping it so hard. But I manage to make my voice more teasing than breathily full of longing. 'I wasn't aware acting ability was high on your list of requirements.'

I might've gone too far. Tony's extensive back catalogue of ex-girlfriends and one-night stands include several contenders for world's least talented actress. Thankfully, he absolutely roars with laughter. 'Yeah, only it might not've been their acting I was focused on. But my standards have gone up a fair bit lately.'

Angharad is certainly convincing when she's telling us that this make-up or that supplement will solve all our problems, so perhaps that's true. But I'm not sure that counts as acting, so I make 'Really?' coolly enquiring.

Tony softens his smile, so presumably, we're not on the same page. 'Yeah, really.' He reaches for another glass, and it's not until he's done drying it that he asks, 'Is that why you turned me down? All the stuff in the press?'

'When?'

'When what?'

'When did I turn you down?'

'Like pretty much every day.'

'But that's never serious.' My hands are still in the sink but I'm looking at Tony directly and his face is every bit as confused as I feel.

He shakes his head. 'Not all of it. But I asked you to dinner, remember?'

'That was just a thank you.'

He shrugs. 'Not from my perspective it weren't. But if you didn't see it that way, I'm asking you for real now. How 'bout coming out with me some time?' He watches my face intently.

For half a second, I almost say yes, let's go now, this minute. But then it floods back, that there's no way I'll live up to what he's used to. That, and all the other things that make getting involved with Tony a spectacularly bad idea. So, even if my voice isn't as firm as it should be, I manage, 'I'm sorry, but I can't.'

He sighs and takes a step away. 'All right, I'll leave it. 'Cept can you stop being polite and just tell me it's not what you want? Not you can't or you shouldn't, or whatever. Cos I dunno, maybe I've got it all wrong, but I'm getting seriously mixed signals.'

I shouldn't complain, Tony's dog-with-a-bone impression is a big part of why he can single-handedly keep three defenders fully occupied. But it also means, for a man who claims he can take no for an answer, he's remarkably hard to deflect.

I try looking not quite into his eyes because that's too distracting, but close enough that it should mimic eye contact. 'Except, Tony, I'm not being polite. I would like to. Very much, actually.' That should sound convincing, because it's one hundred per cent true. The next bit is true if incomplete, so hopefully he'll accept that too. 'But I've told you before, the staff contracts have a no fraternization clause, and I like my job.'

He smiles gently. 'And you're pretty good at it and all.' The smile gets turned up several watts. 'But someone's got to find out, for that to be a problem, haven't they?'

'I suppose, but it's not easy, keeping things quiet around here.' I tilt my head at Monica's discreet home security system.

Tony grins. 'I dunno. Maybe you didn't spend enough time snogging behind the bike sheds as a kid.'

'I went to an all-girls school,' I grin.

'Then I wanna hear all about you snogging behind the bike sheds. Like, for starters, did the uniform involve knee-high socks?'

95

I hit him with a spare tea towel. 'It did not, no.'

He grabs the towel with one hand and my wrist with the other. 'Pity.'

His voice is close to a laugh, but both of us are leaning in, our faces close and the towel pulled taut between us. And that's not the only connection. His eyes are locked with mine, and I think my smile is the same as his, lips parted, half jokey, half hungry. I can't stop myself from waiting for the kiss that feels like it's got to be coming. Instead, Tony glances at the tiny camera tucked above the door, then pulls my hand below the rim of the brushed steel sink. His fingers relax, just enough that his dry thumb can caress the soapy skin on the inside of my wrist.

'You should be wearing gloves for this, beauty. You don't wanna go spoiling them lovely hands.'

He doesn't sound like he's teasing any more. Suddenly, his closeness is so claustrophobic, I wrench my hand away.

Before either of us can say anything, Skylar's voice comes from the doorway. 'Sorry, Tony, Monica's looking for you.'

Nothing in her face suggests she saw anything more than two people innocently washing up, but I've seen Sky play poker, so that doesn't mean much. Tony must be just as good at cards. Because he turns to her, pulling a face and complaining about having to go back to the party. No one would believe a minute before, there'd been enough sexual tension fizzing to fill every one of the champagne glasses lined up on the snow-white countertop.

13

After the last guest has left, Monica makes a point of giving a thank-you speech to the staff. It's a nice gesture, especially since the annual party has to be a strain, given Monica prefers spreadsheets to small talk. My presence can't make it any easier, so I slip outside. I pull the front door closed as softly as I can, and wrap my arms tight around my waist. I'd like to say that's a reflex response to the cool of the evening, but it's more that I've felt empty ever since Tony strolled out of the kitchen. Looking down at the York-stone path, my eyes even start to well up with sorry-for-myself tears.

Crying alone on my ex-husband's golf-course-perfect lawn would be the definition of pathetic. And I'm not pathetic any more. Unwrapping my arms, I remember that men are not compatible with the capable, in-control version of me, that's all. Or not men like Tony, anyway. So I'll stay away from him, unless it's work, obviously. There you go. Simple, problem sorted. Tears gone.

I head for the side of the house. Earlier, the cobbles surrounding the red-brick garage were awash with luxury vehicles. Now, there are only staff cars left, apart from LeMar's Merc and a shiny black Range Rover. And leaning against the driver's door, there's Tony, looking dangerously handsome in the twilight.

'There's no need to wait. Monica let the players go ages ago,' I call across. I'm sure he knows that already, but I need to hurry him away. The needy, useless, not-in-control version of me isn't buried deep enough yet for a one-on-one.

'Yeah, only I wanted a word before I left.' It's his normal voice, no louder, but even from the other side of the yard, I can hear him clearly against the soft quiet that comes when there are no near neighbours.

I totter across, using the stones as an excuse to look down, as I ask, 'Is there something you need?' like I'm expecting a work request.

Tony waits until I'm close enough, he'd only need to reach out a hand to touch me. 'Just to apologize, I reckon.' There's a lopsided smile. 'Which you must be well fed-up with, cos I'm making a bit of a habit of it where you're concerned.'

I look up at him and get lost for a minute. I must've triggered the security system, because Tony's bathed in gold-green light. It's so close to how he looks under flood-lights, it brings back all the times I've watched him play and drifted into imagining us alone together. That's profoundly unhelpful when I'm trying to project cool and capable. And when I ask, 'Apologize for what?' it's less business-like than I was aiming for.

'Saying the wrong thing.'

I'm not sure if he means calling me a bitch or the sexual suggestions, neither of which I particularly object to.

'About the gloves.' His face is cringingly uncomfortable. 'You told me once you don't appreciate that, being told

how you should behave, and then I goes and does it again.'
He looks down at his shoes. 'Sorry. It ruined it, didn't it?'

It shocks me that he can connect the thing with the
house key and me pulling my hand away, and if not quite
get to the right answer, come pretty close. Because it's not
exactly that I resent being told what to do, more that I hate
it when men dress up instructions and interfering as caring.
But even if Tony's slightly off target, it absolutely stuns me
that he, Tony Garratt, soccer superstar and tabloid darling, understands it matters enough to be genuinely sorry.
Before I can stop myself, I'm looking up at him under my
lashes. 'Nothing's ruined.'

'Promise?'

'Promise.' My voice's gone soft and sweet as the smell of
honeysuckle, cascading over the wall of the garage. Damn it.

He grins broadly, the penance of a moment ago washed
away. 'Great. And I know I'm on thin ice with this, but am
I allowed to ask if you're cold?'

He's so unselfconsciously relieved, I feel incredibly
immature for being scared of letting him see I want him.
That's not me. That's old Genie, who started dressing like
a nun the second Gavin dropped a few hints that tailored
clothes made her look cheap. New Genie allows herself to
be attractive and attracted. Within limits. Limits that guarantee old, unattractively clingy Genie stays firmly locked
away. With Tony, that means light flirtation, no touching
and, apparently, no washing-up. Fine. New Genie can stick
to that. She's excellent at boundaries.

I narrow my eyes. 'So long as you're not about to tell me
I should've brought a coat, you're fine.'

He laughs. 'Wouldn't dare. But I've got a jacket in the car, if you wants it?'

I'm about to refuse when I realize, one, that would be churlish, and two, I'm chilly. Turning Tony down to prove I loathe being looked after would be ridiculous. 'Yes, please.'

Tony comes dangerously close to giving me a 'you're a good girl' smile, but manages to rein it in. He leans in to hunt around in the back of the car, providing me with a pleasant reminder of what hours of fitness training can achieve on a body. The late summer evening with the start of stars twinkling has a movie-like quality, and I'm half expecting something beautifully cut in lambswool. Only this is reality, so Tony actually holds out a first-team training jacket, steel grey, waterproof, and deeply unglamorous. But he helps me into it, his hands slipping over my shoulders, and I have to say, that feels nice. And standing side by side with our backs against the cool metal of the car, wearing something that smells of his aftershave, it's almost like I'm Tony's girl.

That feels much, much too nice. New Genie is not as good with boundaries as she'd led me to believe. Got to get those fences back up. 'Sky's giving me a lift. There's no need to wait, if you're ready to leave.'

He shrugs lazily. 'I don't mind, or I can give you a ride, if you want.'

I tell him Sky's expecting me, and I think I maybe manage to avoid sounding regretful. Tony doesn't say anything back, but his shoulder stays almost touching mine. We stare up at the crescent moon, until he turns his face to me. 'By the way, that doc and the Craigs earlier, they were talking about a Charlotte. Isn't that your name?'

And that's all the dreaminess gone.

'Yes.' My voice is sharp and my back has gone fence-post straight. He won't let me break his gaze. I shrug and make an uncomfortable little movement with my mouth. I try to make myself relax, so I'll sound back to normal. 'The name Genie came from a joke I used to have with Gary King, when I first started at the club. He'd ask for something, something crazy usually, a life-sized foam elephant, that sort of thing. And I'd find it and then we'd go through a whole "your wish is my command" routine.' I look at my hands. 'It was just a game, but the Genie thing stuck.'

Only it wasn't just a game. It was Gary making sure I had the contacts I needed to do my job, and his way of giving a shy little mouse the confidence necessary to do it well. And Gavin absolutely hated it.

Tony's shoulder bumps mine. 'That's kind of sweet.' He waits a moment, then looks away. 'You and Gary, was that a thing?'

My voice is adamant. 'No, not at all. He's just a nice guy.'

Tony nods. 'Yeah, sounds like maybe he is.' He pulls a face. 'Can't say I'd have guessed it from playing against him, but there you go.'

I laugh, glad that the tension's gone. 'His defending was a little old school.'

Tony laughs back. 'You can say that again. I was lucky to come out of some of them games with any shinbones left, I can tell you.' He stays staring ahead, but his voice changes to softly enquiring, like when he's probing the defence, looking for a weak spot. 'Do you mind if I ask you something else?'

I try to stay jokey. 'That depends on what it is.'

He smiles, but it's obvious he doesn't plan on getting distracted. 'Well, you don't have to answer, if you don't wanna. But have you been ill or something?'

'No, not in the least. Whatever gave you that idea?'

Even from his profile, I can tell he's uncomfortable. 'When I had to go look at that stuff with the doc. He and them blokes, the Craigs, they were talking 'bout Charlotte, and I just got the impression, like maybe there'd been an issue, or something.'

I give an exasperated sigh. I can imagine exactly what was said. Lots of coy questions. Was I doing better? Had I started to sort myself out? All in hushed tones, like I'd had a breakdown. Which would be maddening even if I'd been remotely in that kind of state after the divorce. But I wasn't. Being discarded like yesterday's socks left a few scars on my pride, but that's it. There's absolutely no reason for Gavin and the Craigs to go on like I'm damaged. And the best way to prove it is to be completely casual.

'It's nothing, a misunderstanding maybe, that's all. Can we leave it?' That didn't go as well as I'd hoped. I sound, even to myself, edgy.

Tony makes a move with his hand like he's sweeping something away. 'Yeah, course.' It looks like he doesn't know what to say, but then he gives me a sly smile. 'So, if we're not going to talk 'bout that, and we're going to be hanging round waiting for Sky, how 'bout you clarify the rules of this no fraternization thing.'

It's probably a hangover from thinking about Gavin, but suddenly I'm dead set on proving I'm not a scared little mouse any more. So, my voice is every bit as flirty as my smile, when I ask, 'What exactly are you unclear on?'

'Katia and LeMar, for a start.'

'They were already together when we hired her. Monica made an exception.'

'So, it's no dating, no serious relationships, yeah?'

'That's right.'

Tony smiles his best naughty schoolboy smile. 'What about stuff that's just fun, then?'

'You've met Monica, so you must realize she especially frowns on fun,' I grin, meeting his direct gaze.

'Good point. But, like, where are the boundaries of that?' he asks, his face mock serious now.

'For example?' I quip.

Tony steps to face me and, without putting a hand on me, kisses my forehead. It's light, a brush of his lips on my skin, but it's enough to make my throat tighten. 'Would that cross the line?'

Given that all I can think about is how badly I want to reach up and start unbuttoning his shirt, it would. But a forehead kiss could fall within the realms of goal celebration, so I shake my head. 'No, I think that would be considered acceptable.'

'OK, good to know. How about this?'

His lips graze my cheek, and if it's not quite a greeting between acquaintances, it's close enough. Which means I can shake my head again. 'No, I think that's still all right.'

He smiles softly. 'Then I reckon this should be too?'

This time, his lips touch mine, but it's a closed-mouth, gentle sort of kiss. And if I'm having trouble keeping my breathing steady, that's more about Tony's closeness than the kiss itself.

'That's probably on the borderline.'

He looks serious. 'Is it? That's a pity, cos there's this thing you do in meetings that gets me all distracted. Where you stroke along here.' He runs a finger along my neck and smiles at my sharp intake of breath, his teeth white in the half-light. 'And you've got me worried, this might not be quite kosher neither.' He leans in and runs his mouth along the line traced by his finger, the roughness of stubble mixed in with the softness of his lips.

I manage to say, 'No, I think anything below the chin is out,' but my voice isn't as firm as it should be.

'Shame. And, just so I'm one hundred per cent clear, how 'bout this?'

His hand is on the back of my neck, his thumb stroking where he knows is sensitive, as he kisses me hard on the mouth, his tongue probing between my lips. I should push him away, or at least politely disentangle myself. But I don't and in the end, it's Tony who slows the pace until we're not kissing any more, but his forehead is against mine. 'That still counts as a kiss between mates, right?'

I try to laugh lightly. 'No, no, sadly I don't think it does.'

Tony's smile is wide. 'OK, I think I've got it then. Me kissing you, that's fine. It's you kissing me back that makes it a problem.'

I side-step away and I'm not smiling any more. 'Actually,

that's absolutely right. Which is why my contract has the fraternization clause and yours doesn't.'

He looks at me, head on one side. His face is genuinely serious, not the play solemnity of a few minutes ago. 'Yeah, well, I get why that pisses you off.'

I try to soften my voice. 'You don't make the rules though, do you?'

He shakes his head. 'No, love, I don't. But I've got pretty good at breaking 'em without getting found out. So, if you ever fancy trying out being bad Genie, just for a bit of a change, you knows where I am.'

As he says it, he glances up at the security camera, high on the wall of the garage, and I realize we're standing in the only blind spot. Tony almost certainly worked that out when he was first deciding where to put his car. And yes, I fully understand that should be a warning sign, but right now, I'm too floaty to care. So OK, you might have a point. New Genie absolutely sucks at boundaries.

14

I'd love it if the next bit was me doing what every atom of my body wants to do, which is drag Tony off to bed. But what actually happens is that we're interrupted by the staff spilling out of the house, all pent-up laughter and heels clickity-clacking on the paving.

Sky bounds over the second she sees us. Kat and LeMar follow more sedately, his arm solicitous around her waist.

'Come out with us, Genie.' Skylar's voice is imploring, so I'm betting Katia and LeMar aren't keen. I can't say I'm crazy about the idea either, so I make a non-committal noise. Skylar interprets that as a yes, snapping round to Tony. 'How about you? You'll come too, won't you?'

'Come where?' he asks, warily.

'There's a club in town that's got a Sunday funday drum and bass night.' Skylar sounds like she's holding out a treat, but Tony shakes his head.

'Sorry, Sky. I would, but clubs aren't a good look for me right now. Plus, I dunno as anything that good ever happens in 'em on a Sunday night.'

'See, Sky? No one wants to. Let's go home,' says LeMar.

'You're all so boring, it's not even late.'

I do sympathize with Sky. She's been on her best behaviour all night and she's fidgeting on the spot, she's so desperate to burn off some energy. But Katia and LeMar are sensitive about being the dullest couple in football, so I try a distraction. 'Sorry, Sky, but I've got to take these shoes off. Why not come to mine instead?'

Skylar skulks her shoulders down. 'That sounds thrilling.'

Tony shrugs. 'I dunno, don't you reckon the afterparty's usually better than the club?'

Skylar gives him a toothpaste ad smile. 'Can we go to yours instead? Genie says your pool's to die for.'

He smiles at me, trying not to laugh. 'Does she now? Cos I can't say she's been as keen on trying it out as I'd hoped she'd be.'

I give an embarrassed little smile. 'That's because I wouldn't dream of inviting myself into a player's home. Honestly, Sky, do we really have to have the professionalism conversation again?'

Tony raises his eyebrows. He's so obviously thinking 'pot and kettle', I blush. Thankfully, all he says is, 'Don't worry 'bout it. It'd be nice, having some company.'

That's probably true so I try to funnel a mental hug into my smile as I thank him.

Skylar's practically dancing, she's so ready to leave. 'OK, great. Let's go before Monica hunts us down over an unwashed glass.'

'You wanna come with me, Genie?' Tony asks.

I glance up at the security camera, and he gives me a little nod. 'Yeah, on second thoughts, maybe it makes sense for you to keep Sky on the straight and narrow.'

I'm turning to follow Skylar to her car, when Katia taps my elbow. 'Genie, can we stop at yours first?'

It takes me a second to guess what's on her mind, then it hits me, and I murmur, 'Swimsuit?'

She nods briskly.

'Yes, of course.'

Katia still looks anxious. I guess she's thinking nothing of mine will give her much coverage, since she's lovely and curvy while I'm boringly flat.

'My rash guard should fit you, if that's all right?'

She nods again and smiles to show I've understood what she was worried about.

'Sky, we need to call in at mine so I can check on Roudie, OK?'

Tony touches my shoulder. 'Bring him, if you like.'

'That's nice, but he can be a bit unpredictable in houses he doesn't know.'

'That's all right. I bring him back with me sometimes, after his walk. I reckon it's lonely for him, getting dropped off right after.' Tony shifts his weight and there's an embarrassed twitch of his mouth. 'And he'll be sad tonight, won't he? If you comes home then goes straight out again.'

That probably explains why, even when Tony texts me pictures of a mud-caked Roudie, I come home to a paw-print-free cottage. And it's so sweet, it's lucky I'm not diabetic.

For the first five minutes of the drive back, I'm all warm and hot chocolatey over Tony. Then, Sky does a dodgem-style swerve to get past someone hogging the outside lane of the bypass, and it hits me, I'll be expected to swim too.

Just like that, there's the start of a nervy over-caffeinated gnawing in my stomach. That can only mean one thing: any minute now, the little monster's going to start clawing its way into my head. I try to block it out, but even Swedish House Mafia blaring at top volume isn't enough to keep it at bay. Because here it is, digging its nails in, hissing, *'It's going to be quite the contrast, isn't it? You in swimwear, when he's used to Angharad.'* I snatch my phone out of my bag, and pull up her Instagram, like I'm going to prove it wrong.

Only obviously, now it's laughing its horrible little head off, because here's Angharad draped across a pool lounger. And she's not just pretty or sexy, she's film-star beautiful. There's no way Tony could want me, after her. Except he keeps saying he does. And God knows, I want him, so what's the matter with me? Why can't I just believe him? And here's the monster, raring to tell me that it's because I'm not new Genie. I'm not even old Genie. I'm scared little mouse Charlotte, scuttling away. And I always will be.

Sky glances across and catches me agonizing over the shimmery gold perfection of Angharad's legs. She turns down the music, which for her borders on an intervention. 'Are you checking if she and Tony are done?'

I can't talk to her. Not about Tony, not when I'm like this. 'No, not really. I was just curious.'

Surprisingly, she doesn't tease. 'Whatever people are saying, I think they must be. She's called the office a few times, when I've been on the phones.'

I shrug, like it doesn't matter. 'That doesn't sound very done to me.'

Skylar shakes her head. 'No, it does. Otherwise, she'd call him, wouldn't she? Not leave a message.'

'Except he's terrible about his phone.'

Skylar shrugs. 'Even if they're not done-done, I shouldn't worry about it. She sounds like a bitch.'

I'm about to say she shouldn't make assumptions from a few phone messages, but Sky's already turned the music up.

By the time we get to the lodge, I've got the headache of the century. At least it's an excuse not to swim and to refuse the drink that, given I'm wallowing in self-pity, would be disastrous. Skylar nags about the pool, but Tony's quick to jump in with, 'Leave Genie alone. If she don't wanna swim, she don't have to.'

Katia's equally ready to avoid the rash guard, with a claim that she's also too tired for the pool. Tony smiles at her, and of the three of us, it looks like she's become his favourite.

'Yeah, you girls have had a busy evening, haven't you? And I dunno 'bout you, LeMar, but I didn't exactly find tonight a breeze neither.' Tony's voice is open-fire warm and LeMar nods, pulling a face like he's just trekked up Mount Everest. It's kind, Tony saying that. I can't believe he didn't notice LeMar's hopeless at parties. But I'm too busy stopping myself from snarling to show Tony I'm grateful he's making an effort.

'So how about we just relax? Maybe get our breath back?' Tony makes that sound innocent but he's staring at me. I can't be doing too well at behaving like nothing's changed since the kiss.

I don't reply so it's Katia who gratefully agrees, and we drift through to the sitting room. I see now why Roudie sloped off the minute we arrived. He's settled on a brand new bed so comfortable that he looks up, calculates that checking in with me isn't worth the effort, and settles back to sleep. And Tony's not just a good dog host. He's every bit as smooth as you'd expect with human guests, based on how quickly he distracts Sky from mithering me with the offer of his Spotify.

She flicks through. 'Tony, why do you have the musical taste of a teenage girl?'

'I don't. Most of that stuff's not mine, I've just not got round to deleting it.' He at least has the good grace to look shamefaced, since the music is presumably age-appropriate for Angharad. 'If you scan through, there's some stuff that's OK.'

Skylar pulls a disgusted face. 'Thanks, but I've already exceeded my maximum daily dose of Ed Sheeran. We'll use something of Genie's.'

Tony looks sceptical that anything of mine will be an improvement, so it's pleasing that the first thing I find is a playlist that's afterparty drifting into hangover session, all melancholy builds and hypnotic drops. 'How's that?'

Tony walks across and bends over my chair, so close it triggers the familiar wave of something bordering on panic, I want to touch him so badly. He nods and the light from the lamp beside us plays across his cheekbones.

'Yeah, not bad actually.' He tries a smile but the best I can manage in return is a minimal reduction in sulkiness. 'I'd not have had you down as a club head. But then, there's a lot of stuff 'bout you that's a touch unpredictable.'

I come dangerously close to a head toss, as I snap, 'I'm too old for clubs now.'

Tony shakes his head, narrowing down his eyes. 'I don't see that. Me and you aren't too far apart, age-wise anyhow, and I'm not.'

My smile is small and brittle. 'Yes, but you're a man.'

'Why's that matter?' His voice is becoming less indulgent and more irritated. I can't say I blame him. But I can't shrug off being so disappointed in myself, I'm furious with everyone else.

I tense my fingers, then look up at him, all sullen eyes and taut mouth. 'If you ever had to queue any more, all they'd be looking at is if you've got the money for bottle service. For women, it's some random man evaluating if you're attractive enough to let in.'

Tony goes to touch my arm then thinks better of it. 'If that's how it makes you feel, you're going to the wrong places, love.' And he says it nicely, but it'd mean a whole lot more if the sort of clubs we're talking about weren't created for the Tony Garratts of this world. So, it's unfortunate that he chooses to add in an undertone, 'And maybe you should rethink coming out with me after all, cos I reckon I could sort that all right.'

I make a 'whatever' gesture with my hand, and go and slump down next to Roudie. You don't need to tell me I'm behaving badly. I know that, and so does Tony, who ignores me for the rest of the evening. Which is beyond dull, with Tony alternating between desultory flirting with Sky and intensely polite conversation with LeMar and Katia.

The only remotely interesting snippet is between Sky and Tony. They're comparing tattoos, and Sky asks what he plans on getting next.

Tony shrugs. 'Probably nothing. I'm running out of space, cos I'm not into full sleeves.'

Sky points at the space next to the lion over his right bicep. 'How about there?'

I happen to know the lion was done after his first England call-up, not that I'm remotely stalkery. I'd assumed the space was reserved for another lion or two, after a big international win.

But Tony shakes his head. 'Nah, that's waiting for if I get married.' He smiles at Sky, one of his sweeter, softer smiles, as he points to one side of the lion. 'I'm gonna get a lioness there, for my missus.' The smile becomes actually shy, which I don't know that I've seen before, as he runs his finger over the skin below. 'And this is for a couple of cubs, if stuff goes right.'

I bet ninety-nine per cent of women can't resist that, but Sky's not a fan of monogamy, and she looks like she's struggling to suppress a yawn. Then she glances quickly over at me, still huddled up next to Roudie, and asks, 'Is there a lioness on the horizon?'

Tony pulls a face. 'I dunno. I was thinking maybe, but now, I'm not sure me and her are on the same page.'

So, he and Angharad must be in one of those not-quite-on, not-quite-off phases. That'd explain why Tony doesn't seem as happy as I'd expect for a man whose comeback match was as smooth as silk.

15

Seven days and an away win later

I've been searching for Roudie for over an hour. Logically, I should go back to the cottage. Last time Roudie dug an escape tunnel, I found him on the doorstep, tapping his paw over being kept waiting. But what if he's not? What if he's been run over? What if I go home and find him lying on the verge, hurt or worse? I try to push it out of my mind, forcing my way along an overgrown path leading deeper into the woods.

There's a rustle. I stop dead, praying that it's Roudie. But it's only branches I've pushed aside, swinging back into place. I try calling again, my voice ragged with desperation. I should never have gone for a run this morning, not when I've been late home every night this week. I should have taken Roudie for a proper walk first thing. I should have locked the dog door. I should . . .

'Genie, it's all right, I've got him.' It's Tony, shouting from the main path cutting across the woods from the lodge to the road.

The relief is so intense, I'm dizzy. I fight my way back through the brambles, then sprint over the rutted track towards Tony's voice. There's one bend, then Roudie, wagging wildly and straining on the lead to jump up at me. I sink down next to him, cuddling him close, which he takes as an invitation to lick my face. When I do finally look up at Tony, it must be hard for him to see how angry I am, I'm so sticky.

'You need to tell me if you're taking Roudie. I thought he was lost. I thought . . .'

Tony scowls. 'No, you needs to stop screening your calls. He was on my drive. I've been calling you over and over, trying to let you know he was OK.'

'But . . .' I touch my thigh, expecting to find my phone in the pocket of my leggings. It's not. It's on the kitchen work surface, next to the leaning pile of letters. Where I always put it when I get in. Where I left it when I went tearing off to find Roudie. I feel awful. 'Oh. I . . .'

'Was too busy worrying 'bout the pup to remember your phone?' Tony asks.

'Um, yes. I'm sorry, I shouldn't have snapped.' I try to smile, but it comes out more cringing, which fits exactly with how I feel inside.

Tony shrugs. His face is involved, and his hands follow behind, giving extra emphasis to how little he cares. 'Don't matter.'

I gnaw at my cheek. I suppose it doesn't, now we're work acquaintances. Because Tony has kept on dropping by the office, but it's to banter with Sky. All I get is a curt 'hi' and 'bye'. Which is more than I deserve after Monica's party. The hollowness in my stomach wells up into my throat, blocking the words that I want to say, about how I really am sorry, not only for losing my temper just now, but for taking all my self-loathing out on him.

Tony stares at me, head on one side, then crouches down and lifts Roudie's nose until they're eye to eye. 'This, mate, is why you don't go running off. Cos it gets Genie all upset, and we can't be having that. Understood?' He gently nods Roudie's head, then smiles at me. 'See, lesson learnt, no harm done.' He looks back to Roudie, his face mock stern. 'And you could've told me Genie weren't blocking my number. Cos that would've saved me some anxiety and all.'

'Of course I'm not.' I can't believe he thinks I'm that bad at my job. What if he needed something? 'What possible reason would I have for doing that?'

'You tell me.' Tony shoots me a sideways glance, then shakes his head. 'Actually, I dunno this is the time for a deep and meaningful. How about we get the pup home instead?'

Standing is making me woozy, part blood pooling in my feet, part post-run, no-food light-headedness. Tony's hand tightens on my bare arm, pulling me in. The warmth of his body creates a lurch of desire strong enough to push back the little black dots clouding my eyes. Then the washing-powder-fresh smell of his discreetly logo-ed designer t-shirt reminds me that my running vest is coated in sweat and my skin must feel all clammy and disgusting. I step away but Tony keeps his fingers wrapped around my arm.

'You all right?'

I nod.

'And it's OK, is it, me walking back with you?'

I should say there's no need. He's going to want me to explain about the other night, and I'm so muddled about it, about him, I don't think I can. But Roudie's glued himself to Tony's jeans, and I'm not sure I could tempt him away, even if I wanted to.

'We'd like that, if you've got time.'

He smiles at me, a proper, big, Tony smile. It's the first time he's done that since the party. A wave of relief washes over me, every bit as strong as when I first saw Roudie. And maybe it's because I exhausted all my available panic hunting for Roudie, but strolling back is absolutely OK. It helps that Tony keeps up a steady flow of talk. It's nothing that matters, just him telling me he picked up the bracelet for his niece, and that she loves it and he can see why I'm so into the stuff Claudia makes. But Tony should get a tie-in with one of those meditation apps, the gravel rumbling under his soft vowels is the definition of calming.

He waits until we're leaving the dappled shade of the woods to ask, 'Do you know how he got out?'

My shoulders get super tense. Here we go. This is the start of the 'unless we know exactly what went wrong, mistakes will keep happening' talk. 'No, I didn't leave the gate open, or anything like that.'

Tony holds up the hand that isn't busy persuading Roudie to abandon an interesting hole in the verge. 'Course you didn't.'

I've got to stop snapping at him over nothing. I'm about to start apologizing, but he's already talking, voice gentle. 'Even if you had, it'd not be my business. He's your dog.'

I grimace. 'I think he'd rather be yours.'

'He's not an idiot. He knows he couldn't find anyone who'd look after him like you do.'

'Except he came to find you, didn't he? And I can see

why. I mean, I have been walking him. Every day. But they're not like the walks you've been doing with him.'

'Then it's my fault, isn't it? Cos I saw you was working all hours, but I didn't wanna, like, assume you was still OK with me taking him out. If you are, he'll be back on his regular schedule Monday.'

'Are you sure? I don't want it to become a burden.'

'Nah. I've missed this fella all right.' Tony scratches between Roudie's ears, earning an adoring look from both of us. 'And how 'bout I take a quick look at the back yard, see if I can't work out how he got out?'

'I can't ask you to do that.'

He reaches out and ruffles my already messy hair. 'Then it's a good thing I'm offering, huh?'

I've been banished to the kitchen while Tony repairs the gap in the fence. My offer of help was declined with a 'Nah, I'm fine. It's a while since I've done anything handy. I don't reckon an audience'll help.' And he doesn't exactly look the part, since most handymen don't dress in Dolce. But the rips in his jeans are sort of appropriate, and from what I can see from the kitchen window, he's making a surprisingly professional job of it.

It's extremely kind. Only it's a bit unclear exactly how I feel about that. Part of me is definitely grateful. Another bit is all neon-sign glowy over Tony being willing to do manual labour. But they're fully occupied, trying to throttle the side of me that's dying to stalk out and remind Tony that I'm paid to take care of other people's problems so I'm more than capable of handling my own.

The stupid thing is, I know that's about Gavin. He's the one that taught me that helpfulness might start out as cooking dinner, but it becomes little reminders about healthy eating, and if you don't pay enough attention, a fertility-maximizing food delivery service. And if instead of being grateful, you start hiding chocolate in your wardrobe, it ends up with your husband screwing your boss. None of which has anything to do with Tony mending a fence. So I need to go out and thank him like a normal person.

It helps that when I do, he's keen to show me, in minute detail, exactly what he's done. I wait for the usual Tony-style jokes and innuendo, but he's disarmingly earnest. It fits with his hair, which is nowhere near as pristine as usual, thanks to the head scratching that went on during the initial measuring phase. A strand that should be swept up has migrated across his forehead. It's the perfect match for the lopsided smile, when he asks, 'So you reckon this'll keep him in, do you?'

'Yep, you've achieved doggy Alcatraz.'

Tony's smile turns into the one he usually reserves for hat-tricks. He directs it to Roudie, lying on his left foot, 'Hear that, mate? No more ducking out for you, OK? And maybe your mum'll follow your example.'

'I didn't . . .'

'Yeah, you did.' He pushes the stray hair out of his eyes. 'But I get it. I needs the odd reminder sometimes, I can't click my fingers and get whatever I want, straight off, every time. Not even off a genie.'

'It wasn't that.' I flail around, searching for some sort of justification for how I behaved after Monica's party.

Before I can come up with anything that adequately hides the crazy, Tony asks gruffly, 'But it's not been too bad, has it? Having me around this afternoon?'

Letting me off the hook is the nicest thing he's done all day. I bump my shoulder against his arm. 'It could've been worse, I suppose.'

He shakes his head at me. 'And to think I've missed you.'

We're laughing, too much for the joke, and it's mixed in with him grabbing my waist and me wriggling away from his fingers, which are tickling me under my t-shirt.

'OK, OK, I missed you too.'

His hands stop still against my skin. My lips part.

There's a shout from the front of the house.

Damn, it's Chrissie. Tonight is yoga and dinner. I jump away from Tony, just in time. Or I think so, anyway. If not, Chrissie's doing a fantastic job of pretending she didn't see anything, brandishing her neon-blue mat and calling hellos.

I'm saying hello back, stopping Roudie from racing over to jump up at Chrissie, and finishing thanking Tony, all at the same time. I think some of the thank you must've got lost, because Tony's face is stony as he starts gathering his tools together.

I abandon Chrissie to Rouden and focus on Tony. 'Stay. Eat with us.'

Tony backs away, like he'd rather swim through snake-infested waters. That's understandable. Chrissie's a medic at the club. I wouldn't be crazy about having dinner with my doctor either, and she doesn't spend her whole time poking at wherever I'm sore.

16

After the stress of this morning, I'd happily spend all evening lying in corpse on the kitchen floor. Or I would if Chrissie didn't keep reaching across to prod me.

'Stop it, I'm still Namaste-ing.'

Chrissie bounces up into easy pose, flicking her mop of amber curls up into a no-nonsense ponytail en route. 'No time for that. The babysitter can only hold back the chaos for another hour, max.'

I don't like the sound of the babysitter. Tonight must be about more than yoga, if it couldn't wait for Chrissie's husband to be available.

'Katia intimated we need to have "a talk".' Chrissie encloses the last bit in finger quotes.

My sigh is deeper than any of my attempts at ujjayi beathing. This is why you should never employ a hyper-empathizer. 'Because she thinks I've been weird?'

'Since Monica's party, yes.' Chrissie turns up the eye contact. 'She's worried Tony Garratt's upset you.'

I put my hand over my eyes. 'No, no, he hasn't.' Let's hope Katia's restricted herself to sharing that theory with Chrissie, who is my oldest friend and a vault worthy of Fort Knox.

'I assumed not. The pair of you looked decidedly lovey-dovey when I turned up.'

I sneak a look at Chrissie through my fingers. She appears intensely amused. Having this conversation horizontal, I'm at a definite disadvantage. I reluctantly ease myself up until my legs are long, and my arms are out behind me, stretching out the tension that's magically reappeared in my shoulders. 'We're not that either.'

'So, what is going on?' Chrissie's in full interrogation mode, leaning forward, chin on her hands. 'Come on, Genie, you might as well say. Otherwise I'll have to tell Katia I failed, and you know what that means.'

'Her mum.' I shudder. Katia's mum has borderline adopted me, which is lovely, and not just because it gives me priority access to the best rum cake in the Midlands. But when it comes to obtaining confidences, Reenie doesn't pull her punches. 'All right, all right. I give in. It was sort of Tony, what was preoccupying me, but not the way Kat means.'

Chrissie makes the sympathetic, tell-me-more noise she learnt at medical school.

'He's needed extra attention, while he's still settling in.'

Chrissie snorts. 'I can't think of a single situation where that man wouldn't require extra attention.'

I throw a yoga block at her. 'Don't be mean. And anyway, it wasn't any trouble. He just needed someone to joke around with, really.'

'And you were happy to oblige, I take it?' Chrissie's back to trying not to laugh. She knows me far too well.

'More than happy.' I grimace. 'But it got a bit out of hand, and he kissed me at Monica's and . . .'

Chrissie pulls a sympathetic face. 'And it wasn't a good kiss?'

'No, it was amazing. But I got sort of panicky after-wards. And I thought he was angry with me over it, but he found Roudie when he went missing today, and he was nice about it, so I don't think he is. Angry, that is.' It seems me talking about Tony is as chaotic as me thinking about Tony.

Chrissie's started frowning. 'Why were you panicky? Did he do something else?'

'No. Of course not.'

'OK. Good.' Chrissie's relieved-big-sister smile disappears. 'So, what was it?'

My fingernails have become incredibly interesting.

Chrissie clears her throat. 'Come on, Genie, spit it out. I'm on a babysitter deadline, remember.'

When I meet her eye, she gives me the look she uses on the rare occasions her children misbehave.

'Well, HR finding out wouldn't be great.'

Chrissie makes an impatient noise. 'We both know so long as the two of you don't advertise it, they won't come looking.'

That's true. Their standard operating procedure even if they do think something's advertised is an official warning, then no action unless it gets ugly, in which case their back's covered if they need to fire you. But fraternization is the least emotional reason why getting involved with Tony is a bad idea. I'm not letting it go without a fight.

'That's easy for you to say, you're not on Monica's hit list.'

'Monica won't care if you screw Tony Garratt, so long as you don't do the same to your budget line.'

'Except it's an easy excuse, isn't it? To get rid of me.'

'I've told you before, you're overly paranoid about that. So come on, be honest. What's the real issue?'

I scrunch up my face. 'It's so embarrassing.'

'I spend half my life treating half-naked, emotionally stunted young men. Embarrassment is no longer in my emotional repertoire.'

I bow my head. 'I might've got a bit, well, scared he'd be disappointed. With how I look, and stuff.'

Chrissie laughs, proving she made the right decision, choosing sports medicine over psychiatry. 'So, despite Garratt spending the entire evening tripping over himself he was so keen to touch you, you managed to persuade yourself he wasn't all that attracted?'

'Don't say it like that, like I've got zero self-esteem. I'm being a realist. He's an actual superstar, I'm dangerously close to a groupie. I mean, ask Gavin. He used to be quite snippy about how enthused I'd get, watching Tony play.'

Chrissie's mouth becomes disapproving. 'Gavin used to get snippy about a lot of things, as I remember it. And Genie, I know you've done a lot of work since the divorce. But I can't help thinking you've focused on your appearance, when it's the inside that needs attention. I mean, honestly, if you don't think you're worthy of Tony Garratt, there must be an awful lot that still needs to be repaired.'

I jerk back. Chrissie's always blunt, but she doesn't usually take it that far.

Chrissie shuts her eyes for a second. 'I'm sorry, Genie. That came out harsher than I intended. I've just had it up to here with Garratt.'

'How do you mean?' I ask quickly.

'Oh, you know.' She waved her hand in exasperation. 'He doesn't want a consultation with a know-nothing provincial medic like me. All I'm good for is delivering the treatments he's had before. The ones the best doctors prescribed. He's a nightmare. And not just with me. He's the same about physio, nutrition, conditioning, everything.'

I can see how that could grate, but surely she can see what's behind it? 'Don't you think that's to be expected, though? It was such a huge risk, coming here. Tony was always going to take a while to trust how we do things. And if he wants input, that's not all bad, is it? At least he's talking to you.'

'I'm not sure barking orders counts as talking.' Chrissie's literally digging her heels into her mat.

It's my turn to snap. 'Then you need to fix that, sooner rather than later.'

Chrissie narrows her eyes at me. 'Do you know something I don't, Genie?'

'Nothing specific. But after training, Tony's always looking to sit, or lean against something. It's crossed my mind he's suffering from some kind of injury that he's ignoring.'

'And you don't think he'd say, if there was an issue?'

I see-saw my head. 'Maybe, maybe not. He's so keen to prove he's back at his best, you know how they are.'

Chrissie nods quickly. 'OK, I'll try to get to the bottom of it. The last thing I need is him hiding an injury. But I can't help noticing we've stopped talking about you.'

Damn. I was hoping she'd forgotten. 'I don't know there's much more to say. We kissed. I went weird. That's the end of it.'

'Except it's not, is it? Or he wouldn't have been here when I arrived, doing . . . Actually, Genie, what was he doing?'

'Fixing the fence.'

She grins. 'Are you serious? Do you call him when you've got odd jobs that need doing, or does he show up on the off chance?'

'Neither. And it wasn't for me. It was for Roudie. Tony walks him sometimes, he wanted him to be safe.'

Chrissie shrieks with laughter. 'I'm sorry, Genie. I'm not buying it. There's no way Garratt's the Bob the Builder type. Have you cast a spell on him? Or . . .' She leans forward, eyes wide. 'Are you blackmailing him? You always do know all their secrets.'

'Stop it. It's not funny.' I pout.

Chrissie freezes. 'Sorry, Genie. Isn't it?'

'No. I knew the helpfulness was weird. But I've been trying to pretend it wasn't.'

Chrissie tilts her head, like a bird tackling a particularly tricky feeder. 'Is it creepy helpful?'

'No, it's not like he expects something back, or anything like that. But I don't understand why he's doing it.'

'Well, I think it's quite obvious. He's looking for more than a hook-up.'

It's my turn to laugh.

'No, hear me out. When you freaked out, he didn't disappear, did he?'

'No, but he definitely backed off.'

'But Genie, what else could you expect? And it sounds like the minute he got a chance, he was straight back here, chomping at the bit to do DIY. No man does that for a one-night stand. As for walking the dog, well, my actual husband absolutely wouldn't, which is why my poor children are stuck with goldfish. Garratt's serious, he's got to be.'

Actually, she's right. Tony was serious today. Or serious for him, anyway. And when he said he'd missed me, underneath the teasing, that sounded serious too. 'It's possible, I suppose.'

Chrissie comes closer to a squeal than any woman of forty should.

I'm her last single friend and my dating life doesn't produce many squeal-worthy moments, so I feel bad, bursting her bubble. But I've gone cold all over. Because I think I know now why he's bothering with me, when I'm so far from picture perfect. 'That might not be a good thing.'

Chrissie scrunches her brows together. 'But the other night, at Monica's, you seemed to be having so much fun.'

I slump, cancelling out the postural improvement promised by our online yoga teacher. 'I was. But how he was today, and before really, I don't think he's been looking for fun. More the opposite, actually.'

Chrissie looks like I've thrown cold water over her. 'Explain.'

'He's trying so hard to put last season behind him. And I'm the perfect accessory for a player out to prove they're a professional, aren't I?'

Chrissie looks at me, like she's got no idea what I'm getting at.

'A nice low-key girlfriend. Someone who knows the

industry, who'll support his goals. But that won't last. Once he can feel he's back on top, he'll be dying to move on to someone more exciting.'

'You think he's that calculating?'

I shrug. 'No, not consciously. But it's what players are like, isn't it? They do whatever they need to perform. It's who they are.'

Chrissie crawls across to my mat and puts her arm around me. 'I can see why, doing what you do, you think that. And I wouldn't normally advise getting involved with a serial womanizer with an ego the size of the Nou Camp. But when I saw you and Garratt laughing in the corridor the other day, he looked so delighted with you, I almost liked him. And do you know who it reminded me of?'

I shake my head.

'Gary King.'

'I do miss Gary.'

Chrissie strokes my hair. 'I know you do. And I used to think it was such a shame you were both married. The pair of you always seemed to be having an absolute ball. So if there's a chance of something similar with Garratt, don't you think you should at least try being open to it?'

I try to remember the last time Chrissie was wrong, and I genuinely can't.

17

The next day

I've commandeered the coaching staff's meeting room for the academy evening, and LeMar's loving being in control of the white board. Most years, the under-eighteens would be dying to soak up tactical insights from our home-grown striker, fresh from scoring this weekend's winner. Tonight though, they're just waiting for the star of the show.

Only, when Tony does finally arrive, there's none of the usual off-hand charm. Everything about him's pent-up, from how he's tapping his toe to the way he keeps interrupting LeMar. At first, I've no idea why. Maybe he's stressed because he was a bit delayed. LeMar's already told me Tony was last on the medic's list and it might run long. But as Tony jumps from topic to topic with no bridge between them, I'm picking up on a theme. He keeps coming back to how players have to work out who they can trust, or they'll end up getting conned. I try telling myself players get like this over nothing, it'll be the after-effects of a bad training session or the weight of the next game. But each time Tony drags up trust, he glares at me.

After half an hour, I've still no clue what I've done, but

obviously, there's something. And he seems to be getting more worked up every minute, so I suggest taking a break, and pull Tony out into the corridor.

'If there's a problem, it's easier to just tell me.'

'Nah, I can do without a hoard of teenagers hearing my business.'

'OK. In here then.' I'm aiming for ready to listen but my voice comes out harsher than it should. Pushing open the door to the indoor pitch, I hunt around for the lights. They flicker on, a dirty grey-yellow that does nothing to warm up the cavernous space.

'You gonna take them heels off, before you tear up the Astro?' From Tony's tone, you'd think we were on his personal property.

I bend to remove my shoes, adrenaline-fuelled shakiness forcing me to reach for the breeze-block wall. I'd forgotten how much those extra four inches levelled up the height difference between us. Standing a stride or two away, Tony's taking up even more space than usual.

'So, what is it?' I'm looking for eye contact, but he's too busy glowering down at the floor.

'I dunno I'm in the mood to do this now.' His arms are crossed tight, matching his voice.

'Whether you want to or not, you need to tell me what's going on, or I can't help you.'

I'm pushing deliberately, but it takes me by surprise when his head jerks up. 'Oh, you think you're here to help, do you? Well, I've had all the help I can take off of you, I can tell you.'

I lean back against the wall, the rough blocks harsh

where my sheath dress leaves my shoulders bare. 'OK. I get it. I've pissed you off. But you'll need to fill me in on how.'

'What? So you can make it all better, like you reckon you always do?'

'No. Because you're obviously dying to fight, and I can't join in unless you tell me what we're fighting about.'

'Don't talk to me like I'm a fucking kid.'

I shrug. 'Then stop behaving like one.'

'Yeah, well, maybe talking don't come as natural to me as it does to you.' He spits the words out, and I've got a nasty feeling I do know what this is about.

I try to keep my voice relaxed. 'So, I've said something I shouldn't.' I hold his gaze, even though I'm dying to look down. 'Tell me what.'

'Don't pretend you don't know. You've been gossiping with your mate Chrissie, haven't you? 'Bout how I'm not fit to play.'

I keep my focus on his eyes, which have become the colour of smoke, trying to force him to connect with me. 'I did speak with Chrissie, and I'm sorry, maybe I shouldn't have.'

'Too right you fucking shouldn't.' His voice is edging towards a shout.

I keep mine conversational. 'No. I'm getting that message loud and clear, thank you. But I didn't say you weren't fit, just that I thought Chrissie needed to make sure you and she were communicating, in case there was an issue.'

'And what do you reckon gives you the right to stick your nose in?'

'Mainly that I care about you.'

'No, you don't. All you care about is what makes you look good!' His voice is loud enough there's the beginning of an echo off the hard ceiling.

I raise my eyebrows, my mouth hard. 'I'm sorry?'

'You know what I mean.' He's not shouting any more, but his voice is sulky.

'I actually don't.' I let enough anger show that I'm glad Tony isn't between me and the door.

But he doesn't move towards me. Instead, he leans a hand on the wall, bows his head and kicks at the AstroTurf, then looks back up to me. 'You think I'm too dumb to notice? How you're all over me when we're on our own, but the minute someone else shows up, you act like I'm nothing?'

I'm about to say he could never be nothing, but he holds his free hand up. 'I don't need no more excuses. Christ knows, I'm sick of hearing the stuff 'bout your job.'

'That's not an excuse.'

The nasty short laugh is the opposite of his usual roar. 'Well, maybe it ain't. Cos you wouldn't wanna risk the job, would you? Not when it gives you everything you need. And I gets it, why you get off on having all the guys going on 'bout how great you are, how nice, how kind.' His fingers tighten, balling up his free hand. 'What I weren't so sure 'bout was what was in it for you? Getting me following you round like I was on a fucking string.'

'Tony, I'm . . .'

He shakes his head. 'Oh, you don't need to explain. I figured it out all on my own. I mean, it's true, I started out

134

thinking you was just after a bit of a thrill, only you didn't want no one knowing you'd stoop that low. Cos you're too good to go near a player, aren't you? But I worked it out in the end. You thought it'd make me play better, didn't you? And that'd get everyone talking 'bout what a great job you'd done, fixing poor old broken Tony Garratt. Only you was so busy working on it, you forgot there'd come a point where you'd have to drop me or dirty your hands and fuck me. Isn't that right?'

'Tony, that's not true,' I splutter, shocked.

'Then how come you've been freezing me out, ever since I kissed you?'

'I . . . Tony, it's not like that . . . I . . .'

'Just thought you could keep giving me the odd smile, and I'd stay being a good boy?'

'Tony, I'm sorry I made you feel like that but I promise, it wasn't intentional.' I look away from him for the first time. 'This isn't easy for me to talk about. But we can, if you want. Only I need you to calm down first, OK?'

He pulls his mouth into a sneer. 'Nah, like I said, I don't need nothing explained to me. Least of all by you, however much you reckon you're the one round here with all the answers.'

And he's so thick with self-pity, I'm suddenly angry enough, I could breathe fire. But I'm not going to give him the satisfaction of raising my voice. Instead, I make sure it's quieter than before. Quieter and colder. 'Then this is done. And you can storm off like a spoilt brat, or pull yourself together and finish talking to the boys. But either way, leave me alone.'

He starts to say something, but I interrupt. 'Now.'

Tony looks at me, shakes his head, and walks an exaggeratedly massive arc away from me to the door. As he pushes his way out, the anger disappears and I'm just sad. I know it's ridiculous, but it feels like grief. This is the end of the teasing, playful thing that meant every morning, there was a spark of excitement about coming into work. And it's such a grim end. Not just what Tony said, or how he said it. But because I want to claim that was all a reflection of what's broken about him. Only that wouldn't be true. The damage I carry around with me played its part too. And that makes me flat and grey inside, a wave of tiredness pushing aside the jittery leftovers of fight or flight.

I'm still slumped back against the wall, knees drawn up to my chest, when LeMar puts his head round the door an hour or so later.

'Sorry, Genie. I was going to turn the lights out. I didn't realize you were in here.'

I try to sound bright, like it's completely normal to be sitting alone on the indoor pitch on a Monday night. 'Are you finished?'

LeMar shrugs. 'Tony's still in with them, but I wasn't contributing much. I thought I might as well go.'

That doesn't sound like things improved after I left. I should go and shut the evening down, but I can't face it.

LeMar's still looking at me. 'Genie, are you all right? You seem weird.'

I'm tempted to say everything's fine. But then I remember LeMar at fourteen, pacing around my living room after visiting his mum in hospital, raging about the doctors telling white lies.

I sigh, letting it pull my face down into unflattering lines. 'It's just Tony.'

'Did he hurt you?' LeMar asks quickly.

I shut my eyes briefly, forcing back tears. 'No, of course not.' I make myself smile. 'I did something stupid, and Tony was letting me know he didn't appreciate it.'

LeMar, being LeMar, doesn't ask for details. Instead, he shrugs. 'I wouldn't lose sleep over it. Garratt's permanently on the edge of a melt-down.'

That doesn't fit with what I've been told. I mean, the training staff aren't exactly effusive about Tony, but it's more like they're wary he'll slip back to old ways than that he's a current problem. Only there's stuff players see that coaches miss, so I ask, 'Has he got agitated before then?'

'A full-on tantrum?' LeMar's voice is scornful. 'No, but it's been on the cards for a while.'

I raise my eyebrows.

He smiles. 'Yeah, OK. I know what you're thinking.' LeMar sinks down next to me, not touching, but as close as he gets to any woman who isn't Katia. 'And it's not like I don't have some sympathy. I mean, I get it. He's here on his own, he can hear the clock ticking on his career, everyone's watching, waiting for a slip-up. But the life he's lived, it's his choice, isn't it?'

'Not everyone's you.'

'I'm not judging. Just saying actions bring consequences.' He turns his face to me, his cheek flat against the grey of the wall and the shadows adding an extra inch to his high-top. 'And, Genie, I'd steer clear. Do your job and leave out the extra stuff this time.'

'I don't ever really do anything all that extra.'

'You did for me.'

That's the closest he's come to admitting that, when he was the only quiet kid in the academy, the player care office was his safe space. I'd like to hug him, but he'd be horrified, so I settle for a smile.

'I don't remember you being any trouble. And if there's an issue with Tony, he deserves the same help from Player Care, whether you like him or not.'

LeMar draws his hand down his face. 'Only, Genie, I know you. You're seeing him as this lost puppy who needs looking after. And it might be Garratt does need some of that, because how he is, it's weird. Like at training, he's how you'd expect, always has to be the best at everything. But it's not just the technical stuff. He started out like he couldn't be bothered with us. Now, he's got so he has to be everyone's best mate. Do you know what I mean?'

'Yes, I do,' I say, smiling.

LeMar sighs. 'Yeah, I thought you might. Only I don't know as it's something to smile about. Because the minute training's over, it's like he's flipped a switch, he's that keen to leave. And the last week or so, he's hardly been able to keep the buddy stuff up for a full session. I get it's him trying to show he's here to play for the team, but it's got to be adding weight on.'

That's my fault. Suggesting he tried harder with the others was obviously a stupid idea.

LeMar inches his hand a fraction closer to mine. 'So, I get you've got to do your job. But watch out, OK? This puppy, it might bite.'

I make reassuring noises, but I am concerned. Not for me, for Tony.

18

The next morning

I was dreading today, but then I push open my office door. There should be three pairs of heels, one black, one nude and one red, tucked away in their corner, ready for days when I work out on my way in. But instead, they're arranged in a perfect straight line on my desk, and each one is freshly polished. More than that, when I pick up the black stiletto at the end of the row, it's ultra-soft and supple.

That fits with the distinct smell of Vaseline. It's an old trick, smoothing petroleum jelly into the inside of the heel to stop boots rubbing. Bothering with that little detail would make this the most adorable apology I've ever received, even if I didn't recognize the old cliché about how player x isn't fit to clean player y's boots. So, I can't keep pretending I don't owe Tony an apology of my own. Because he's right, I am different when other people are around. But he's miles off about why.

I stalk the first team, until there's the perfect opportunity to catch Tony on his way out of the gym. I smile polite 'hello's and 'how are you's to players and staff thronging around in the corridor, but when I get to Tony, I give him a quick hug. Which isn't remotely suggestive of fraternization, when in this game, we hug all the time, and high five and put an arm round each other's shoulders. But I wouldn't have done it yesterday. And I make sure it's a really good hug, if a fleeting one. Plus, it's just possible, on my way down, I might've briefly nuzzled his neck.

'I wanted to thank you for doing the academy thing yesterday.'

Tony smiles, though it's nowhere close to a back-to-before smile. 'It was nothing.' He draws me into one of the inexplicably frequent corners that break up the hallways, calling over to the coaching staff, 'I'll catch you up, OK? I need to get something sorted with Genie real quick.'

Once the rest of the players have moved on, Tony says, 'What was that hug for?'

I settle back against the wall, painted a loyal, if depressing, grey. My hand grazes his. 'Tony, about what I said to Chrissie. I'm sorry. I had the best of intentions, and I do still think you'd be better off opening up to her properly. But it's not for me to tell you that.'

He shrugs. 'If you'd just said it to me direct, I dunno as I could've objected.'

I frown and shake my head quickly. 'No, you definitely could. It's not an excuse, but I'm used to even our first-team players being so young, they don't just need a bit of guidance, they want it. But you're a proper professional. You know better than anyone what's right for you. And you don't need to hear my thoughts about it.'

'I'm not sure as that's true.' His head is low and his voice sounds tired.

'It is. And even if it wasn't, I shouldn't have said a word

to Chrissie without checking with you. So, I'm sorry, and I promise, it won't happen again.'

He looks up, enough to meet my eyes. 'No, I'm the one who's sorry. Like I'd prefer you'd not done it, but me kicking off like that was a complete over-reaction. And what I said, I didn't mean it. You get that, don't you?'

I think he did, in the heat of the moment. But I say, 'No, I know.'

He drags a hand over his face. 'The anger, it's such a, like, an ugly thing. And I never used to get that way.'

I nod.

'And now, when I do, I hate it. It's like my dad's in the room, you know?'

I put my arm around him, inviting him to lean his weight into me.

'I'm just, like, so disappointed in myself. That I spoke to you that way.'

'It's sort of the same thing though, Tony. I'd rather you hadn't, but there's no harm done.'

He rests his head against mine and takes my hand loosely. 'I dunno 'bout that. I'd never have laid a finger on you, but I'm a big guy. Me throwing my toys out of the pram like that, I get it can be scary.'

I squeeze his hand. 'I've seen worse.'

'That don't make it OK.'

'No, but this is a high-pressure industry, isn't it? And the season's getting to the point where things are starting to build. You're not a robot. Sometimes things bubble over.'

He shakes his head, his stubble rubbing against my hair. 'Yeah, only now you're sounding like my mum, and not in

143

a good way. Making excuses for me, when you should be telling me to get lost.'

I smile. 'Well, as I remember it, I did.'

He makes the noise that's sort of a sigh and sort of a sniff. The one that usually goes along with the first smile after a man's been upset. 'Yeah, you did, didn't you? Quite forcefully, I must say.'

I tighten my fingers for a second, pushing into his. 'Tony, it's really fine, you're not the first player to get frustrated with me.'

Tony turns me to face him. 'That's good to hear. But like I say, that's not who I usually am.'

'No, I know.'

His face changes, so his eyes are stern. 'No, Genie, you don't. So, now's when you run a mile, OK? Cos I can hear myself saying the stuff blokes always say. How they're sorry, how it won't happen again, all that.'

I reach my free hand to his elbow. 'Tony, you don't have to take care of me. It's my job to do that for you, remember?'

He grunts. 'Yeah, only that's sort of the problem, yeah?'

'Is it?'

He turns his head away and there's tension in his jaw, like he's having to say something he'd rather not. 'It's a big part of why I lost it yesterday. Cos I get all the stuff you've done since I arrived, it's been you doing your job, getting me settled. But you're dead good at it. Like more than professional, real kind. And I've not seen a lot of that lately, so I like, latched on a bit strong. Let myself think it was more than it was.'

'Kissing you doesn't exactly fall within my job description.' I'm trying to smile, to lighten this, but he looks back at me with earnest eyes.

'Yeah, and maybe it's not. But that don't excuse nothing I said. If anything, it's worse, cos you get to change your mind whenever. I don't need no sexual harassment seminar to tell me losing my rag cos you don't wanna sleep with me, it's unacceptable.'

I resist asking exactly how many seminars he's had to attend over his career, since we're nowhere near the joking stage. And anyway, I'm only tempted because this next bit isn't easy to say. 'Tony, I'm glad you know that. But I can't pretend I didn't give you mixed signals. And there are lots of reasons, but it comes down to having issues of my own.'

He interrupts. 'Yeah, but I've known that from the start. Cos if you didn't, a woman like you wouldn't be single. And how you are, there'd be kids for sure. But I don't have a clue what the issues are, so I can't do nothing about 'em.'

It's like he's pressed on a bruise, especially about the children. But I'm not going to go into all that with Tony, because really, what's the point? I make a movement with my shoulders. It's meant to be a shrug, but turns into more of a sad little shuffle. 'They're not your problems to do anything about.'

'What if them being our problems meant me and you had a chance of going somewhere?'

There's a spark of what I've got a nasty feeling is hope. But I know, after talking to LeMar, that's got to be stamped out. 'I think the last thing you need is someone else's problems right now.'

'Cos I'm fucked up enough on my own?' he asks, more sad than angry.

I do the thing that's basically an upside-down smile. 'Honestly? Yes.'

He nods, and I think he's on the verge of walking away, so I reach for his wrist. 'Look, Tony, what you said about not being an angry person, I know that's true.'

'How can you know that?'

'Because of how you play. You know how some players are incandescent with rage? Like when they score, they want to burn the stadium down, they're so angry.'

Tony half smiles. 'Yeah, I can think of a few like that.'

'Well, I've always loved that too. The passion of it. But how you play when you're at your best is something different, something really special. Like you're so good, you're not even trying. It's the same as Roudie when he's chasing a Labrador and realizes he can catch it without getting out of second gear. It's . . .' I search for the right word. 'Joyful.'

He smiles properly. 'That's a real nice thing to say.'

'Umm, but it's not true at the moment, is it?'

His brows come together and there's the start of him being offended again.

I make my voice gentle. 'I mean, you're playing well, really well, but it's not effortless yet. But it will be soon. Just like if the anger isn't something you had before, it'll go. Only I think you've maybe got some stuff that needs to heal first.'

He swallows hard. 'Yeah, you might be right 'bout that.'

I slide my hand down from his wrist until our fingers

146

are intertwined. 'So, I think it makes sense for us to be just friends, at least for now. Don't you?'

He nods. 'I'll take mates over how we was last night anyhow.'

I make my smile business-like, even though that's not how I feel. 'And Tony, what I was saying, about how the pressure's starting to build, I do think that fed into last night. So, how about after training, you come and find me and we go through your diary? Work out where we can trim things back?'

He nods. 'I'd appreciate that, thanks, love.' He looks down at his hand in mine. 'But, Genie, only if you're sure. Cos after yesterday, if you wants me to stop bothering you, I'll understand.'

I wrap my fingers a little tighter. 'There's nothing I'd like less than you stopping bothering me.'

19

Tony does come and find me right after training, but his eye contact is more fleeting than usual. I think this conversation needs to be just us, so I take him out to our little outdoor eating area. It's not scenic, tucked between the car park and one of the training pitches, but it's private.

Only when we sit down, I can see flaws. Tony isn't the right build for picnic benches, so he's got his usual problem over where to put his feet. It's also way too early in 'let's be friends' for me to be comfortable, sitting so close our heads almost touch as we hunch over my laptop. I force myself to ignore how close Tony's fingers come to brushing mine as we flick back and forth through his calendar, and focus on how it makes perfect sense that he's feeling overwhelmed. All the first team's diaries are busy, but Tony's looks like it's covered in rainbow vomit, there are so many coloured block-outs. But as we go through, each time I try to delete something, he says there's no need.

Like we've just been over two meet-and-greet slots. I'm not going to claim M&Gs don't matter. It might only be fifteen minutes or so of the player's time, but it means a lot to the fan who gets the one-on-one. Only it doesn't need to be Tony doing it. It could just as easily be a player who's not making the team that week, or who won't be travelling

149

for our European matches. But when I point that out, Tony shakes his head emphatically.

'Nah. Media's already sent me the little bios they does for these two. One's a kid who's had a hard time, the other's an old bloke who's likely seeing his last season. I'm not going to back out on 'em.'

That's sweet, but unhelpful for the diary pruning. I move on to the next appointment, blocked out in an ugly tangerine colour. Tony's hand tenses around the edge of the table. That's odd. It's an interview, but with Felicity Landon, the tamest journalist in Monica's menagerie, so no reason for Tony's knuckles to go white against his tan. Except maybe the date?

'You have an actual rest day then, don't you?'

'Yeah.' He doesn't sound all that bothered. But the first team are so heavily scheduled, it's hard for the coaching staff to find them a whole day off. When they do, it's best they grab it.

'Then I don't know how this ended up on your off day. Shall I have media reschedule?'

There's an uncomfortable twist in his mouth. 'Do you think you could get 'em to cancel, instead?'

'Probably. But you'd owe them a serious favour. She's one of our preferred sources.'

I suspect Tony's more than familiar with just how helpful a friendly journalist can be. And he does say, 'OK. I'll do it.' But he sounds not so much reluctant as truly miserable, and his fingers haven't relaxed. If anything, he's pushing down harder.

'But let's move it to a light training day.' My voice is

smiley, like I'm offering something delightful instead of a mild reduction in inconvenience.

Tony gnaws at his bottom lip, then asks in an unusually small voice, 'Do you think we could do it by phone, or have her come here, instead?'

That's when I notice the interview involves a London trip. Tony's reluctance begins to make sense. 'Of course.' I open up the appointment and look at the details more closely. 'Actually, Tony, I'm sorry, I think there's been a mix-up. They're sending a photographer to do some shots with you at the stadium, so I can't think why this was scheduled for you to have to travel. I'll speak to the media department and try to get it straightened out. But yes, definitely, we'll make sure you don't have to trek down there just for this.'

Tony lets go of the table, stretching his fingers. 'Thanks, love.' He leans in closer, frowning. 'Only don't that being orange mean it got set up by you guys, not the media people?'

I'll never understand why the diary entries have to be colour coded, instead of the responsible department being written in actual legible words. I bend in too, trying to ignore the not unwelcome physical proximity between Tony and me.

'Yes, you're right. That is ours.' I'd already spotted this and had been puzzled by it, thinking it must be some kind of error.

But how did it happen? We never schedule interviews. So, this is another of those weird little mistakes that on their own don't mean much, but seem to be adding up to something more. Then I remember, my problems aren't Tony's problems, and smile briskly. 'But whoever, I'll sort it.'

He nods, quick and serious, like this is a major relief. 'Yeah, that'd be great.'

'Do you have any more like this, where you have to travel?' This has got to be about Tony worrying he'll slip into old ways, if there's something better on offer than the distinctly limited delights of Covenly's nightlife.

Tony scrolls through, grim-faced. He's going fast, like he knows exactly what he's looking for. 'Just this.' He pulls a going-to-the-dentist face. 'It's a photoshoot.' He mentions the name of an athleisure brand that most players would kill to get into bed with.

'You're not keen?'

He shakes his head quickly.

'Are you locked in, or can your agent get you out of it, if you don't feel like doing it?'

It's not like Tony needs the money, surely he can duck it, if it doesn't appeal?

Tony's doom-laden expression deepens, the lines on his forehead turning to furrows. 'They're like allied to my agency, so it's not that simple.'

I narrow my eyes and look at him closely. He's tapping a toe, and he only does that when he's really bothered. Maybe I'm wrong, and this is about more than going to London. Except I can't get any other vibes from Tony. Though I've got to admit, my intuition failure might be connected to how, each time Tony moves his foot, his joggers brush my bare knee. In the end, I resort to simply asking, 'What would make it less bad?'

Tony struggles free from the bench and walks a few strides away, hands deep in his pockets. Without turning he says, 'It was in my diary from before I transferred, yeah?'

I make an agreeing noise.

'So, there's someone who'll know 'bout it, and I don't wanna see 'em.' He turns back to me with a less-than-convincing smile. 'Sorry, I'm being a right baby over this, aren't I?'

'No, if it makes you uncomfortable, we need to fix it.'

He looks down at the floor. 'All it is, is the last girl, the one from before I got here. I don't wanna see her, and end up going back over old ground. Do you get me?'

That sounds like Angharad is currently out of the picture. But if that was ever my business, it certainly isn't now. I make sure nothing in my face pries for details. 'I understand, you've other things to think about, with the games you've got coming up.'

'Yeah, only I don't wanna put you out over something I ought to sort for myself.'

I shake my head briskly. 'No, this is an easy one. I'll get in touch with their PR, say you have a club commitment, and you need to reschedule.'

He runs his fingers across his hair, so his face is hidden by his forearm, as he says, 'If you could, that'd be good.'

'Although, actually, Tony, I might have a better idea. You know LeMar's got a deal with them too?'

'Yeah, maybe. It's hard to keep track.'

I smile. 'It certainly can be. But I know LeMar's got a shoot scheduled for tomorrow. He's going to leave straight after training. Why don't I see if you can go together?'

Tony laughs, though it's not massively happy. 'You

thinking he's the best sheepdog you've got for a trip to the big bad city?'

'Well, can you think of anyone less likely to lead you astray?'

He nods, eyes amused. 'Fair point. Only do you reckon I'll have to take him to the Science Museum after?'

It still surprises me, LeMar being blessed with sporting talent when he seems so much better suited to coding. But I shouldn't laugh, and I almost don't.

'If they've got an exhibition on gaming technology, I can't see how you'll avoid it. But think of it as teambuilding.'

Tony grunts, then runs a hand along the line of his fade, which is getting progressively higher with every game. 'Do you reckon this is OK, or do I need it cut for this?'

'Put your head down a second.' He sits beside me, bending his neck so I can study the shave. 'It looks fine to me.' He has these three darts that I've been dying to touch ever since he had them cut in. And I'm going to take my chance to run my fingers over them, even if we are just friends. 'Except, is it OK that these feel the tiniest bit furry? They still look clean enough.'

'Nah, they'll do, I reckon.' He straightens and smiles. 'And I can see the vanity, so don't feel you've gotta point it out.'

'I wasn't going to. I'd be even less enthused than LeMar about having my photo taken over and over.'

He gives me the smile that sends shivers up my spine. 'Pity. Cos you're a whole lot prettier than either of us.' He looks up under his lashes. 'If I'm allowed to say that to a mate.'

'You are, but I doubt Katia would agree.' The look

between us isn't the between-friends sort. I'm not sure we're going to be great at our new arrangement. But maybe it's just a question of practice? 'Is that everything? Because if it is, I should go and make these things happen.'

'Yeah, it is.' He looks at the floor, lines up a few pebbles with his trainer, then darts a quick glance at me. "Cept what you said, 'bout working with Chrissie, I wanted you to know I'm going to give it a go.'

I'm glad, but I don't want to make it into a big deal. I start picking up my things, waving away Tony's offer to help. I want him to go home and relax, not trek back to the office with me.

At the bottom of the stairs, Tony stops to say goodbye. His hand skims my upper arm, just as the manager glides round the corner, blessing us with his most beatific of smiles. 'Ah, Tony, I had heard you and Genie were becoming better acquainted.'

Tony smiles, half respectful, half amused. 'We are, boss.'

The manager nods sagely. 'In my experience, Genie is a woman worth knowing.'

The ratio tips in favour of amused. 'Yeah, I reckon I'm finding that out.'

'And of course, she is always so ingenious in the face of a problem.'

Tony's clearly unsure if that's a pun or a genuine observation. Personally, I'd lean towards the latter, but I wouldn't put money on it. Tony settles for, 'Um, yeah, she's that, all right.'

'Indeed. A woman to value.' The manager strokes his perfectly manicured beard before drifting away, his expression serious and his mind presumably full of false nines and inverted fullbacks.

Tony waits until he's rounded the next twist in the corridor, before asking, 'Why'd that feel like he was wishing me interesting times?'

'Did it? I thought he was being sweet. But then he always is, except when he's flustered.'

'Dunno as you'd say that if it was you he was screaming at from the sidelines.'

I pout. 'But he is flustered then. And you've only got yourselves to blame.'

'How's that?'

'Try tracking back like you mean it, and maybe he'll stop yelling.' There's more irritation in my voice than is strictly merited.

Annoyance flickers between us, then Tony laughs like he's thoroughly entertained. 'Christ, don't tell me I've been treading on his toes.'

'No, of course not.' I can't help smiling. 'Though honestly, it's lucky he's never asked. I simply can't say no to him.'

'Thank God for that then, cos I'm way too old to be playing away with the manager's missus.'

I touch Tony's elbow. 'Hang on, are you telling me that story's true?'

So, Tony does end up walking me back to the office, sharing a salacious story from early in his career. It's farcical, to the point that I have to redo my eye make-up afterwards, I've been laughing so hard. Perhaps we'll be better at just friends than I'd thought.

20

From: Beth Christie (bchristie@Media.CovenlyFC.co.uk)
To: Charlotte Edwards (cedwards@Playercare.CovenlyFC.co.uk)
Sent: 09.34 Wednesday 26 August
Subject: Felicity Landon interview

Hi Genie,

Just spoke to Landon's PA. Landon's on board with doing a
'power couples in football' piece on Monica and Gavin, and
she's more than happy to interview Garratt at the same time.
But before I book her in with him for after training on Thursday,
I wanted to 100 per cent confirm he's on board with that?
Landon's PA said that's what she'd tried to set up originally, but
Garratt wanted to meet in London. The puff piece on Monica is
Landon doing us a favour, so I don't want to mess her around if
there's a miscommunication on our end.

Thanks

Beth

That's weird. Only actually, it probably isn't. I can think
of multiple reasons why Tony might've originally wanted
a London trip on his calendar. Including one whose first
Instagram post of the day involved a yoga pose I could
only achieve by dislocating my hip. And I know gossip isn't

reliable, but if there's even a smidgen of truth in what's been said about Tony and Angharad, their relationship status changes more often than her filters. If Tony wanted to meet and then decided he didn't, it's not like he's got to explain that, is it? Not when we're just friends.

So, I send a quick non-nosy Slack message back:

> Thanks for checking. Tony definitely wants to do the interview here. But before you schedule, I'd confirm he can fit it in. First team leave at 3 pm.

See, I'm such a good friend, I'm even giving him a chance to change his mind again. Except there's something that doesn't make sense.

> Sorry, one other thing. Did Landon's PA happen to say if she spoke to Tony directly or someone from the club? It looked like that interview was set up by Player Care, but none of us remember talking to her.

> She didn't. I can ask, if you want?

> No, it's not a big deal. Just wanted to be sure we hadn't been stepping on Media's toes.

I'm still trying to figure out how that interview ended up in Player-Care tangerine when Skylar races in.

'Sorry, Genie, sorry. I know I'm late, conditioning ran over.'

It's the second time this week, and it's only Tuesday. I

try to look disapproving. But she can't exactly walk out of training early, and she's still in gym clothes so she hasn't dawdled.

'I've got a present though, to make up.' She holds out a package. 'Well, not from me. From Tony.'

It's squishy. Probably clothes he wants returned, since we are now definitely outside gift-giving territory. Only there's no return address label. I open it, hoping for an explanation inside about what I'm supposed to do with it. Whatever it is, it's wrapped in tissue paper, and as I ease it out, my fingers brush silky softness that can only be cashmere. Shaking the empty parcel doesn't produce a note. I look up at Sky. 'Did he say . . .'

'Oh, yeah.' She pulls a crumpled scrap from the pocket of her joggers. 'He gave me this.'

It takes me a minute to decipher the scrawl: *This was looking for a home. Thought you might like it.*

'Did he say who it's for?'

'You obviously.'

'Not obviously. There's no name. He might want me to send it on.'

'Nope, it's definitely for you. He couldn't exactly write a full-scale love letter, Sanchez was in his face over being late.'

I'm surprised Tony managed to write anything. Sanchez, one of our wingers, did his junior years at a club that fines by the minute for lateness. His timekeeping is impeccable bordering on pathological.

I unwrap the tissue paper and shake out a woman's hoodie. Skylar's whirlwind arrival didn't shake Katia's laser-focus off a player's council tax paperwork, but clothes are her kryptonite. The minute she sees it, she's at my desk, fingering the gold and purple zebra stripes.

'Isn't it lush? I've been trying to get my hands on one ever since they came out.' Kat looks at Sky. 'Did Tony say how he managed to get past the waitlist?'

I check the label. 'Oh, it's just free merch, I think. This is the brand Tony and LeMar did the shoot for, isn't it?'

Katia mimes gnashing her teeth. 'Urgh. LeMar's so weird about freebies. But I've been going on for ages about how I wanted one. If they were giving them away, he could've accepted, just this once.'

I completely understand why she's annoyed. It would look amazing on Katia. But even if it is too bright for me, there's no way I'm giving it up.

Skylar snorts. 'Only, obviously they weren't.'

Katia and I both look at her, heads to one side, like puppies surprised by a squeaky toy.

'You don't have to be a genius to work it out. Tony paid for it.'

I begin to say no but Skylar talks over me, her voice husky as an old-style radio ad. 'Zebra stripes, the perfect gift for the lioness who won't accept anything.'

I restart explaining this is just a friendly gesture. Because Tony definitely seems to have fully bought in to the friends thing. As in, yesterday, he was so deep in conversation with Steph, the club photographer, he barely managed to smile hello. Obviously, I didn't butt in, though I was tempted to offer her a scrunchie. She seemed to be having terrible trouble keeping her hair out of her eyes, based on how much she was flicking it around. Well, I say her hair, but I mean her not particularly convincing extensions, which I can't help noticing have appeared since she travelled with the first team for Saturday's game. And no, of course I'm not jealous. Whatever gave you that idea?

Only, right now, that doesn't matter. Neither does exactly how Tony obtained the top, because it's just hit me.

'Skylar, how are Tony and Sanchez running late? If you saw them on your way up, they should've been easily in time for training.'

Skylar stops correcting the effects of deadlifts on her platinum ponytail for long enough to say, 'They're skipping training. To meet the medics, I think. Does it matter?'

I must look horrified, because Katia rushes to reassure. 'Tony's not injured. Today's the demo for that new shock-wave machine at the hospital, to see if we want one of our own. Don't you remember, you sent me the list of players missing training?'

'But was Tony on it?' I'd swear he wasn't.

Katia rushes over to her computer. 'No, no, he isn't.'

I try calling Tony. It goes straight to voicemail. Typical.

That's a problem. A big one. Players have to tell the FA's whereabouts team if they're absent from training. If they don't, and the anti-doping people show up for a random check, that's a strike. Three strikes equal a one-year suspension. And it doesn't matter if it's the club's fault or the player's, a strike's a strike.

I check my watch. Training's just started. Can't add Tony to the list now. But maybe the medics are still here? If Tony's at the training ground, we can report him as being late for training, instead of missing training. It's a technicality, but within the rules. Or it is, so long as he doesn't leave before we make the change.

I kick off my heels and start running.

I round the corner to the treatment room like a 100-metre sprinter. And thank God, they're all there, hanging around in the hallway, Tony, Sanchez, Leon Wite from the academy, and Gavin. Shiny concrete and bare feet don't mix, so as Chrissie emerges from the medic's office, I'm struggling to stop myself sliding into Tony.

'Genie, what on earth's the matter?' she asks.

'Tony's not . . .' Gaspy breathing. 'Tony's not on the whereabouts list.' More gasping, I can't be doing enough cardio. 'You need to wait for us to . . .'

'What do you mean, he's not on the list?' Gavin snaps. 'I emailed you on Friday. I was perfectly clear. Garratt, Sanchez and Wite would all be absent from Tuesday's session.'

'I'm sorry, I . . .' I'm baffled, how could I have missed that email?

'There's no point making excuses. This is exactly why I've always said Player Care shouldn't be trusted to handle whereabouts reporting.'

It's true. Gavin's told everyone who'll listen, it's a job for the medical team. It's me who's resisted. Because it's not always a medical issue. What if a player's missing training for something personal? Something they don't want to share with the doctor who weighs in on whether they're fit to play? Only now, I've proved Gavin right.

Player Care can't be trusted, and I couldn't be more mortified if I tried.

Gavin's mouth tightens. That only happens when he's really angry. 'You know the anti-doping brigade can turn up for any session. What if today had been the day? It's common knowledge they're after scalps this season. How many times do you have to be told, we've got to be careful?' Gavin looks pointedly at Tony. 'Especially with certain players.'

That's a low blow, but I doubt Gavin realizes how low. Gavin considers the gossipy side of football beneath him, so he's probably referring to a story that's practically Jurassic, about an off-season trip to Amsterdam which briefly cost Tony his place on the England youth team. Gavin won't have heard of Angharad Jones, let alone her bestie Caliste, a wellness guru and fervent advocate for microdosing. So there's no chance he'll be familiar with the (almost certainly) slanderous rumours that Tony's loss of form reflected a more macro approach.

Only Tony doesn't know that, judging by how his fingers are curling around his thumbs. 'I don't dope. Not for performance and I don't do recreational stuff neither.'

Gavin raises his eyebrows. Even if he's unaware Tony's currently on a hair trigger, that wasn't a good idea.

Tony takes a step away from the wall. 'I've never had a bad test, not once. And I've done a fuck of a lot more of 'em than most people, I can tell you.' He's not raising his voice but his eyes have turned to ice.

Sanchez stares fixedly at the wall immediately above Chrissie's shoulder, and she's finding the club badge on his jacket fascinating. Leon shuffles his feet. So everyone gets this has got very flammable, very fast.

Everyone except Gavin. 'Nonsense, it's an entirely random system.'

'Random my arse,' Tony sneers. 'But if you wanna test me, go ahead, try me.'

You don't have to be a body language expert to see that's a thinly veiled threat. But Gavin spends more time in the board room than the treatment room these days. He's probably got so used to passive aggressive, he's forgotten what active aggression looks like.

'If it was up to me, I would.' Gavin's top lip curls.

Tony shifts his weight fractionally more onto the balls of his feet.

This needs to stop. Now. I step not completely in front of Gavin, but enough to create a barrier. 'Gavin would do the same for everyone, if he had his way. You've always talked about setting up an internal testing system, haven't you?' I turn and smile encouragingly at Gavin. 'So we're on the front foot, isn't that how you put it?'

Thankfully, Gavin takes the bait and begins a monologue about the advantages of in-house detection. Chrissie yawns expansively. Tony shakes himself, like Roudie straight out of the river, and grins at Chrissie. Crisis averted.

Sanchez breaks in when Gavin pauses for breath. 'I'm sorry, doctor, but Genie, I need to be clear, I am on the list, yes? And the young boy?' Sanchez points at Leon.

'Yes, absolutely. The only person missing is Tony. I'm so sorry for the confusion. I really don't think I got an email but I will look into it.'

Gavin sighs. He's not angry any more, he's educating. That's so much worse. 'And you see now, don't you, how this kind of error can have real consequences? I mean, I know you're more comfortable with the emotional aspects of player care. But even if administrative details aren't your strong suit, you must understand, they . . .'

Tony holds up his hand. 'Yeah, all right, mate, let's leave it, shall we?' He turns to me and everything about him, from his eyes to his hands, softens. 'I dunno why everyone's getting so wound up over this. We've not left yet. If you just text the whereabouts people at the FA now, we're all Gucci, aren't we?'

My hackles spring up. I know I look pathetic, letting Gavin run through all my failings without even trying to defend myself. Only I can't exactly argue, everything Gavin's saying is accurate. And even if it wasn't, Tony's got no right to swoop in. I can look out for . . . oh, actually, I've got this completely wrong, haven't I? Because there's a tiny shift in Tony's face, turning his smile from sympathetic to an invitation to play. So, the extra-niceness isn't patronizing or interfering, it's for Gavin's benefit.

I almost laugh, it's such an effective prod. I mean, can you think of anything more dismissive than going from raring to fight to boundless tolerance, just like that? Judging by Gavin's eaten-a-wasp expression, he's fully aware of the alpha subtext. So it's probably for the best that Chrissie frowns and clears her throat. 'But I still don't understand why Garratt's coming with us at all? I'm not aware of any evidence this modality has preventative benefits, and there's no acute damage in the hamstring.'

Gavin begins to argue.

Tony interrupts. 'No offence, doc, but it's Chrissie I'm working with. If she don't rate this, I'm not interested.'

Gavin begins a variant of the speech he trots out annually for physio appreciation week. But Tony's talking over him, before Gavin's more than thirty seconds into explaining how the medics at Covenly are a team within a team.

'The way I sees it, treatments aren't so different from when I take my car in. And it's the mechanic I want doing my tune-up, not some bloke whose missus owns the shop, thanks all the same.'

Gavin's opening and closing his mouth, but words aren't coming out.

Tony adopts the expression of extreme innocence usually reserved for immediately after goading a defender into disorderly conduct. 'So I'd best be off to training, I guess. Cos like you say, you never knows if today's the day.'

I'm not even back in the office when Chrissie pops up in my Slack:

> I take back anything negative I've said about Garratt. What an absolute poppet.

> I thought you found male posturing the most tedious part of a tedious game?

Chrissie is fascinated by sports injuries, not sport itself.

> I make an exception when Gavin's on the receiving end. But I meant more how he is with you.

She adds a gif of a pitbull licking a tiny kitten.

> That's not exactly flattering to either of us.

> But so accurate. Now be a good girl and thank him in the manner he's clearly very much hoping for.

> We've agreed we're just friends.

Chrissie's laughing emojis last most of the screen.

21

My afternoon is consumed by the monster that is my to-do list, and it's not until Kat and Sky have left that I get a chance to hunt through my deleted emails. Had I somehow deleted one before even reading it? Even if I didn't spend ninety per cent of my time thinking about Tony, we've three weeks until our first European away match. There's no way I'd have missed a hospital visit for the player who lifts our midfield from solid to sublime.

Only it seems I did, because there it is: Sanchez, Wite, Garratt. The names are even followed by player numbers, because Gavin's a stickler for detail. This has to be my mistake. And sure enough, here's my email, asking Kat to list Wite and Sanchez at an alternative location.

So yep, entirely my fault. Gavin's right, I am useless at forms and paperwork. For half a second, I'm tempted to pretend it never happened. But the manager is big on players owning their errors, so I'll have to do the same. WhatsApp seems like the least humiliating option:

To: Sanchez, Tony, Leon Wite, Gavin

I wanted to let you know, I checked the information given to me by Dr Harrison. All 3 of you were listed as missing training. I was at fault and I can't apologize enough. I'd like to reassure you that Player Care takes the whereabouts protocol very seriously, and if

you'd like to be kept updated as to whether you're listed as at an alternative location, let me know and I'll have Katia message you directly.
17.52

Sanchez replies:

> I will message Katia about updates.
> 17.53

So I'm not trusted even to talk to Katia. That's upsetting but understandable.

Leon sends a smiley face and:

> Kat can message me anytime but I don't need updates on that
> 17.59

That's quite baller for someone with two years left in the academy. Must keep him away from LeMar.

No reply from Tony, which I get. However kind he was in front of other people, he's got to be furious over this. But as I'm putting my coat on, my phone pings with a private message from Tony. I steel myself to read exactly how incompetent I am, but he actually says:

> Don't beat yourself up. I've screwed up the whereabouts stuff a few times over the years myself. It's why you get 3 strikes a season
> 18.17

So once again, Chrissie's completely right. He's an absolute poppet. Not that I can tell him that.

> Thank you for being so understanding
> 18.18

> > I should be thanking you for getting between me &
> > the doc. I'm honestly working on not popping off the
> > whole time, but he hit a nerve
> > 18.20

> I know, but I really don't think he understood why doping is a
> sensitive topic
> 18.21

Hmm, I could've worded that better. I can't imagine Tony wants to dwell on the exact nature of last season's gossip.

He sends a shrugging emoji and:

> > It was more how he spoke to you that set me off
> > 18.22

> > Sorry-scratch that. I should've said it's not right,
> > talking to staff like that in front of players. You can't
> > exactly answer back to Mr boss
> > 18.24

Maybe Tony wasn't only taunting Gavin. Worryingly, that makes me surprisingly smiley, for someone who got all prickly about Tony interfering.

Honestly, I think Gavin was more than justified to be annoyed. But you're right, I'd have preferred it if he'd spoken to me privately. I hate players feeling they can't trust me, so I appreciated you doing some damage limitation
18.26

> Having each other's backs, it's what mates do, yeh?
> 18.27

I didn't exactly have yours & I feel horrible about it
18.28

> Don't
> 18.28

> Me risking death by rondo to save you the trouble of texting the FA, maybe it can be the start of evening up the score between us? After the other night
> 18.30

That's already forgotten
18.31

> By you maybe. It's still pretty fresh in my mind
> 18.32

I miss . . . delete, delete . . . *I want . . .* that's worse . . . *Can we . . .* What is the actual matter with me?

> You don't need to say nothing to that
> 18.36

Except, I do. Because turning to switch off the lights, I see the hoodie, neatly folded on my desk.

> BTW I completely forgot in this morning's panic, thank you for the
> top. It's lovely and very kind of you to pass it on to me
> 18.37

>> You're welcome. They owed you. Having me there
>> winding him up made LeMar's photos way better than
>> usual
>> 18.38

I should screenshot that for Skylar. It's definitely a freebie.

> Katia showed me. You're right, they're SO much better-LeMar
> actually looks like who he is
> 18.39

And he really does. Before, the camera's always transformed LeMar back to an awkward teenager, but in these pictures, he's precisely the elegant young man he's become.

>> If you mean a stuck-up little prince, then yeah, I guess
>> he does
>> 18.39

> He told me the two of you got on fine
> 18.40

Depends what you mean by fine. He wasn't exactly chatty
18.41

Give him time. LeMar's cautious about letting people get close
18.42

Time fixes that, does it?
18.43

Yes-it's best not to rush him
18.44

I wasn't asking about LeMar
18.45

Weren't y . . . I don't ne . . . Let's start ov . . .

Sorry, ignore that. I'm going to go now x
18.49

I pick up the hoodie and stroke along the soft stripes. Would it be so wrong to message him back? I mean, after today, I can't pretend obsessing over Tony isn't affecting my work. But he sounds sad, and . . . Gavin picks that exact moment, when I'm behaving like a child with a blankie, to snake his head around the door.

I try to make my voice absolutely assured. 'Oh Gavin, I'm glad you looked in. It saves me emailing to confirm I've double checked the whereabouts details for the rest of the month.'

Gavin hovers in the doorway, presumably due to a misplaced fear I might pounce. But he nods in a kindly way, which I shouldn't find annoying, before launching into a series of suggestions for improving our processes. All of which would be great, if we were monitoring high-security prisoners. I'm trying to find a non-defensive way to get rid of him, when he does his rueful 'I can laugh at myself' smile. 'But this can wait. I only came up to reassure you, I won't mention the mix-up to Monica.'

'Oh.' That's kind. And unexpected. My understanding was Gavin kept Monica fully informed of every operational detail. I'd assumed it was part of the attraction. 'Thank you.'

'Well, we both know the budget's tight this year. It's not in anyone's interests to highlight issues in Player Care.' Which is code for Monica thinking we're an unnecessary expense, while Gavin grudgingly accepts we're an unfortunate necessity. Gavin pushes his curtain of mousy blond hair off his forehead. 'And on reflection, I may have been a little abrupt this morning.' Except we both know, if I hadn't left Tony off the list, Gavin wouldn't have snapped. Before I can begin grovelling, Gavin's busy recovering from his own apology, by adding, 'But you know how I feel about doping.'

I nod. Gavin's a big fan of fair play. Seriously, it borders on a fetish for him. Like, I have seen, with my own eyes, Gavin attempt to persuade the manager that tactical fouls damage the club's reputation. It's the only time I've heard Monica really laugh.

'But it can't happen again. Garratt's purchase, the

European place, it all means extra scrutiny on Monica, on the club, on all of us. You understand that, don't you? The last thing we need is negative press attention.'

'Absolutely. I'll be extra careful from now on.'

'Well, good night.' Gavin steps into the corridor, then turns back. 'Except, well, this is a little, um, unfortunate. But on the subject of negative attention, there's been some banter among the lads, about you and Garratt. Not all of it in the best possible taste. I thought you ought to know.'

I shrug, doing my best to hide the worry I feel that we've been noticed. 'It'll be because he's been in and out of here a few times. Just for the usual new player stuff. But you know what they're like. It'll be something new next week.'

'Perhaps, but it might be wise to distance yourself. Given your contract.'

Gavin walks away, before I can find the words for how ridiculous that is. Much as I hate Gavin's helpful hints, he does mean well. I thought we'd been discreet, but clearly not enough. I flash back to an end-of-season barbeque, not long after we'd arrived at Covenly. Mark, one of the physios, had asked who I'd sign if we had all the money in the world. I said Tony, because who wouldn't? But there was a bit of back and forth over exactly which of Tony's stats had attracted my attention. And Gavin had made it crystal clear that wasn't something he found amusing. Which it seems still bothers me, because my palms are every bit as sweaty now as on that drive home.

22

Eight days and a home win later

Gavin glares at me as I slink into the conference room. To be fair, I'm late. But when I got to work, Sanchez was already fidgeting outside our office. After checking three times, he finally accepted Wednesday is Katia's late start, and deigned to tell me he needed somewhere to sleep tonight, because his new son doesn't sleep at all.

That took a while to unpick. Eventually, I managed to prise out of him that his wife is reluctant to go to pick up the baby too quickly when he cries, so she has to leave him, which makes her cry. That's more tears than Sanchez can cope with, so it's lucky that, however bad I am at paperwork, I'm an expert on childcare emergencies. All the same, it's the sort of problem that always takes forever to fix.

So, really, Gavin should be grateful I'm only five minutes late. And there's no reason to have waited for me. The meeting's to go over the travel details for our upcoming European away match. I've triple checked everything that's my responsibility, my only input will be nodding along. Not that I mind. As vice-captain, Tony's one of the two player representatives, lounging behind the white elm conference table. I'd planned on sitting roughly opposite him, so I could make gazing at him look like I'm drifting off. But Gavin's icy stare attracts Tony's attention. He looks from Gavin to me, grins and pushes out the chair beside him.

'Managed to escape the lake of tears, have you, Genie?' asks Devo, our captain.

His concern is real, even if he sounds jokey. Sinking down into my chair, I mutter that Mrs and baby Sanchez are fine and being fussed over in the players' lounge, if they want to say hello later. Tony smiles one of his softer smiles, and Gavin's expression approaches absolute zero. When I said I was only five minutes late, that's honestly true. So, Gavin's reaction seems over the top, even for a man obsessed with punctuality. But then he wheels round to Monica's PA, Fiona, demanding she inform our gracious leader that we're all assembled. Now it makes sense, keeping Monica waiting is obviously unforgivable.

Only, I don't get why Monica wants to bother with this. I mean, she's massively overinvolved compared to other owners, but this is basically housekeeping. Monica must agree, because Fiona hisses something to Gavin. And maybe it is Monica he loves, not her bank balance. Because he certainly looks disconsolate enough as he announces he'll chair, as Monica's otherwise engaged. Devo's sigh is equally doleful. I fully understand why; Gavin's bound to insist on exactly the level of detail you'd expect from a man who considers arriving at the airport four hours early to be cutting it fine. I prepare to blot out past holiday PTSD by focusing on Tony's profile. Only I can't, because Fiona's gesticulating at me.

I reluctantly abandon Tony's square chin and smile across at Fiona. She's an earnest woman in her mid-fifties, unremarkable except for her Yorkshire Terrier-style top-knot. Being Monica's PA must be a dog's life, so I suspect Fiona's woolly exterior hides an ironic sense of humour. But she doesn't look amused now. She's too busy pointing at the meeting agenda, then staring up at the PowerPoint, over and over.

Gavin stops mid-sentence and looks sharply at Fiona. 'Is there something you wish to contribute?'

She mutters apologetically at me, then more intelligibly, 'The dates . . .'

Suddenly, I can see exactly what she means. The hotel check-in is the day after the flight arrives. We're playing in Spain, so it's nothing to do with the time difference. If those were the actual booking dates, it would be a major disaster. There'd be no hope of making alternative arrangements for the entire first team and their entourage at two weeks' notice. But I know the dates were right when I checked last night, and when Gavin demands clarification, my 'No, there's an error on the PowerPoint,' is confident bordering on dismissive.

Gavin becomes sarcastically polite. 'Could you confirm that, simply to reassure the group?'

I snap open my laptop, and go straight to the carefully organized folder on my desktop. Thank God, the booking confirmation is right there, exactly where it should be. I'm just starting to say, 'See, check-in is the sixteenth,' when I stop and look more closely. And now, I want the earth to open and swallow me up. There's the booking date, staring at me in black and white, and it's the 17th. I can feel the ugly red blush flaring up from my throat to my cheeks as I stutter, 'I'm sorry. There must be some mistake. The dates were correct when I checked yesterday.'

Gavin cuts in, his voice like a scalpel. 'That can't possibly be the case. This can only be an error made during booking.' His eyes dart between Devo and Tony. 'You may choose to associate with those who behave as if you're infallible . . .'

'No, doc, you're wrong there. We all know Genie's got form when it comes to mistakes,' interrupts a grinning Devo. His knee knocks mine. It's kind, coming from a man who sent me a bottle of Dom Pérignon when Gavin left, complete with giant congratulatory balloon. If anything, it makes me feel worse.

Gavin ignores Devo, except his frown deepens. 'But this type of mistake is inevitable when Player Care is focused on the personal rather than the practical.' Gavin's gaze settles on Tony, and he's got the exact same expression as when he'd catch me watching trashy TV. 'Which is becoming rather a pattern, I'm afraid.'

I try to make my excuses. The sooner I leave, the sooner I can call the hotel. There's probably no chance of changing the booking, but it's torture, sitting here, not knowing.

Gavin shakes his head. 'No. We should finish checking there are no other errors, before attempting to salvage this one.'

He's switched to his 'this hurts me more than it hurts you' expression. I've always found that one particularly irritating, and it's the only thing stopping the hot, angry tears that are welling up. Well, that, and Tony's foot, resting gently on mine.

The meeting finally ends without uncovering more catastrophes. I should rush to make frantic calls. But I know, if anyone speaks to me on the way out, I'll lose it. I scrunch down, pretending to hunt for something in my bag, until I hear the glass door glide closed. When I sit up, there's a scrap from a club notebook on the table in front of me. It's a doodle of a lioness savaging a stick man holding a doctor's bag. That makes me smile. It's the smallest of smiles, but it's enough to push the tears out.

Holding them back seems to have doubled their volume. I search for tissues, but I guess weeping in our conference room is less common than you'd think. In the end, I give up trying to stem the flow and opt for standing at the floor-to-ceiling windows. Hopefully, anyone walking by will think there's something worth looking at on the empty training pitches below.

23

There's the sound of the door sliding open. 'Genie, you OK?'

I keep my back to Tony and try to reduce the snuffling to a minimum. 'Yes, fine.'

The door snaps closed. The conference room carpet soaks up sound, so there's a gap, then Tony's hand is on my back. 'You don't sound fine.'

'I am. It's nothing.'

'Then how 'bout turning round, letting me look at you?'

I shake my head. It's stupid, obviously Tony knows I'm crying, but I can't bear the idea of him seeing tears on my cheeks. He stays with his shoulder behind mine and his palm against the small of my back. His thumb strokes along my spine, over and over. He keeps that going, firm and even, until I can't help but lean into him.

His hand slips round to my waist, pulling me closer. 'That's right, beauty. You put the weight on me for a minute.' It's so completely what I want to do that I twist to look up at him. It's still not direct eye contact, but I can see enough of his face to know he's smiling. 'See, that's not so bad, is it?'

I shake my head, biting my lip.

'You know none of this is worth crying over, don't you? It's nothing that can't be mended.'

That makes me cry more. It's just about intelligible when I say, 'It's not about the thing with the hotel, though. Not really.'

'Isn't it?' His voice is extra gentle. 'Then I'm making a bit of a habit of getting stuff wrong with you, aren't I? Maybe it'd be best if I gives you a proper hug, 'stead of talking. You all right with that?'

I bury my head in his chest. He wraps his arms around me, his chin on my hair, and rocks his body slightly side to side. We stay like that until my breathing stops being gulpy. He waits until just before I've got up the strength of character to pull away. 'Do you think filling me in 'bout what's going on, that might help?'

I lift my face and look at him properly. 'I'm meant to be keeping my problems to myself.'

Tony tightens his arms. 'Thing is, I'm quite into having a kip before I play. So, this one, it's sort of my problem already?'

'Maybe.'

'Definitely. But let's get you sitting down first, shall we?'

He unwinds himself and leads me over to the cream sofa, artfully placed in one corner. I perch on the edge as Tony investigates the drinks table. He looks at the fancy coffee machine, head on one side, exactly like Rouden when he first saw the automatic feeder. 'I think this is a bit beyond me. You OK with water?'

'Water's fine.' Actually, more than fine. Tony remembers I prefer Perrier with lime and a chunk of ice. That might not sound like much, but usually, it's me remembering other people's drinks. When Tony brings the glass across, I'm still trying to make minimal contact with the sofa. How today's going, I'm bound to spill my drink, or do something equally stupid to mark the pristine leather.

Predictably, that doesn't seem to cross Tony's mind. He sprawls, one arm along the back of the sofa, legs wide enough his knee touches mine. 'So, what's got you all upset, then? If it's not the mix-up with the hotel.'

I pinch the bridge of my nose, determined not to cry again. 'When I was making the booking, it's true, you came into the office, and maybe I was distracted for a minute. But I know, absolutely know, after you left, I looked at the fixture list on the UEFA website again, before I finalized the reservation. And I definitely re-checked them yesterday.'

Tony's face is more serious than I'm used to. 'Yeah, I don't doubt that.'

It's calming, having him say that. I let myself lean back properly.

He looks at me, a long look, like he's weighing something up. 'What exactly are you saying?'

I sip my drink, then try not to sound crazy. 'I don't know how, but I think someone changed the reservation.'

Tony makes a movement with his mouth, sort of like he's wincing. 'Why'd anyone wanna do that?'

I wave my hand in a vague gesture of despair. 'I don't know. But it's not the first time something like this has happened. Since before the start of the season, mistakes keep happening. Mostly little things. The estate agent claiming I'd got the days wrong, or the interview in London. I never booked that. And I don't know, I think the whereabouts thing must've been me, but the others . . .'

Tony slips his hand from the back of the sofa to my shoulder and gives it a little squeeze. 'Genie love, it's not that I don't believe you. But it's struck me, once or twice, you're over-worked. And there's no shame in making the odd mistake in that scenario. This place, it's got big quick. The staffing, it's a bit behind, maybe? Like you're running a top-four club, but the number of back-room people, it could still be a Championship team knocking on the door. Do you know what I mean?'

I nod.

'And I knows you're the best, but is it possible even Wonder Woman could've made the odd slip-up?'

I smile, he's putting so much effort into making me feel better. 'But I've been doing this since we were straight out of the Championship. I didn't make mistakes then, and it was just me. Comparatively, I'm spoilt for help now, and I know my job . . .'

He interrupts. 'I know that – better than anyone, probably. So, OK, it's not you. Who'd wanna make it look like it was? And don't say you don't know, cos I reckon you've got an idea.'

'All right. I've no proof, but I think it's Monica.'

He turns his head from side to side, trying that on for size. 'Yeah, OK. I could buy that. But you'll have to fill me in on the backstory. Like why's she always such a bitch to you? Just cos it pisses her off, everyone liking you better?'

I can't help laughing. 'That's probably the least effusive compliment you've ever paid me.'

'How do you mean?'

'Well, everyone loathes Monica, to varying degrees.

Apart from Gavin. And it doesn't seem to worry her.' I look down at my fingernails. 'I think it's more that since we've got properly successful, she's around more. Having me in the background, well, it's got to be awkward. Only it would upset people if she sacked me. But if I start screwing up, it won't be long before everyone accepts, I have to go.'

Tony pulls his eyebrows together, puzzled. 'I'm not so sure 'bout that. If she fired you, I reckon half the guys at least'd refuse to play. And I don't get what's awkward 'bout you being here.'

'Oh, you don't know, do you? I suppose no one bothers about it any more, apart from me and them. I was Gavin's first wife. We divorced three years ago.'

Tony half laughs, half chokes. 'Hang on a minute. You're seriously telling me you used to be married to grizzly Gavin? You, a woman who I'd give my right foot to have on my arm?'

I do laugh back, but I probably shouldn't, and I definitely shouldn't say, 'That would be a major tactical error. It's by far your most attractive feature, or what you can do with it is, anyway.'

He grins. 'We'll come back to that later. Cos I dunno about you, but this whole being mates thing, it's not exactly ticking my boxes. And I'm not above taking advantage of your weird fetish for midfielders.'

It's true, I'm convinced midfielders are the most attractive players because everything they do is about feeding someone else. But I don't get a chance to ask how on earth Tony knows that, because he's already more serious.

'But let's clear this up first. How'd you end up with Gavin?'

'He honestly didn't used to be so awful. Or, I don't think he was, I might've been blind to it.'

'But the scales, they dropped from your eyes and you left him. And he took up with Monica on the rebound, and she don't like being second best, right?'

'No. Not right at all. He left me. Gavin came home one day and told me he'd outgrown me and it would be for the best if I stepped aside, to clear the way for Monica.'

'What a dick.' Tony's hand tightens on my shoulder, pulling me close. And I know Gavin's right, Tony's a distraction that I should be trying to resist, but I can't stop myself nestling in. Tony wraps his fingers around mine. 'Hope you smashed up a good few of his stupid collectibles before he left.'

'No. I oddly wasn't that upset. I mean, finding out they'd been seeing each other for months, it was a shock. But once the dust settled, it was honestly a relief.'

Tony's lips brush my hair. 'Glad to hear it. But I still don't get how a woman as fine as you ended up with a bloke like him in the first place.'

I squeeze his fingers this time. 'To be fair, he was a bit different back then, and he took me on with good intentions too. He was convinced he could fix me.'

'I don't see nothing about you that needs fixing.'

'That's sweet, but not true, and definitely not when Gavin met me. He was a junior doctor and I was the world's worst medical student.'

'You're a doctor, too?'

'No, I dropped out.'

I expect Tony to look at me like I'm the definition of failure. Only he doesn't. From his face, you'd think he was still listening to a functioning human, which means, for once, I can try to explain.

'I thought medicine was about people, but it's not, it's about what's wrong with them. I hated that, but I was good at the academic side, so when I gave up, everyone said it was a terrible waste. And I was a bit lost afterwards. So when Gavin started checking in, it felt, well, comforting, I suppose. And I think Gavin thought all I'd need was a little push, and I'd go back and finish my training. But I knew even then, deep down it wasn't this big tragedy. I'd just made a mistake, picked the wrong path, you know?'

Tony nods. 'Yeah, I think I do. And I reckon that's pretty brave, walking away when you know it's not for you. Even when people are judging.'

Tony's the first person who's ever said that. I have to turn away for a second before I can look back at him. 'That's not how Gavin saw it. But he did try to accept it. It's a big part of how we ended up back here. I wasn't earning much, and the medical role at the club started as a way of supplementing Gavin's pay while he was still a junior doctor. And he put loads of effort into helping me find another career. Like he was very into the idea of primary school teaching, but I wasn't. I mean, I like children, but I don't like telling them what to do. And it makes me laugh when they're naughty, so I'd have been a hopeless teacher.'

Tony smiles enough that the edges of his eyes crinkle. 'Makes you dead good at this job though, don't it?'

'Funnily enough, it's the perfect mindset for babysitting players. And it was Gavin who got me the job here, once he'd got used to the idea I wasn't one of life's professionals.

So, I should be grateful, but it was probably the final nail in the coffin for our marriage.'

'How's that?'

'He was getting life and death calls from the hospital, and I was taking just as many midnight phone calls. Only mine were from guys who'd locked themselves out, or left their second phone in a taxi, or forgotten their girlfriend's birthday. You know the sort of thing.'

'Yeah, I do. And I'm betting you was quite a lifesaver yourself. But he should've been pleased, you finding what you enjoyed doing. And was good at.'

'But he thought it was just a little job, something to keep me occupied till I got pregnant.' The words catch in my throat and I push my hair back from my face. 'Only I didn't get pregnant.'

I suddenly realize I've told Tony far more than I intended, more than I've ever told anyone about me and Gavin. He doesn't say anything, just stands and walks over to stare out of the window. Watching him, I know I'm completely over Gavin and everything that happened before. Because all I'm thinking is how much I want to run my hand down from Tony's shoulder, along the curve of his spine, to the waist of his jeans. But now he knows all this messy complicated stuff about me. Though complicated, well, everyone knows that's not what Tony Garratt's looking for.

Even if what he said before about being more than friends was for real, I'll have put him off now. I'm half expecting him to say that, to get it done with right away. But when he turns, he looks every bit as determined as before he takes a penalty.

'All right then, Genie, my beauty. We're going to make sure you keep your job.'

'Are we?' I ask, almost laughing at his absolute confidence.

'Yeah, we are.' He looks me up and down, then shakes his head, staring up at the ceiling. 'And I hopes you know, what I wanna do most in the world is take you home. So we can pick up where we left off just now, talking about how my long passes get you all hot under the collar.'

I laugh out loud this time. 'I don't recall saying anything of the sort.'

'But we both knows that's what you meant. Only, I'm a much nicer bloke than you give me credit for, so you'll have to make do with clips of my finest moments tonight. Cos I'm gonna be busy getting that booking switched to the right day.'

My confidence dips. 'I'm not sure that's possible.'

'It's the hotel visiting clubs always use, yeah? The white stone one off the main square?'

'That's right.'

'Well, it just so happens, I'm on friendly terms with one of the reception girls.'

'Why doesn't that surprise me?'

He shrugs. 'We've both been in this industry a while. You've got your contacts, I've got mine.'

'I think I picked them up slightly differently, but if you don't mind calling her, I'd be grateful.'

'You know I'm gonna hold you to that, don't you?'

Walking out of the door, I can't help smiling over my shoulder. 'I certainly hope so.'

24

I'm on the sofa, a quarter of a bottle of wine in, when WhatsApp buzzes:

> Sorry, took a while to get hold of her. All sorted.
> Monica's PA will get a call in the morning saying
> there was a problem on their end and the dates are
> fixed
> 20.17

Thank you, I do really appreciate it
20.19

Was that grateful enough, when Tony's probably saved my job?

Apparently yes, because next there's a string of YouTube links to Tony's greatest free kicks, top ten assists, etc., etc., followed by:

> Some passing porn for you. Let me know if you need a
> helping hand xxx
> 20.28

That properly makes me laugh, which is saying something after today. And I shouldn't have had a drink when I'm tired and still a bit weepy. That's what I'm blaming it on anyway, when I reply:

> Believe me, you've already given me everything I need
> 20.33

> > Then I'll definitely be dreaming of Genie. But I do that every night tbh. If you change your mind, call me xxx
> > 20.35

The whole way to work, I can't stop thinking about that text. I've tried telling myself it's no different from how we've joked around before. But it is. And Tony's car's already in the car park and I'm all hot and prickly. I can't do this, not yet. But he's already bounding across the tarmac, shouting, 'Morning, beauty.' God, everything about him is extra glossy. The second he opens his mouth, he's going to tease.

Except he doesn't. He stops dead in front of me and says, 'You look nice. Very boss lady.'

That's exactly the look I was aiming for when I went for a pinstriped blazer and black, high-waisted jeans. Which helps me manage to start walking in with him, instead of running off to hide. And it's how, when Tony looks at me out of the corner of his eye and asks, 'So, how was your night?' I can manage to reply, 'Fine, thank you.'

'Is that all? Cos I'm scheduled with the analytics boys this morning.'

'Are you?' My voice remains admirably monotone.

'I am. So, if what I sent you yesterday didn't hit the spot, let me know what does, and I'll have 'em pull the clips.'

I cover my eyes. 'Don't.'

'Don't what?' he asks, exaggeratedly innocent.

'Tease.'

'Who says I'm teasing?' He dips his head, trying to see my face. 'Hang on, are you blushing?'

'Urgh, yes, a bit.'

Tony laughs like he's been holding it in for a while. 'I don't see why. I mean, when Sky said 'bout your midfielder thing . . .'

'Skylar told you?'

The grin is extra toothy. 'So what if she did? I mean, it's a touch unusual, but it's not like weird. So long as it's just appreciating nice passing, or whatever. If it's OBV stats and xGs that are getting you all hot under the collar, then yeah, OK, you've got a problem.'

'Actually, sorry, Tony, but could we not?' My voice is tight.

He side-steps away. He must think I'm such a child. 'Course. Sorry.'

'No, I'm sorry. It's just, if someone heard us. After yesterday . . .'

His face becomes ultra-serious. 'Oh, yeah. I didn't think.' He glances up and down the empty hallway. 'But have you got a sec for a quick chat?'

'Umm, come in.' I push open my office door and let it close behind us.

I go to pull a chair across to my desk, but he holds his hand up. 'Nah, this won't take a minute. I just thought, you've cleared stuff up for me a bit, 'bout where I stand, so I ought to do the same back.'

I prepare my face to hear that he's only looking for a casual fling, something to keep him occupied until things are back on track with Angharad.

He rakes a hand through his hair, turning it into more porcupine than pompadour. 'So what you told me, about babies, was that to warn me off, after I'd said about wanting kids?'

'Um, no, I . . .'

'OK, good.' His face changes from earnest to exaggeratedly casual. 'Cos just as a like general thing, I'd be a hundred per cent up for adopting, if I was with the right person.'

I couldn't be more astonished if he'd pulled a white rabbit out of his training jacket. 'I have literally no idea what to say to that.'

He smiles as he shrugs. 'Then don't say nothing. Just keep it in your back pocket. And I'd better go hit the gym, or the fitness guys'll be wondering where I am.'

I'm at my desk, staring into space, when Katia walks in.

She sees my face and laughs. 'What's up, Genie?'

I give myself a shake. 'Oh, nothing. I just had a . . . a surprising conversation with Tony.'

Katia's grin is mischievous. 'About a night away?'

'What?'

She looks mortified. 'Oh, sorry. It's none of my business. I didn't mean to . . .' Her voice fades away.

'No, Kat, it's not that. I've just got no idea what you're talking about.'

Her eyes widen and for a second, her mouth's frozen,

lips parted. 'I must've misunderstood. Sorry.' She starts fussing in her bag. 'But, um, Genie, you might want to check Tony's diary? For after tomorrow's game.'

My stomach's heavy. I change the subject, but the minute she's at her desk, I pull up Tony's calendar. Tomorrow night's blocked out as personal. Underneath, there are the details of a London hotel booking. It's in Player-Care tangerine, so I guess Katia set it up. Not that I'm going to ask. I can't think of anything worse than Katia feeling sorry for poor desperate Genie. I mean, could I be any more deluded? I was honestly starting to believe the great Tony Garratt cared about me.

It's obvious now. Management hate players travelling back separately from the team. Tony must've made hand-on-heart promises that he'd be back in time for the post-match recovery session the next day. And with Tony, it won't be a family thing. It'll be a woman. And the hotel fits. Men, even ludicrously well-paid men, don't spend that kind of money unless they're out to impress. And at that price, it's someone highly desirable. Someone like Angharad.

But it's not like Tony and I owe each other anything. I wouldn't mind, or OK, I'd mind, but I wouldn't be quite so hurt, if he hadn't said what he did about adopting. Dangling that in front of me was cruel. I was already panting after him, he didn't need to tempt me with false promises. So, when Tony texts me from the team bus, I ignore it. And when I get a call, right around when they'll be settling into their pre-match hotel, I ignore that too.

25

The next day

I can't bring myself to watch the match, and I can't concentrate on anything else. Running's the one thing that might shut my brain down, but I'm not even a mile from home when I'm stopped in my tracks by a waterfall coming from Tony's lodge – water is cascading through the gates and over the road. I'm tempted to leave it, what do I care if Tony's garden floods? Except it'll end up as my problem to fix.

I clamber over a low spot in the wall, then wish I hadn't. The sprinklers are spraying at full capacity and the lawn's like an Amazonian tributary. By the time I've worked out how to shut the water off, I'm absolutely drenched. Trying to ward off hypothermia, I shove my hands into the pouch of my top and feel my keyring, zipped into the inner pocket.

My keyring, which has Tony's front door key. And obviously, I wouldn't usually let myself into a player's home uninvited. But I'm freezing, and it's not like Tony will ever know. He's far too busy ordering room service for whoever's sharing his Egyptian cotton sheets. So why shouldn't I unlock the lodge's weathered oak door? It's not like running my clothes through the drier will do any harm. I won't snoop. I'll just shiver in the laundry room until they're done. Only, on top of the washing machine, there's a pile of freshly folded, pillowy white towels. And that reminds me where in this house is very, very warm.

Before I know it, the hot tub's on and I'm lying back, eyes shut, letting the heat soak into my bones and the noise of the bubbles drown out what's been going through my head all day. Because I'm still getting mental flashes of Tony naked. But it's not me with him, it's someone younger and prettier and infinitely less messed up.

I'm telling myself this absolutely has to be my last five more minutes, when there's a familiar drawl from immediately above me. 'Can I get you anything, love? Glass of wine maybe, or how 'bout some company?'

I shriek, snap open my eyes and struggle to cover what I can with my hands all at the same time. Tony's looking down at me, in a sweatshirt and jeans but his feet are bare, so it makes sense, him getting so close without me hearing. And now, we're acting out my worst nightmare, me naked and Tony laughing like he'll never stop. But he just about manages to get some words out. 'It's all right, Genie. No need to look like that.'

'What on earth are you doing here?' I demand, my heart still pounding.

'I live here. Remember?'

'But you're not supposed to be back till tomorrow.'

He stops looking entertained for long enough to show he's confused. 'I dunno where you got that from. I came back with everyone else. What else'd I be doing?'

It's so offhand, it sounds true. But I'm light-headed enough, more from the shock than the steam, that I can't trust my instincts, let alone come up with an alternative explanation for the hotel booking. And I can't exactly interrogate Tony when I'm midway through a home invasion. Not that he seems upset. He's back to laughing, though at least now, he's trying not to. 'How 'bout I find you a dressing gown?'

'Please, yes, thank you.' I was aiming for dignified, but it comes out more mortified.

Tony's still grinning, but his hands are over his eyes. ''K, you wait here. I'll chuck you something over.'

He turns, drops his hands and strolls over to the pegs on the wall. Without looking back, he throws a robe and towels to land perfectly at the foot of the tub.

I put my head around the sitting-room door, the fluffy white dressing gown tied corset tight. 'Tony, I'm so sorry. I'll grab my clothes from the drier and go.'

He twists over the back of the sofa to grin at me. 'Come in here a sec.'

I tiptoe inside the door. 'Tony, really, I can't apologize enough.'

I launch into a complicated explanation about sprinklers. Tony shakes his head. It's pitch black outside now and with only the lamps lit, his face is all shadows. 'I'm not bothered 'bout none of that, I just wanna know what's got you all worked up.'

Obviously, now is not the time to get into the hotel thing, since jealous and delusional aren't personality traits I want to highlight. 'Me being here. It's a huge abuse of your privacy.'

He shrugs. 'Then go ahead, abuse my privacy any time you like.' I start trying to apologize again but he carries on over me. 'Seriously, I completely get why they call you Genie now. The whole time, coming back here, I was dreading an empty house. Walking in and finding a gorgeous, naked woman in my hot tub, for a minute, I honestly thought I must've conjured you up.'

My smile is embarrassed, but I feel a little better. 'Maybe you did. Otherwise, I don't know what possessed me . . .'

'I do. Cos you've been dying to get in that hot tub from the minute you saw it, haven't you?'

I bite my lip. 'They're my secret vice.'

'I can think of worse. And like I've said before, you're welcome, anytime. Feel free to make use of the gym, the hot tub, my bed. Whatever takes your fancy,' he adds with a wink.

He begins to lounge over to me. I still don't trust him, but I'm not sure I care. All I can think about is how much I want him. But when I laugh, it's nervous, not seductive. 'If every girl you said that to took you up on it, I imagine this place would get rather crowded.'

'I'm off girls for the foreseeable.'

'I can't see that lasting.'

He shakes his head. 'You're wrong 'bout that. I don't reckon I'll have any problem sticking to women. They're less trouble and a whole load more fun and all.'

He's at the end of the sofa now, nowhere near close enough to touch. But still, I'm struggling to come up with a line that matches his grin. The best I can do is, 'So, you've been flirting with me because I'm old and not much effort?'

His face gets more serious. 'Nah. Your body completely does it for me too. And, if you wanna check that out, I'm still hard from walking in on you.'

I'd give anything to be the sort of woman who'd do just that. But I'm not. I'm the type who looks down at the floor, blushing, which is maddening.

Tony watches me for what feels like forever, then comes close enough that his toes touch mine when he lifts my chin.

'The last couple of times I played, I was all miserable over you wanting to be just mates. This time it was cos of you not picking up the phone. I'd got myself convinced, you getting standoffish anytime it felt like we was going somewhere, it was cos you weren't sure I was worth the bother.' He reaches and strokes along the line of my jaw to the collar of the robe. 'But you was proper upset, wasn't you? Over me walking in. That don't make sense, unless you've got no clue how gorgeous you are.'

I make an inarticulate noise.

'And that'd fit with you not wanting to swim the other night. So, love, am I on the money? Was them sulks partly cos you didn't wanna get your kit off?'

I bite my lip and the hand under my chin drifts down my throat, until it joins his other, loose over my shoulder.

'Come on. I reckon it's time you got straight with me. Was that it?'

Now feels like the time when I should pull back, but it's like he's drawing words out of me. 'Maybe. A bit. And, well, Kat and Sky are so beautiful, and so young.' I shrug. 'The comparison, it's hardly flattering.'

His eyes are laughing but he manages to keep his voice steady. 'Exactly how old are you?'

'Thirty-three.'

'So hardly ancient.'

'It's a long way from twenty-three.'

He smiles and shakes his head once. 'And like I said, that don't need to be a bad thing.'

'Because it's less trouble?' I ask, my voice small.

This time the shake of his head is emphatic. 'Nah, I've got a feeling you could cause me a whole load of trouble.' He stops smiling and looks down at his hands on my shoulders. 'Look, I don't wanna come over like I'm one of them blokes that goes round paying women false compliments, or whatever, cos he read on the internet that that will get him what he wants.'

That does make me smile, and I almost forget how awkward I feel. 'Don't worry. I can't believe you've ever had to google a solution to that particular problem.'

'Nah, I haven't. Which is why you should believe me, when I tells you, you don't have to worry 'bout comparisons with your girls. Cos Katia, she's dead pretty, but she's a bit dull, isn't she?'

'Katia's a very sweet girl.'

'Exactly, that's what I just said. And I'm not into little girls.'

'Skylar's perhaps more to your tastes.' I manage to make my voice teasing.

He strokes my cheek so lightly it tingles. 'Even if it's just on looks, I'd go for you over Sky every time. Cos I know it's not fashionable to say it, but the whole rock-solid abs, zero body

204

fat thing, I don't like it.' Tony runs his fingertips over my waist, then places the back of his hand flat against my stomach, and I find myself longing for him to undo the dressing gown. 'Like, to me you are perfect. And that move in your back, the thing you did when I first touched you, that's so fucking sexy. But what I don't get is, if you wants this, wants me, why do you keep getting all flighty, anytime we get close?'

I look down. 'My job, everything I told you before.'

'Bollocks.' His hand edges down between my thighs, and this time he does part the dressing gown, and before I know it he's stroking my bare skin. 'If it was just that, me and you, we'd have been at it for weeks and keeping it quiet.' His voice is dropping into a growl. 'And it's not that I've got it all wrong and you're not into this, cos, Jesus, I can feel you are. So, what is it? Is it that a nice educated woman like you shouldn't be getting all hot and bothered over a bloke with an accent like mine, all tatted up, and vulgar new money? Cos you're better than that?'

'No, of course not.' My voice is sharp, I'm so offended he'd even suggest that, and my eyes leap straight to his. 'You know what I think about you, your talent.'

He laughs softly. 'Oh yeah, I was forgetting. You're a connoisseur of the midfield.'

I start to pull away from him, but he shakes his head. 'No, love, don't go getting all offended. You just relax and enjoy yourself. Cos you like this, don't you, Genie?' He slides his hand higher up, until he's touching my most intimate parts. I whimper, his fingers feel so good. Tony grins, all teeth and stubble. 'Is this what you were planning? When you got in my hot tub?'

I try to say no, but it comes out more as a moan as I sink against him.

'Having a bit of trouble talking, Genie?' he murmurs, twisting me around with his free hand, pulling my back tight against his chest.

I try again to say it's not true, that I didn't know he'd be back, that none of this is what I want. But he's started to kiss my neck and that's all I can think about. That, and his fingers.

'Can't get the words out, beauty? Well, that's all right, I can probably guess, or we can go by trial and error. Oh, you like that idea, do you?' His laugh tickles my throat. 'Who'd have thought? Perfect, put-together Genie letting me . . .'

I pull at his hand on my waist. 'Tony. Can you stop it, please? Now.'

He lets me go, holding his hands in the air. 'Sorry. Too fast?'

I'm struggling to get the dressing gown re-tied as tight as possible.

'I'm sorry if I upset you. You wanna go back a few steps?' he asks, voice back to everyday.

I shake my head. 'No. I'm sorry, Tony, this was a mistake. I didn't come here for any of this.'

He nods and sighs. 'OK, I'm sorry if I read it wrong. Go and get some clothes on and I'll drive you home, all right?' he adds, more gently.

'No, it's fine. I'll pick the clothes up some other time.' I hurry out into the hall and grab my shoes, keeping my back to him, so he can't see the state I'm in.

'Genie, don't be fucking stupid. You can't walk out of here in a dressing gown and running shoes.'

'I'll take the track through the woods. No one will see.'

'I'm not worried about no one seeing you coming out of here. I'm worried 'bout you wandering round half-dressed in the dark.'

'Don't be.' I slam the door and run off down the drive.

26

Every time I think about last night, I want to squirm deeper underground. Roudie's not helping, keeping me standing around on the rickety wooden bridge, while he sniffs every rabbit hole on the river bank. I've almost given up hope we'll ever get home when his head shoots up. I follow his gaze and damn it, there's Tony, jogging across the meadow.

'Genie, you got a minute?' he calls, when close enough. He sounds unusually hesitant.

Every bit of me wants to shake my head and run. Only, obviously, I can't, so I call back, 'Of course.'

'Good. I was wanting to have a chat anyhow and when I saw you from the road, now seemed as good a time as any. If that's all right with you?'

He's only a step away now. Any closer and he'll pick up on the pulse rushing through my head so loud, I can barely hear myself saying, 'Umm. But I'll have to keep an eye on Roudie. He's got a one-track mind when it comes to rabbits.'

Tony grins down at Rouden, precariously balanced on the bank. 'Yeah, well, I can get a bit caught up in stuff myself. Which is kind of what I wanted to say. 'Bout last night, I . . .'

'Tony, I'm sorry. I didn't . . .'

'Actually, Genie, can I go first? I've been thinking out

how to say this ever since you left. I'll only screw it up if I don't get it done in one go.'

'OK. But . . .'

'OK. Good. All I wanted to say is, I'm sorry. I came on way too strong. I read the whole thing wrong. I . . .'

'That's the thing. I don't think you did. Read it wrong, that is.'

He hesitates, but pulls a face, the same one as when a set-piece doesn't go as planned. 'Nah, I did. Going in all full-blooded like that, it was stupid of me.' He reaches towards my elbow, then tugs his hand back without touching me. 'Only I'm not making excuses or nothing, but I reckon there's been a few mixed signals.'

I step back from him. 'That's not fair.' Even though I'm aware that maybe it is.

There's the same reaching of his hand that he pulls back before it gets to me. 'I don't mean anything bad. But you come off cool. Like you're holding back. And I thought if I didn't do something brave, dial it up a bit, we'd stay kind of stuck. Do you get me?'

I nod. 'Only I wasn't cool with it.'

'I get that now, all right. And I'm very sorry, truly.' He pulls his mouth sideways. 'But I didn't just want to talk about last night. Cos me saying what I did about kids, I knew like two minutes after it came out of my mouth, I'd been an idiot. So you blanking me, it weren't exactly unexpected, but it still felt like a bit of a slap in the face. And I dunno, I guess a bit of me thought OK, if the Tony Garratt experience is all you're after, fine, I'll give it you.'

'That wasn't wh—'

'No, I know now, I got that so wrong. Course that wasn't what you wanted. But I've got a reputation, haven't I?'

He's still wrong. I try to say that wasn't why I pulled back, but he talks over me.

'I'm not making out I didn't earn it, cos I did. But it means the women that are into me, if it's not about the money, it's cos they wanna do the stuff they don't want their boyfriends knowing they're into. And then they go back to their nice life, no harm done.' He leans back against the bridge until he can watch my face, then looks over my shoulder across the meadow. 'But that's not you. And I've gone and fucked up something I reckon I'm going to regret, big time.'

It's not what I expected, and I think it cost him a fair amount to say it. Whatever I say back, it needs to be honest. I look down at the water and feel the heat from the iron rail of the bridge under my hands.

'Actually, I'm not so sure that isn't me.' I look at him from the side of my eye and his face is the same, still, waiting. 'Well, maybe not quite that. But obviously, I'm attracted to you. You already know that.'

If he looks the tiniest bit pleased, I can't blame him. That was the understatement of the century.

'And I've watched you play for years. Admired you, just like so many other women. Taken pleasure in your talent. Last night, I think I let myself get carried away with that. But then I realized, at the last minute, that I was pretending at being someone I want to be. But that's not who I am. Does that make sense?'

He shrugs. 'To me? Honestly, no.'

I stare into the dark water, the light drifting through it in little ripples. 'Well, maybe all it is, is what you said about Katia, and maybe it applies more to me. I think I want something, and then when I come close to it, I run a mile.'

Tony tilts back on the rail, trying to look me in the eye. 'Nah. I don't reckon it's the sex you're scared of, not really, anyhow. Cos me and you, you can't tell me there's not like proper sparks.'

He waits, eyebrows raised. When I nod, half smiling, half shy, he grins. Then his face softens. 'But I can see now, you needs me to go way more gently. Cos I know exactly when you froze up last night. It was when I said that stupid stuff 'bout what people would think. I was only teasing, but it hit a nerve, didn't it, love?'

He turns and puts his hand on my waist, no pressure, just his palm and the tips of his fingers.

'But that's sort of what you meant before, isn't it? About the other women,' I ask.

He shakes his head quickly. 'Nah, it's not. That's where I learnt that line of talk. And it don't usually end up with 'em running off, I can tell you. Which got me wondering if someone's been none too nice to you? Got you worried you're gonna get hurt?'

I bite my lip, then look at him directly. 'Not in the way you mean, no.'

'But in a way that means something to you?'

'Maybe.'

I look up at the absolute blue of the sky and the white of the clouds, because looking at him is getting far too much.

'It's all right, Genie, you don't owe me nothing. No need to say anything more if you don't want to.'

I swallow hard. 'No. I do want to, to clear the air if nothing else. And honestly, it's not that big a thing. It's just, when Gavin and I split, like I told you, there were lots of reasons. But part of it was that he didn't find me attractive. Certainly not by the end.'

Even without turning to him, I know Tony's watching me. And now there is pressure on my waist, him drawing me in.

'Must've been something wrong with him, then. Cos what I was saying last night, I might've been a bit crude 'bout it, but I meant it, you're beautiful.'

'That's kind,' I blush.

'Nah. Just true. Look, you've been in this industry a fair while, haven't you?'

'Nine years or so.'

'Well, I reckon that's long enough for you to have got things a bit distorted. Cos a lot of the women in our field, their looks are their livelihoods, aren't they?'

'Don't let Skylar hear you say that,' I say, but my voice isn't right for the line.

'I mean the wives and girlfriends. And a lot of what you do, it's with them, yeah?'

'Some of it,' I admit.

'Yeah, yeah. I'm sure they're all great girls. But what I'm getting at is most of 'em are got up to look like models. You don't look like that. You could, but it's not how you present yourself. So, when you walk in a room, maybe you don't get the same instant attention. But it's not that you're not sexy. It's that you're more slow-burn, and there's nothing wrong with that.'

I smile at him. 'That's a lovely compliment.'

'Like I said, it's just true. If your ex didn't see it, or didn't let you know it, that's his problem.'

'Except when we split, I didn't look great. I hadn't been happy and it showed.'

'Hence all the exercise and stuff now?' he asks, softly.

'Maybe, yes.'

Tony rests his head against mine, and I breathe him in, the mix of fresh from the shower and the hint of the sweat that follows it. 'But how you are now, you must know, you looks fantastic. And you all calm and collected at work, that's sexy as fuck and . . .'

I move away far enough that when I lean forward, I can meet his eye. 'Tony, as I said, this is lovely. But I've been doing this long enough, I know players like you don't have the time or the patience to waste on boosting anyone's self-esteem.'

He smiles wryly. 'Only don't you reckon that's a bit one-sided? Us all going on like we're rappers, wanting women confident enough to ignore our past ways, or however it goes. When what you do, half the time, it's psychological physio, more or less?'

That makes me laugh. 'If you can tell I'm doing it, I'm not as good as I thought.'

'I'm not complaining. My ego needs every bit as much attention as my hamstrings, I can tell you. But I dunno as there's anything wrong in you needing a bit of that in return.' He puts a hand over mine. ''Specially if it might help make you agree to give me another go.'

I try to smile. 'I don't think it would.'

He holds the eye contact. 'Then can you tell me what'd do it? Cos I don't buy you worrying 'bout your job and nothing more. Or you fretting over what I think 'bout your body, cos I reckon we've established, I'm a fan. There's something else you're not telling me.'

I pull my hand free and lock my fingers together, my elbows on the rail and my mouth resting against my hands.

'No pressure, love, to say any more. Just if you want to.' Tony's voice is quiet.

'I . . . oh, Tony, this is so embarrassing.'

'That's all right. I won't laugh or nothing.'

'And you won't tell anyone?'

He shakes his head vigorously. 'Course not.'

'OK then. So it was only partly about Gavin no longer finding me that attractive. It went a bit further than that. He also didn't enjoy what I wanted, in bed and things. So, you saying about what other people would think, it brought that back.'

Tony's about to say something, but I hold my hand up. This is something I haven't told anyone before, and if I don't get it out now, I never will. 'And there have been one or two others since, no one serious, but nice, ordinary guys. And with them, I could keep that side of things fairly locked down. Just fulfilling their expectations, I suppose you could say. But with you, I'm not sure I can do that. And I can't face all the . . . the shame again.'

Tony isn't laughing, his face is dead serious. 'Um, OK. Not going to lie, that's not quite what I thought you was going to say. But I think it might be I was the right person to tell. Cos you was pretty young when you met the doc, weren't you?'

I nod, miserably.

'Well then, I think you might've got unlucky, and ended up with a bloke that wasn't right for you from the start. Not cos there was anything out of the ordinary 'bout you, but cos of stuff about him. And if I'm wrong, and what you want is really out there, one of my few good qualities is I don't judge.'

There's a quick twitch of a grin. 'And if it's a bit of both, that's perfect. Cos I get bored easy and some variety, well, I likes that. So, me and you, we might end up being a real nice combination, you know?'

His voice is a caress now, and his fingers on my back are matching it. 'And look, I've learnt my lesson 'bout putting pressure on. So, I'll just say I dunno how this'll play out. Like from what you've said, I can see a bit of fun behind closed doors might be all you're after. And that's fine with me, but if it turns into something more, I reckon I might be open to that. So, how about I work on earning some trust, and you have a go at letting your guard down? You think that might work?'

'It might.'

He beams. 'Sweet. I'm going to leave you alone for a bit then, cos I'm going to have to think this one out. But you'll be on my mind, Genie love, I can promise you that.'

He turns to walk away and I touch his elbow. 'Wait, Tony, before you go, I should've said, me not responding to your calls yesterday, it was because I saw you had last night blocked out on your calendar and I . . .'

'Thought I was with someone else?'

I nod.

He frowns, and I'm convinced he's going to tell me jealousy isn't something he can deal with, but what he actually says is, 'Then there is something I want off you soon as possible, and that's a full list of the stuff that's gone wrong at work that you're surprised by, and your laptop. Cos I wasn't ever booked out last night, promise.'

As soon as Tony is on his way home I text Katia, ultra-casually, to find out who asked her to set up the calendar entry. Her reply is a super confused, 'Wasn't it you who put that in?????'

27

*Two Sundays, one home and
one European (!!!) win later*

'Charlotte, dear. You look . . .' Mum visibly searches for a positive way to describe the stripey top. 'Very celebratory.'

I force a smile as I add my gift to the pile on the carefully polished sideboard. 'Well, I thought birthday.'

That's not true. I actually thought if anything's going to get me through the nightmare which is Mum's annual birthday brunch, it's Tony. Only I couldn't invite him because, one, he's playing today, and two, we're miles off meeting the parents. So, I'm making do with the hoodie.

My sister's staring with obvious disapproval. 'Why are you wearing that?'

For the record, Eleanor is nice, generally. It's just with me, she still plays the older sibling, patrolling my behaviour in case I embarrass her. And I almost make the sort of excuse I usually do, about needing something warm for the train, or how I'd spilt coffee on my intended outfit and the hoodie was all I had that was clean. But then I remember Tony's voicenote reply to the thank-you photo I sent this morning, which consisted of a single flame emoji, and I smile.

'Because I like it.' Then I fix my eyes on her tasteful

oatmeal sweater and ask sweetly, 'Why are you wearing that?'

Mum breaks off from an in-depth discussion about the front room's new curtains. 'Charlotte, have you seen what Thomas is doing? So clever . . .'

As I crouch down, ready to inspect my nephew's Lego empire, my aunt reaches to snap her handbag closed. She's a second too slow, and I catch a glimpse of the Sunday supplement. It's crumpled, like it's been squished into the bag in a hurry, which it probably was, right as I walked in.

'Oh, is that Monica and Gavin's power couples in football piece?' I ask, in a dazzlingly bright voice. 'It's a nice article, isn't it? Especially that photo of Monica and the twins.'

'Oh, yes, very,' my aunt stutters, with a quick guilty glance at Mum.

Ah, exactly as I thought, the pair of them have been poring over that interview. I'm surprised I couldn't hear the gnashing of teeth from the station. Mum's clearly still upset over me letting the perfect son-in-law slip through my fingers. Which, to be fair, Gavin was. Well, apart from the cheating. Only Mum doesn't know about that. I might not've signed an NDA, but I'm crystal clear on why I walked away from the divorce with the deposit for the cottage. So, I bite my tongue when Mum gives me an 'Aren't you brave?' look, and focus on obeying my nephew's instructions regarding model road construction.

I've graduated to being allowed to sort blocks when my phone buzzes. As I reach for it, Mum sighs. 'Must you, Charlotte?'

I smile apologetically. 'Sorry, it'll be work.'

And it is Tony, only it's not a player care request. It's him asking:

> How do you feel about meeting up?
> 10.41

Almost before I've read it, there's another message:

> No pressure. I've just got something I want to run by you
> 10.42

My aunt laughs. 'I wish my work made me smile like that.'

She's right, the corners of my mouth are actually aching.

Mum frowns, then remembers that we have company and exaggeratedly pouts at her friend Elaine. 'It seems grown men can't take care of themselves, even for one day.'

She definitely meant that to sound jokey, but it doesn't. I try to brush it off. 'Oh, it's not something anyone needs. Just some good news. Something I've been waiting to hear for a while.'

Since we spoke by the river, apart from the handover of my laptop and my list of supposed mistakes, Tony's been keeping his distance. And the little monster in my head has been busy the whole time telling me that's because Tony only said what he did to be kind, of course he's not really interested. The sane bit of my brain has pointed out repeatedly, that doesn't fit with the number of messages Tony's sent. And I'm now going to allow it to do a spot of raised arms, 'What's the score?' style chanting while I come up with a reply that's not off-puttingly overeager.

The best I can do is:

I'd love to. Come over to mine tonight?
10.46

Tony doesn't reply. I'm not letting the monster have a bite at that. It's early kick-off, Tony's phone should probably have been off fifteen minutes ago. So, there's no reason why I shouldn't stay as bubbly as my pre-lunch half-glass of Cava. Which is helpful, because Dad is busy corralling us for photos, and he won't be satisfied with anything less than manic grins. Though it looks like he's met his match in my niece, Olivia. Dad's trying to coax her into letting her hair down, and Livy looks positively mutinous.

I pull a sympathetic face over Dad's shoulder. It's one of his things, how girls look so much prettier with their hair framing their face. As a kid, every time he said it, I'd want to punch someone in the face. Which might sound like an over-reaction, but it's really not, because it's code for how women should be delicate and feminine, and not interested in nasty rough things, like football, just as an example. But Livy's quite a girly girl, so I'm surprised it bothers her. And I'm even more surprised when she scowls at me, as only an angry nine-year-old can.

My brother-in-law mimes looking up at the heavens. 'Sorry. Ignore her, she's sulking.'

'About anything specific, or just pre-teen angst?' I ask, and hopefully it's sympathetic enough, he won't notice that

I'm a tiny bit pleased. Not that Livy's unhappy, obviously. It's just, after playing with my nephew, it's refreshing to see children aren't always adorable. Perhaps that will stop me re-running what Tony said about adoption a million times a day, then having to remind myself he's already told me he regrets saying it.

My sister leans across to straighten her husband's collar. 'It's nothing serious. She was agitating to go to some make-up sale in Covenly on our way home, and we had to say no. She's far too young.'

I pull a guilty face. 'Sorry, that might be my fault. I let her try out an eyeshadow or two last time I babysat. I hope I haven't created a monster.'

Based on how her lips narrow, Eleanor's unimpressed, but she limits herself to saying, 'I think it's mainly coming from school. One of the other mothers is, well, not as careful as we are about social media. This beauty thing, it's run by some model from TikTok, I think.'

Why would a model from TikTok be coming to Covenly of all places? And then my mind races as my paranoia builds. Unless it's someone with another, and much better reason to be here.

Now, when I feel like my insides have been hollowed out, is the moment Dad shouts, 'Happy smiles, everyone.'

Mine is going to look more like a death's head, but there's no way I'm going to hang around for another shot. I take my chance, while Dad's distracted by rearranging the grandchildren, to sprint upstairs. As soon as the bathroom door's safety locked, I pull out my phone. I know this is mad, but I can't help it. Ever since what Tony said about trust, I've

223

been stopping myself from cyber-stalking Angharad. But even with shaky hands, it only takes a second to pull up her Instagram. And I'm right. There are already nine posts reminding her followers that today's pop-up beauty event in Covenly runs from noon until six. How convenient. She'll have a good hour to spruce herself up before Tony arrives home with the rest of the first team.

Because that's why he hasn't replied, isn't it? Of course he doesn't want to spend the evening with me, when she's in town. There's a flash of raw, hair-pulling jealousy, so strong it scares me. Except it's not fair, is it? I bet Angharad doesn't even know I exist. It's Tony I should be raging at. Only I don't think I can. Because I look back at his message, and I misunderstood it, didn't I? 'I've just got something I want to run by you' is basically the same as 'we need to talk', isn't it? And what good ever came of that?

Flicking back to Angharad's posts, I decide that Angharad can squeal as much as she likes about how Covenly's historic market hall is super-cute, but the set-up looks pretty amateur compared to her usual carefully curated perfection. If this is a last-minute event, then I guess the two of them reconnecting is new too. And that explains why Tony messaged me when he should've been getting into game mode, doesn't it? Because the new improved Tony Garratt tells women he's moving on, instead of letting them find out from the tabloids. I guess I should be grateful.

How could I have been so stupid? Why did I say I'd love to see him? Why did I wear this top, the one that feels like he's hugging me? And why can't I yank the thing off, without it getting caught in my hair? Oh, and now Mum's calling, so I can't even sort out my lopsided ponytail, let alone wallow. Back to happy families . . .

I abandon my phone in the kitchen. If I'm not in the same room, maybe I won't be so tempted to keep torturing myself with Angharad's posts. And perhaps then, the nasty, bitter taste in my mouth will fade before I have to choke down food? But I'm only halfway through laying the table when Livy skips over, sulks forgotten, holding out my phone and calling, 'Auntie Charlotte, you've got a message.'

I think she's trying to make up for the scowl, so I force my thank you into being extra grateful. How I feel now, if I reply to whoever it is, I'm bound to say something wrong. But Livy's looking at me expectantly, so I'll have to at least look at it:

> Tony Garratt
> Great, I've been wanting to see you so bad-is it OK if I
> come straight there? Like 7.30ish?
> 11.46

And just like that, the heavy, grey weight has gone from my shoulders, and I'm helium-light, floating-to-the-ceiling happy. I manage to calm that down enough that my reply doesn't sound deranged:

> 7.30 sounds good. BTW are you OK? Shouldn't you be in the tunnel
> any minute?
> 11.47

I'm racing back upstairs to fetch the hoodie, when his reply comes through:

> Officially, I'm doing an emergency boot change. But it's more that it's been no phones since I messaged you & no way could I fully focus till I'd heard back 11.48

Why he'd think there was even the slightest possibility I wouldn't want to see him, I don't know. But it must seriously matter to him, if he's willing to risk the manager's wrath right before kick-off. And obviously, I don't want to encourage that sort of behaviour, but I can't pretend it doesn't make me disgustingly happy. Because I am stupid, aren't I? But not for trusting Tony. I mean, I still think the only reason Angharad's in Covenly is because she wants to see him. But maybe he doesn't feel the same, if he's planning on being with me by seven thirty. So, I promise, I'm never going to look at Angharad's social media ever again. Because yes, I'm aware my little meltdown was the most ridiculous thing you've ever seen.

28

A knock at the door later that evening triggers an undignified competition between me and Roudie over who gets there first. And when it is indeed Tony, eleven minutes early and still in match-day jacket and joggers, there's an even less dignified tussle over who gets their paws on him. In the end, I manage to push past the pup and wrap my arms around Tony's neck. I wait for him to pull me in, but he doesn't.

There's an awkward moment, when I've held him a fraction too long without any response, and have to step back and politely ask him in. He's holding a bottle of red. I try to pretend he didn't hug me back because he was worried about dropping it, but that doesn't explain why he shuffles away until his back's against the door. The light from the hall's bare bulb picks out the lines on his forehead.

'Tired?' I ask.

He nods. 'Knackered.'

'I'm not surprised, today didn't look like much fun.' I try to force my voice into soothing instead of scratchy. I streamed the game when I got home, so it's ridiculous to be on edge over Tony not being all over me, when I knew he'd hate losing. Top-class players always do. It's part of their DNA, as is the struggle LeMar has when we do our children's hospital visits and I have to bribe him to let sick kids beat him at board games. I should just be glad Tony's here with me, not . . . except I'm not thinking about her any more, am I?

Tony narrows his eyes and turns his head. 'Hang on a sec, you saw the game, then?'

I nod and search for a non-patronizing way to say continuously meddling with the system is the manager's vice, not a reflection on Tony's ability. And anyway, it wasn't Tony's deeper-lying role that was the problem, it was LeMar getting over-eager, playing off the shoulder.

Tony cuts in. 'All of it, not just the first half?'

'Of course.' I mirror the tilt of his head, we both seem equally confused. 'Why?'

'Just I don't wanna be taking nothing under false pretences.'

That hasn't made things any clearer. 'Like what?'

He looks down at his hands. 'The hug and stuff.' There's a quick glance up under his lashes, the confiding child expression I can't resist. 'I wasn't sure I'd be welcome, after how today went.'

I step back. Surely he can't think I'm just another ball bunny, only interested in him after a win? 'You're always welcome. Win or lose, it makes no difference.'

Tony grimaces. 'Not cos of the result. Cos of the thing with LeMar. Could you not see what went on?'

I smile, relieved that this is only a misunderstanding. It was the crowd getting after LeMar for being caught offside that got him flustered, not Tony. And it was LeMar who got in Tony's face, over what I guess he thought were mistimed passes, not the other way around.

I make my voice teasing. 'It was just about noticeable. But you did have to be watching ever so closely. I can't imagine it'll make it onto *Match of the Day*.'

Tony shakes his head at me, but some of the tension's gone from his hands. 'It's nice you can take the piss, love. And to think the whole way back here, I was worried sick you'd want done with me over it.'

'Over what?' I ask, trying to be serious when I want to grin. The 'done with' has got to mean he already thinks there's something real between us.

'Well, LeMar, he's your boy, isn't he?'

I shrug. 'That doesn't mean he's never wrong. And Tony, don't you think you should be happy about it?'

'How'd you mean?'

'Well, you didn't lose your temper, did you?' Better than that, when LeMar blew up, Tony walked away. And yes, LeMar might not have got quite so angry if Tony hadn't provided a few home truths about his positioning. And Tony could perhaps have tried harder not to laugh, but he's not a saint, is he?

Tony bends over to pet Roudie, but not fast enough to hide the smile, like he's genuinely pleased. 'Yeah, I reckon I've got that under control all right. But then, I've had a bit of help, haven't I?'

I might've pulled the odd string to stop Tony being top of the list for every club commitment, but I'm not going to take credit for his work. Instead, I stretch out my hand for the wine.

He hands it over. 'I know genies have mixed feelings over bottles, but I reckon you'll like this one OK.'

I glance at the label. 'Umm, thank you. I'd happily live in this one. Should I open it now?'

I'm expecting the usual request for water, but Tony looks at me, eyes shy. 'You can, but I'm dying for a beer, if that's OK?' He hands over a bag of beers I hadn't spotted in his other hand. Before I can say anything, he hurries to add, 'The nutrition people here are all right 'bout it, if it's like just the one.'

I smile. 'I know. Carbohydrate reloading and all that.'

I herd Tony through to the sitting room, which the log burner has made invitingly cosy, despite the limited furnishings. And as I open a couple of lagers, I'm beaming. Tony feeling he can have a drink is the strongest sign yet that he's settling. Plus, if he's ready to relax the iron discipline, there's a chance he'll be able to sustain it.

I'm not sure it's physically possible to smile more, but it makes me even happier to see Tony settled on the sofa with Roudie pressed up against his feet in a cravenly obvious ploy to stop him leaving. As I hand Tony the bottle, he smiles a thank you. But when his fingers brush mine, he pulls away like it burns. I sit beside him, close but careful not to touch, since it seems that's unwelcome.

He points at my stripy sleeve. 'That looks great on you, by the way. But I should probably let on it was more of a gift than something going spare.'

Is that what he's worried about? That I'm going to over-react about a tiny half-truth? I meet his eye. 'Then I like it even more.'

There's an odd pause, then he pulls at the knee of his joggers. 'Er, Genie, is it OK if I, um, put my arm round you?'

'Of course, there's no need to ask.'

His mouth tightens. 'Only there is, isn't there?'

Suddenly all the careful avoidance of physical contact makes sense. I snap, 'No, there isn't. I'm not frigid.'

Tony tries not to smile and fails miserably. 'Nah, you're definitely not that.' His face becomes earnest. 'But it's gone wrong a couple of times now, hasn't it? Me touching you and it going nought to sixty in like two seconds, then it being too much and you sprinting off.'

I chew at my lip and nod.

He leans in towards me until our foreheads almost touch. 'And it's been killing me, holding off from you the last couple of weeks, trying to give you space. So I hopes you don't mind, but I had a session with my psych guy first thing, and I asked him 'bout you. Well, 'bout us.'

I can't believe he'd do that. After how angry he was when I spoke to Chrissie, it sounds like he might have shared with Martin, our sports psychologist, the most personal, humiliating thing I've ever told anyone. To make it worse, Martin's one of Gavin's cronies. The shock and the disappointment must show, because Tony goes to take my hand, then pulls his away.

'Genie, beauty, don't look like that.'

'Please tell me you didn't tell Martin what I said?' I ask, unable to process why he can't see the issue.

'No, course not. I'd never talk to no one at the club 'bout anything private that came from you. I, um . . .' He looks at his fingernails. 'I, um, have this, like, I guess you'd call him a counsellor, that I've seen off and on for a few years. Not cos I'm crazy or nothing, just when stuff's building up . . .'

Well, now I feel awful. This is what I'm supposed to be good at, sensing how people feel, what they need. And Tony's the person I want to do that for most in the world. So why do I keep rushing to think the worst of him, when all he does is prove me wrong?

I take his hand and squeeze gently. 'That sounds like a really good idea.'

He nods, still looking shamefaced. 'Yeah, well, I let it slip a bit last season, so I'm getting back into it now. Trying to keep things level, you know?'

I nod, earnestly. 'The ups and downs have to be hard.'

He shrugs. 'Yeah, but I'm not here to talk 'bout me. What I told Daniel, the bloke I do the sessions with, it weren't the stuff you asked me not to tell no one, the sex stuff, promise.'

I tighten my fingers around his. 'You could've done.'

'Nah, I couldn't, cos I said I wouldn't. But I mentioned that thing you said, 'bout how having watched me play, and how you had come to feel like you knew me through that, but the reality of being with me isn't quite the same?'

Tony's face is still close to mine. On one level that's nice. But it's hard, having this conversation when he's so near, I can smell the product in his hair and the faint hint of citrus from his aftershave. He must pick up on that, because he sits back but keeps his hand in mine, and this time, it's him squeezing my fingers.

'I didn't quite get it, but he got me to see how it would be weird. Have I remembered right what you said?'

It is right, or almost. Close enough anyway, that I don't have to say it's not just that Tony's nicer than I'd imagined, or that he's more vulnerable. On top of that, I've spent so much time fantasizing about touching him, his body's both familiar and foreign at the same time.

I nod.

'Once he got that through to me, I could see how that'd freak you out. 'Specially if the person you was with before was pretending they cared when they was really standing back from you, judging when you was trying to be intimate with them.'

That is right, so right that I can't look at him any more. I twist away, staring at the flames of the log burner, reflected in the dark of the window. Tony waits for a minute or two. 'Don't go getting upset, cos we're going to sort it, aren't we?' He pushes his fingers into my palm. 'Promise, OK?'

My laugh is watery, but I can look back at him and smile. 'OK.'

He grins. 'That's better. The only downside is Daniel reckons the fastest way to fix it is to cool it, physically. Let you get to know the real Tony, 'stead of Tony Garratt, star midfielder. So I reckon it's best if, till we get you feeling safe, I ask before I touch. How's that sound?'

It sounds like an unnecessary delay when I'm fizzing with desire, to the point where I can barely sit still. I lower my voice, aiming for seductive and I think making a reasonable job of it. 'Do I have to ask before I touch you?'

He grins. 'No, you can wrap yourself round me as much as you like.'

'And can I ask you to touch me?'

'Yeah, course.'

I smile slowly. 'Then I can see it has potential.'

Tony laughs, my favourite roaring laugh. 'It does, don't it? And to think I weren't the one to see it.' He leans back from me. 'But I think we ought to put that on ice for now. Until you feel more comfortable with this. What do you reckon?'

'Yes, absolutely, of course,' I say, biting down the disappointment.

Tony drops his chin and looks at me with narrowed eyes. 'Then why are you doing that thing where you yank at stuff?'

He's right, my hand is on the string of my hoodie.

'Come on, what is it?' he asks, taking my hand and drawing it down onto the sofa.

I pull at his fingers, then decide we're past the point where I gloss over things that need to be said. 'Don't you think you might, well, get bored?'

'Tonight, I reckon a bit of a cuddle's all I'm good for.'

He turns to look at me full on, his face end-of-the-season, critical-three-points serious. 'I have to tell you, Genie, you and the pup running up to me tonight, that was like I was coming home. And I dunno if I can remember the last time I felt that way.'

I want to tie myself in knots around him but I settle for looking down at his fingers interlaced with mine. 'It's lovely, you saying that . . .'

'What's with them big sad eyes, then?'

'It's just I think it might make me feel more self-conscious, having to have a full-scale negotiation, every time you touch me. Sorry.'

He smiles. 'Nah, you telling me that straight is you

holding up your side of the deal. How 'bout we adjust it a bit? I'll check any time I'm not sure, but if I reckon you'll be good with something, I'll do it. Only you've got to tell me the second I get that wrong. All right?'

'Yep. Perfect.'

And it is. We watch TV, and as the second episode cues up, I lift my feet onto the sofa, snuggling back against Tony.

He rests a hand lightly on my navel and murmurs, 'OK?'

I draw his hand under my top to the curve of my stomach. The warmth of his fingers melts into my skin. 'This is better.'

'Yeah, beauty, you're right, way better.'

29

Eleven and a half days later (not that I'm counting)

It would be great if the next step was moving beyond company and cuddles. But Tony was straight off to an away game for the league. The minute he was back, he was laser focused on our next European match in which, incidentally, he played like an angel. So, I've barely seen him except on FaceTime, and I'm dying to engineer a quick meeting in the hallway as he traipses in from training. Only I can't because my morning is fully occupied trying to set up a match-day visit for a junior we're trying to tempt into our academy.

Callum's a sweet kid, but his parents love him and loathe each other with an equal passion. I'm stuck as negotiator and when a message comes through, I'm dreading opening it, expecting it to be from one of them. But it's Tony asking:

> The roof is pretty much the only bit of this place not
> covered by security cameras, right?
> 11.47

Yes. Should I ask why you're asking or is it better not to know?
11.48

Tell you in a minute, meet me up there?
11.50

OK SYS
11.51

As I push open the door onto the roof, the bitingly cold wind swooshes past me into the stairwell. Pulling my faux fur coat tight around me, I hurry over to Tony, who comes to meet me, smiling like sunshine.

'Hello, love. Bit chilly, huh?' He slips an arm around my waist and turns so his back blocks the icy gusts.

'It is.' I slide a hand under his jacket, searching under the layers until I can run my palm over the hard curve of muscle sloping into his spine. 'You're nice and warm though.'

He pulls me closer. 'Snuggle in then.'

I don't need to be asked twice, and he holds me tight, burying his face in my hair. There's a stab of desire so sharp it hurts, and I almost pull away. But he's already slackening his arms and asking gently, 'All right?' And that's enough that I can let myself enjoy the closeness, the softness of his sweatshirt against my cheek, the strength of his hands on my back. But I did tell Sky I wouldn't be long, so eventually, I untangle myself just enough to look up at him. 'Did you need something?'

Tony smiles gently. 'Turns out, I've been needing that all morning.'

I nuzzle back into his chest. 'Bad day?'

'Nah, not really. Training was a bit of a bitch, is all.'

'Are you hurt?' I ask, taking half a step back so I can see him properly.

He extends his arms to keep me close and shakes his head.

'You're sure?'

He nods. 'Yeah, I'm fine. Promise. You know how it is sometimes. I weren't feeling it, and I could do without this weather.' His smile is still soft. 'But nothing a bit of a cuddle with you can't put right. Not that I dragged you out into the freezing cold just for that.'

'I wouldn't have minded. I've had quite an irritating morning myself.'

He stops smiling. 'Yeah, it's 'bout your workplace irritations that I got you up here.' Tony lets me go with one hand and guides me over to the little hut that forms the top of the stairwell, out of the wind. We stand side by side, backs against the wall, Tony's arm around me, his trainer against the edge of my ankle boot.

'You know how I said I'd talk to someone, 'bout what's been going on with the mistakes that keep happening? And about your computer?' Tony asks.

I nod. Part of me doesn't want to hear what's coming next.

'Well, there's this bloke, Christian, who's done some work for me in the past. He runs like a consultancy, doing digital security. So, he knows what he's about.'

I nod again, an anxious twinge in my stomach.

'And he used a load of fancy terms. But basically, he found some spyware stuff on your laptop that'd let someone come in remotely, see what you're doing, make changes, that sort of thing.'

The shock is intense. Why would anyone do that? Tony senses it and squeezes my waist. I know he's out to comfort, so I turn to let him and try to raise a smile. 'But that's good, isn't it?' I say, trying to convince myself. 'Well, I mean, obviously it's bad. But it's better than it being someone at the club, or me becoming incompetent.'

There's a twitch in his mouth that's closer to pain than the start of a smile. 'I dunno that it means it's not someone here.'

I hesitate. 'But it's much more likely to be a rival club, or a journalist even, isn't it?'

Tony sways his head back and forth, like a weighing scale. 'I don't think so.' He covers my hand with his. 'Cos, I'm not putting down what you do, or nothing. But targeting Player Care, it's too much work for not enough back, don't you think? Like if I wanted inside information, I'd target the coaching staff, the medics, that side of things. And if I wanted to cause trouble, the players' phones'd be where I'd start.'

'I suppose so.' I lean my head against his shoulder, and he pushes his thumb into my palm.

'But the biggest reason I think it's someone here is it feels personal. Like it's all designed to make you look bad.'

I sigh, and my breath is misty against the cold air. 'It certainly feels that way.'

'And that does kind of beg the question, who'd wanna hurt you?' Tony rests his chin on my hair, and his voice is grim.

'Well, like we discussed before, maybe Monica? I mean,

I don't think she'd be interested in hurting me particularly, but dispensing with me . . .' I shrug.

'Thing is, I don't see it being her.'

'Why not?'

Tony reorganizes us, so both his arms are around me and I can see his face. 'You know when I first arrived and I was late?'

I nod.

'Cos I got that text, changing the time?'

I bite my cheek. 'You think it's part of the same thing?'

Tony purses his lips. 'Yeah, I do.'

'Well, I can completely see why you don't think that was Monica. If you hadn't shown, it would've been incredibly embarrassing for her.'

He nods. 'More than that, she'd have lost sway over the board. After she pressured 'em into approving the transfer when half of 'em was convinced I'd be toxic.'

I'm about to say no one could think that now, when something strikes me. Something horrifying, given how Tony and I have been messaging back and forth. 'But Tony, if you got a text I didn't send, then it's not just my computer that someone has access to, it's the phone too.'

'You could be right, and we should definitely get your phone checked. Christian managed to retrieve the text, and it wasn't from your number, it was just signed off "Player Care" so I assumed it was you.'

'Could he trace it?'

'Just to a burner phone. So, not massively helpful, 'cept the timing's weird.'

'Weird how?'

'Well, that's the start of all of this, innit? The first time you had any issues.' His gaze has become intense, his grey eyes more green against the sooty winter sky.

I think about it, then shrug. 'It's the first thing I remember. But some of the little things might not have made much of an impression, until they started to become a pattern.'

'Nah, I'm pretty sure, it was the first.' Tony's voice borders on impatient.

'Why?'

'Cos it's amateur, innit? And a gamble, cos I could be like you and leave all my texts to mount up, case I need them later. Which actually, turns out, you're absolutely right to do.' He smiles at me, back to sweet and soft. 'And the software, Christian dates it to 'bout a week after that. So, it feels like this was maybe something to do with my arrival here. I'd think it might be about the instant attraction between us but that doesn't make sense of that first text.'

I can feel myself blushing at the instant attraction comment. Tony shakes his head once. 'Don't bother coming up with something to bat that away. You know I think you're beautiful, and I think it was obvious from the start. Which you can accept since I'm not coming on to you, or no more than usual, cos now's not the time.'

I slide my hands from his spine to the back pockets of his jeans, and smile up at him. 'Isn't it?'

He shuts his eyes for a moment, then they're back to diamonds. 'Nah, it's not. I've made the mistake of moving too fast once when you was vulnerable. I don't plan on doing it twice.'

My smile is the one that softens now. Tony's here, and

I don't feel vulnerable. It's impossible to be scared with his arms around me. Not even when someone's gone to a huge amount of effort to cause me trouble. But I know that'll change when I'm on my own again and that will gnaw at me. Maybe I am trying to force things on, just to delay him leaving.

I go to draw my hands away, but he shakes his head. 'Leave 'em, love, for the warmth if nothing else. Which kind of gets me back on to why I got you up here in the cold. Cos it crossed my mind, you and me, we've been careful, but there's been the odd hug in the corridor when no one was around, that sort of thing. Someone with access to the cameras, they could've seen. So, there's no one in Security you've pissed off, is there?'

'No. I'm not super close with any of them, but we're cordial.'

'And none of 'em have a stalker vibe?'

I think for a second. 'No, not at all.'

'You're sure, not even someone who just gives you a bad feeling?'

I shake my head. 'No. They're all boringly normal family guys. And anyway, that wouldn't make sense, would it?'

Tony gives me a slow look. 'Why's that?'

'Well, if the first thing was the text message, that was before you even arrived. So, someone who's jealous that we're friends or whatev—'

Tony interrupts with one of his wider smiles. 'We're whatever. I've got zero interest in being friend-zoned again, thanks.'

I smile back. 'OK, so it couldn't have been someone

who's jealous that we're two emotionally damaged people working out how to have some sort of relationship without anyone losing their job or getting hurt . . .'

Tony laughs. 'You know that's actually progress, don't you? You saying "relationship" out loud.'

I hide my head in his sweatshirt. 'I know. I'm sorry. I get scared.'

Tony does his best bear hug. 'I know, beauty. But that's why we're going slow, right?'

I mutter into his chest, and he laughs. 'Did you just say, like a glacier?'

I pull back from him and pout. 'That's what it feels like some days.'

Tony nods. 'Yeah, I know. And I've got an idea for moving things on a bit. Which we'll talk 'bout in a minute, when you're done making your point.'

'OK, so someone who was jealous over me and you, why would they send the text before we'd even met? It makes more sense for it to be someone who wants Player Care to look bad.'

'You reckon there's someone who fits the bill?'

'Not off the top of my head, no. But I'll put some thought into it.'

Tony lets me go for a second, then slides his hands inside my coat. 'You do that, and I'll do some thinking of my own. But if you're sure it's not Security, there's no reason for me to keep you out here. You must be freezing.' My cranberry sweater dress is actually quite warm under my thick coat, but I don't say that, in case it makes him take his hands off my waist.

'Before we go in though, Tony . . .' I reach up and kiss him lightly, letting my lips linger on his cheek, which is marginally warmer than mine. 'Thank you, for doing all that.'

He smiles like that means something, but his voice is offhand. 'Yeah, it weren't no bother.'

He lets me go and holds the door open. As I walk into the warmth of the stairwell, I try to sound just as casual as I ask, 'Would you let me pay Christian's fees?'

Tony grins as he shakes his head in exasperation. 'No, I fucking wouldn't.' He wraps an arm around my shoulders. 'But I appreciate you asking.'

I reach up and touch his hand. 'Thank you. But I don't want you to think I assume you'll pay for things.'

'I know. Which is mainly cos you're one of the good ones, but there's a bit of you not accepting stuff in there too. And that's something we're working on, right?'

I nod and slide my hand away, ready to walk down the stairs ahead of him.

'Hang on a sec, Genie.'

I look up at him.

'So, real quick, you know I get a whole day off tomorrow?'

'Umm.'

'Well, I know you're busy, but I was thinking, me and you, we've not been anywhere together. Like on a date, or nothing.' Tony twists his sweatshirt with one hand, and I realize he's nervous. That makes me smile, which seems to make it worse. His voice becomes almost unrecognizably hesitant. 'So, I was, um, wondering if you're . . . you could free up any time, if you wanna, um, come out with me?'

I try not to smile again, but maybe overdo it a bit,

because Tony says, 'But I get it, if you're tied up. Like, it's short notice and I know you've got a lot on . . .'

I'm going to have to interrupt. 'No, I'd love to. I am due some time off.'

Tony grins. 'Great, that's great. Cos I've got this idea that I reckon you might really go for.'

I let the smile come out now, all beaming and happy. 'I'm sure I will.' A text comes through on my phone. 'Sorry, I'd better get this. It's Skylar, she's probably worried I've died of exposure.'

We walk downstairs. At the bottom, he says, 'See you tomorrow, then,' and begins to wander off towards the car park. I head in the opposite direction, then realize we are literally the two least relationship-functional people ever and call out, 'Tony, what time tomorrow?'

'Early, like eight. And wear something you don't mind getting muddy.'

30

I get up ridiculously early, telling myself it's so I can walk Roudie before Tony arrives. But the pup doesn't seem convinced a double-speed rush round the village makes up for being forced out of bed at five thirty. He's currently sitting at the top of the stairs, staring accusingly at me as I attempt the no-make-up make-up look. I've watched enough YouTube videos to write a thesis on achieving an 'Oh, I just woke up like this' dewy glow. But the wind is already getting up, and unhelpfully, none of the videos mentioned which setting powder best withstands a full-on gale.

In the end, I give up, take everything off and settle for less is more. A light swipe of foundation, a tiny bit of concealer, a dusting of pale pink eye shadow and plenty of clear lip balm might just about hold up to the weather. Which brings us to what to wear. Tony's compliments might be more 'you look nice' than 'that's a nice dress', but I don't believe he doesn't notice clothes. I mean, I can't pretend his style is to everyone's taste. But even my mother would have to admit, everything fits him perfectly.

I suspect he likes his women equally well turned out. Only I'm not sure how to combine stylish with muddy. I frenziedly pull things out of the wardrobe then throw them back, until Roudie wanders in. He gazes at me, head on one side. I definitely don't want today to include Tony being equally confused over why I can't understand a weather forecast. So, I opt for comfort over fashion. Except I do make sure the leggings I choose aren't just thermal. They also provide a little artificial boost to what nature and a depressingly large number of squats can achieve. And the sweatshirt is a soft lilac, which I've decided is the optimal colour for the naturally pale.

Next, I attempt a tight, high ponytail. But however much I straighten the ends, they keep kinking out at weird angles. The straightening introduces bumps, and let's just say, no one's going to mistake me for an influencer. I consider rewashing it and starting from scratch. Except, it's already seven thirty, and I can't possibly get that done in time. Admitting defeat, I brush my hair out, pull it back loosely and clip it up. Looking in the mirror, I suppose there's a chance Tony will think it's deliberately dishevelled, rather than merely messy.

Mirrors aren't my friend. Especially now I'm ready, with nothing practical to distract me from the flaws. And thank you, but I don't need reminding there are people really suffering while I'm fretting over uneven skin tone or a less than perfect jawline. It's just when I daydream about Tony, which let's face it, is most of the time, everything's perfect. Including me. The thought of spending the day with him, knowing that inevitably, he'll be comparing me to Angharad, and that the comparisons won't be in my favour, well, it's dispiriting. I consider texting that I've a headache or it's too cold or something's come up at work. But my excuse selection is interrupted by the doorbell.

I grit my teeth and walk downstairs behind Roudie, hurtling down three steps at a time. When I open the door, Roudie goes into an orgy of delight, leaping and wagging. Looking at Tony, I can't blame him. Predictably, he's dressed like one of the Corleones out for a day in the country. That means suspiciously new walking boots, jeans and a black cable-knit sweater, tight over his shoulders and fractionally looser over the torso. Plus, he's holding two cups of coffee, so his sleeve has ridden up to show the gold of his watch. And though he's shaved, there's already the hint of stubble, and his hair is freshly washed and gelled. Which is all to say, if I had a tail to wag, I absolutely would.

He grins at me, all white teeth and toothpaste.

'Hello, beauty. Do you think you could get the pup to cool it, before I spill these?' he asks, holding up the coffee.

'Sorry, yes, of course. Come on, Roudie, that's enough. Basket.'

For once, Roudie takes direction. That's particularly surprising given I sound hesitant, which is an accurate reflection of how I feel. This isn't like meeting Tony at work or the definitely-not-dates we've done before. The nerves last until we get into the kitchen and Tony puts down the coffee cups and wraps his arms around me, nosing into my neck. I'm glad I went for Coco perfume. Whenever I wear it, his hugs last longer.

After a minute or so, he murmurs, 'Hello properly, Genie, love,' his voice muffled by my shoulder.

And as I say, 'Hello, Tony,' I don't feel awkward any more, or anxious. I'm just happy he's here.

He pulls back, sliding his hands up to my shoulders.

There's a long look between us, until Tony smiles his closed-mouth, serious smile. 'You look really pretty.'

I make an intense effort not to say anything negative. I guess he can tell because the smile becomes fractionally more teasing.

'Is this all right for what you've got planned? I can easily change into something dressier, if you prefer.'

He shakes his head and his smile is back to gentle. 'Nah. You're just right.' Then he grins. 'You'll need a nice big coat though.'

'Do I get to know what we're doing?'

'Not till we're driving. That way you can't back out.'

I squeeze his arm. 'I wouldn't anyway.'

He lets me go. 'Hope not. But I've got a favour to ask, before we get going. Can we take your car? I'm happy to drive, but I fancy going under the radar today and mine are a bit flash. Plus, yours is comfier for the pup.'

'Does Roudie get to come too?'

Tony returns my full-beam smile. 'Yeah, course. I need my wingman for this one.'

It's only once we're halfway out of the village that I take a sip of the coffee. The cup sleeve has the wolf logo of Lupa, my favourite coffee shop.

'Oh, you've been all the way into town already.'

His voice is gruff, like he's embarrassed. 'Yeah, it's the right place, is it? The one you like?'

I smile. 'It is. How did you know?'

'It's where Sky goes, when she wants to get on your good side so you'll let her go early, or so I heard?'

I laugh. 'It is. I'm obviously easily bought.'

He tilts his head. 'Let's hope so.'

I smile back. We talk nonsense until we're nearly at the motorway, when Tony becomes suddenly serious. 'So, listen, I knows you like water, being outside, running, all that. And me and Roudie put our heads together and thought, how 'bout taking you for a walk on the beach? Does that sound all right?'

It does, absolutely right. I love the sea. But, on a good day, the nearest coast is a two-hour drive. Getting on the motorway always means the sort of traffic I hate, so I hardly ever get up the courage to go. The beach is also completely different to my first date with Gavin. That involved a classical music concert and extremely uncomfortable chairs.

'That sounds perfect.'

31

Roudie races across the sand, leaping across pools left by the tide and skittering away any time the waves get close to his toes. He sprints back to us, play bows and dashes off again. It's his way of inviting us to join the only game that isn't beneath his dignity. Tony drops my hand and darts towards Roudie, so he must already know the rules. Roudie careers away, helter-skelter, then stops stock still, panting, and pretending not to watch us out of the corner of his eye.

This time I hunch down, stalking him with slow strides. Roudie waits, then when I'm almost within touching distance, he sprints away towards Tony. The chase runs round and round, the two of us pursuing Roudie, until I cross paths with Tony. He stretches out an arm to catch my waist, pulling me in. I'm half panting, half laughing up at him. His lips are parted, the tip of his tongue between his teeth, as he reaches up and removes a strand of hair from my eyes. When it's tucked safely behind my ear, he stares at me, like it's the first time he's seen me.

'God, you are fucking irresistible when you're happy.'

He kisses me, the wind whipping round us and his teeth pulling at my lip, then mine at his. Before, this sort of kiss has been like being up high, exhilaration followed by the fear of falling. I'm waiting for it, that sense I'm slipping out of control. But it doesn't come. I could keep going forever, just me and Tony and the taste of sea salt on his lips. But Roudie pushes at us with his nose, and Tony slowly releases me and strokes Roudie's head. 'Sorry, mate, keeping you waiting, are we?'

Tony smiles at me and we walk off down the beach, hand in hand, Roudie between us like a toddler. And we don't talk much. It's so blustery, words get blown away. But his hand is in mine, or on my shoulder, or round my waist the whole time. Or it is, until there's a sudden onslaught of rain. Not just drops, but sheets of water pelting against us. We race for the car, heads down, Roudie's tail tucked tight.

Once we're inside, doors slammed shut against the storm, Tony looks at the snakes of hair plastered against the white of my cheeks, and my puffa jacket heavy with rain.

'You and the pup are soaked, aren't you?'

I shake my head. 'No. Roudie will hardly be wet at all under his topcoat, and I'll dry off quickly enough.'

He reaches for my hand and squeezes it tight. 'No, you won't. You're shivering.' He looks away, but I catch the wince before his profile's quite out of sight. 'I'm sorry, Genie. I wanted this to be perfect. But it was a stupid idea, coming out here on a day like this.'

'No, it wasn't. I can't think of a nicer way to spend the afternoon.'

He looks back at me. 'You're a special woman all right.' Then his smile becomes properly happy. 'And I've just had an idea, so get your seatbelt on.'

We drive, Tony leaning forward to squint through the

rain, until he pulls into the car park of a gym we passed driving into town. He bends across to kiss my cheek. 'You wait here with the pup. I'll be right back.'

By the time Tony returns, the rain's stopped. 'Make the most of the showers. Cos I've just bought a membership, which is coals to Newcastle, I can tell you.'

I start to thank him, but he waves it away. 'Me and the pup have got an errand to run. So, you go and get dry, then meet us out here, OK?'

The showers are blissfully warm. There isn't a hair drier, but there are enough towels that I can get my hair close to dry, even if it is a bit on the tangled side. I'm facing up to putting back on my wet clothes when the blonde from reception puts her head around the door. 'Your boyfriend asked me to give you these.' She bundles supermarket carrier bags towards me.

Looking inside, Tony's errand obviously paid off. So, when I hurry out to meet him, I'm considerably warmer, if not exactly glam, in black leggings that are slightly too short and an oversized grey sweatshirt. It's got an unusually threatening Welsh dragon on the front, but I'm more focused on the new-born lamb soft fleecy lining.

When I get to the car, Roudie's coat is like a hedgehog where it's been rubbed dry, using towels I guess Tony bought for the purpose. Tony's working on his last paw, and watching, I can't help smiling. He's being so painstakingly careful, just like when he pushed the hair away from my eyes earlier. And that's the thing with Tony. He's such a big boisterous person, being gentle or careful takes him superhuman effort. But because he has to try so hard, it's amplified, so he's a hundred times more gentle, more careful than anyone else. And suddenly, I know this is no longer just attraction. I love Tony. Absolutely.

It's so obvious, I almost say it when he turns and grins at me. But I don't, because who says I love you on a first date? Instead, I smile back and he's the one that speaks first.

'Better, beauty?'

'Umm, much better, thank you. And I'll finish Roudie, you go and get warm.'

When I tell Tony he's taken a wrong turn, he shakes his head without explaining, until we pull into the car park of a pub just off the high street.

'You all right with us seeing if dog-friendly extends to wet ones?'

I nod enthusiastically. 'Absolutely, I'm starving.'

Tony smiles. 'Thought you might be. I had a look at the menu on my phone. It does veggie, but it's not exactly healthy eating. Only I reckon you and me can afford a day off from that.'

His arm is wrapped extra-tight around me as we walk in. The landlady, a grey-haired, round woman, is more than happy to accommodate Roudie. As Tony goes to fetch him and I take my first sip of gin and tonic, she gestures to an elderly Labrador, deeply asleep in a basket behind the bar. 'It warms your heart, doesn't it? When they're soppy over the dog.'

I beam at her. 'It certainly does.'

I turn to watch Tony stroll in. You'd think he'd look ordinary, just any other normal person, with his hair still wet, and wearing non-descript joggers and a supermarket own-brand sweatshirt. But he doesn't, he looks how he always does. Special.

As we finish eating, in my case ridiculously good chocolate pudding, Tony smiles at me.

'This has to be one of the best meals I've had in a while, even if it's not the swankiest place I've ever taken a woman.'

That's part of why this was a genius idea. If we'd gone to a smart restaurant, I'd have spent the whole time wondering if he'd been there with someone else, and how I measured up. But I'm pretty confident this is the first time Tony's taken a girlfriend to a Welsh beach in the first week in October.

Only saying that would ruin it, so I glance down at my sweatshirt. 'Well, I'm not exactly dressed for anywhere posher.'

Tony grins. 'I dunno, that dragon's doing stuff for me, all right.' He reaches across the table and takes my hand, his face becoming more serious. 'And you like that, it's nice. I mean, I likes you all dolled up, obviously. But loads of people see you that way. You a bit softer, that feels like it's just for me. You know?'

I nod and stroke his fingers, and he's back to grinning as he turns my palm upward.

'So, I'm guessing you reckon palm reading's all women's magazine bullshit?'

'I'm afraid so.'

He bows his head over my hand, but looks up at me.

257

'And you might be on the money. But my old gran, she was a believer all right.'

'And let me guess, you inherited the sight?' I ask, my voice teasing.

'Take the piss all you like. But you never know, you open your mind and you might hear something to your advantage.'

'I can't claim psychic powers, but I think that's a certainty.'

He grins. 'I dunno. It's just possible your palm might let on you're a sarky bitch.'

'Oh, I think we both know that already.' I soften my smile. 'But go on, tell me my destiny. Only isn't that the wrong hand?'

'Nah. Most people use the right, but my nan reckoned the left was stronger. Cos of what sits here.' He lines the nail of his thumb up with where a wedding band would sit, then reaches round to stroke from my wrist, across my palm to the tip of my little finger.

'So, for starters, you've got water hands, all long and slinky. Which ought to get you thinking, cos they're supposed to go with being sensitive. Like exactly what I'd expect for a lady who can read what other people are needing from the other side of the room.'

He slides his thumb back and runs it across the first curving line. 'And this one, it's your heart line. See how it runs right up between your fingers? That's a sign of a woman who'll put all she's got into taking care of her man.' He glances up into my eyes. 'So, for your job, that's kind of appropriate, innit?

'But it's these that are real interesting.' He traces the

258

grooves below my little finger. 'Your lines of affection. There's differences of opinion on 'em, but Nan used to reckon they tell 'bout your lovers. And maybe she was right, cos you've got this one that's barely there and don't go far. I'm thinking we both know who that is. Then there's these little ones that hardly show. I'm guessing they're the guys you didn't care 'bout enough to let 'em see you properly. Then you've got this one. It might start a bit unsteady, but it gets all long, and straight, and deep, don't it? He's the one you belong with.'

'Why do I get the sneaking suspicion you've done this before?'

He winks and slips my hand under his. 'Thing is, I might've given the odd reading in the past. But see how I've got all them little lines, what's underneath 'em?'

And it's true, the last line matches mine. Only his runs hard and steady without any of the wavering at the start.

We're still looking at each other, not quite smiling when the waitress places the bill between us. I reach for it, then pull my hand back. Tony grins but doesn't say anything until we're on our way out to the car. He stretches an arm around my shoulder, pulling me in. 'You, beauty, have done brilliant today, haven't you?'

I look up, getting lost for a second in how he manages to look incredibly handsome, even in the yellow light of the car park. But then I remember I'm supposed to be asking him a question, and he realizes and gives me a big smile, then kisses my forehead.

'Cos you've taken compliments without trying to twist 'em or duck out of 'em. And even better, you've let yourself be looked after, and you've hardly fought it at all.' He softens the smile. 'And I know that's real hard. Having someone else take charge of the caring for a change.'

'Sometimes.' I rest my head on his shoulder for a step or two.

'And it's taken me a while, but I think maybe I do get why. Seeing how Gavin is with you. It's got me wondering if you're scared, letting someone take care of you, it's going to end up with 'em telling you how you should be?'

I bury my head in his shoulder, trying to hide how much that means. 'Maybe you are psychic after all.'

He stops and looks down at me, his eyes grave. 'I dunno that you've gotta be a mind reader to come up with that one. Or to work out that if someone's always going on 'bout how you could be better, it'd get you feeling like you're not good enough now. And I don't need no special powers to see how a few years of that could end up so it's claustrophobic, any time a bloke comes along wanting to treat you nice.' I can feel the tears coming, but Tony won't let them. 'Nah, beauty. Don't you be sad 'bout nothing. I've got no interest in improving you, promise.'

I bite my lip then smile up at him. 'Tony, that's why today was so perfect. Everything you've done, it's been you working out what I like, and giving me that, not what you think would be better.'

He smiles. 'Yeah, that's how this dating thing works.'

32

Skylar interrupting my quiet Sunday isn't unexpected. She got subbed off twenty minutes into yesterday's game. As usual, she took it as a personal insult and since her house-mates are better at 'let's go have fun' than 'I'm sorry you're sad', she'll be looking for sympathy, and knowing Sky, food.

After my specialty, pasta and random vegetables that happen to be in the fridge, we retreat to the sitting room. An hour later, Sky's still immobile on the sofa. There's a distinct resemblance to a wolf that's eaten so much elk, it can only lie upside down digesting. So, I'm not surprised she's unenthused about taking Roudie out.

'Don't you do the guilt walk earlier?' she asks, wiggling her shoulders deeper into the cushions.

It's true. Normally, when the first team play away, I try to make amends for all the weekends I work by taking Roudie for an extra-long morning walk. But that means having to do a post-match stroll around the village in the evening. Lately, I'm not keen on being out by myself after dark. It's silly. I didn't used to worry, Halsbury has to be the safest village in England. All the stuff at work must've got inside my head. Since Tony took my laptop I've been using a new one and the mistakes have stopped, but still, it's hard to let go of the fear someone's spying.

Or it might be I've got spoilt. Spending every evening

last week at the lodge meant Tony walking me and Roudie home. But yesterday, Tony was travelling for today's game and stepping out into the dark without his arm around me, there was a tightness in my chest that never used to be there. And we'd barely been out five minutes when a cat slinking out of the shadows was enough to get me dragging Roudie home.

I'm not admitting any of that to Skylar, who's the definition of fearless. So, instead of explaining an afternoon walk means I can justify letting Roudie out in the garden last thing, I shrug and try to sound nonchalant. 'Oh, we just fancied a lazy morning.'

She does drag herself off the sofa, but there's a fair amount of semi-audible muttering about how a lazy afternoon sounds better. Opening the door, I can see her point. After the warmth of the log burner, the cold is bitter. But Roudie pulls me through the porch, dying to find out which animals have been where. And once I'm out, it's worth it for the unbroken bird's-egg-blue sky.

Trying to stop Roudie wrenching his lead out of my hands, I fiddle with the key in the lock.

'Is that Tony's request?' says Skylar.

'No. What makes you ask that?' I ask, meaning more, why are you asking like you disapprove?

Sky shrugs. 'Just you never used to bother.'

I say something vague about being more security aware, and let Roudie tow me down the path. I stop at the garden gate, peering out. Hopefully, Sky will think I'm checking for traffic. Which I am, but I'm also seeing if there's a car in the gateway, half-hidden from the cottage by a bend in the road. And there is, the same one that was there yesterday, a red Ford Fiesta. Logically, I know it's probably nothing. Someone visiting family, or something like that. But why park here, right on the edge of the village?

Obviously, the sensible thing is to walk past it to prove there's no one lurking inside. Only, I don't want to, not even with Skylar next to me. So, we start off in the opposite direction. It's not as much of a cop-out as it sounds. The loop we're doing takes us back past the car. Unless it's gone. Because it might have, mightn't it?

Sky's quiet, hands deep in her pockets, eyes fixed on the floor. She's not a player who wants to compulsively discuss a bad game, picking apart each error. I focus on Roudie instead, running with his nose low on the chocolate-brown plough furrow, tracking long-gone hares.

It's not until we're almost at the top of the hill, looking down at the village, that Sky asks, 'So, you and Tony, is that a thing now?'

She sounds angry. I don't understand why.

'Sort of.'

She raises her eyebrows, mouth a flat line. Maybe she's upset I didn't tell her?

'It's early days. We're trying to keep it low key, take things slowly.'

Skylar laughs, harsh and snorty. 'That doesn't sound like Tony.'

I'm not sure if she's out to hurt, just because misery likes company, or if there's more to it. I try to stop my voice getting defensive. 'Well, he's been doing quite a few things differently, ever since he got here.'

She shrugs. 'So the papers say.'

Obviously, I see the implication, that Tony's good behaviour is all an act. It could be sour grapes. Tony's been playing like a man possessed and Sky's as competitive as they come. Everyone going on about how great he's doing must be salt in the wound when she's off form. But it catches like a stone in my shoe. Because there's already a little mental blister that's been brewing since last week's date. Only Sky doesn't know about that. I should ignore her. Concentrate instead on how nice it's been, coming home to Tony every night. Almost like we're a real couple.

Re-running cuddling on the sofa gets me happily over the brow of the hill. There's a little crack in the general rosiness when I pick out the red car. At this distance, it's toy-like. But it hasn't moved from the gateway. I make myself remember dancing in the kitchen. That could easily get me all the way home, and yes, I'm aware how nauseating that sounds. Only Skylar spoils it.

'So, how's the sex?'

Usually, I wouldn't mind her asking. But even if she hadn't made it sound like a challenge, I wouldn't want to talk about it. Not because she'd spread gossip at the club. She's the opposite of a tale-teller, plus there's a certain central defender who's no stranger to Sky's bed. And not because I think Tony would object.

He's told me there are things in his past he regrets. Mainly from when he was younger. Times when he thought something was casual but the woman involved wasn't on the same page. But he's not ashamed of the tabloid stories, or the more salacious rumours that go round the circuit, about his particular tastes. The reverse, if anything. It's something I like about him, part of his general swagger, which makes me feel free when I'm with him. So, if we were having fantastic, chandelier-swinging sex, he'd definitely be OK with me sharing the details with Sky. The problem is we're not.

I must've thought too long. Sky pulls a sympathetic face, though her voice doesn't match. 'Oh dear. Not as good as you'd hoped?'

I look away quickly, so she won't see me biting my lip. 'We haven't. Yet, anyway. Like I said, we're not in any rush.'

Or I think that's what I said. The last bit might have come out a bit jumbled. Skylar stops walking and tries to look at me properly. Luckily, Roudie chooses that moment to check in, making sure he isn't lost before racing off again. I bend over, fussing his ears. As I straighten, I rub my forearm quickly over my eyes. It can't have been as discreet as I'd hoped, because Skylar reaches a hand for my shoulder.

'Oh. Genie, I'm sorry. You know I'm just being mean, don't you?'

'Because you hate everything and everyone. I know.'

Smiling was a mistake. It's pushed tears forward, so I'm not actually crying but my eyes are watery.

Skylar's face becomes earnest, which is rare enough that it makes me feel worse. 'You should take it as a compliment. Tony's so into you, it's hardly surprising, him choking the first couple of times.'

'No. It's not that. I think . . .' I take a gulp of breath. 'I think he doesn't want to.'

It's almost a relief, saying what's been at the back of my mind ever since we got home from the sea.

Skylar laughs, pushing her shoulder into mine. 'Don't be stupid. All he's done since he got here is go on about how much he wants to. It's completely normal, Genie, honestly. You've just forgotten because it's been a while. All you have to do is tell him he's amazing. You're already the world expert on boosting Tony's ego, it'll be the easiest shift you've ever put in.'

'Only it's not that we start and it doesn't, you know, progress.' I focus on a row of poplars three fields over. 'It's that he never tries to initiate anything.'

'Hang on. I've seen him try and initiate, as you put it – which I can't imagine gets Tony all hot under the collar, by the way – in the office. Are you sure you're not missing the signals?'

I swallow hard. 'I might've been, when it seemed like he was just looking for a one-time thing. But since things have got more serious, he's different when it's just us. Like he wants to cuddle, and he'll kiss me. Really kiss me. But any time there's a chance of it being more than that, he stops.'

I know what you're thinking, Tony's trying to stick to taking things slowly. Only you're wrong. Take the date. On the beach, that was an 'I want to rip your clothes off' kiss, for sure. I'll accept there are logistical issues with that on a public beach in October. But when we got home, Tony walked me to the door, kissed my cheek and left. And yes, I get sex on the first date doesn't fit with taking our time. Except you can't tell me there's no middle ground between

266

lifting me up on the kitchen cabinets and a kiss that'd work for a grandparent. Just like there's no point pretending a man who's dying to go to bed would be happy walking me home night after night, then giving me exactly the same sort of kiss.

I call Roudie back before the road and Skylar waits until I've got the lead wrapped round my wrist before she scrunches up her nose.

'He must've gone mushy. Sorry, Genie. What a downer.'

I look at her blankly.

'You know. He's caught feels. And now he's scared to touch his precious one.'

I hadn't considered that. Skylar doesn't give me much time to think about it before she's back to commiserating. 'I know, it's the worst. But you can usually get them over it. You just need to tell him, you're good to go.'

'That's not going to happen.' I don't say because I don't want to ask and hear no, but I think it's implied.

'Then try being super-enthusiastic, any time he comes near you. He should get the message.'

'If I get any more enthusiastic, he'll think I'm auditioning for porn.'

'Based on past girlfriends, I doubt he'd have a problem with it.' Then her voice is back to serious. 'But Genie, I'd tread carefully. I mean, I know he's been fine, since he got here. But last season, if half of what's said is true, he'd not got the best handle on himself. If Tony thinks you're the love of his life, and you don't feel the same, it might go off the rails, big time.'

'I can't see that happening.'

A tractor drives by, forcing us into single file. When it's quiet enough to talk again, Skylar asks, 'You mean you don't think he'll kick off, right, Genie?'

'Umm.'

'Not that you're making wedding mood boards, or anything like that?'

She sounds so disgusted, I almost laugh. 'No, of course I'm not. But I do like him.'

Skylar turns on her heel and faces me. 'How much?'

I shut my eyes. There's an image of Sanchez's wife and son outside our office. I'd dragged myself out to admire him with everyone else, just as the first team emerged from a tactics session. The minute he saw the baby, Tony was right beside me. He didn't say anything, but his body became a shield, hiding his hand caressing my back. Playing down how I feel, it's not going to work. 'Honestly? I think I love him.'

'Oh.' She looks appalled, which I hope says more about her than Tony. 'You don't sound exactly happy about it.'

'Would you be, after what I've just told you?'

Skylar shakes her head. 'But that's easy. If you've both gone all lovey-dovey, you can skip the fun part and go straight to boring relationship sex.'

'Except I think you're wrong, about Tony feeling that way.'

We start walking again, as Sky says, 'I don't see why else he'd be like that.'

I take what my yoga instructor would call a deep cleansing breath. 'I think I've become the green juice girlfriend.'

In my mind, that makes perfect sense. But I've been

thinking about it solidly, ever since Tony got on the team bus yesterday. It's not unreasonable that Skylar's response is, 'What?'

I force a wry smile. 'You know, the one you should want, because it's good for you. But when it comes down to it, you'd far rather have a cocktail.'

Sky narrows her eyes. 'You think you're part of his training strategy?'

I give a small sad nod. 'Not consciously. But yes, I think that's what it comes down to.' I bend over and stroke Roudie, who looks up at me like I'm insane, since he's not one of life's therapy dogs. 'When Tony first started taking an interest, I told Chrissie I thought he was more looking for support than anything else. But I didn't want to believe it, so I let him persuade me he was genuinely keen. How he is now, I think I was right.'

Because it's not just that he doesn't seem to want sex. It's that he wants everything else so much. Even the snuggly, cuddly evenings we've spent together fit. Tony's let slip that physical affection wasn't a big feature of his childhood. So, I can see how our Friday night could have been filling a void, with Tony absent-mindedly stroking my hair as he runs through pre-match analytics. But I bet he never watched an analytics package when Angharad was available.

Sky laughs. 'Sorry, Genie, but you're crazy. Only I suppose you don't get to see Tony watching you any time you walk out of a room. He genuinely looks like he's soaking up Beyoncé carrying the Ballon d'Or.'

As we follow the dense hawthorn hedge round to the

cottage, I'm so busy hoping she's right, I almost forget to check out the red car. And then I wish I hadn't, because glancing back, I'm sure I see something move. But, by the time I turn round properly, there's nothing there except a newish, cleanish, empty red hatchback.

33

A week later, Tony and I haven't talked about the sex situation, because God forbid we behave like emotionally competent humans. I'm in the friends and family box, watching Tony play in the pouring rain. And I keep thinking, how can he read LeMar's mind, but have no idea what's going on in mine? There's a lovely give and go between the two of them. It should end in a goal but Tony pulls up short. I'd have sworn it was nothing major but Tony goes off for treatment, and it's not long before a text pings through from our senior physio, Mark. 'Could you get down to the physio room asap? I've got a bit of a situation.'

I reply instantly, 'On my way.'

Hurtling through the maze of corridors leading to the back-room area of the stadium, I keep telling myself this will be something administrative. Tony hobbled off like it was a hamstring injury, it can't possibly be anything really serious. But when I knock on the physio room door, Mark comes out, pulling the door closed firmly behind him. He takes my elbow and draws me far enough away that a low-voiced near-whisper won't be audible to Tony inside. From his expression, I know he's going to tell me something awful.

'How bad?' I ask, trying to keep my face professionally concerned. Only there must be at least a hint of panic because Mark becomes apologetic.

'Sorry, didn't mean to make it sound life or death.'

I wave my hand impatiently, trying not to show I'm massively relieved. 'So, what is it?'

'Hammie. Not too serious, I think, but bad enough he can't go back on now. We can MRI tomorrow. But I could do a quick ultrasound now, get an initial picture.'

He stops and looks at me expectantly. I'm confused. 'Sorry, Mark. Do you need me to set up a car, get an appointment?'

Mark shakes his closely shaven head. 'No. Look, Genie, this is a weird one. Tony, he's agitated, very insistent he wants you. And I don't think I can get him scanned and sorted until he's calmed down. Do you think you could work your magic?'

'I'll see what I can do. Could you give us a minute?'

Mark nods and drifts towards the end of the hallway.

I knock on the door but open it before I get an answer.

Tony's on his feet, leaning both hands on the physio table, neck bent. He raises his head to me without speaking. And just like when he's happy, he's the world's happiest person, now he's the picture of utter misery. I walk across to him, talking gently, like he's a spooked horse.

'How are you doing? Feeling sore?'

He nods, biting his lip.

I put my hand between his shoulder blades. 'Poor Tony. This isn't very sensible though, is it? Let's get you sitting down, shall we?'

I coax him over to a chair and pull another round, for keeping the leg elevated. Once I've hunted out an icepack and wrapped it in a towel, I place it where the swelling's starting at the back of his thigh. 'Mark said you were a bit upset. Do you want to tell me about it?'

He looks at me, kneeling next to him, then ducks his head away. 'This one, it's bad.'

His voice has a break in it. That's, well, odd. It's not unusual for young players to freak out over something minor, convinced it's career-ending. But Tony's experienced enough to know the drill. And I've seen him furious he's not allowed to keep playing after he's been knocked out or while he's actively bleeding. So, presumably, this isn't about the pain itself.

'Mark doesn't seem to think so.'

Tony looks away but not before I see the tears starting. 'I felt it go.' He wipes his eyes with his forearm. 'Fuck it, Genie, sorry.'

I perch on the table, pulling his head into me and rubbing his back. 'It's all right, darling. It's all right. I know it hurts.'

'It's not that.' His voice is muffled by my sweater.

'Then can you tell me? So I can try to make it better?'

He shakes his head without lifting it, and I can tell from his breathing, he's still crying.

'That's OK. We'll just stay like this for a bit, shall we?'

He nods into my jumper and I kiss his hair, still damp from the rain. Mark pops up at the window in the door, but I shake my head and he disappears. I keep stroking along Tony's spine, like he's woken from a bad dream, then scratch at him gently with my fingertips, trying to bring him back to me. 'You're getting cold. Shall I find you a blanket or something?'

'No, don't go.'

'OK, it's OK. I've got you.'

Gradually, his breathing changes from uneven gulps back to slow and steady and he stops pushing into me quite so hard. I relax my arms, letting him decide when he's ready to break away. And when he does, it's sudden, like he can't bear to be touched. Tony sniffs hard and lifts his arm to wipe his eyes, keeping his face turned away from me. I get up to find tissues and a spare dry top he can change into. It seems like that makes it easier, my back to him. Because he says, in something close to his usual voice, 'Sorry. You must think I'm such a wetwipe.'

I turn to him, holding out tissues and a towel. 'Of course not. You've been playing so well. Having to be out for a bit, it's only natural to be disappointed.'

He takes the towel and begins drying his hair. 'It's not that I'm disappointed over.'

I have this horrible feeling he's going to say Covenly doesn't suit him, he's tried really hard, but it hasn't worked out here, just like we don't work. And that's not me jumping to the worst-case scenario, out of nowhere. It fits with being so upset. Tony's been insanely good all season. If he wants a transfer, the only thing that might put a buyer off is an injury. But even if that's true, he needs someone to listen.

'Isn't it?' I ask, making my voice as open as I can.

'You know it's not.' There's an undertone of anger that I wasn't expecting.

'I'm sorry, Tony. I'm not sure I understand?'

'Yeah, you do. Cos it's you who's disappointed.'

I look at him questioningly.

'Like I'm supposed to be showing you can trust me, and this is what you said'd happen. Buy an overpriced has-been, and watch 'em spend half the season out injured and the rest on and off the bench. Cos there's no chance they'll do ninety minutes. That about right?'

I kneel to his eye level, turning his face to me with a finger under his chin. 'No, Tony. You know I never meant that, even when I said it, not about you. I was just being horrid because I was annoyed.'

'Doesn't mean it weren't true.'

'Except it wasn't. I was talking like this would be your last season, but you've got at least another three or four, probably more. Lots of time to tick off those last few wins you want to add to the collection, I promise.'

'It's not even about that though. Not really.'

I hold his gaze and wait.

'I wanna like pay you back for helping me, being kind, all that. And now, my hamstring's fucked again, and you'll be thinking you've wasted your time.' His voice is thick, like he might cry again any minute.

This feels like we're back to the academy evening. And I don't understand what I'm doing wrong. Because it must be something, or we wouldn't keep treading water, would we? About this, or sex, or anything else.

I try speaking slowly, as if I'm explaining something to a child. 'No, Tony. That's not how it works. If you hadn't put the effort in, hadn't shown up for us, then yes, I'd be thinking that. And that I couldn't trust you, because you'd have been telling me one thing and doing another. But that's not true, is it?'

He shakes his head.

'No, because you've done everything perfectly, from the minute you arrived. Being injured, that's not your fault. And whatever I said when you first got here, that's not how we treat people. Like they're performance cars, or something that can just be discarded as soon as there's a problem. I care about you, so does Mark, so does Chrissie.'

'Cos you're paid to.'

'You must know for me, it's not that. Maybe, to begin with, I didn't show you properly, but I thought I'd stopped hiding it. If I haven't, you must've guessed how much I love . . .' I stop myself, just in time. 'Being around you.'

He does look at me, but his eyes are sulky. 'I don't want you saying stuff like that cos you feels sorry for me.' There's a quick glance at the ceiling, biting down on his lower lip, then an emphatic chop of the hand. 'I want you to be fucking proud of me. Like I am of you.'

'Except that's not always true, is it?'

'Yeah, it is. Course it is.'

'No. We both know, there've been times when you've been lovely to me, not because you think I'm great, but because you wanted to make me feel better.' I stroke his sleeve, where a captain's armband would sit. 'And you're always telling me, I've got to get better at accepting that. So, how about leading by example?'

He reaches for my hand and kisses my fingers. ''Cept I can't get enough of that off of you. So, I should be able to win you some stupid trophy in return, shouldn't I?'

'I don't care about trophies.'

'Yeah, you do. Or I hope so, anyhow. Cos your thing

about midfielders has been my main motivator all season, I can tell you.'

I laugh, the relief of feeling wanted again bubbling through. 'But Tony, what if I don't want the Premier League one? Then you're getting all upset over nothing, aren't you?'

He almost smiles. 'So, which one do you want? And don't say the league cup, cos I don't like being patronized.'

I pull away so he can see my face is exaggeratedly arch. 'Oh no, darling. Obviously, I want the Champions League. After all, if I'd been ready to settle for anything less than the absolute best, I wouldn't be free to cuddle with you now, would I?'

That does make him laugh, a quick short burst, despite himself. 'Well, yeah, obviously I'd like to get you that one, not least cos I reckon there's no limit on what you'd do for me afterwards. Only, Genie, my beauty, it might not be realistic, not first season anyhow. But if my leg's not fucked, I'll give it my best.'

I smile more softly. 'That's all I can ever ask. And seriously, Tony, I do care about you. You, not your stats or your minutes played. And if this is a bad injury, we'll all help you get back. But I don't get the impression Mark thinks it is, so why don't we let him take a look?'

Tony nods. 'Yeah, OK.' He looks away again, and I think there's a last tear, because his arm is up at his face again. 'Genie?'

'Yep.'

'You're really nice, you know? Like I'm not just into you for your looks, I like properly likes you. You get that, right?'

I don't look at him, because I don't think he'd welcome it. 'I like you too,' I say, heading for the door.

When I beckon to Mark, he mimes closing the door and I walk to meet him.

'All sorted?' he whispers.

'I think so. He just panicked that it'd be like last season, with him out for ages.'

Mark gives me a long look. 'If you say so. Come with me, will you? While I do the scan?'

When we walk in, it's obvious Tony's got himself together, because he's back to looking like the room belongs to him. He makes a play of being shamefaced. 'Sorry, Mark, mate. Got myself in a bit of a state.'

Mark shrugs as he gets the ultrasound ready. 'No worries. Let's take a look see.'

Tony reaches for my hand. I can't believe Mark would say anything to anyone, so I take it and let Tony squeeze down on my fingers as the probe pushes into the injured muscle.

Mark scans back and forth, then looks up at Tony. 'I'll run the images by Chrissie after the game, and she'll maybe want the MRI to be a hundred per cent sure, but it looks like a grade one, maybe borderline two to me. So, probably two weeks out max.'

Tony laughs like a slightly embarrassed lion. 'I look a right idiot now, don't I? Crying like some snotty-nosed kid over a minor tear. I just, you know, like felt it, and it seemed worse.'

Mark makes polite noises as he begins placing a compression bandage. I squeeze Tony's hand and he looks up at me. 'Any excuse to get time up close and personal with you, hey?'

I laugh but Mark looks distinctly disapproving. 'God, Tony. It's to be hoped Monica's insurance covers sexual harassment claims.'

Tony grins up at me. 'I confine it to Genie, cos she understands me. Don't you, love?'

I grin. 'I'm not sure I'd go as far as that, and really, I am only hanging around to watch you change your shirt. So, can you get on with it, or I'll miss the end of the second half?'

Tony pulls off the damp shirt slowly, stretching each muscle. I smile my most lascivious smile. Mark laughs, so I think he buys the back and forth between me and Tony being at least ninety per cent play-acting.

Tony starts hobbling out. 'I'd best be getting back out on the bench myself. Don't want it all over the papers tomorrow that I'm seriously crocked again.'

I go to leave too, but Mark gestures for me to stay. He waits until Tony's out of earshot. 'Genie, I'll have to pass this on to the coaching staff.'

'Pass what on?' I ask warily.

'How he was before you came down. The leg might not be too bad, but psych wise, something's not right for him to be getting like that.'

I sigh. 'Honestly, it's not a big issue. What he said to me, I won't go into the details, but I think he's feeling like he's got something to prove.'

Mark shrugs. 'Well, yeah, he has.'

'But not to us. Or it shouldn't be, anyway.'

'Family till we die, or they transfer out for bigger wages,' Mark says, his face ironic.

'Or we push them out because they're not performing or they're injured.' I know I sound snappy but I don't feel apologetic.

Mark shakes his head. 'You're too soft-hearted, talking like they're racehorses off to the dog food factory. If Tony crashes and burns here, he'll go to Saudi or the States and get a massive pay-out for doing nothing.'

'Except that's not what Tony wants. And the last thing he needs is everyone watching to see if he's about to crack up. So, couldn't you just pretend today didn't happen?'

'Genie . . .'

'Please?'

He grimaces. 'All right, if it means that much to you. But be careful, OK?'

'Don't worry, I know, he's a huge asset.'

'I meant careful of him, not with him.' His hand brushes my elbow. 'Look, I know it's not my business, but there's been talk about you and him, and him and that model, or whatever she is. And honestly, I just think you deserve better than that, second time around.'

If he'd said that yesterday, it might've bothered me. But how Tony was just now, I trust that a hundred times more than club gossip.

34

Tony leapt at my offer of a lift home, but he's quiet until we're done with busy roads. Once we hit winding lanes, he says, 'Sorry, Genie. About earlier.'

I glance across quickly, smiling. 'Don't be.'

There's a pause, then, 'And me and you, we're OK, are we?'

'Of course. Better than OK.'

He touches my hand on the gear stick. 'That's good. Cos the last week or so, it's felt like maybe you've been pulling back a bit.'

I suspect that played into this afternoon, but I keep staring down the path of the headlights. 'Not really. I got a tiny bit insecure over something that's not important. That's all.'

His hand closes over mine. 'Yeah, well, I reckon I've just shown you, I'm not exactly slow to get that way myself – where you're concerned, anyhow. But, like, for the future, it'd be easier if you just tells me what you're thinking.' There's a flicker of real pain in his voice. The last thing I want is to make his life harder.

'Sorry. It's hard sometimes, staying open. But I'm trying.'

'I know, beauty. And I'd been thinking you was ready to step things up a bit. But if you're not, I can hold off, if that's what you need.'

'It's not.' My voice is firm.

'Thank Christ for that.'

I look across to him, and he's grinning. We don't talk any more. But anytime I can take my eyes off the road, the smile between us feels like everything's going to be all right. So, I'm ashamed to say, when we pull up outside the cottage, I'm irritated to see Skylar sitting on the doorstep. That would be mean at the best of times, but it's even worse today. She looks bereft, arms tight around her knees and her face all pinched.

I make a disappointed face at Tony. 'I'm sorry. I was looking forward to it being just us.'

He reaches over and brushes my cheek. 'Me too. Want me to get lost, so you can deal with this?'

'Actually, would you mind helping me out?'

There's a dart of his eyes, searching for an escape. 'I dunno. I'm not exactly the best person when it comes to relationship advice.'

It's lucky Sky wasn't able to hear that. People cry over her, not the other way around. 'It won't be that. And honestly, you're probably uniquely qualified to get her feeling better.' I smile at him. 'But if you can't face it, I do understand.'

He still looks unenthusiastic. Comforting Skylar has to be the last thing he wants to do when he's in pain, but he shrugs. 'Nah, I reckon with you, there's always going to be a fair number of waifs and strays. I might as well get used to it early.'

I have to suppress an excessively bright smile before I wave to Skylar. I mean, he wouldn't say that if he wasn't serious about us, would he? As I get out of the car, I do my reflex check for the red Ford I saw lurking the other day, but I'm not really expecting it to be there. I haven't seen it since Tony got back last week. So, it was probably nothing. Just a valuable lesson about not getting worked up over shadows.

Walking up the path, I think Tony's exaggerating the hobbling a touch, making sure I get to Skylar first to mop up any major hysterics. But today, it seems like it's too serious for dramatics. As I reach her, she gets up and asks quietly, 'Can I have a hug?'

I wrap her up in my arms. Skylar burrows her head into my shoulder. Holding her tight with one hand, I pull my keys out of my pocket with the other and pass them back to Tony. The minute he's got the door open, Roudie bursts out. Tony catches my eye over Skylar's shoulder. 'I'll take care of the pup, shall I? Get him fed while you two have a bit of a cuddle?'

'Please.' I guide Skylar round to my side, keeping my arm around her. 'Come on. Let's go and sit down.'

By the time we're on the sofa, the tears have started. I stroke her hair and make soothing noises, until Tony can't draw out looking after Roudie any longer. He puts a box of tissues on my lap and takes his time getting settled, leg elevated. Skylar blows her nose loudly and wipes at her eyes, spreading salty kohl streaks down her cheeks. She glares, determined not to cry in front of Tony. It exaggerates how young she looks when she's upset. I feel like the mother of an overly determined twelve-year-old, when I ask, 'Did you not get picked, sweetie?'

'No. Jenny'll start and Nas will be reserve. I don't travel.'

She sounds tyre-slashing mad, but I think that's mainly for Tony's benefit. Sky's been fighting all season to keep her first-team slot, so losing it has to cut deep.

I say I'm sorry, but then I leave space, willing Tony to take over. Whatever he has to say will be a hundred times more helpful.

Skylar's less patient. 'It's so unfair,' comes out in a wail.

Tony sits back and sniffs, almost as if he's amused.

Skylar looks at him. 'What would you know about it?'

He smiles, and at least it's soft. 'A fair bit, actually, love. I used to get like you and then some, if I didn't get picked. Till it was pointed out to me, you're not owed your spot, you earns it.'

'It's not the same for you,' Skylar retorts, eyes sulky.

'What, because I'm a man?' asks Tony, his eyes blazing.

I force myself to sound calm. 'It's not about that. But you've never had to take a second job. What Sky's paid for playing barely covers her bills.'

Maddeningly, Tony shrugs. 'Yeah, but who plays isn't 'bout who's got the hardest-luck story. All that counts is performance.' He looks over to Sky. 'So how big's the difference between you and this Jenny?'

I'm expecting Skylar to snap, but she tilts her head back and forth. 'She's not way better, just sharper. Or for the last few weeks, anyway.'

Tony glances at me and sighs. 'Look, Sky, I'm gonna have time on my hands this week. How about I have a go at a spot of coaching, see if we can't close the gap?'

I'd expect her to bite Tony's hand off, but she looks ready to turn him down. Then she shakes her head. It's not a no, more like she's trying to dislodge something that's stuck. 'Yeah. All right, if you like,' she manages, finally.

Tony ignores the missing thank you. 'Might as well start now then. You got some replays we can look over?'

Skylar goes to fetch her bag, discarded in the hall. While she's washing her face, Tony smiles at me, like there's a shared joke.

'Be nice, Tony, won't you? She's more fragile than she looks.'

Tony grins. 'Fragile like a tank.' I'm about to tell him he's wrong, when he says more seriously, 'Trust me, Genie. It's what she needs. She'll work a hell of a lot harder if she hates me.'

And maybe it's not just Skylar he can read. Because his fingers stay intertwined with mine, even as he stops the match recordings every few minutes to pick up a positioning error or a lost opportunity for a run. And when it's time to leave, the goodnight kiss isn't quite the full-on passion I want, but it's definitely turned up a few notches.

35

Two Thursdays later

Pulling around the last sweep of the lodge's gravel drive, my headlights catch the shine of LeMar's silver Merc. I'm already giddy over Tony offering to host Katia's employment anniversary dinner, but that pushes me into an-under-ten-on-Christmas-morning territory. Because Tony's told me he's been busy building bridges, but LeMar being here is the first evidence it's working.

That could be just what Tony and I need. Because we're still not actually sleeping together, unless you count me drifting off, head in Tony's lap, while he catches up on the NBA. But goodnights have progressed to heavy breathing, back-against-the-wall kisses, and when Tony's pressed against me, it certainly feels like he wants more. And a very effusive thank you, maybe that's all it will take to get us there?

I've spent enough time at Tony's, I don't think he'll care if I let myself in. But as I close the lodge's heavy front door, Skylar comes dancing across the hall. She's draped in a towel, still dripping from the pool. There's no use pretending she doesn't look gorgeous. Her summer tan is beginning to fade so her tattoos show bright against her skin. And she's completely fit, healthy and, based on her wide-open smile, extremely happy.

I should play fair and let them know I'm here. But instead, I sink back into the darkness, knowing Skylar won't notice me as she practically pirouettes into the kitchen, calling, 'Tony?'

There's a gilt-framed mirror giving a view into the kitchen. Tony's like one of those Dutch oil paintings, the gold light picking out the movement in his face as he smiles. The chances of this being a scene I want to watch are basically zero, but I stay frozen where I am, my hand on the panelling behind me.

'You look pleased with yourself,' Tony says, with a laugh mixed in.

The mirror only shows Skylar's back, but I can tell from her voice she's grinning. 'So I should be. I'm starting Saturday. Mo just called.'

Tony gives her one of his more serious smiles this time. 'That's great, love. You deserve it, the work you've put in.'

Skylar lets the towel drop. 'And that you put in.' She takes a step towards him, her arms wide, ready to embrace him.

Tony holds his hands out, keeping the distance between them.

Skylar laughs. 'Don't you want me to say thank you?'

Tony shakes his head. 'Not necessary, Sky.'

'It might be fun,' she says, her voice softer now.

Tony's face is grave. 'I'm sure it would. But not the sort I'm looking for right now. And Sky, don't be offended or nothing, but I've gotta say something you might not wanna hear.'

'Go ahead, my skin's quite thick.' Skylar's voice borders on sulky, and I hope he's going to do this nicely.

'All right then. You wanna be taken serious, right? As serious as the men.'

'Obviously.'

'Well then, look. I never kissed nobody for training me. And I've not slept with 'em neither. So maybe it'd be a good idea to have a think 'bout that?'

It says a lot for Skylar's strength of character that her response is 'Fair enough,' as she rearranges her towel. Once it's secure, she follows up with, 'I am grateful though.'

Tony shakes his head. 'Don't be. I mean, I don't mind helping out. But it's not like I did it out of the goodness of my heart. I just thought it'd help me get in your boss's good books, doing something for someone that matters to her.'

'And now you think I'm a bad person, because I came on to you when you're into Genie?'

'Nah. I dunno as Genie's decided she wants me yet. But till she tells me no, I'm not looking to do nothing that'll push her in that direction. So, you're a good-looking girl and all that, but . . .' He opens his hands.

'But I'm not Genie.'

'Exactly. And she's what I'm needing.' His smile is apologetic.

Skylar laughs. 'Not a mouthy kid with an ego as big as yours?'

'Fraid not. Not even a real pretty one.'

'Probably for the best. You'd only get jealous when my stats got better than yours.' She turns to walk out, then looks over her shoulder. 'By the way, I can't see Genie telling you no.'

Honestly, I do feel bad for eavesdropping, but I can't pretend I'm sorry to have overheard. I'm not upset with Skylar, or not really anyway. It's not like I didn't have some warning. Every time Tony strolled into the office to collect her for a training session, she'd get weirdly hostile. You didn't have to be a genius to guess at the start of a crush. And Sky's still at the age where other people's boyfriends, or more realistically, other people's possible future boyfriends, are fair game. Plus, Tony's basically irresistible, so I'm at most mildly annoyed. And it's lovely, seeing Tony taking care to turn her down so gently.

All the same, I decide this is the moment for me to appear. I sneak back to ease the front door open, then slam it behind me, calling, 'Tony, do you mind? I let myself in.'

He comes out of the kitchen beaming. Skylar's a step or two behind, looking, for her, ever so slightly sheepish.

'Genie, love, you made it.' He hugs me then holds me away from him. 'Hard day?'

'Not particularly, just long.'

Tony looks like he's about to joke but then he looks at Skylar, fidgeting like a toddler anxious to show her latest fingerpainting masterpiece, and asks, 'You wanna tell Genie?'

'Tell me what?'

'I'm back in the team.'

I smile at her, and hope it looks adequately spontaneous. 'Oh, that's wonderful. I'm so pleased. I'd hug you instead, but you're all damp, and Tony's nice and dry.'

Skylar laughs. 'And nice and toney?'

I laugh back but it's Tony I'm staring up at as I stroke the hard muscle of his arm through the long-sleeved black t-shirt. 'Yes, and nice and Tony.'

He looks borderline embarrassed. It's one of his more charming expressions, not least because he doesn't use it often. 'Food will be about ten, fifteen minutes. So, Sky, you go change and tell Katia and LeMar to do the same, all right?'

She drifts off towards the pool as Tony and I walk into the kitchen, his arm still around me. I lean back against the work surface, watching as Tony pours a glass of red.

He hands it across, letting his fingers touch mine. 'Sounds like you deserve this, from what Katia was saying.'

I shake my head. 'It wasn't that big a problem to unpick.' That's not quite true. But we should be doing this at mine. Tony only offered to host because I got trapped at work, figuring out why my quarterly accounts had suddenly stopped adding up. And I don't want him thinking about that. I need Tony thoroughly relaxed, not worrying that the troublemaker's back. God knows, it makes me tense enough that I reach round to rub my shoulders.

'You achy, love?' Tony asks.

'A bit. It's hunching over the computer all day.'

'Do you want me to do something about it?' Tony asks, and there's an endearing touch of hesitancy.

I make sure the eye contact is direct when I nod, trying to show this won't be a repeat of the night he found me in the hot tub. 'Yes, please.'

His smile is extra broad. 'Bring your wine, then.'

I take his hand, but walk behind him. He looks back

over his shoulder. 'We'll do this in the living room. It's not as good as using a bed, but I don't want the kids getting the wrong idea, OK?'

I smile and nod.

He pushes open the door to the sitting room, but it's me who shuts it.

'You wearing a bra that'll give you a bit of coverage, or do you want me to get you a towel?'

I'm not remotely worried about it, it's nothing he hasn't seen before. 'The bra's fine.'

I stay facing him as I unbutton my shirt, taking my time, letting the silk slip between my fingers. Tony stares, his eyes fixed on me even as he slumps down onto the sofa. I'm just about to shrug the blouse to the floor when he stands up. 'You know what? This isn't a good idea.'

His voice is ice-bath cold and even before he's finished saying it, he's walking out. And it's like I've run into a glass door, the shock hitting before the pain.

Dinner's torture. As soon as I decently can, I begin making noises about it having been a long day.

The others try to get me to stay, apart from Tony, who's straight on his feet. 'I'll drive you.'

So, no nice romantic stroll home then. I guess whatever he has to say can't be going to take long. All the same, I'm not sure I'm ready to hear it. And I point out my car is here, that being the perfect excuse to get out of it, for now, anyway.

'You've had a drink.'

'One glass. It'll be fine.'

'I'll drive you,' he says firmly.

I look at him, trying to decide what he's thinking and failing miserably. 'OK, you drive.'

We walk out together, but Tony doesn't use the cold night air as an excuse to cuddle. Instead, he heads to the driver's door of my car, hand stretched behind him for the keys. And he forces the car into gear, roaring off before my seatbelt is even done up. We don't talk, until we're almost at the cottage, when I can't bear it any more. Even though I know it sounds pathetic, I ask, 'Did I do something wrong?'

He still doesn't look at me. 'Worried you've overplayed your hand, love?'

'I wasn't playing.'

Tony pulls onto the verge outside my house and turns the engine off.

'You sure about that?' His voice is granite hard.

'Very,' comes out too small to sound confident, but I think we've reached the point where that doesn't matter. I mutter something about it being all right and reach for the door handle. Tony slumps forward, head against his hands on the steering wheel. 'Give me a sec, Genie.'

I'm not sure if that means go or stay. I freeze, hand still halfway to the door. There's a minute or two of silence, then Tony clenches his fist.

'Fuck it.' His voice is quiet. He turns his head sideways, cheek on his hand, eyes on me. 'I can't win, can I?'

'What do you mean?'

He sits up sharply, running his fingers through his hair. 'Cos you're like leading me on, but the minute I go near you, you run a mile. Isn't that right?'

I pull my hand into my lap, shrinking back in my seat at the harshness of his voice. 'No. I was trying to show you, I'm ready.' I push at my hair, trying to hide the hurt on my face. 'I understand why you might not believe that, after how I behaved before. But trust me, it's not one way, Tony.'

He shuts his eyes, then looks back at me. His gaze is softer, even if his mouth is still tense. 'Sorry, I'm not having a go. What I'm trying to say, it's coming out wrong. But, you know what I said, 'bout making a break?'

'When you first arrived, yes.' I try to sound bright, like it isn't obvious he's missing everything he left behind.

'A big part of that was breaking from my ex.'

'Angharad?'

He looks surprised, or maybe caught out. 'You know 'bout that?'

I try to maintain unbothered. 'Umm. I mean, I know you kept it out of the papers, but this is a small world, isn't it? There are always rumours.'

'I guess. But they don't always cover the full extent of what's gone on.'

'No, probably never the full extent.'

He nods. 'Yeah, like with Angharad, I got in properly over my head, you know?'

'I didn't, but tell me.' I go to touch his knee, but he pulls away.

'Leave it, can you, Genie?'

'Sorry.'

'I can't go through all this with you like that.'

'OK.'

He stares straight ahead. 'So, Angharad, she's probably

the best-looking woman I've ever seen, on the surface.' I want to crawl away, but if Tony realizes I don't want to hear this, it doesn't show. 'And she's a good bit younger than me.'

I nod, which he probably can't see.

'At the age where she's starting to enjoy having a bit of power. Wanting to find out what her looks get her, you know?'

I make a non-committal noise. If he still loves her, he can criticize but I can't.

'And I should have enough mileage on me not to have got drawn into that. But I couldn't resist her. Like I'd know she was pulling my strings, but I'd go for it every time. And that was playing into the fitness issues, the discipline issues. She couldn't get enough of that. Of knowing I was throwing everything away. Cos it was proof I'd do anything for her, I guess.'

'And tonight, you realized you still feel that way about her?' I ask, my voice over-controlled.

He does look at me now. 'No, Christ, no. It was that I felt for a minute, watching you, like you was doing the same. Playing with me, seeing how far you can push.'

'Oh, Tony, no.'

'So, what was that then? If it weren't you testing me out?'

I look out of the window at the darkness for a minute, then back at him.

'I was playing. But not like you mean. One of the things I like about you is how you can make me feel desirable, when I don't feel that way very often.'

He starts to say something, but I shake my head. 'No,

I'm not fishing for compliments. What I'm saying is, yes, I was letting myself tease you, just a little. And I was enjoying it, and sort of thinking, maybe tonight, we'd end up in bed and everything would start properly. But not so I could hurt you, not to see what I could get from you. Just because it's part of it, isn't it? The teasing, the playfulness. Part of lust or desire, or however you want to put it.' I have to look away for a second, so he doesn't see the start of a tear. 'And we're good at that, me and you. Or we are when it doesn't count. But any time there's a hint of things going anywhere, it stops. And I can see now, it's not me who isn't ready, it's you.' This time when I reach for his knee, he doesn't pull away. 'And Tony, that's OK. All you'll need to get back to that is time. But I'm not the right person to help you get there.'

'I need you.'

'But you don't want me, or we wouldn't be having this conversation.' I shift my hand from his knee to take his fingers, and squeeze gently.

'You really think that?'

'Umm, I'm afraid so.'

'Then I'm no use to you, am I?' His voice is flat and he's still not looking at me. ''Cos you'd had as much rejection as you could take, hadn't you? Before I ever showed up.'

I nod. 'And that means I can't be the one who pulls you back in. It's no one's fault, no one's to blame. But there's no point pretending this is going to work.'

He starts to say something but I don't think I can hold it together much longer. 'No, Tony, let's leave it, shall we?'

'For now, or for permanent?'

296

'Permanent, I think.' I lean over, kiss his cheek lightly, take the keys from the ignition and get out of the car. It's not until I close the front door that I hear the driver's door slam shut. I sink onto the cold tiles in the hall. Rouden comes to lick my face dry. Tears freak him out.

36

I must have slept because a ping from WhatsApp wakes me. But my brain's so fuzzy, it takes effort to process Tony's message:

> I can't let you go over something that's not even true. You thinking I don't want you makes no sense. I'm beyond attracted to you and have been since day one. Please come over tonight & let me prove it. I swear I won't bottle it again
> 07.01

It breaks my heart, but that doesn't really change anything.

We both know you're trying to force yourself into committing to me because you think it's the right thing to do. Being your safe, boring choice isn't enough for me
07.05

> If you was safe, I'd not be losing my mind over you
> 07.06

I thought that's how you feel about Angharad?
07.07

It's not until I press send that I realize the jealousy is obvious.

> I don't feel nothing for her any more. And if this is
> about you thinking you're second best, that's so easy
> to fix. You're my number one, all-time best, 🐹 , no
> question. What've you got to lose by giving me one
> last chance to show you?
> 07.09

I stare at the empty pillow beside me.

> OK. I'll come over after work.
> 07.15

> Thank you, thank you, thank you
> xxxxxxxxxxxxxxxxxxxx
> 07.16

We always check deliveries on arrival, so while the leather-clad courier exaggeratedly checks his watch, I snap open boxes from Claudia's Fine Jewellery. Two are pieces commissioned back in September, since Claudia won't sacrifice quality for speed, even when it's a player needing a Christmas present. The last is a square box, in Claudia's signature purple.

The ring inside is distinctively hers too. The band is broader than a typical engagement ring. But the square-cut diamond is so perfect in its simplicity, it couldn't be anything else. Only it's not the diamond that holds my attention, it's the little rubies, scattered through the gold like drops of blood. The courier coughs. I scrawl a signature, but I'm fixed back on the ring before he's even out of the door. Well, on the ring and the genie's lamp on my desk, because the similarity's obvious. I check the package, it's addressed to Tony, and it must've been included with the others by mistake, because the address is the lodge, not the club. So, I guess I wasn't meant to see it.

I sit, staring at the ring, a cold, dead feeling creeping up inside. Skylar saunters in and launches into a story about training. I make noises like I'm listening, until she stops mid-sentence.

'What's wrong, Genie?'

I hold out the ring box. 'Guess whose?'

She looks at the ring.

'Yours?' Her voice is chilly, so even if I said it was, I doubt there'd be congratulations.

'No, I just signed for it.' I sound surprisingly normal.

Skylar prods the open box. 'Is it me or does it remind you of your lamp?'

I give a small shrug. Skylar's been in Player Care long enough to learn men are magpies. Borrowing something here, something there, until when they put it all together, it seems like it's just for you. And the genie thing, it's a lovely little morsel to add to the collection. I'd bet you anything, Tony's got a whole make-my-wish-come-true routine worked out to go with the ring.

'He'd have ordered it when, end of August, beginning of September?' Skylar asks. That's another thing she's picked up working here, the wait time for custom jewellery.

I nod and she says flatly, 'For Angharad then, you think?'

'Umm.'

Skylar snorts. 'What a bastard.'

Everything feels just out of reach, and my voice has the same far-away quality when I say, 'That's not necessarily fair.'

'Don't defend him. He's been all over you from the start. Now it turns out he's still tangled up with her.'

'You don't know that. Like you say, he must've ordered this almost as soon as he got here. Just because it wasn't over between them then, doesn't mean things didn't change.'

I say it like that would make everything fine between me and Tony, only obviously, it wouldn't. The picture Tony painted last night doesn't fit with an engagement ring. But now, I know when Tony was standing in my garden, saying he'd missed me, he was planning at one point on asking Angharad to marry him. So, he's lied to me, it's just the size of the lie that's up for debate.

Skylar pulls out her phone, shaking her head. She scrolls for a second, then pokes it at me. 'Only there's this, too.'

The screen's open on Angharad's social media. Or, more specifically, on a photo of Angharad wearing a Covenly shirt. There's a match playing on the TV behind her, and the caption is three grey heart emojis. I'm about to say that's not necessarily anything to do with Tony, when Skylar says, 'I asked in the shop. She was on the last players' list.'

Players constantly get shirt requests from friends, family and fans, and each player has an allowance of freebies.

The latest list would have been a month ago, about when Tony and I were walking on the beach. So, the same time that I was making a conscious effort not to think about Angharad, let alone internet stalk her.

'Oh.' I can't say any more.

'I'm sorry, Genie. I should've told you right away.' Skylar puts a hand on my shoulder. 'Only I didn't want to upset you if it was just a misunderstanding, or a mistake or something.'

Suddenly her training with Tony takes on a different light. Or it would, if I hadn't seen her in Tony's kitchen. I narrow my eyes. 'Why come on to Tony, then?'

'He told you?'

'No, of course not. I saw, when I walked in.'

Skylar shuffles her feet. 'Well, there've been a few rumours about Tony and Angharad, right from when he started, but I wasn't convinced they were true. And at first, you didn't seem to want anything serious, so I didn't think it mattered much either way. Only when you, um, said you . . .'

She looks down and I finish for her. 'Love him?'

She nods. 'I decided to look into it a bit more, so I started going through her socials. And I thought the shirt probably was nothing. I mean, it's their agents half the time, isn't it? Putting in the requests. Only I knew, if I asked, he'd say that, so . . .'

'You thought you'd test him?' I ask, flatly.

Skylar nods, then crinkles up her brow. 'And when he didn't go for it, I thought it was OK, that proved he was only interested in you. So I didn't need to tell you.' She waits for my face to change. When it doesn't, she sighs. 'Sorry, Genie, it was a stupid thing to do, wasn't it?'

I tell myself she doesn't have much experience of actual adult relationships. 'No, it's all right. It's just not quite how things work.' Even with how awful I feel, I almost laugh. 'I mean, I know you're gorgeous. But with Kat and LeMar in the next room, and me about to turn up, did you honestly expect him to pounce on you?'

She shrugs. 'The old Tony would've done.' She reaches out a hand to rest tentatively on my shoulder. 'So, maybe the ring is old news?'

I sigh. 'I don't know. Tony and I will have to talk.'

I don't hear what Skylar says next, because the whole time we've been talking, I've been scrolling. It's been an endless stream of Angharad in workout wear, or pyjamas with her girlfriends, or showing off some product. There are coy little messages mixed in, all variants of 'Why is it men find it so hard to say what they feel?' They're suggestive, but not out of line with Tony's version of their relationship. But then a photo stops me dead. It's Angharad with tiger-striped eye-shadow and a chirpy caption about how her new sweatshirt is such a generous gift and it's arrived just in time for her fierce Halloween make-up tutorial. And she's wearing a gold and purple zebra-striped top. My zebra-striped top.

I jerk my shoulder to get rid of Skylar's hand. 'I've got to go. Call me if something comes up, OK?'

I rush to the car, grabbing a padded envelope from the supply closet on my way. But I don't go straight home. I stop at the lodge, let myself in and leave the re-packaged ring on the kitchen table, as if the cleaner signed for it.

No pressure, but any idea what time you'll get here?
20.01

I won't be coming
20.05

Something come up at work? Because I don't care if
it's late
20.06

No
20.07

What's happened?
20.08

I don't reply.

Trying to do this by text is stupid. I'm coming over. OK?
20.17

There's no need
20.18

He doesn't respond.

There's a knock on the door loud enough to wake
Roudie. I shut him in my bedroom, I can't face seeing his
delight at Tony's mere presence.

I stand in the doorway, my arm stretched across to the
opposite side of the frame.

Tony looks at me, head to one side. 'We're going to do this on the doorstep, are we?'

'I think that's best.'

Tony shrugs. 'Whatever works for you. But I dunno what's got you so het up you can't bring yourself to let me in.' His face becomes exquisitely gentle. 'So how's about you have a go at telling me, beauty?'

I can't bring myself to say anything about the ring, so I hold out my phone. He looks at the photo of Angharad. 'What of it?'

'If you can't see it, this conversation is even more pointless than I thought.'

He looks at the photo more closely and doubles down on his thinking face. 'You upset it's the same as yours?' His voice is questioning, and if anything, that fuels my temper.

'Ten out of ten.'

He breathes out hard, like he's taken a blow. 'Cos you think I gave it her?'

I give him a nasty, closed-mouthed smile. 'Aren't you doing well?'

He shakes his head. 'I swear I didn't. The whole time she was with me, she was on at me 'bout setting up a deal with 'em. They must've sent it her.'

It sounds so convincing, I almost believe him. But I've seen the ring, so I know he's capable of recycling a romantic gesture. At least this time, it's one of his. 'What a coincidence.'

'That's all it is, though, love.' He takes a step towards me, dropping his chin, making sure his puppy dog eyes have maximum effect. 'That top, I got it for you cos it's zebra stripes for my lioness. You know that, right?'

'Then it's a shame I've no interest in being part of a pride.'

'Genie, you're not hearing me. It's you I want, just you, no one else. And 'specially not her.' He reaches out but I wrench my arm back. He sighs. 'Look, I don't like talking bad 'bout women I've been with. But if you need details, I can give you 'em. Cos honestly, she was a nightmare, start to finish. Like she was only ever interested in using my profile to boost hers. Well, that and my money, maybe. Not that I didn't deserve it, cos I wasn't doing nothing more than following her round too. And we'd row all the time over me not wanting to go public, and every time, she'd cheat. Then I would, just to prove I could.'

He drops a beat, waiting for me to say something. When I don't, the words start pouring out again. 'It wasn't like we even liked each other much. Like you, you can really make me laugh, but God, I used to find her so fucking boring. And I know, I should've cut it off, soon as I felt like that. But it ended up being this stupid competition. And I knew that's all it was, but I'd got into that mindset, you know, 'bout not backing out of a tackle. It took coming here to break me out of it. Coming here, and meeting you. It's you that's sorted me out, got me playing again, got me back to who I was. I promise, I've not spoken to her, not touched her, not been near her, since.' He fixes his eyes on mine. 'Please, Genie, you've gotta believe me, I've never done nothing behind your back.'

Everything about him screams that he's telling the truth.

But if he really felt that way, he'd never have bought that ring. So, all Tony's doing is proving that off the field, he's every bit as good a player as he is on it.

'Except I don't.'

'Don't what?' he asks.

'Believe you.'

'Then how about you try listening?' It sounds like it's a struggle, keeping his voice soft.

'No, Tony. You forget, I know this world. You think I'm the sort of woman who'll help you make your targets. But I'm not the nice girl who cooks the right food, gets you up in time for training, sucks you off when you can't sleep. The one you come home to after you're done with whoever's younger and prettier this week.'

He steps back sharply. 'I dunno how you can talk like that. When all I've done is try and take care of you.'

'I don't remember asking for that.'

'No, but you never ask for nothing, do you? Cos you don't need no one. Cos you're so fucking happy as you are, aren't you? That's why you're measuring your portions and working out the whole time, and spending half your life slapping on make-up. Cos you're so satisfied with what you've got.' The anger drains away, as fast as it came. He puts his hand to his face. 'Sorry, love. Sorry, I shouldn't have said none of that.'

'At least it's honest,' I say quietly.

'Only it's not. Not really.'

'Except we both know it is. And Tony, that's exactly why this doesn't work, why me and you don't work.'

'I don't understand.'

I can't bring myself to say it's because you don't like me, let alone want me, you just think you should. And anyway, I don't think it's necessary, I'm sure he knows it already. 'Tony, you do. So, now's the time to go.'

He turns his head away and wipes an elbow over his eyes. 'If you can't trust me, maybe it is.' He walks down the path without looking back.

This time, I'm awake before the early-morning message comes through because I haven't slept.

> Please don't delete this before you've read it. I can see now, I come with a ton of baggage and that's more weight than you can carry. I wanted to make it clear I'll respect that, and won't be making stuff difficult for you at the club or nothing. I wish we could've worked but I hope you find a good guy who can give you the security you couldn't get off me. Till then, if there's anything you need, you know where I am.
> 06.47

> I just realized that last bit sounded like I'm still looking for an in. But all I meant was we never finish sorting the stuff with your computer. If you ever don't feel safe, I want you to know you can come to me.
> 06.49

The thing I hate about WhatsApp is how the sender can tell the minute you've read the message. There's no chance to think before you reply. Or cry, which is what I want to do more than anything in the world. Because I love him so much, and those messages sound like he feels the same. But he proved last night he can lie to me like it's nothing, so that doesn't mean anything.

I settle for:

> Thank you. I appreciate you being kind, but I think we both said what we needed to, and it's best to put an end to going back and forth. If there's anything you need from the club, I'm always happy to help.
> 06.52

He messages back:

> You don't have to worry. I'm done behaving like a spoilt brat anytime things don't go my way. I plan on keeping my form up
> 06.54

> That wasn't what I meant
> 06.55

The two ticks turn blue but he doesn't reply. I suppose I should be happy. It's exactly what I asked for.

37

I've just met Tony in the hallway. You'd think almost a month and a half after we stopped something that never really started, that wouldn't matter. But it does. Enough that the semi-greeting between two people who aren't talking, simply because there's nothing to say, is the worst thing that's happened today. That's saying something. We're in the frantic run-up to the Christmas season and the players are scheduled so tight, they don't know if they're coming or going. Every time I see anyone, they need something. Apart from Tony, obviously, unless it's to hurry away as fast as he can.

So, it's unfortunate that the first thing I do when I get into the office is knock over a precariously balanced plate of biscuits. And it's even more unfortunate that the first person I see is Katia.

'What on earth are those doing there?' My voice is sharp with the exhausted irritation that's been prickling away since I woke up.

Katia's already scrabbling around on the floor for cookie fragments. 'I'm sorry, Genie. I'll clear it up.'

'That wasn't what I asked. Why are they there? And come to that, why is any of this here?' I sweep my arm around, to encompass the stacks of pastries, bowls of sweets and platters of biscuits that fill every available surface. 'It looks like we're working on a gingerbread house to trap the academy kids.' Which would be appropriate, given what a witch I sound. But I can't stop myself adding, 'And there's no point just picking up those big bits, there are crumbs everywhere. We'll end up with vermin.'

'I'll get a dustpan and brush.' Katia straightens and scuttles toward the door, scooping food off the desks as she goes. 'Sorry, Genie, sorry.'

Suddenly, my irritation disappears and all I feel is awful. If it were Sky, it wouldn't matter. She'd think 'Genie's being a bitch', then get back to whatever was on her mind before, probably something to do with formations. And by lunchtime, it'd be forgotten. But Katia will be genuinely blaming herself for me having overturned a plate. That means all the confidence she's been building up will be knocked back again, just because I can't control my temper.

I try to make my voice gentle. 'No, Kat. Stop. I'm sorry.' She freezes, awkwardly mid-stretch for a bowl of chocolates. 'I'm the one who knocked it over, I'll clear it up.'

Katia shakes her head quickly, her eyes still wide. 'I don't mind.'

'Well, I do. Go and sit down, and I'll find some cleaning stuff.'

When I get back to the office, Katia looks so miserable, I ignore the crumbs and go and sit on the edge of her desk. I touch her shoulder briefly. 'I am sorry, Kat. Really, please forget it. I'm just in a mood. It's nothing to do with you.'

She nods, but turns her head away, like a guilty child.

'Is there something else?'

Katia looks back at me, and pulls an apologetic face. 'It was me, who put the biscuits there.'

I make myself laugh, since it takes a conscious effort these days. 'Is that all? I thought you must've booked the under twenty-threes into the same hotel as a strippers' convention, at the very least.'

Katia doesn't actually laugh, but she moves her face like she's trying to. She only does that when she's super uncomfortable.

'Come on, Kat. It's obviously not just you putting the plate there, or me behaving like an evil stepmother. So, what is it?'

Katia pulls at a strand of hair. 'It's Tony.'

I really don't want to talk about Tony, but I make my voice light. 'Well, that shouldn't be too hard to sort. I know he and I aren't as friendly as we were, but I can still help you with whatever he needs.'

Katia shakes her head. 'No, it's not a player-care thing. It's the biscuits.'

I make a confused face. 'How's our office turning into a bakery anything to do with Tony?'

'I bumped into him on my way out a couple of days ago, and he um, he said . . .'

There's the start of tears and I put my arm around her. 'Did he upset you, sweetie? Because if he did, that's not OK. And you know I'll deal with it, don't you?'

Katia straightens her shoulders. 'No, he didn't. Well, not really anyway. He was just, sort of intense.'

Having been on the receiving end of Tony's version of intensity, I suspect she was upset. Honestly, I could do without this, but I'll have to steel myself to sort it out. 'Intense about what?'

'About you.' She looks down at her desk and re-arranges her pens. 'He was saying you looked tired, and how you'd lost weight, and that you couldn't be eating properly. And how you always look out for me and Sky, and let us get away with things . . .'

The words are spilling out so fast, it's hard to interrupt, but I can't let that pass. 'That's absolutely not true, you both do excellent work.' Then, even I have to admit, that's stretching the truth. 'Well, you do anyway. Sky does adequate to good work.'

Katia shakes her head, her eyes gloomy. 'Except what Tony said was true. You let me go early to do things with LeMar, almost as much as you let Sky slope off for training. And you're working late almost every night and . . .'

I shrug. 'And that's why I'm the boss.'

'But you've always been the boss, and you've always worked late, but you weren't how you are now. And me and Sky have been so busy with our own things, we didn't notice.'

'Is that what Tony said?'

Katia nods.

I tighten my arm around her shoulder and she reaches up to squeeze my hand. 'And when he said it, I was annoyed. But then I thought about it, and it's true. Especially the bit about you losing weight. You've been slim for as long as I've worked here, but you know, healthy slim. Now, you're thin.' There's a tear now, rolling down her cheek. 'And that's what happened when LeMar's mum got sick, so I thought you might be too and . . .'

'Oh Kat, sweetie, you should've just asked. I'm fine, you don't need to worry about me.'

'But you'd say that, even if you weren't. And I know weight's a sensitive thing, so I thought if I made sure there was lots of food around and you didn't eat it, it'd be because you were sad about Tony. But if you were eating and still getting thinner, then I'd know you were ill. And maybe you'd talk to LeMar, if I got him to ask, because the two of you are close.'

I pull her into me. 'Kat, *we're* close.' Stepping away, I crouch down so I can look at her properly. 'And I promise, there's nothing physically wrong with me, except I'm not sleeping that well.'

Which is about Tony. Tony, and the red car I'd noticed, which is back lurking on and off. And me being so tired, I slump on the sofa the minute I get home, then can't get myself together enough to go to bed. But I can't face going through any of that with Kat. So, I carry on, slow and steady, nails in my palms to hold back tears. 'And that's making everything more of a struggle, so I don't have much energy left for cooking.' I don't add, 'and I'm too miserable to eat.' Although, oddly for someone who's always consumed their feelings, that's true.

Katia nods, her face solemn. 'I understand.' She reaches to brush my hand. 'Except, I don't. Because I don't understand the thing with Tony.'

I smile slightly. 'I know you're not keen.'

Katia leans forward she's so keen to make her point. 'No, no, it's not that. I mean, I didn't like him, not at first. But the two of you always seemed so happy, just being in the same room. I don't understand what's changed. He must still care about you, or he wouldn't have spoken to me about the weight and stuff.'

My smile is at best lopsided. 'I think he feels guilty.'

'Yes, but why? We had a nice dinner, then the two of you were in the car for all of fifteen minutes and everything was over. What can possibly change in that time?'

'Nothing changed. We just clarified something that had been there all along.' She looks unconvinced and I pull at the oversized dog-hairy jumper that's become my work-wear staple. 'Angharad. It turned out to be more serious than I'd thought.'

'Oh.' Katia looks as glum as is humanly possible while wearing a fuzzy bubble-gum pink sweater dress. Then she changes to puzzled. 'Do you think they're back together now?'

'Yes.' To begin with, I wasn't sure. But most nights, I hear a car engine that can only be Tony's, driving through the village. It's always roughly when I get back from Roudie's evening walk. Which is about right, for going to London straight after training, and staying an hour or two. And who else would he be coming back from, night after night?

'Then why's he so miserable?' Katia asks.

'I don't think he is. He's playing too well.' Plus, he's doing extra stuff for the academy, media requests, M&Gs, everything you could possibly ask of a player. So, I guess it wasn't just that he didn't want me, he doesn't need me either.

Katia pulls her mouth to one side. 'But he's not smiley any more.'

I shrug. 'Probably doesn't have the energy, with how fast games are coming up until after New Year. But Kat, if Tony's playing fine, that's not our concern. And honestly, you don't have to worry about any of this. I'm not going crazy or starving myself. I'm just sad, but I'll get over it.'

She bites at her lip. 'All right, Genie, but do you mind if I say something that's a bit, well, in your business?'

'No, go on.'

'It's just, I know you don't think so, but I've had to fight for LeMar, plenty of times. There are always girls messaging him, coming up to him, trying to get his attention.'

I can't help smiling. 'But he's not remotely interested in them.'

'Yes, but there've been times when he could've been, if I hadn't made sure he wasn't.' She's not complaining, it's like it's a fact of life. But it makes me see there must've been times when she's needed more from me than I've given. Katia puts her hand over mine. 'So, if you want Tony, who cares about Angharad? It's not like they're married, or living together, or anything serious. Why should you just let her have him?'

The phone rings and she turns to answer. I watch her, smiling as she talks, making her voice fur-coat warm. And I do wonder if there isn't quite a bit more to Kat than meets the eye. And if maybe it isn't about time I started taking her advice?

She puts the phone down, pulling a face. 'Sorry, Genie. Monica wants you. Now.'

38

Monica has the office of a serial killer. It's so aggressively tidy, sitting opposite her, I must look like I should be swept away. And everything's absolutely modern and perfectly straight. Except, she's drinking tea from a porcelain cup, covered in delicate pink roses.

There's the briefest of greetings, then she launches straight in with, 'Genie, you must find a boyfriend before the start of January.'

Is 'how' or 'why' the appropriate first response to that? I settle for, 'Um . . .'

A normal person would take that as an invitation to fill in the gaps. But Monica passes across six sheets of A4, each with a headshot and a brief bio. 'If you don't have anyone in mind, here are possibilities.'

Against my better judgement, I leaf through the papers. Each man is from Monica's business circle. Given Monica's people skills, she may not've noticed one of them is gay. Alternatively, this might be more of a business arrangement than an intervention for my personal happiness. Actually, that's almost certainly the case. But unless she's looking to add madaming to her already impressive CV, I still don't get it.

'I'm not sure I quite understand?'

Monica drums her nails on the desk. The office is so

quiet, it's like gunshots on the polished glass. 'I require Garratt to clarify his position before the January transfer window.'

'You're not selling Tony?' comes out before I can stop it. Obviously, I've known that might be coming. The model player stuff fits with Tony putting himself in the shop-window. But it makes me feel sick, saying it out loud.

She sighs. 'Not if I can avoid it.'

I'm ridiculously relieved. 'Then I don't see the connection. Between Tony and transfers, or me getting a boyfriend.'

Monica flexes her hands. 'It's quite simple. I assume you're aware of the buyout clause in Garratt's contract?'

'Vaguely. It's something like if there's an offer of twenty million plus and he wants to go, you have to sell, isn't it?'

'Exactly. And twenty million is a laughably low price.' She looks down and shakes her head. For once, her irritation seems self-directed. 'I should never have agreed to it. But he was adamant he wouldn't move to a smaller club unless he had the option to leave. I took a gamble.' She sounds like she's admitting to something despicable.

'And an offer's coming?'

'No.' There's a flicker of her blood-red fingernails. 'Not yet. But I know for a fact, in the last month, two La Liga scouts and a Serie A director of football have been in touch with Garratt's agent. When I put that to Garratt, he didn't deny it. But he did commit to stay until the summer.'

I turn my face away, hoping to hide that I can't bear the thought of not even passing Tony in the hallways any more.

Monica clears her throat, demanding a return of my attention. 'Obviously, I'd prefer to retain Garratt, given his current form. But if that's not an option, January's the time to invest in a replacement.'

'So they're integrated into the system by the autumn?' I ask, mechanically. When Tony leaves, it will be like working in the Sahara.

'I suppose.' Monica's voice suggests that hadn't crossed her mind. 'More to the point, we can drive a harder bargain with Garratt in place. The minute there are rumours that he's leaving, it will be obvious we need someone urgently. And you know agents, once they smell blood.' She crinkles up her nose, though I'm sure sharks are her favourite animal.

'But I still don't . . .'

Monica interrupts. 'Garratt won't confirm that he definitely plans to leave. If he's still here next season, we'll have spent a great deal of money on an unnecessary understudy. Uncertainty is the enemy of business.'

'I can see that, but . . .'

This time, Monica sighs like she's taken up breath work. 'Basically, Garratt has made it clear that his future depends on your relationship status. Which isn't ideal, obviously.'

Half of me is melting. The other half is furious that he'd suggest that to Monica. Oddly for her, it seems like she can read it in my face. Well, the anger, anyway.

'He's vehemently denied any romantic relationship between you.' She sniffs, which somehow manages to convey irritation. 'He's also made it crystal clear if the club activates the termination clause in your contract, he will instigate a transfer. And he'll ensure the purchase price is twenty million and not a penny more. If we move to sell before he's ready to go, he'll do the same.' That might not sound like a threat, but given what Tony cost, it would be a serious loss for the club. She draws her brows together. 'I have to say, it's extremely trying. Not least because it's completely unnecessary.'

'Is it?'

'Of course. I obviously can't sack you over fraternization.'

'Can't you?'

'No, not after Gavin. That would be entirely unreasonable.' She says it like that's obvious. And maybe it should be. Monica needs to be right, even when it means doing something she finds unappealing. And she can't bear things to be unbalanced, whether it's an account or the arrangement of items on her desk. Suddenly, it doesn't seem remotely likely she's behind the sneaky attempts to make me look incompetent.

Monica takes a dignified little sip of her tea. 'And beyond that, I simply can't understand Garratt's position. I suggested the club could encourage a relationship between you . . .'

'You did?'

'Of course.'

'It didn't cross your mind that might not be your call?' I ask, unable to hold my tongue.

Monica's eyes widen. Perhaps this is the first time anyone's pointed out club staff aren't her personal possessions? 'Not in the least. It seemed like the obvious solution for stabilizing the situation.'

I half sigh and half laugh, because what's the point of doing anything else?

She frowns. 'But he insists that he has no interest in a relationship.'

So, melty was premature. And stupid. I mean, I know about the ring, and beautiful Angharad, and the late-night drives. Of course he doesn't want a relationship. Not with me, anyway. What I said to Katia must've been right. Tony's feeling guilty over how things ended. He promised he'd be there for me in tough times. Living up to that will be a salve for his conscience. Making it part of his transfer decision is taking it to an extreme, but Tony doesn't do anything by halves. And a promise is probably something else he thinks of as roughly the same as a tackle. Something you can't back out of without losing face. I'm sure I'd think that was sweet, if it wasn't so depressing.

Monica shrugs. 'So, really, I've no idea. But he's a player.' She raises her brows. 'Players do inexplicable things.' There's a faraway look in her eyes. I'd bet my life she's fantasizing about player robots. Monica gives herself a little shake, abandoning her dream of perfect predictability. 'Objectively, you finding a boyfriend makes the best of a bad lot. We can set in motion buying a replacement for Garratt. And we can agree his sale at a price of our choosing, rather than his.'

'It's not quite as simple as that.'

'Those men aren't to your tastes?' she asks, waving a hand at the papers.

'No, and even if . . .'

She cuts me off. 'There is another option.'

I push my hair back and try to be patient. 'Is there?'

'Of course. Garratt might say he isn't looking to pursue a relationship, but that isn't at all the same as him not being ready to take one, if it were offered. In fact, in many ways, that's the ideal scenario. It would certainly secure his services for the foreseeable future.'

'I don't think that's a viable possibility,' I say, flatly. Tony has Angharad now. And since he's playing beautifully, I guess they've worked out their issues.

'Genie, I've avoided being part of your annual reviews, because of, well, the situation with Gavin.' Monica straightens the sleeves of her already perfect suit jacket. 'Not that I've ever felt remotely guilty. Gavin suits me very well and you never seemed the slightest bit keen to keep him.'

That's so obviously true that I smile, which she ignores.

'But if you'll accept some feedback, I am told, frequently, that you are extremely good at what you do. But you downplay your own abilities. You make yourself small. I would expect Garratt to worsen that.' She tightens her mouth. 'I meet so many men like him. Big personalities, I suppose people would say. Usually, they suck their wives dry, until they become dowdy little women. But when I've seen you with Garratt, it's quite the opposite. You are more when you're with him and so is he with you. Personally, I believe every woman should make that a rule, that they will seek to make themselves bigger than they are.' There's a little shake of her head, and I'm dismissed with, 'But all I require is that you resolve the matter by the first of January. Whether it's Garratt or another man is entirely up to you.'

39

The staff Christmas party is compulsory, because noth-ing says fun liked forced attendance. But this year, I can't face it and I've got my last-minute work emergency ready to roll. Only I'm starting to think maybe I should go? Walking out of Monica's office this afternoon, missing Tony hit me like a boulder. I've been trying to tell myself all I've got are withdrawal symptoms. Once they wear off, I'll be back to how I was before, content on my own, look-ing out for myself. Now, I know that's not true. Hearing that Tony plans on staying until I find someone else, for a second, it was like being back in the warmth of his arms. That felt so good, almost like being happy again. Because it turns out, I do like being taken care of after all. By Tony, anyway.

And I keep replaying Katia's advice. Normally, I'd shrug off the whole fight-for-your-man thing as desperate, border-ing on demeaning. But let's face it, I am desperate. So, maybe I should forget self-respect and make a Hail Mary attempt to get Tony back? I mean, isn't it possible this is the one and only time Monica's read someone right, and Tony really does want me? And yes, I know that's unlikely. But what's the worst that could happen? OK, obviously, him laughing in my face. Only, honestly, I doubt that'd make me feel worse than I do already.

If I'm going to try a last-gasp thirty-yard shot at goal, tonight's probably my best chance. For morale-boosting purposes, players are required to show their faces, so Tony won't be able to do his usual staring at the floor, dash off in the opposite direction. But standing in front of my wardrobe, I'm struggling to find anything that says desirable.

I try the dress from Monica's party. Where the burgundy fabric used to hug, now it hangs in unflattering bunches. That turns out to be true of most things. In the end, I settle for a black strapless baby doll dress. At least it's supposed to skim rather than cling, even if the effect is more bin bag than haute couture. I try hair up, since it needs cutting, but I can't get it to work. I settle for brushing it out with tons of volumizing mousse. If it's not well-lit, it might pass for tousled rather than tangled. Make-up is even less success-ful. There's only so much concealer can do. And I'm so pale, the contouring is clown-like. In the end, I take most of it off and try dark smudgy eyes and red lips.

Looking in the mirror, I guess I've become more con-sumptive nineteenth-century prostitute and less clinically depressed middle-aged spinster. But I'm nowhere near Angharad's glossy beauty. I slump on the bed, summon-ing up the energy to change into something more suitable for an evening at home, feeling sorry for myself. When a text comes through, it seems like too much effort to reach a hand out to look. Only it's probably work, and if it is, it's late enough that it might be urgent. I haven't quite got to the stage where I'd ignore an actual crisis, so I do check the phone. It's Katia:

> Don't be mad. I asked Devo about Tony because
> LeMar's clueless. He says if Tony is with anyone, it
> can't be going well, because he's miserable as sin
> under the top professional act. Direct quote. So, get
> here soon, before the players start leaving.

I take a deep breath and call a cab. Waiting, a drink feels like a good idea. All I can find is tequila that's been at the back of the cupboard since forever. But it's not like alcohol goes off, is it?

One shot might've been a good idea. Four on an empty stomach definitely wasn't. Not in heels, anyway. Staggering through the lobby of the hotel, there aren't any major disasters. But it takes super-human concentration to navigate the steps into the ballroom. I just about manage it, though not elegantly.

And of course, the first person I see is Tony. He's lolling against the bar, in a white shirt and jeans that probably cost more than my monthly mortgage payment, they fit so well. There's something clear in his glass. I'm betting mineral water, one of the more depressing aspects of the annual staff party being that we get to drink, but the players can't. Officially, that's because they travel tomorrow ahead of their Sunday fixture, but it's more to do with regrettable incidents in the past. Understandably, they usually huddle resentfully in morose, sober groups until they're allowed to leave.

Although Tony doesn't appear to have the typical ghost-of-Christmas-bored expression. He's laughing at something Katia must've said. Or he was, until he notices me, looking at him. He returns my gaze for half a second, then looks away. I guess tubercular doesn't get him going. I should walk straight out, before I do anything stupid. I begin pretending to look for something in my bag. But before I can slip away to 'fetch' the 'forgotten' thing, Monica taps a glass.

That signals the start of the worst part of the evening, Secret Santa. In theory, it's not a bad idea, each player picking a staff member out of the hat. That way, they don't feel obliged to get something for everyone, and there's no risk of someone being forgotten. But the price limit reflects their wages. And it feels wrong, sitting in a circle, admiring presents that cost more than most of us earn in a week, when we all know it's loose change for the players. Or maybe I'm just churlish. Then it's my turn, and I have to fix a smile as I unwrap a kitchen gadget.

It doesn't matter what, it's never something I'd use. But for the record, this time it's an extremely fancy tin for making a cake I've never heard of. Objectively, that's no worse than in previous years. Except Tony makes it harder to be politely grateful. About half a second into my fake enthusiasm, he asks Katia in a distinctly audible whisper, 'Why does Genie get that thing?'

'It's a joke. I think, anyway,' Katia hisses back.

Tony doesn't reply. But he looks at me properly for the first time since I walked in, and his face is thoughtful. I try to work out why, but I can't. Then Skylar brings me a bourbon. I can't say it makes me feel better, but it does slow down the loop of 'you love him but he doesn't love you'. If I keep drinking, maybe it'll stop altogether?

*

The alcohol catches up with me, midway through giving Skylar an intense lecture on how trust is overrated. An unclear amount of time later, Tony lounges over. 'I'm taking Genie home.'

LeMar gives his tom-cat eyes. They only come out when he's seriously annoyed and intent on not showing it. 'That's up to Genie.'

Tony smiles, but his face is hard. 'Fine with me.' He reaches out and runs a finger over my wrist. 'Do you wanna go home with me, Genie?'

I've been too busy not putting my head down on the table to take much interest in the conversation. But Tony's touch is enough to get my attention. 'Yes, please.'

Tony smirks at LeMar. 'Schoolboy error, that. Never suggest asking the lady unless you're sure what she's gonna say.'

LeMar ignores him, and leans forward until his face is close to mine. 'Genie, that's not a good idea.'

I stand up. LeMar follows but I shrug him away, putting my arm through Tony's. 'It's time to go home now, isn't it, Tony?'

He grins. 'Yeah. It's definitely time we got you home.'

Waiting for the car, the cold of the night sobers me up enough to realize I've behaved badly. 'Do you think I should go back and say sorry to LeMar?'

Tony pulls me into the warmth of his chest. 'Nah. Best leave it, I reckon. I'll have a chat tomorrow. Make sure he knows there's nothing to worry 'bout if you're with me.'

I nod into his shirt. Then we're in his car without me being completely sure how that happened.

I reach to stroke the white of his collar, luminous in the street lights. He pushes my hand away. 'Not just now, Genie, love.'

'Why not?'

'Cos I'm driving.'

'Would you say that if it wasn't me?' I want to add, if it was Angharad, but even I can hear, that would sound petulant.

'Probably. You're a bit of an above-average distraction, though.'

He glances at me, my legs crossed and my hands tightly clasped in my lap, and laughs.

'What?'

'You, looking all prim and proper.'

'Except you know I'm not.' I think I manage that without getting the you and I muddled, but I wouldn't swear to it.

'Not tonight you're not, anyhow.'

'Not any time, really.' I lean back against the cool of the window and shut my eyes.

'You need me to open that for you?'

I half open my eyes. 'No, I'm just having a rest.'

'That's good. But if you're gonna throw up, that's OK. Only tell me first, cos I'm pretty fond of this interior.'

'I'm never sick, however much I drink. It's one of my absolutely best qualities.'

He laughs. 'I'll add it to the list.'

'You're in a good mood.' My voice matches my eyelids, sleepy.

'Right now I am, yeah.'

'That's nice, I can't remember the last time I was happy.'

'I can.'

'Can I ask you something, Tony?'

'Yeah, love, you ask me whatever you want.'

'And you'll tell me the truth?'

'Why not? It's not like you'll remember in the morning.'

I point at him, or maybe miss him and point at the window behind him. 'That is very, very true.' I lean forward, elbows on my knees, so I'm as close as I can be without touching him. 'Do you regret it? Coming here?'

He crinkles his brows together. 'Honest answer, no, I don't. I regret some of the stuff with you, though. I'll admit that.'

'The stuff at the start?'

'Yeah, some of that weren't great. But more the end bit. And how it is now.' He keeps staring dead ahead. 'Cos I didn't intend on you getting hurt. But I'm coming in every day, seeing you all miserable, and getting skinnier and skinnier. And half the time, even when you're inside, you look like you're freezing. And it kills me, knowing that's my doing.'

'Actually, I'm starting to think it's mine. Do you know what I regret, Tony?'

'Getting sucked in in the first place?'

'No, not getting you into bed the minute I had a chance.'

'That's the bourbon talking, I reckon, Genie.'

I shake my head, more emphatically than I intended, so my chin slips off my folded hands.

He ignores it, or maybe doesn't see, he's trying to pull into traffic. 'Can I ask you something back?'

'If it's quick, I'm going to be having a nap shortly.'

'Sounds like a plan. All I wanted to ask was, did you honestly like your Secret Santa present?'

'Did you buy it?' He probably can't tell through the slur that I'm wary.

Tony's eyes are hurt and his voice is offended. 'No. Course I fucking didn't. Why'd I buy you something for the kitchen?' He clearly realizes a second too late that could be insulting. 'I mean your food, it's fine. Good, actually. But it's like a knife, two pans, something to stir it with, max, yeh? Why'd you want some baking gadget? Like, have you baked anything, ever?'

'I did, quite often, when I was married. I went through a domestic phase, but it didn't stick. I wasn't very good at it.'

'I don't imagine you was.'

'So, what would you buy me? Running shoes?'

'Nah. Something pretty and expensive. Like the other girls got, only better, obviously. Cos you're my best girl.'

It would spoil the moment to add, 'at the club'. So, I smile and say, 'That sounds nice.'

'It would be. So, like I asked before, why don't you get something like that?'

'I don't know. I just never have. Katia's probably right, that it started out as a joke. Most things do, don't they?'

'This one, I'm starting to wonder if it might pay to look into the punchline.'

'I don't understand, and I'm too sleepy to think about it now.'

He nods, eyes all serious. 'OK. You leave this one with me.'

*

'Genie, where're your keys?'

'Here.' I hand Tony my bag and lean against the cool bricks of the porch. That way, I can drink him in without getting distracted by how everything's starting to spin. The electric light is cold, so the lines of his face are harsh as he hunts for the keys. 'You have such nice cheekbones.'

He keeps searching through the bag, not looking at me. But the laugh in his voice is obvious. 'Thanks, love.'

'You're not driving any more, so can I touch them?'

'In a minute. Let's get you inside first.' Once he's got the door open, Tony puts his arm around my waist. I move an experimental inch from the wall. The spinning gets considerably worse. Tony's arm tightens. 'Big step, beauty. You gonna be able to manage that? Or do I need to pick you up?'

'I can do it.'

'If you say so.'

I do just fine with the step. It's an over-enthusiastic Rouden mixed with slippery terracotta tiles that's almost my undoing. I lurch into Tony, and even I can't pretend that was remotely lady-like. He's rock-solid, even under the combination of my weight and Roudie's front paws. And I have to say, the idea of spending the rest of the night with my head on Tony's chest is extremely attractive. But I manage to pull myself together enough to at least lift my head to look at him. 'Sorry.'

'Nothing to be sorry for. Do you think you could calm the pup down though? Before you get tangled up with him.'

I wrap my arm tight around Tony, kind of like lashing myself to the mast. That way, I can lean over enough to stroke Roudie's ears. 'Hello, sweetie, that's enough now.' It's not the most commanding of instructions. But Roudie takes the hint, and prances off in front of us towards the sitting room. I inch my way up Tony until my head is on his shoulder. 'You smell nice too.'

'So I should, at the price this stuff is.'

'Not the aftershave, you.'

He laughs properly this time. 'Well, that's good. But I'm not sure it's relevant just now. Do I need to do something with the pup, before I put you to bed?'

'Before you take me to bed.'

'Yeah, we'll discuss that in a bit. But let's focus on one thing at a time, shall we?'

I nod. 'Then could you let Roudie out in the garden for a minute?'

'Yeah, I can do that.' He walks me through to the sitting room, puts his hands on my shoulders and gently pushes me onto the sofa. His face is very close to mine when he says, 'Stay there, OK?'

I consider kissing him, but settle for stroking his stubble, enjoying the roughness against my fingers. 'OK, but don't be long.'

'Anyone'd think you were trying to lead me astray, Genie.' He shakes his head at me, then pulls away. I lean back and shut my eyes for what I think is a moment. When I open them, Roudie's on his bed and Tony's sitting beside me holding a glass of water. He takes my hand, positioning my fingers around the icy glass.

I'd like to say thank you but the furthest I get is a smile. Once the water's gone, Tony takes the glass. 'Time for bed then.'

I try to smile seductively, but I've got a nasty feeling I'm swaying slightly. 'That sounds like a good idea.'

Tony's back to trying not to laugh as he says, 'Yeah, I think it might be.' He stands, then pulls me up by my hands. 'But I'm gonna carry you for this bit, OK? Otherwise it'll take forever.'

'Don't hurt your back. I'll be terribly unpopular if you can't play on Sunday.'

'I reckon you're well under my weight limit. Just put your arms round me.' I reach up and link my hands behind his neck. 'That's right. Good girl. Up you come.'

Thankfully, I am easily within his lifting capacity, and he carries me upstairs as if it's minimal effort. He sits me on the bed and kneels down, taking off one of my stilettoes and then the other. I can't resist leaning over and stroking the back of his neck, where the hair is freshly shaved.

He looks up at me, grinning. 'Let me guess, beauty, that feels nice?'

'Umm, very, like a horse's nose.'

Tony laughs. 'I'll have to take your word for it. What do you usually sleep in?'

'Pyjamas, but I don't need them yet.' I've moved from his neck to his shoulders, tracing out the muscles under the crisp cotton.

Tony reaches for my hands and lifts them away as he stands. 'Yeah, I'm not so sure 'bout that.' He picks up the striped top lying at the foot of the bed, looks at the buttons and shakes his head. 'I reckon it's gonna be tricky for me to put these on you. Hang on a sec.'

He begins to hunt through my wardrobe. If I was fractionally more sober, I'd be embarrassed he's getting a glimpse of the chaos. He turns back to me, holding a baggy grey t-shirt. It's got to be the single least attractive thing I own, something to wear for cleaning and odd jobs. But I know why he's picked it. And I can't pretend I'm not disappointed, as he says, 'Arms up,' and pulls it over my head. Once it's down almost over my knees, he gets me up onto my feet and reaches under the t-shirt to unzip my dress. It's falling to the floor as I wrap my arms around his neck.

'Tony, do you really not want me?'

He rubs his cheek against mine. 'Course I fucking want you. Just not like this.'

That's genuinely crushing. Everyone knows, Tony's quite discerning about actual girlfriends, but when it comes to one-night stands, he's not been so picky. I must be in even more of a state than I realized, if I'm below his standards. I gather together the last shreds of my dignity and let him go. Luckily, he keeps his arms around my waist. The room is seriously whirling, and dignity and falling over are definitely incompatible.

'No, of course not. I'm sorry, I don't usually get like this.' My voice sounds brittle.

Tony pulls my head into his chest and strokes my back. 'You, Genie, don't need to tell me you're sorry, for having a nice time with your mates.'

I pull away, enough to look up at him. 'I didn't have a nice time. And it's not attractive, is it?'

He smiles, more gently than usual. 'Nah, you're wrong there. You happen to be a seriously adorable drunk.'

'But not as adorable as Angharad?'

'She don't drink. And if she did, I can't see her being anywhere near as entertaining as you. Or as sweet.' I wish my head was clearer, so I could be sure I understood that right. He rests his lips on my forehead for a second. 'But the first time between me and you, I don't want there to be no risk of regrets in the morning. You get me?'

I reach up and stroke his cheek, thinking about Katia and the biscuits, and Tony factoring me into his transfer decisions. 'You're so lovely, Tony.'

He smiles, the same half-sad, half-happy smile as before. 'That's one thing I hope you do remember when you wakes up tomorrow.'

'I will. And anyway, I've known for ages. I just got confused.'

This time the smile is almost all happy. 'If that's true, it's the best thing I've heard in a long time.'

'Tony?'

'Yeah?'

'My bed's so big and empty.'

'Is it, beauty?' he asks, his face grave, except his eyes.

'It is. So, why don't you stay, and just not fuck me?'

'Cos honestly, I'm not sure I could.'

'But you could kiss me goodnight?'

'Yeah, I can manage that all right,' he says, his voice growly. He leans forward, one hand on my waist. The other's light on my back, so I could stop any time I want. But I don't want to. The kiss is exactly what I want, long and deep, his tongue hard against mine. Until Tony pulls away. 'I think I'd better call it a day, love, or I'll be getting carried away.'

I nod and sink down onto the bed. He waits until I'm lying down, then leans over and touches his lips against my cheek before he leaves.

40

Roudie's such a good boy, he must be starving but he waits until almost eleven to wake me. It's quite an effort, opening my eyes. When I do, there's a bottle of water and an upturned bowl beside the bed. Next to them is a note scribbled on the back of one of my unopened letters:

Hello beauty,
Hope you had a good sleep. Ibuprofen is under the bowl,
coz I didn't want the dog getting into it.
Xxx

I swallow the pills and stagger down to let Roudie out into the garden. His walk will have to wait until I feel more human. As I inch towards the kitchen, I'm so intent on coffee, I almost miss the envelope and slim purple box on the doormat. Reaching for them, my head's pounding. But I'm glad I did. 'Genie' is carefully printed on the envelope and underneath, there's a scrawled:

The box is your pretty expensive thing. Please accept it. It's
to say you'll always be my lioness even if I'm not your lion.
There're no strings attached, promise. You don't even have to
open the envelope if you don't want to, but if you could see
your way to reading what's inside, I'd appreciate it.

Standing's getting tiring, so I slip down onto the cool tiles to rip open the envelope. Inside, there's a note. The cream paper is thick, with a watermark. I can't imagine Tony writes many letters, so I guess he bought it specially. That fits with the painstakingly neat handwriting, and even a quick glance is enough to see it doesn't have Tony's usual free-wheeling approach to grammar. So, I'm betting this isn't a first attempt, and that at some point, there was a typed, spell-checked version. He must have been up half the night writing it.

Dear Genie,

This isn't anything I haven't tried to say to you, but when we talk, it never comes out how I want. I thought if I got it down in black and white, that might help. The last few weeks, I've tried like a hundred different versions and none of them are right, but maybe this one kind of gets over what I feel about you.

For starters, I need you to know I only ever walked away because I thought you couldn't trust me. If that's true, you need to give up being miserable over me, and find someone who'll make you happy. Not just for you, for me too. I've been trying real hard to keep it together, because I knew you'd got hold of some stupid idea I was only after you to help with the professional stuff. But even if I look OK on the outside, I miss you so bad, seeing you, it hurts. So, if you can't believe me, you've got to find someone who'll have your back, and let me get out of here.

But before I let you go I need to be sure you still feel that way. Because you might not remember, but you said stuff last night that made me think you don't. If that's true, I

*can't accept us not being together when we obviously should
be. And if it's not that you trust me yet, more that you're
starting to think you might've been wrong, I swear on you,
on Rouden, on whatever you need, you're all I want. There's
been no one else, and if you'll have me, there never will be.
Honestly, the last time I had sex was the first week I got
here, when me and you hated each other. That was just a
random hook-up, nothing more. And I've not even been
messaging with anyone since, especially not my ex.*

*Anything else you've heard, or think you've seen, is
bollocks. I'll do whatever you want to prove it. But maybe
you know already, because how you were yesterday, it made
me think this is as simple for you as it is for me. We're
happy when we're together and miserable when we're not, and
that should be all that matters. I know I can make it OK
with the club for us to be a couple, and that's what I want, to
be with you in public, 100% committed.*

*If all that's keeping you back from that is background
noise about who I've been with in the past, we've got to find
a way to put that to bed. And if you're still thinking I don't
fancy you, I honestly can't get my head round that, it's so far
from the truth. But I get this is scary for you, only I know
how strong you are, even if you don't. So, how about being
brave like a lioness and at least trying to talk to me?*

*Yours, if you'll have me,
Tony Garratt*

It's the full signature that means the most. Tony's spent his
whole adult life one hotel room away from a kiss and tell

story. Putting his name like that, if it isn't true, is a huge risk. And I do remember last night, or most of it, anyway. Enough that even before I read the letter, I was wondering if I hadn't blown things out of proportion.

It was seeing the ring that did it. But I'm a grown-up. I know things don't always end tidily. Even after it was over with Angharad, he might've been lonely enough, or nostalgic enough that, for a moment, a big gesture felt right. And if he'd been honest, and admitted there had been that little back slip, would I have wanted to hear it? Probably not.

And why swear it's over with Angharad if it's not? The little monster claws back into my head for a second, telling me why have one woman when you can have two? But that doesn't make sense, not when he's talking about making things official. The monster doesn't have anything to say to that. So, that just leaves the night-time drives. And I'm starting to think they might have another explanation . . .

But before I get into that, I can't resist any longer, and I reach for the box. Inside, hanging from a gold chain is the face of a lioness, complete with little emerald eyes. I stroke the charm between my thumb and forefinger. And Tony's right, it is time to be brave.

I walk across to the sitting room, its floorboards cold on my feet, and peep through the curtains. But all ready to burst my bubble, the red car's back.

I decide I've had enough. When I knock on the window, the man dozing on the front seat jumps, tipping up the peak of his baseball cap. I realize I recognize him, hold out a coffee cup and mouth hello.

He winds down the window.

'It's Darren, isn't it? Mike from Security's eldest?'

He must be at least nineteen, but he looks more like a fourteen-year-old caught smoking. 'Miss Edwards, it's not what it looks like, honest.'

I smile. 'Actually, I think it probably is. Can I get in?'

He pushes open the passenger door, shoving aside take-away wrappers.

'I take it someone at the club requested this?'

He's less panicked now, more embarrassed, based on how he can't meet my eye. 'Tony Garratt. He went to the manager, like early October.' I think back, realizing that was right about when we found the spyware. 'Said you were having some issues, like maybe a stalker, something like that. He was worried about you when he was playing away, what with you walking the dog by yourself, running on your own, all that. And he was wanting to sit a league cup game out, while he got something sorted. But you're like a favourite with the manager . . .'

I shrug. 'More a necessary cog in his beautiful machine I think, but anyway, go on.'

'So, he went crazy to Dad about fixing you up with some security.' Darren looks at me, his lips pulled back to show clenched teeth. 'And Dad said you needed to know, so it wasn't, like, creepy. But Mr Garratt was dead set against it. I don't get why, honestly. But he said it was his problem, being worried, and he didn't want you taking it as him saying you shouldn't be out on your own. Does that make any sense?'

I can't help smiling. 'Yes, it does. Complete sense,

actually.' And the exact reverse of making controlling little suggestions. I know exactly what Gavin would've said, or my parents come to that. Why don't I stick to the treadmill? Get a dog walker for Roudie? Whatever it takes to make sure I'm indoors after dark.

Darren takes a gulp of coffee. 'It's not like weird, though. Honest.' He holds out his phone. 'Mr Garratt was clear on that. All he wanted was a text in the evening, saying you were in for the night safe and sound. Not what you'd been up to, who you'd seen, nothing like that.'

'No, of course not. And it's only away matches that you're here, isn't it?'

Darren nods quickly. 'Yeah, absolutely. Mr Garratt does a check-in with you, if he's here, doesn't he?'

So, the luxury car engine last thing at night isn't Tony roaring back from seeing Angharad.

'He does, yes.'

Darren looks at me through calf-like eyelashes. 'You're not mad, are you?'

'No, I'm not. But you can head home. I'll text Tony myself tonight, OK?'

Darren smiles. 'I think he'd like that.'

I pick up the necklace, ready for the next step in being brave. That's getting out my phone and pulling up WhatsApp:

> Thank you for the letter and the necklace but I'm done talking.
> We've wasted so much time on it and it never changes anything
> between us. If you want me, come and get me.
> 11.47

Seriously? Coz I'm on the bus now, but I'll hijack it if
you mean it
11.48

I can wait till you're done playing. Just.
11.49

Be there the second I get back
11.50

The minute the door's open, Tony's inside. 'You've not changed your mind, have you, beauty?'

I reach around his neck, pressing into him, kissing him hard. 'Does it feel like I've changed my mind?'

He pulls back just far enough to look at me. 'Nah, it don't. And thank Christ for that. I've been counting down to this ever since you texted me. I honestly dunno what I'd have done, if it'd turned out you didn't want me after all.'

'Let's go to bed.'

'When I'm finished kissing you.'

The force of his lips on my hair, my neck, my mouth, is enough to push me back, one hand braced against the bare bricks. The kisses are mixed in with Tony murmuring my name, that I'm beautiful, that he's missed me, that he wants me. And I can tell that's true because he's pushing against me, one leg between mine, his hand on my back pulling me close.

'Tony, Tony, I can't wait any longer.'

'Come on, then. Upstairs.'

The second he lets me go, I'm pulling him along behind me. I push him down onto the foot of my bed and step back. There's a moment of self-consciousness, looking at him looking at me.

'I was going to dress up for you. But then I thought,

this time, the first time, maybe it's best just real, no tease, no games.'

He smiles softly. 'Yeah, this is perfect. You're perfect.' His smile broadens. 'Now get those fucking clothes off. But leave the necklace.'

I pull my t-shirt off. Not slowly or seductively, just trying to get rid of it, ripping off sweatpants too.

'Now come here.'

I try to say something but it's more of a wanting sort of noise, as I step over to Tony. He reaches up to unhook my bra, slipping it off my shoulders and waiting for it to fall to the floor before he slides my knickers off. I go to climb onto his knee, but he holds me away, hands on my hips. 'Let me drink you in a minute. This is one I wanna remember.'

He looks at me, head to toe, then closes his eyes for a moment. 'You, Genie, are solid gold. You knows that, don't you? And gorgeous with it. Even if I'm gonna have to feed you up.' Tony points at the floor-length mirror in the corner, 'See what an absolute beauty you are?'

'All I can see is that you're wearing far too many clothes.'

'That I am.' His voice is muffled as he starts pulling off t-shirt and hoodie together. Before he can untangle himself, I'm already scrabbling at the buttons of his jeans. His hand holds mine still as he reaches into his pocket then holds out a condom.

'Genie, you run the show this time, OK?'

His eyes are grave and I match him as I nod, then we're both smiling and he's kicking off jeans and briefs. And I know I'm supposed to say it's Hollywood perfect, but it's not. There's the scrambling rush of wanting all of each other all at once, and the fumbling that's part of finding out how we best fit together. But none of that matters, because Tony reaches up to my waist and his hands guide me into the rhythm that he needs. The second it's right, he makes a noise in the back of his throat that's half growl half groan. And that is perfect, knowing for once I can be as noisy as I want, because my voice will be wrapped up in his. Not that either of us manages actual words, until Tony's almost there. As he climaxes, he's panting, 'Genie, Genie, you fucking angel. I fucking love you.'

We lie side by side, his arm under my neck, our bodies touching wherever they can. Tony waits until his breathing is close to normal, then says, 'Genie, love, I'm sorry. I didn't quite get you there, did I?'

My voice is sleepy and deeper than normal. 'Nearly, though. Much closer than I usually get.' I reach up to stroke his hand on my shoulder. 'Sorry. Mostly, I fake, but I thought with you, that probably wasn't necessary.'

He kisses the hair just above my ear. 'It's not. And honestly, I'd rather you didn't. Cos I'm gonna have loads of fun working out all the stuff that does it for you, but it'll be easier if you're not play-acting.' He runs his fingertips over me, tracing the line of the necklace first, then drawing rectangles over my stomach and figures of eight around my breasts. 'Like I think you're into this. Is that right?'

'Umm, definitely.'

He begins to circle my nipple. 'So this is probably nice too, yeah?'

'Bliss.'

'Which means this should work?' He tugs my nipple,

gently at first, then just to the edge of pain, until I moan and arch my back.

He begins to slide his hand down, finding my hip, then my thigh. 'And if I remember right, you're keen on this and all.'

He runs his fingers over my wetness, stroking and circling. It's gentle at first, then firmer, with me lifting my hips, trying to rush him into building the pressure.

'There's no hurry, beauty. Just relax, let me take care of you.' He keeps that up, murmuring into my ear that we've got all night, that he wants to take his time, that I feel good. And his fingers feel good too. So good that I let myself sink into the sensation, moaning and whimpering until I think I can't bear it any longer.

'Try to stay with me one more minute, OK?'

That's enough to push me into pure pleasure, my head buried against Tony's chest. It takes me a moment to come back to conscious thought and when I do, it's nothing clever. Just, 'Oh, Tony.'

'You all right, love? Had a nice time?'

I prop myself up on my elbow so I can look at him. 'The absolute best time.'

He grins. 'Me too, beauty. Me too.' He reaches up and strokes my face. 'And Genie, I know it's not the classiest time to have said it, but what I said, I meant it. I love you. And that's not the sex talking. I've loved you for ages. I just weren't sure, like, I dunno, about how to tell you, or maybe more, if I should, when I might not be right for you. All that.'

I shake my head and bend to kiss him gently. 'You

couldn't be more right, Tony. And obviously, I love you too. Completely.'

'You don't have to say that, not if you're not ready.'

'Except I am. And it's nothing to do with you being Tony Garratt, the best of his generation.' I make my face thoughtful. 'Though you do know, darling, I think that might have quite a lot to do with how much I want to fuck you.'

Tony laughs, the one that's close to a roar. 'Believe me, I've no complaints 'bout that. Cos, Genie, I love all the sides of you. Like sensible, smart Genie, she's dead impressive. And worrier Genie, who needs a bit of looking after, it's nice knowing I can give her what she needs. And sweet Genie, like tonight, obviously she's my favourite. But slutty Genie, she gives her quite a run for her money, I can tell you.'

I run my fingers over his chest. 'I'm pleased to hear it. Because I think she'll be putting in another appearance shortly, if you're going to be ready to go again any time soon?'

He smiles, lifts my fingers to his lips and sucks them, letting his teeth rake over the skin as he releases them. 'Any minute, I'd say.'

Which makes it absolutely maddening that the doorbell rings. I make a disappointed noise, and Tony says, 'Ignore it.'

But it keeps ringing and Roudie starts barking, and whoever it is, they're not going away. I pull a face at Tony. 'Sorry, it's probably Sky, wanting to tell me how her game went. I'll get rid of her.'

I'm at the bedroom door, when Tony calls, 'Genie, aren't you forgetting something? Like I know Sky reckons clothes are pretty much always an optional extra, but what if it's a Jehovah's Witness or one of your ancient neighbours looking for their lost cat or something?'

I shrug. 'Well, if it scares them off . . .' But I do pull on knickers and Tony's t-shirt, which is long enough to skim my thighs. As I head for the stairs, Tony shouts, 'That'd not scare me off, I can tell you. Fact there'd be no getting rid of me.' So, I'm laughing when I open the door. But I stop right away because it's Gavin.

42

'Gavin, what on earth are you doing here?'

'We need to talk.'

'This isn't a good time.'

You'd think even Gavin would pick up on the hints that this is actually a spectacularly bad time. But he clearly can't, because he starts walking in. 'This won't wait.'

I want to push him back, but I'm hampered by having to make a grab for Roudie's collar. Rouden's always had an inconsistent approach to security, sleeping through some visitors and barking like mad at others. But he never bites. Only today looks like it would have been an exception, if I hadn't caught him mid-lunge. I'm trying to calm Roudie down and repel Gavin when Tony appears at the top of the stairs. He's shirtless and buttoning his jeans.

'It's all right, Genie. Let the doc in. As it happens, I've been wanting to have a chat with him and all.'

I look over my shoulder to make eye contact with him.

'It'll be all right, beauty, promise.' Tony looks confident to the point of cocky. That's intriguing. I step back, dragging Roudie with me.

'All right, Gavin. If you must come in, I suppose you must.'

Gavin stands in the hall. The puffed-out-chest power pose has gone. Instead, it's like the rain dripping off his

Barbour is pulling his shoulders down. Tony, on the other hand, is racing downstairs two at a time, until he's behind me, arm around my waist. Roudie must find that comforting. He nudges Tony, allows his ears to be fondled then slinks away.

Tony shows his lovely white teeth. 'The lounge, I think. Don't you, Genie? It'll be nice and cosy in there. You'll catch your death out here, with what you're wearing.' He begins to propel me towards the sitting room. I can't see his face, but I suspect from how much he's exaggerating his accent that he's doing his best leer, as he says, 'Or not wearing, I suppose I should say.' He reaches up under the t-shirt to squeeze my ass and I just about manage not to laugh. Now I'm absolutely clear what game we're playing.

Tony looks over his shoulder. 'Leave the jacket in the hall, doc. Can't have you dripping on the upholstery now, can we?'

That time, I don't quite keep the laugh in, but it's not much more than a snort.

Tony leads me to the sofa and sits so close, I can smell sweat and sex. He strokes my thigh slowly with one finger. 'Legs up, I think.' I lift them across his thighs and he begins to trace patterns over my knees, as he wraps his other arm around me. 'That's it. You cuddle up with me, all nice and safe.'

Gavin sits opposite us, upright in the hard armchair that I'm too lazy to replace. He runs his fingers through his floppy hair, noticeably not quite as thick as it once was. It's obvious this isn't going as he'd expected. There's a brown envelope on his lap. It must've been inside his jacket, because there's only the odd raindrop visible on it, already drying in the heat from the log burner.

Tony smiles over at him. 'So, you wanna go first, or shall I?'

Gavin looks down his nose. 'I'm here to talk to Charlotte.'

'We'll stick with Genie, I think. Cos she prefers it. But go ahead. I'd say she's all yours, only obviously she's not.' Tony's tone is still exaggeratedly good-humoured, but the sneer is implied.

Gavin shrugs. 'By the time I'm finished, I think you'd have preferred not to stay, but it's your choice.'

Tony inclines his head. 'Do your worst.'

Gavin leans over to me, holding out the envelope. 'I'm sorry. If I'd known how far things had gone, I'd have told you earlier. But I wanted to give you hard evidence, so you'd know this is me trying to protect you, not interfere.' He's using his bedside-manner voice, the one that makes me want to punch him in the mouth.

I take the envelope. Inside there are five photos, grainy but clear enough to make out an extremely attractive woman walking to a car in a hotel car park. They are time-stamped two days ago, and from the quality, I'm assuming they're CCTV not paparazzi. I hold one of the photos out to Tony. 'Is that Angharad?'

Tony looks me in the eye. 'It is, yeah.'

I try to keep my voice softly enquiring when I ask Gavin, 'And I suppose she was at the team hotel to see Tony?'

'I'm afraid she was.' Gavin puts on his fatherly concern face.

I take Tony's hand, but keep looking at Gavin. 'And you think I'm going to care about that?'

Gavin gives an exasperated half sniff half snort. 'Genie,

355

or actually, I don't know why I'm using that stupid nick-name, Charlotte, there's no point pretending you're that sort of woman.'

'And what sort of woman would that be, exactly?' I ask, my voice less soft now due to the hint of disdain.

'The sort who's happy to be one of several. Just low-level entertainment for a man who doesn't care about you.'

I smile slowly, sliding my hand up Tony's arm, enjoying the curve of his bicep. 'Oh, Tony takes excellent care of me, I can assure you.'

Tony gives me a long, slow smile but doesn't say anything.

Gavin's face is angry now, a look I remember. 'So that's it, is it? You're so caught up by him, you're grateful for what you can get. Even if he's more interested in someone else. I thought even you had more dignity than that.'

Tony leans forward, but I tighten my hand on his arm. 'No, darling. I can deal with this.'

I sit back and look hard at Gavin, until he breaks my gaze. 'If Tony was more interested in Angharad, why wouldn't he tell me that?'

'Don't be a child. You know players, you know how they operate. The sense of entitlement. Stringing women along until they've served their purpose. The lies.'

I smile. 'But that's exactly the point. One man in this room has lied to me, about working late, and on-call shifts and weekend conferences. But it's not Tony.' I turn to Tony, 'So, did you invite her there?'

Tony's face is serious. 'No.'

I nod. 'I thought perhaps you hadn't. She just turned up?'

'She did, yeah.'

I look at Tony for a moment, trying to work out if he and I are running on the same lines. 'And did you think that was rather odd?'

'It struck me as strange, yeah.'

'Because how would she know where we put our players before that particular away match? Unless someone told her.'

Tony crinkles up his eyes. 'Yeah, and why'd she think I wanted to see her? When all I've done since I got here is block her number.'

'Unless someone told her?' I ask again.

Tony smiles his partner-in-crime smile. 'Exactly, love.' He looks across at Gavin. 'And that touches on what I wanted to talk to the doc about.' His smile gets nastier. 'Cos ever since Genie told me she reckoned someone was out to cause her trouble, I've thought it had to be over something personal. So, you've always been in the running, but it took her getting that cake tin thing for me to be sure.'

Gavin begins to bluster but Tony cuts through. 'See, I had a little something lined up for Genie's Christmas present.' He strokes the necklace where it crosses my collar bone. 'And I knew she'd not take it, if I gave it her direct. So, I thinks to myself, why not just make sure I get her Secret Santa ticket? Only no one had it, and what's more, none of 'em had ever picked Genie. The odds, well, let's just say I'm betting they're slim enough they could do with a few cakes of their own. So, I thought to myself, who'd wanna make sure they got to decide what Genie'd get, year after year?'

Gavin splutters, in what I assume is an attempt at denial. Tony ignores him.

'And that baking tin, it was a bit of a hint, weren't it? Cos from what Genie's told me, you're the only bloke round here who'd think the kitchen's the best place for her. So, I texted Monica's PA, asking who puts the slips in the jar. Turns out she's quite a fan of yours, ain't she, doc? What with you being so helpful, doing that every year.'

Gavin draws himself upright. 'That's hardly proof of, well, whatever you're insinuating.'

Tony shrugs. 'Nah, it's not. But you not wanting Genie to know she's appreciated, getting her believing all the lads see her as like domestic help, well, it's suggestive. So, while I was hanging round waiting to play yesterday, I did a bit of research. And you know, Genie, beauty, you should start paying more attention to boring blokes at parties. Cos it turns out, Gavin's old mates the Craigs, their firm's not just software, it's more spyware.'

'Really?' I should've guessed, they were always sneaky, even when I knew them as students.

Tony grins at me, back to furiously cheerful. 'Yeah, really. And when I passed that on to my security guy, he matched up bits of the code on your laptop to some of their commercial stuff.'

Gavin's mouth has tightened. 'I fail to see the connection.'

Tony laughs. 'Maybe you'd better get some glasses then, doc. Cos your best mates playing nasty tricks on your ex-missus, that don't feel like a coincidence.'

Gavin mutters about circumstantial evidence, and slander might be scattered in too.

Tony shakes his head. 'Thing is, there's plenty more where that came from. Like I feel a bit sorry for Angharad. Cos me and her did have a little chat.' Tony looks at me. 'With LeMar in the room the whole time.'

I smile, I've no more anxieties in that direction.

'And she was going on 'bout how I'd sent her stuff. Personal stuff, that'd seemed like it'd be off me. Like she got a shirt, apparently, and a real nice top. Only obviously, they weren't from me, but they came from someone at the club all right. So, when she got an email, from a Covenly account, saying come to the hotel, I'm wanting to see her, she believed it, didn't she?'

'Poor Angharad.' I mean it. I can't think of anything worse than believing Tony wanted to meet, then finding out he didn't.

Tony strokes my fingers. 'It's all right. I'm gonna send a mate of mine her way. Retired out of the game six months, bored, loves being in the tabs, made of money. And all the emotional sensitivity of a breeze block.'

'Oh, that sounds perfect.' I smile.

'Don't you go getting ideas, you're stuck with me now.' Tony kisses my hair, then looks back to Gavin. 'Thing is, doc, that was you getting too clever for your own good. Cos the club's security took a look at that email, and it might be a false account but it was sent off your laptop all right.'

Gavin's cheeks had been flushed, but they now drain white except for irregular red blotches. 'Will you tell Monica?'

Tony looks at me, eyes soft. 'Up to you, beauty.'

I think about how Monica was nice to me, or nice for her anyway, last time we spoke. And how what she said has as much to do with me and Tony being back together as Katia's advice. And about her beautiful twins, and that decides me.

'So long as there's no repeat of any of this, personally, I'd let it go.' I turn to Tony. 'But it doesn't just affect me. You've been worried too, haven't you?' And actually, I think Gavin's caused Tony far more anxiety than me. I was too busy getting myself muddled over Tony to take much notice of any of this.

Tony chews his lip. 'How you handle this, it's gotta be your decision. But if anything happened to you . . .' His eyes dart away.

I squeeze his hand. 'It's all right, darling. It's not that Gavin's stalking me because he's obsessed with me, or anything like that, is it, Gavin?'

Gavin's eyes open wide, and he's so obviously horrified by the idea, I almost laugh.

'No, of course not, far from it. I wanted to stop you making a fool of yourself, or me. Or Monica.'

Tony pulls a confused face. 'This whole thing, Genie, dunno if you've noticed, but it's dead weird.' He looks across at Gavin. 'Give us a minute, will you, doc? Me and Genie have to figure something out.' Tony takes my hand. 'Cos I think we needs to think 'bout what we're doing next. Like if you've got a hankering to try your hand at player care somewhere new, we can do that. But I like the club, and I wanna buy the house. So, I'd prefer to stay, if that's all right with you?'

I nod quickly, smiling. 'That's exactly what I want.'

Tony grins. 'That's good, cos the pup'd find Spain a bit hot. But it means I reckon we need more of a guarantee than a promise this won't happen again. Cos me and Gary King exchanged a few texts, when I was on my way back tonight. And he reckons he didn't get a contract extension here after a medical that weren't exactly kosher, and it struck me, it was Chrissie that did mine, not the doc.'

I bite at my lip, thinking it through. 'What if Gavin told Monica he wanted to give up his role at the club? To focus on the twins, something like that?'

Tony weighs it up. 'Yeah. I reckon that'd be OK with me. How 'bout you, doc?'

There's an almost imperceptible nod from Gavin.

I give him a hard stare. 'But I am going to go to HR. I'll tell them I've got better things to do than bother with you now. But if anything like this ever happens again, to me or anyone else, all this will be on record, ready to go straight to Monica. Understood?'

Gavin nods again.

Tony grins at me. 'All sorted, then. And I dunno 'bout you, but I'm ready to get on with being like disgustingly happy.'

I nuzzle into Tony's neck. 'Umm, me too. So, Gavin, it's time you left.'

Gavin starts to scurry out, but as he passes, he reaches out a hand like an appeal. Tony's arm blocks him. 'Nah, I don't think so, mate. No one's gonna touch my girl without her say so, OK?'

43

Tony leans into the sofa cushions. His face is like Roudie's when he sees an automatic door. 'I still don't get why he did it.'

'I'm not sure I do either.' I play with Tony's fingers, thinking it over, then look back into his eyes. 'It might be that leaving me for Monica and all her lovely money, it didn't fit with Gavin's idea of himself, you know?'

Tony shrugs. 'Can't have much self-knowledge then. It's exactly what I'd expect of a wanker like him.'

I smile. 'Umm, but Gavin sees himself as such an upstanding citizen. And he always thought I had terrible judgement. So, this whole thing might've been his twisted idea of making amends.' I roll my eyes. 'Stopping me from doing something "unwise".'

It does sort of fit with how Gavin was about the divorce. He was always so solicitous, like it was an illness I'd inflicted on myself, not a separation he'd chosen.

But Tony shakes his head. 'Nah, I don't buy it. What he did, it wasn't just him trying to keep me away from you, it was nasty. He was trying to make it look like you weren't doing your job properly and get you into trouble.'

I shrug. 'Well, who knows, really?' I look up at Tony, half hesitant, in case he's offended by what I say. 'But from what he said, I think it might be more that everything about you is, well, big. Isn't it, darling?'

Tony laughs. 'Glad you've noticed.'

I laugh back. 'I had. But I meant more loud. Flashy, maybe.'

Tony tilts his head with a smile. 'Yeah, perhaps. What of it?'

'Well, Gavin's like my family. Conservative with a small "c".'

Tony looks confused.

'They think the worst thing in the world is to draw attention to yourself, to get people talking.'

'And you reckon he's worried it'll stir up gossip, his ex-missus turning out to be the woman who tamed Tony Garratt?'

I giggle. 'I'm not sure I want you too tame, darling.'

Tony kisses me to prove he isn't, and it takes me a second to get my breath back. 'It could be something like that. Gavin's ego took quite a hit, when I wasn't devastated after the divorce. He kept hinting to anyone who'd listen that underneath, I was barely coping. That I'd been unstable, a burden, all through the marriage, and he just couldn't keep supporting me any longer. Because I was too damaged to ever be a functional partner.'

'And that don't fit with us being in-your-face together, all over each other in public?'

'No. And I've always been, well, a bit of a fan, so Gavin would've known I couldn't resist you, if you took the slightest interest. I think he might've been worried a story about us would draw attention to exactly how he and Monica got together. We'd always hushed up exactly how much overlap there was. And it's the sort of little snippet the press loves, isn't it? How the owner's husband cheated on the star player's new girlfriend. Gavin would hate everyone knowing. He can't bear being in the wrong.' I pull a don't-care face. 'But why he did this doesn't really matter, so long as we're rid of him.'

Tony hugs me, holding me tight. 'Only you sure you're OK, are you, beauty?'

'I am. Very sure, thank you. And Tony, I'm sorry you had to be part of that.'

He shakes his head, vigorously, like Roudie after a bath. 'Nah, I'm sorry you had to go through it. Not just tonight, any of it. Cos I think I'm only starting to see now how, like, controlling he must've been.' His hand rests on mine. 'The stuff with Mike and Darren, the red car, it was never like that, promise. It was just I was dead worried 'bout you. And . . .' He looks down for a second, then straight into my eyes. 'I needed to know you was OK, when I weren't around. But I didn't wanna come over like I was telling you not to go out, or nothing like that.'

I kiss his forehead. 'I know. But next time, talk to me, OK?'

He nods quickly. 'Yeah, for sure. And you know, don't you, you don't need to worry about nothing any more? Cos I'm going to make you, like, boringly happy. Like from now on, you're in clover. It'll just be kisses and cuddles and me telling you how amazing you are, how I'm dead proud of you, all that. Till you're sick of hearing it, OK?'

I lean into him, my arms tight around him, my cheek flat against his chest, his chin on my hair. He holds me for a long time, until I look up at him. 'Tony, do you see now, when I said you were right for me, that you are? It's what I love about you the most, that there's no chill to you. You're all warmth.'

He kisses my forehead. 'That's a real nice way of putting it, love. And I can see, hundred per cent, why you need warming up a bit. And I'm, like, over the moon glad you trust me enough to take the line you did. But I don't get why. I mean, isn't Angharad where the trouble between us came from? Well, that and me not knowing how to get a woman I actually care 'bout into bed, without screwing it up?'

I snuggle into him. 'Umm, but I got the wrong idea, didn't I?'

'You did. But I was trying to explain I didn't love her or nothing, it was only ever lust and feeling old and being a bit of an idiot. Nothing like what I feel for you. But it came out wrong, cos I was that wound up over thinking you was done with me.' He nuzzles my hair. 'Sorry, beauty.'

'No, I'm sorry. And embarrassed, about getting so silly and jealous. But it was the thing with the ring . . .'

'What ring?'

'I signed for the custom ring you ordered.' He's trying to interrupt and I hold my hand up. 'No, darling, it's all right. I thought you buying an engagement ring for her, it showed things weren't really finished between the two of you, when you first arrived. Only you'd told me they were, and I got in a bit of a state about you, well, editing the truth, I suppose. But I'm over that. And of course, I know there's nothing between you now. If there was, you'd never have said you loved me.'

Tony looks confused. 'But what I don't get is why'd you think I was planning on giving Angharad your ring?'

I sit up, eyes wide. '*My* ring?'

'Yeah. Didn't you see the rubies in the band?'

'I saw them.'

'And you didn't think that looks like your lamp?'

'Um, well, yes, I did sort of think that might've given you the idea for the design.'

He cuddles me in. 'Ah, I think I'm getting an inkling 'bout why you was so upset. Poor Genie. You thought I'd taken something special to you and used it for someone else?'

I nod and swallow hard.

Tony kisses my forehead, my brows, the lids of my eyes, my cheekbones, then rubs his nose against mine. 'No, I'd never do that, promise.'

I want to believe him, but the timing doesn't work. I look down and pull at the rip in his jeans. 'But Tony, I know how long custom orders take. You must've put in the commission almost as soon as you joined us.'

'Yeah, I did.' He drags his hand over his face. 'Look, Genie, when we're done with this conversation, you're gonna need to put in a good twenty, thirty minutes of telling me how fucking great I am. All right? Cos this is gonna be like toe-curling for me.'

I smile. 'We could watch today's game, if you like? And I'll spend the whole ninety minutes pointing out how you're not only the most tactically gifted player on the pitch, but also by far the handsomest.'

He grins. 'Yeah, I'd like that.'

'I thought you might. But you need to do your explaining first.'

'Yeah, OK. So, I'm not saying I knew you was for me right from day one . . .'

I laugh. 'No, I'm sure you didn't. I was a complete bitch to you on your first day.'

'About me, not to me. There's a difference. And that didn't stop me fancying you, obviously. But it might've delayed me noticing you was the love of my life by a day or two. Only I did start to see it real early. Like you love the pup more than anything, don't you?'

'Well, apart from you,' I whisper, covering Roudie's ears.

Tony smiles and strokes Roudie. 'But you shared him with me. Just cos you knew that's what I needed, a bit of unconditional affection and country air. And that was like the most generous thing anyone's ever done for me. But the thing that sealed it was seeing you can stand up to me. Cos I reckon that means you could handle me day to day.'

I lean over and kiss his hair. 'It's not that difficult.'

'You ask one or two of my exes, they might feel different. But anyhow, you know when me and you was joking around at Monica's party?'

I nod.

He wraps his little finger around mine and his face is serious. 'Well, that's when I first decided, me and you fitted, one hundred per cent.'

I lean my head into him, breathing him in.

'Only I wasn't sure you was getting the same vibe.'

'Sorry, Tony. I got scared.'

'I know. And I get why you'd be frightened I was gonna

368

hurt you. Cos I did some dumb stuff when I was younger that's followed me round since. But like I've told you before, you're dead good at hiding stuff. So, it took me a while to cotton on to what was going on in your head.'

I nod, my teeth sinking into my lower lip.

'So, when I went and picked up that present for my niece, I wasn't feeling great, 'bout how stuff was going between us. And then I saw this ring sitting in a display case. It was just a band with the little rubies all scattered through it, and I got the idea I could commission one that looked kind of like your lamp. So I thought, you know, if you was who I wanted to be with, I should, like, dig in. Properly commit.'

I narrow my eyes at him. 'Hang on, you're seriously telling me, you commissioned an engagement ring, when you'd kissed me once, and we were barely talking?'

Tony grimaces. 'Yeah, yeah, I am. But I wasn't like totally sure I was ever gonna give it you. I was just thinking wouldn't it be dead romantic, if I got lucky and you ended up on the same page as me, if I could show you the receipt for the ring? And you'd know I bought it like a month after I met you. So, I paid for it and picked out the stones. But then I had to have Claudia wait till I could check I'd got your ring size about right . . .'

I rack my brains and then it comes to me. 'That's what the palm reading was about?' I ask, laughing.

He covers his eyes. 'Yeah, yeah, it was. Cos I needed to know that before I could say to her, go ahead, put the diamond on it. And it's been sitting in my sock drawer ever since, waiting for you to realize you can't live without me.'

I run my hand over his chest. 'Oh, Tony. But why didn't you tell me when we spoke in the meadow? Not about the ring, obviously, but that you definitely wanted something serious?'

He laughed. 'Well, I'm not an idiot, am I? I mean, the last time I'd seen you, you was running out the house half-naked after I'd borderline assaulted you. You don't need to be the most sensitive to see that's not the ideal starter for the "I wanna wake up next to you for the rest of my life" conversation.'

'You didn't assault me.'

'Nah, but what I did was all wrong. And me being all clumsy with you, that was tied up with me saying about adopting and it scaring you off. So I wanted to make sure, if we was starting fresh, I wasn't putting on no pressure.'

'But I told you, that wasn't why I stopped picking up the phone.'

'Yeah, but that was you glossing over it, wasn't it? To be kind.'

'No, no, it definitely wasn't.'

His smile is dazzling. 'That's great, cos I've got to admit, sometimes I see how you are, with Sky and stuff, and I can't stop thinking how you'll be a lovely mum. But I know it's still early doors. I'm only telling you about the ring cos you kind of forced my hand. Obviously, I'm not asking you for an answer now. I get you'll need to feel this out, check being with me works for you, before you start making big commitments. But see, it's your ring. And I promise you, Genie, it's never crossed my mind for a minute to give it to no one but you.'

I reach up and kiss him, dragging his mouth down onto mine. 'Thank you.'

'What for?'

'Being so lovely.'

'You might wanna hang on till I've got the game loaded before you start that. Cos you've promised me a solid ninety minutes of it, and anything before that, it'll not go on the clock.'

'I don't mind putting in a bit of extra time. But Tony, I think we should move this to yours.'

He sighs. 'Why's that? Your internet not working or something?'

'No, it's just I'll do a much better job of the praise if I'm wearing my ring.'

He looks at me, like he wants to be sure, then smiles slowly. 'So, not too soon?'

I shake my head. 'No. Not too soon at all.'

He kisses me so hard I'm bent back against the sofa cushions, and his hands are busy trying to work out how to get my knickers off without interrupting the kiss. I break away from him. 'I'd wait, darling. Until we get to yours, anyway. Because I think you're going to love the things I'll do for diamonds.'

He laughs, his best, happy lion laugh. 'Yeah, I bet I will.' He practically drags me onto my feet. 'Almost as much as I'm gonna love being married to you.'